"A CORKER . . .

RUBICON ONE

A MINOR MASTERPIECE OF ITS KIND."

The Toronto Star

RUBICON ONE

"A NOVEL OF NAIL BITING TENSION . . . HIGHLY RECOMMENDED."

Library Journal

RUBICON ONE

"TAKES OFF LIKE A VERY SOPHISTICATED MISSILE."

Publishers Weekly

"FAST MOVING AND FAR RANGING . . . ABSORBING . . . The novel paints a realistic and logical picture."

Best Sellers

"NEVER STOPS BOILING . . .

RUBICON ONE

as it moves from Moscow to Washington to Jerusalem."

Ottawa Citizen

"A DAMNED GOOD BOOK . . . A CRACKLING GOOD STORY"

Los Angeles Times

RUBICON
ONE

A NOVEL
DENNIS JONES

A Division of General Publishing Co. Ltd.
Toronto, Canada

General Publishing edition
published in 1983

General Paperbacks edition
published in 1984

Cover design: Brant Cowie/Artplus

Illustration: Terry Hadler

ISBN 0-7736-7070-X

Printed and bound in Canada

To my wife

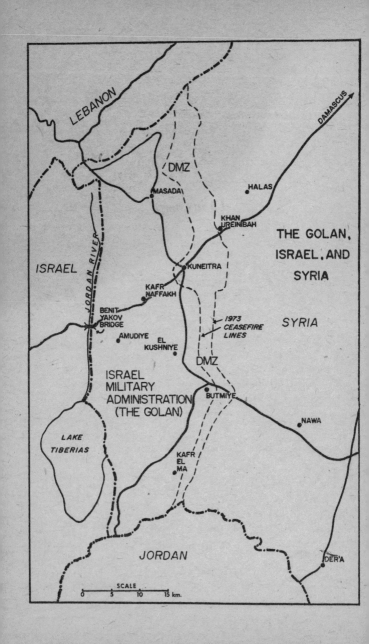

THE GOLAN,
ISRAEL, AND
SYRIA

LEBANON

DMZ

DAMASCUS

MASADA

HALAS

KHAN
UREINIBAH

KUNEITRA

ISRAEL

JORDAN RIVER

KAFR
NAFFAKH

SYRIA

BENIT
YAKOV
BRIDGE

1973
CEASEFIRE
LINES

AMUDIYE

EL
KUSHNIYE

DMZ

ISRAEL
MILITARY
ADMINISTRATION
(THE GOLAN)

BUTMIYE

NAWA

LAKE
TIBERIAS

KAFR
EL
MA

JORDAN

DER'A

SCALE
0   5   10   15 km.

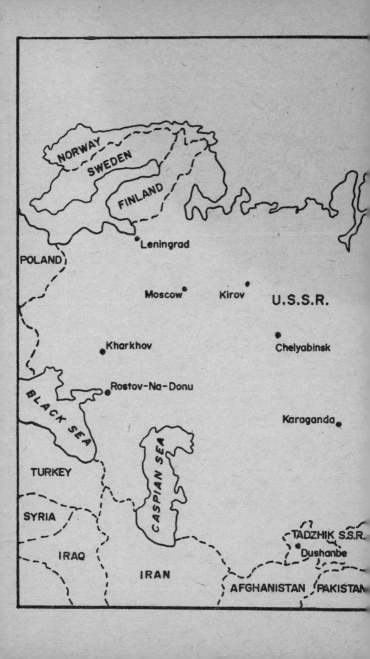

Dushanbe
Tadzikh Soviet Socialist Republic
June 7

MAJOR NIKOLAI ANDREYEV stood on the stone porch of Communications House watching the flow of traffic past the white limestone facades and dusty foliage of Lenin Square. There were more of the rural folk about than usual, most on foot, others clinging haphazardly to the chassis and beds of rattletrap trucks from the Vakhsh cotton collectives. Their robes, faded cloth in stripes of red or blue or blue-gray, flapped around their calves in the hot wind blowing down the Lenin Prospekt.

There wasn't much cotton on the trucks, Major Andreyev noticed. He wiped a drop of perspiration from the end of his nose and watched a particularly disreputable-looking pair of Tadzikh peasants disappear up Lenin Prospekt towards the Old Town. One of the two was wearing a green sash.

Green, thought Major Andreyev. That could be significant. There were green sashes at the Karaganda riot.

"Is this normal traffic for a Monday?" he asked his companion.

"I've seen it more crowded around Ramadan," said Colonel Khomenko. He worked for the KGB; in what capacity Major Andreyev wasn't sure. Andreyev suspected Khomenko to be in charge of counterespionage for the Tadzikh capital district. All Andreyev had been told by his battalion commander was that Colonel Khomenko was their liaison with the local KGB and the MVD militia.

"What about now?" pressed Andreyev.

"It's a little busy for a market day," admitted Colonel Khomenko. "A little. There's been nothing unusual reported, though, not through our normal channels."

Major Andreyev, through his own efforts to set up an intelligence net in the area to the northeast of Dushanbe, had learned how uncommunicative the rural Tadzhiks could be. He had little faith in Khomenko's "normal channels." He also hoped that the KGB man was unaware of Andreyev's own activities in the region. Although listed on the battalion's personnel roster as an executive officer, Andreyev was also a major in the GRU, army military intelligence. That wouldn't please Khomenko if he knew about it, for reasons that went back to Stalin's and Khrushchev's days. Stalin had transferred some of the GRU's responsibilities to the KGB in 1948. Ten years later, Khrushchev purged the GRU's senior officers, replacing them with KGB men. For a long time the KGB had maintained its control of the GRU, but after Andropov's death, a power struggle in the Kremlin allowed the GRU to regain most of its autonomy. The two organizations worked reasonably well together at the lower levels, but there was an unspoken awareness that they had become rival services in some fundamental manner. In senior GRU and KBG circles the rivalry was bitter, with the GRU constantly fighting off KGB attempts to devour it again. One result of the tension was that local KGB people were especially irritated by intelligence nets run by the GRU, particularly when the information gathered was unshared.

Major Andreyev had absolutely no intention of sharing his current suspicions with the KGB colonel. He barely dared think about them himself.

To get rid of the thought, he asked, "Would you be informed if there were anything in the wind?"

"Of course." Colonel Khomenko sounded very sure of himself.

"What do you think will happen at sundown? At the evening prayer?"

"Well, the muezzins don't howl from the minarets like they did in Afghanistan," said Khomenko. "They pray in the mosques, of course, when they can. The Khadzi mosque was open until last week, but it had to be closed for repairs. It was becoming a public danger."

Andreyev could guess how long the repairs would take: a long time. "Any reactions?"

"No. At the moment people's minds are more on their bellies than their souls. There isn't much food."

"Oh," said Andreyev, playing the part of the economically ignorant soldier.

"Still," said the colonel, "we might like some of your unit to be present this evening. No use taking chances with hooligans. It's possible the closing of the mosque has been misunderstood. The villagers are extremely ignorant. They'd pray in the building till it fell on their heads, then say it was the will of Allah."

"Maybe you should let it fall on them," said Andreyev. "They might be made to see it as a sign of divine disapproval of religion."

Khomenko grinned uncertainly, then frowned. Major Andreyev remembered the KGB's well-known shortage of humor and said hastily, "I'll see the lieutenant-colonel immediately." If he's sober, he added to himself. "We'll be on the outskirts, prepared to move, unless you'd rather have us in town immediately."

"No," said Colonel Khomenko. "That sort of provocation was what set off the Karaganda riot. I've had strict orders on that. Were you in the area when that happened?"

"No. The battalion was moved down here from Alma-Ata in April. I heard about Karaganda, though." He paused and then said, "By the way, we've tied our field switchboard into your police-communications net. You can reach us through MVD headquarters any time you need to."

"Good." Khomenko looked at his watch. "It's three o'clock. Will you be back at your headquarters by half past?"

"Easily."

"I'll have the militia patrols increased until midnight. If nothing's happened by then, nothing will."

"Very well. We'll keep one company on alert from then until morning, though, just in case."

"Whatever you like. Stop by tomorrow and we'll have a drink."

Major Andreyev nodded and went down the steps to the BRDM scout car. The metal of its door handle was hot enough to burn his hand. He got in and the driver pulled away, heading north on Lenin Prospekt towards the suburb of Sari-Asiya and the battalion bivouac area beyond it. Leading off either side of the avenue were small, twisted streets lined with mud-brick buildings, mostly condemned but still inhabited. They formed a drastic contrast to the monolithic white official buildings and memorials on the avenue. Andreyev disliked the look of the Old Town's streets; they would be unpleasant to fight in.

The battalion concentration area was a dusty field on the north edge of Dushanbe. The tents of the three infantry companies and the support company huddled under the scrappy shade of a few dried-up trees on the field's western perimeter. The vehicle park was in the full sun, where the BMP troop carriers hulked black on their tracks, turrets squat and ugly. The command post was set up in a small house that sidled up to the largest of the trees.

Andreyev got out of the BRDM and went into the house. It had only two rooms; in the larger they had established the battalion communications center. Snores issued from the adjoining cubicle. Rybalko, the captain commanding the support company, looked up from a metal table which was stacked with maps. Major Andreyev jerked his head questioningly at the cubicle.

Captain Rybalko lifted an imaginary glass to his lips and drank. Then he motioned Andreyev outside. The private manning the radio console looked up, then quickly returned to his machinery.

"What's going on?" asked Rybalko when they were outside.

"Just be ready. We may have to move quickly if there's trouble in the city. What's the situation here?"

"There's not enough water. Captain Balan took a squad from First Company to get some. Is there going to be trouble?"

"KGB doesn't think so."

"Good."

"They might be wrong. Where are Tchigorin and Polyarkov?"

"Overseeing maintenance on the BMPs."

Major Andreyev, by virtue of his rank of battalion executive officer and because he had fought in Afghanistan, was de facto battalion commander whenever the lieutenant-colonel was drunk. "All right," he said. "We'll be called if there's trouble. Two companies – first and second – will be ready to go until midnight. After that the second can stand down. Until then the third will rest in reserve. Your support company, the fourth, will operate as base defense if that's necessary. We won't need heavy mortars in the city, anyway."

"We're operating as though we were in hostile territory?'

"We might be."

Captain Rybalko, who had not been in Afghanistan, did not comment. Andreyev felt uncomfortable and wondered if he were overreacting. But he had discovered in Afghanistan that units taking too few precautions were in far more danger than those that took too many.

"When do you think he'll wake up?" he asked, meaning the lieutenant-colonel.

"Probably any time. He's been asleep since noon."

"Is Captain Suchkov around?"

Except for the required political-education meetings, the battalion political officer was rarely in evidence. He was not very well liked.

"He was sitting under a tree over by the road when I last saw him."

"Find him, please. I'd rather he woke the colonel up than me. We have to plan things for this evening. It all has to be cleared with the regiment as soon as possible."

Captain Rybalko knew that the commander would pick at a few details of Andreyev's tactical proposals and then leave the overall plan as Andreyev had arranged it. The wrath of his hangover would be reserved for the unfortunate Captain Suchkov. The two men exchanged a look of understanding.

"I'll go and get Suchkov," said Rybalko. Andreyev went back into the house to find the street map of Dushanbe.

By seven o'clock in the evening the lieutenant-colonel was nursing his headache on a wooden chair at the door of the command post. He was only thirty-five, but he looked older because of lack of sleep. Andreyev and Captain Rybalko sat on the stone steps beside him.

"Light's going," said the lieutenant-colonel.

The black ridge of the mountains to their northwest cut a hard line against the incandescent sky. The sun had just dipped below the highest peaks. The air was already much cooler, although the baked earth still radiated the day's heat. Andreyev wondered what the weather was like at home in Smolensk, and wished he were there.

"Should we be doing something constructive?" asked Captain Suchkov from the open door behind the three officers.

"What would you suggest?" asked the battalion commander.

"Well – "

The telephone rang inside. Captain Polyarkov answered it. Thirty seconds later he put his head outside and said, "KGB wants to talk to you, sir."

The lieutenant-colonel went into the house. Andreyev forced himself to relax and then followed, Captain Rybalko on his heels. The battalion commander was standing at the table tracing a finger over the Dushanbe map as the caller chattered in his ear. "Good," he said finally. "We'll be behind them in fifteen minutes. Can the militia deal with it that long?" He grimaced. "All right. We'll hurry." He put the receiver down and turned to his officers. "There's a mob moving towards Lenin Square. Hill men, students, down-and-outs from the Old Town. They came out of that warren up Lenin Prospekt about twenty minutes ago. A few of them tried to get into the Khadzi mosque; the militia turned them back. Then they started throwing stones and broke into the mosque anyway. The militia's falling back towards Lenin Square. We'll go straight in from here. First Company, down the Lenin Prospekt. Second, peel off at the Sanreddin Monument, go down Druzhbi Narodov Street and then come in on their flank from Komsomolskaya Street. We'll push them towards the river. Once they're dispersed, take up the positions we selected this afternoon. Let's go."

The darkness was thickening as the ten BMP armored personnel carriers of the First Company roared and clattered along the road into Dushanbe. Behind them clanked the two battalion headquarters BMPs and after these the vehicles of the Second Company. At the Sanreddin Monument the lead BMP slowed and the column accordioned until the carriers were only ten meters apart. They slowed still more until they were traveling at no more than a fast walk. There was no traffic on the avenue and the BMPs fanned out until they were proceeding south in a double column. The flat blare of their exhausts rattled back and forth among the limestone facades above them. Most of the windows were darkened.

Major Andreyev, riding in the sixth vehicle of the left-hand column, scanned the street from the BMP's command hatch as the driver swung left to follow the colonel's machine along Druzhbi Narodov Street. They were driving without lights and the glimmer of the streetlights seemed weak and fitful in the faint afterglow of sunset. A lot of dust had been kicked up by the BMPs' tracks; it hung in the air a long time before settling.

The command vehicle turned right at Komsomolskaya Street. Andreyev's driver went on to the next main cross street and turned there, followed by the vehicles of the Third Company.

"We've stopped a hundred meters from the Lenin Prospekt," crackled the lieutenant-colonel's voice over Andreyev's headset. "Are you in position yet, major?"

Andreyev waited for a moment as his driver slowed. "Yes, we are now."

"Report, First Company."

Captain Balan, in the lead BMP coming down Lenin Prospekt, said over the radio, "We're at the Botanical Gardens. There are about two hundred people in front of the mosque up ahead. They're watching us."

"Major Andreyev, what do you see?"

"From what I can see of the avenue there's a big crowd on it. They've lit some torches."

"Same up here. That crowd you see has likely moved along from the mosque. All right. Captain Balan, if the group at the mosque isn't doing anything, drive past it and back us up as we move into Lenin Square. Second Company, start up slowly and begin dispersing them. Don't get into any back alleys. We want to start by moving them out of the square."

"Go on," said Andreyev to his driver, whose head protruded like a cannonball from the right hatch. "Move slowly, so they have a chance to get out of our way. Riflemen, fire on my command, but over their heads."

He heard a rattle as the riflemen, chest-deep in the BMP's fighting compartment, cocked their assault rifles. The engine roared and the armored carrier, followed by its companions, clattered towards Lenin Prospekt. A few people in the crowd gestured violently at the oncoming vehicles. Some took to their heels; most did not. As the vehicles swung around the corner onto the avenue a fusillade of stones clanked and rattled on the BMP's hull.

"Button up?" asked the gunner from his position in the 73-mm-gun turret above and behind Andreyev.

"When ordered," snapped Andreyev. A larger stone, a cobble likely, struck the turret with a heavy clang. "All right. Close down."

The gunner and the riflemen ducked into their nests and closed their hatches. The driver glanced at Andreyev, shrugged and stayed up. The risk of being hit by a stone was less than the strain of driving with only the view through the periscopes.

"We're on the Lenin Prospekt," said the lieutenant-colonel's voice over the headphones. "Some of them are going off down the side streets already. Company commanders, report."

"They're throwing stones," said Captain Polyarkov. "But they're moving."

"Same here," said Balan, from the northern column.

"Major Andreyev?"

"We're almost at Lenin Square. There are about two

thousand people in it, mostly men. They're still throwing stones." A black blur plummeted towards him, grazed his shoulder and clanged against the armor. He dropped deeper into his hatch. "They're concentrating on us. I think the militia are keeping them off the steps of Communications House and Government House. I think they'll break up as soon as we're out among them."

"Captain Polyarkov," said the lieutenant-colonel, "as soon as you're in position have your first platoon fire two rounds, each man, over their heads."

"Yes, sir."

Andreyev's command vehicle ground steadily on into the broad expanse of Lenin Square. It was lined with government buildings, square-columned and many-windowed. The windows glimmered fitfully now in the torch glow.

"Stop," Andreyev told the driver. "First Platoon. Major Andreyev here. Are you in position?"

"We are now," said Polyarkov. "Fire will start in a few seconds."

Andreyev waited. The mob swirled in front of him, roaring, fists raised; stones fell out of the night. Mixed with the roar were ululations that sounded like chants. Torchlight sheened on distorted, sweating faces. Thirty meters away from Andreyev's BMP a long pole dipped and soared. Fastened to its tip was a long green banner: green, the color of Islam. Farther over near the south edge of the square were two more green banners.

The BMP to Andreyev's left had rolled a few meters beyond his, then stopped. It hulked, black and efficient, against the light stone of the buildings behind it. Its gun turret tracked back and forth, sniffing. The driver and commander had gone under the hatches. Andreyev peered to the right, to where the dark trees of the War Memorial Park lined the south edge of the square. The trees were lit intermittently by the torches and by the steadier glow of the streetlights.

Andreyev saw movement among the tree trunks and felt a sudden apprehension. "Gunner," he said into his microphone, "train the turret right. Target may be in the park."

A spatter of shots, flat and dry, snapped out from behind him. First Company had opened fire. The mob swayed and began to unravel at the edges.

A sudden flare of light blazed across the facades of Lenin Square. Andreyev jerked back against the hatch rim, bruising his shoulder blades. Something incandescent shot in front of his vehicle and struck the BMP left and ahead of him. There was an ear-splitting bang and the BMP was instantly enveloped in smoke and flame. The flame was blue-white: the BMP's magnesium armor was burning.

"It came from the park!" screamed the gunner.

"Open fire with the MG!"

The gunner began to hose the park with the machine gun. "Back up!" Andreyev shouted at the driver, forgetting, momentarily, the intercom. They had to get out of the open square.

Another flash from the park. Andreyev knew what it was: the exhaust flame of a portable antitank missile. The missile roared straight at them, then swerved and streaked overhead. Andreyev felt its heat on his face. It struck Communications House with a dull boom. Masonry sleeted down into the square.

The other BMPs were raking the park with machine-gun fire. Someone with presence of mind fired a flare, but its light did not penetrate beneath the trees.

As the flare expired there were two explosions in the park. Somebody had opened up with a 73-mm gun. Trees began to burn. Andreyev spared a glance ahead as his BMP backed out of the square and stopped. The mob was breaking up, streaming off into the side streets. The damaged BMP was still burning furiously, lighting up the surroundings with a savage, actinic glare. Shots had been fired into the crowd; scores of bodies sprawled untidily about the pavement. One of them, Andreyev noted with an odd detachment, lay too close to the burning BMP and had caught fire.

No more missiles screamed out of the park.

"Cease fire," said Andreyev. The machine gun fell silent. The air reeked of nitrous oxide. The shooting trailed off and then died.

Andreyev stared at the furnace of the BMP. More than any other death, he feared that by fire.

Where did they get the missiles, he wondered, as burning ammunition began to explode, driving splinters of metal across the square. There's going to be trouble over that. A great deal of trouble, indeed.

Islamabad, Pakistan
June 8

HIS NAME WAS MUSTAQ NASIR AKHTAR and he had waited in a cell in the sub-basement of the National Security Headquarters for an hour before two uniformed men came for him. Walking through the corridors, he fantasized: his KGB control officer appearing from nowhere, leading armed men, a firefight, freedom; or perhaps an earthquake breaking open the ceiling, killing the guards, letting in the sunlight; or a terrorist bomb. It was impossible that one of these things should not happen, impossible that he should actually be stopping now in front of this door.

One of the guards knocked.

"Enter."

They opened the door and took him in. There was a table behind which sat two men in civilian clothes, an older and a younger. The older man had a hawklike beak of a nose. Two meters from the table stood a piece of interrogation equipment. When he saw it, Akhtar's knees buckled and the guards had to hold him up.

"No," he said.

"Put him on it," said the hawk-nosed one.

He struggled weakly, but it was no use. The two civilians watched impatiently as he was strapped naked to the wooden platform, his legs spread out in front of him. His back and arms were secured to an upright. The platform and the upright were suspended from a pulley in the ceiling, and could be raised or lowered by a small winch bolted to one wall. There was a round hole in the platform, and under the hole was the sharpened tip of a two-centimeter thick steel spike. The spike was three feet long and was cemented to the floor.

"Arrange him," said the younger man.

One of the guards lowered the platform little by little. Akhtar whimpered and closed his eyes very tightly. The second guard guided the tip of the spike into Akhtar's anus. Tears leaked from under Akhtar's eyelashes. The lowering stopped.

"Now," said the man with the hooked nose, "I am Riaz Hasan, director of counterintelligence, among other things. Do you realize why you are being examined at this level?"

Akhtar shook his head. He was trying not to feel the pressure between his buttocks. It hurt only a little as long as he kept relaxed.

"Because," said the man beside Hasan, "you are – were – a trusted planning clerk at the Institute of Nuclear Science and Technology. Because you have sold information about our nuclear-weapon and missile programs. Because we wish to find out exactly what information you have given to your control and who helped you obtain what you could not get yourself. Because you are to be an example to others."

"To whom were you providing information?" Hasan asked.

The Russian had told Akhtar what could happen to agents who betrayed their control officers. "The Indians," he croaked. His tongue felt like sandpaper.

Hasan gestured. The platform dropped a centimeter. Akhtar strained rigid against the upright, drawing in his breath with a great whoop. Urine spread over the platform and began to drip onto the floor.

"You will be lowered a centimeter each time I do not believe you," said Hasan. "We have watched you for a long time. You have never met any Indians. Two weeks ago, however, you did see a man who works at the Russian Embassy. Is he your control?"

"Yes," gasped Akhtar. He felt distended, ripped, and it had hardly begun.

"His name?"

"I don't know. He never told me."

Hasan raised his hand. Akhtar screamed in anticipation. Nothing happened.

"That's likely," said Hasan, lowering his hand. "His name

is Stychkov. He's an embassy KGB officer. How long has he been controlling you?"

O Allah, Allah, thought Akhtar, how long was it? Was it three months or four or. . . .

"Four months."

This time he had reason to scream. Small beads of blood rolled down the spike and diffused pinkly into the pool of urine.

"It has been five. We knew there was a leak, but we weren't sure it was you until you saw the Russian. I should tell you that if you cooperate we will lower you very slowly, if at all, and shoot you when you have answered all our questions. If you do not answer us, the stake will kill you by centimeters."

Akhtar managed to nod. The younger man took a syringe from a box on the table and gave Akhtar an injection. He felt his heartbeat strengthen and the gray that had clouded his vision began to dissipate.

"You took a bus from here to the Old City in Rawalpindi to make a drop today. In the drop you stated the date of the cruise-missile test. Was the drop in the Old City your normal method of communication?"

"Yes."

"Did you know we were following you?"

"I was afraid you might be. I saw a gray Fiat several times."

"Have you ever told your control you thought you might be followed?"

"No."

"Why were you giving this information to the Russians?"

"For money."

"How much?"

"Several hundred rupees. Please give me some water."

"Is that the only reason?"

"My brother has a daughter. She is crippled, she needs drugs. Some of the money was for her."

"If you do not cooperate we will put her on the platform instead of you."

"I will cooperate. Please. Water."

Hasan ignored him. "What else have you told the Russians?"

"The expected warhead yield. The missile's range. Anything I found out about the guidance system."

"Which was?"

Akhtar told him. Hasan pondered this and said, "You said you normally used the drop. Why did you meet the Russian?"

"I asked to. I wanted more money."

Something tore deep and softly within him as the winch clicked. When Akhtar stopped wriggling the younger man gave him another injection. There was a faint odor of feces in the interrogation room.

"What else?"

"All, all, all, nothing else."

"You could not have known some of this material in the course of your normal work. Where did you obtain it?"

"Everywhere. People left drawers unlocked, put papers in wastebaskets, not the shredders. They talked."

Hasan frowned. "The guidance system. Much of that work was not carried on at the institute. Who provided you with that information?"

Akhtar had hoped against all reason that they would not ask him this. His cousin, how could he tell them that?

"It was your cousin Nabi Mansuri, wasn't it?"

"No."

This time the scream went on for a full five seconds. When it ended, Akhtar was unconscious.

"Wake him up," said Hasan. He glanced at his watch. "I want to be done by ten."

In fact they managed to get the rest of the information out of Akhtar by 9:50. Hasan was initially reluctant to believe that his security at the institute was so poor that the clerk could have come by so much information, but by the time the stake had penetrated Akhtar to a depth of some twenty centimeters, Hasan had accepted that the cousin was the only other one involved.

At twenty centimeters, of course, there was really nothing left to do with Akhtar but shoot him, which they did.

"It wasn't at the fallback drop, either?" asked Vladislav Kochin.

"No," answered Mikhail Stychkov, ostensibly a Russian

embassy chauffeur but actually a KGB lieutenant. Kochin was deputy chief of the Islamabad KGB station. "I think he's been picked up," added Stychkov.

"Shit," said Kochin. "And their counterintelligence is usually such a joke. He was going to give us the date of the test today, wasn't he?"

"He said so."

Kochin rubbed his nose and then shrugged. "Well, it doesn't really matter. We've got sources for that information much better placed than Akhtar. He would have been useful confirmation, but. . . ." A thought struck him. "Even if he does turn up again, I'd be suspicious, if I were you. They might decide to use him to pass false information."

"Close him down?"

"Yes, for now – if Hasan's thugs haven't already closed him down for us."

"All right. Anything else?"

"No," said Kochin. "Not for the moment."

THE NEW YORK TIMES
Pakistan Tests Cruise Missile

ISLAMABAD, June 11 (Reuters) — President Zia of Pakistan yesterday announced the successful test of a Pakistan-designed and built cruise missile, possessing a range of more than 500 kilometers. Zia emphasized that the weapon was intended for defensive purposes only, and gave no indication that the missile could transport the recently announced Pakistani atomic bomb. In an immediate reaction to the test, US Defence Secretary Nathan McKay said the missile's development "is a disturbing renewal of the trend towards the proliferation of nuclear weapons and delivery systems."

Round Lake, New Hampshire
June 20

THE RAFT WAS MOORED in fifteen feet of water about twenty yards from the end of the floating boat dock. Beyond the raft, half a mile away, the far edge of the lake was clad in oak, maple and pine. Only three summer cottages were visible through the trees on the shoreline. The cottages were not yet inhabited. The lake was rather isolated and thinly populated even in summer; its few seasonal residents would not arrive until the fourth-of-July weekend.

One of the lake's few year-round residences was at the end of a stone-flagged path that led up from the boat dock. A two-story white-frame building constructed at the end of the last century, the house had a high-pitched shingled roof and a screened veranda along two sides. One wing faced the lake, the other the gravel drive running down from the main road. Like the rest of the shoreline, the area around the house was thickly wooded.

It was ten o'clock in the morning, sunny and warm.

David Thorne closed the door on the lake side of the veranda and ambled down the flagged path towards the boat dock. In one hand he carried a thermos, in the other a copy of *The Roman War Machine AD 14 – 378* in a plastic freezer bag. He was six-feet-one inch tall and quite thin. The height of his forehead was only partly reduced by a fringe of light-brown hair cut off horizontally above his eyebrows; the hair was rather too long over the ears and at the back. Two lines ran from the corners of his straight nose to the corners of his mouth. His was not a very happy face.

He reached the dock, stuck the thermos in the waistband of his trunks and lowered himself carefully into the water. It was still quite cold. He turned on his back and began an awkward one-armed sidestroke towards the raft, towing the book behind him. At the raft he climbed out of the water, poured a cup of coffee – there was rum in it – took the book out of the bag, flopped over on his stomach and began to read. He read very quickly, absorbing everything. The level of liquid in the thermos sank lower and lower.

After an hour he turned on his back, put the book aside and closed his eyes. He would give himself half an hour more of sun, and then go back to the house and the manuscript that was sitting, half-typed, beside his Selectric. He began to doze.

Beep.

Thorne sat up instantly, pressed the stud on his wristwatch to silence the audible alarm, put the book and the thermos into the bag and rolled off the raft into the water.

The raft sat on oil drums; there was an eight-inch airspace under the boards forming its deck. Thorne surfaced under the raft, put the bag on the shelf he had built under it and waited, watching the boat dock.

The red alarm eye on his watch still glowed. He turned it off, wondering momentarily whether he had invited anyone to the house and then forgotten it. Nothing surfaced in his memory, nor did he really expect it to. Thorne was very careful about his visitors.

He heard brakes squeak, then the crunch of gravel under the wheels of a car. The trees at the lake's edge obscured his vision. A car door slammed. There was nothing stealthy about the approach, at least.

He submerged until only his nostrils were above the water. The angle of the noon sun would make it very difficult for an observer on shore to detect him in the shadows under the raft.

Faint knocking, once, twice, three times, at the screen door. A silence.

A man appeared on the dock and walked out to its end, scanning the water, left hand shading his eyes. He limped slightly. Sunlight glanced from his bald head. He stopped, pulled out a red-and-white checked handkerchief and mopped his face.

Thorne exhaled slowly, grabbed the bag and sculled from under the raft.

"Hello? David?"

Thorne trod water. "Hello, Isser. Just a minute." He swam to the dock and pulled himself out of the water. Isser Stein looked down at him with some amusement. "You don't change much. It's a good thing I remembered to use the handkerchief."

"I knew it was you anyway," said Thorne. He shook water off the bag and stood up. He was taller than the Israeli by a good three inches. "But it's preferable to be sure. How are you?"

"Well, myself." They shook hands. "Do you have a little time?" asked Stein.

"Nothing but. Let's go up to the house."

They started up the path. "How did you know I was coming down to the water?" asked Stein after a moment's climb. "Or do you usually reside under your raft when bathing?"

"The driveway's bugged," said Thorne uninformatively. They were at the veranda. He went through the screen door and held it open for Stein. "It's cooler in the kitchen. The veranda catches the lake breeze, but there isn't much today."

Stein glanced briefly around the kitchen. There were no alarm strips at the windows, which were open. Ultrasonics, at least, then, he thought. But well hidden, and independently powered. He certainly hasn't changed.

"It's a nice room," he said a little awkwardly. They hadn't spoken in five years.

It was indeed a pleasant kitchen. A long wooden counter ran along one side, a microwave oven and a stove at one end of it. A neatly proportioned teak table with wicker chairs was separated from the cooking area by a small island that enclosed a dishwasher. Windows lined all of the lake wall; the glint of water and part of the dock were visible through the trees.

"Pull up a chair," said Thorne. "This is the most civilized room in the house – everywhere else has rough drafts on every horizontal surface. Beer? Coffee? Rum?"

Stein was hot. "Beer would be fine." He sat at the table,

watching Thorne open the brown bottles and pour with deft, precise movements.

Thorne put the two full glasses on the table and sat across from Stein. The two men looked at each other for a moment. Thorne raised his glass and they both drank.

"What do you want, Isser?" asked Thorne.

Stein regarded him for a moment, trying to consider the changes five years might have made. Then he glanced down at the ring of foam on the surface of the beer and looked back up. "Your advice on a certain matter. Perhaps your assistance."

I never could make out the color of his eyes, thought Stein. Sometimes they are gray, sometimes blue. They change with the light.

"What about?" asked Thorne neutrally. "You must know I've retired."

"Yes. I know that. But this is a situation that might hold unusual interest."

"What?"

"You know," said Stein, moving away from the point, "that we've always been ready to deal swiftly with threats to Israel, regardless of the source of the threat. Remember the *Liberty* fiasco?"

Thorne did. During the Six Day War in 1967, the CIA spy ship *Liberty* had been cruising in the Mediterranean some fifteen miles north of Sinai. She was receiving the total signal output of the Israeli armed forces and relaying it to Washington. After a warning to the United States that the vessel was endangering their security and should stop the rebroadcasts, the Israeli general staff had waited for several hours. The radio traffic continued. On June eighth, Israeli air and torpedo-boat strikes were launched against the ship, disabling her. Thirty-four American personnel were killed and more than twice that number injured. The Pentagon rumbled and then was still. The radio relay was not resumed.

"I remember," said Thorne. He had been nineteen during the Six-Day War. He had not found out about the background of the *Liberty* action until 1973, when he had been brought into the disinformation task group formed, at very short notice, during the Arab-Israeli October War. "You were taking a chance, doing that."

"We told your people, but they ignored it, or the warning was lost in transit. We had no time to waste."

"Yes," said Thorne. He got up, opened a cupboard and got out a packet of cigarillos. He lit one carefully and sat down, pushing the packet towards Stein. Stein shook his head.

"You used to smoke them."

"Heart. I had to stop two years ago."

We're both getting old, Thorne mused. I'm thirty-eight but some days I feel seventy. Maybe Isser does, too. But he's into his sixties, anyway.

"What does Mossad want, Isser?" he asked. "I presume you're still with them." He paused, then probed. "What would Israeli intelligence in Washington want with a superannuated CIA ex-desk man, ex-analyst, turned military historian, moreover?"

"How's the book coming, by the way?"

"All right. But, Isser, you're station chief in Washington. What the hell are you doing in New Hampshire?"

The cigar had gone out. Thorne put it on the edge of the table.

Stein removed three newspaper clippings from his shirt pocket and put them on the teak. "I presume you've seen these?"

Thorne glanced at them. One was quite small and outlined the successful test firing of a Pakistani cruise missile earlier in June. The second, dated the previous year, was much longer and announced the acquisition by Pakistan of small-scale nuclear-weapons capability.

"This is the important one," said Stein. He tapped the third clipping. It was headlined *LIBYA, PAKISTAN NEGOTIATE REPAYMENT OF OIL DEBTS* and bore a handwritten note: "*Far Eastern Economic Review,* Jan 15/86."

"I'd seen the other two," Thorne said. "Not that one."

"They're calling in their debts," said Stein.

Thorne eased his back. It felt crinkly from the sun he had absorbed on the raft. "Would Pakistan give them bombs?"

"Libya gave Pakistan a hundred million US dollars in 1973," Stein pointed out. "To work on a nuclear capability. That was under Bhutto. When Zia took over in '76 they went at it full tilt. Pakistan got some money from the Saudis in 1981 but Libya financed most of the work. The Pakistanis have been expanding the plants at Sihala and Chasma for five years. And they've built others at Campbellpore and Talagang. Libyan money again. Qaddifi's been sending them oil, too. We think he's going to let them have the oil in return for the other things."

Thorne listened to the birds in the pines and to the wind's faint hiss through the veranda screens. The breeze had been growing stronger since they sat down. "How many devices have they been able to put together?"

Stein looked at him. "This is very classified."

"I know that."

"About twenty. Low yield, likely very dirty. Two to ten kilotons each. They're really tactical warheads, by superpower standards."

"But enough to flatten Tel Aviv."

"Undoubtedly."

Thorne realized with a start that his glass of beer sat untouched. He drank half of it. Stein's glass was nearly empty. "Another?"

"Thank you," said the Israeli.

Thorne poured and opened a second bottle for himself. He drank the rest of the beer in his glass and refilled it. Stein watched him.

"Do you drink a lot of beer, David?"

Thorne put the empty bottle down. "Sometimes."

"Why?"

"My business."

"You're bored, aren't you?" It was a statement rather than a question.

"No," said Thorne. "Will Islamabad give – lend – the Libyans some of their warheads?"

"They've already committed themselves to do so. Our reports say that ten warheads will be provided, with the cruise-missile delivery system described in the clipping."

"Is there any intention of using them?"

"We don't know. The Libyans may not know themselves."

"Why bother, then?"

Stein shrugged tiredly. "Who knows? It just goes on and on. We're all trapped by history."

Thorne said, "That's why I got out."

"Was it?" asked Stein. "I wish I could." He shrugged again and said, "Anyway, they're going to move the weapons next month. We have somebody in Islamabad who's in a position to know."

"What are your people going to do about it?"

"Stop them, of course. But we can't move directly against installations on Pakistan's soil. It has to be done while the weapons are in transit."

"You could shoot the transport aircraft down."

"They're not going by aircraft. Ship."

"Slow." Thorne considered. "And vulnerable."

"We believe they're depending on secrecy and the freedom of the seas. They don't think we'll risk the accusation of piracy. We will, of course. In any case, we've organized things so that the devices won't arrive. And done so with great difficulty, I might add."

"What are your chances?"

"Good. We've had a contingency plan for this sort of thing for some time."

"What do you want with me?"

"We would like you to come along on the raid, to examine the warheads before we sink them."

Thorne relit the cigar, staring at the Israeli.

"You'd be very well paid," said Stein. "You're a professional, remember. Even if retired."

"You have experts of your own," Thorne pointed out.

"There is a finite possibility that the raid will fail," Stein observed.

"And you don't want to risk losing any of your domestic experts."

Stein shrugged delicately. "I would be a fool to deny that's a consideration."

"Have you told my . . . previous employers that this proposition was being made?"

"No."

"Are you going to?"

Again the delicate shrug.

Thorne regarded the pine trees and the mosaic of the lake beyond them. At length Stein asked, "What do you think of the idea?"

"No," said Thorne. "I'm not interested." His cigar had gone out again.

Stein finished his beer and got up. "Please consider it. If I don't hear from you by the twenty-seventh I'll assume you're really not interested. You can call me at this number if you change your mind." He scribbled on the *Economic Review* clipping. "It's just a travel agency. Ask for Mr. Roth."

"Perhaps," said Thorne.

"You realize the security breach I've committed by telling you this," Stein said, hand on the doorknob.

"I appreciate it, Isser. But no."

Stein regarded him for several seconds and then left Thorne alone at the kitchen table. Thorne didn't see him to his car.

Central Intelligence Statistics and
Evaluation Center
Langley, Virginia
June 21

THE CENTRAL COMPUTER ROOM was seventy feet down and very air-conditioned. There were three floors between it and ground level. If visitors approached the installation from the road, they saw only a neutral building of two stories, built in russet brick, with very few windows. The building housed a clutch of late-model IBM computers, which processed data overflow from several federal agencies and provided statistical projections for the Bureau of the Census.

The center's actual business – which was not a very closely guarded secret, since the existence of the installation would have been impossible to hide from determined searchers anyway – was the computer evaluation of intelligence and the generation of political and military scenarios based on those evaluations. The core of the system was in the center of the complex of rooms on level four: a Cyber 220 mainframe computer, backed up by an older Cray-1 and a pair of Cyber 205s. The 220 was the most powerful computer ever built, and there were only twelve of them in North America. Two of them controlled the Minuteman III ICBMs in their silos in North Dakota, the NORAD defense net, the AWACS warning-and-control systems and the Strategic Air Command alert systems. They continually advised the center's 220 in Langley of the data they had collected from satellite-reconnaissance systems and from electronic surveillance of Russian and Chinese air, land and naval forces; they also kept the Langley 220 up to date on the state of US readiness and military capabilities. In return, the Langley 220 furnished profiles of likely Chinese, Russian and Third World behavior under various conditions, some of them of crisis proportions. It did this using a very large computer program, probably the largest ever written, which had only partially been created by humans. The 220 was one of the first big machines to use automatic-program generation for sophisticated purposes; a very large chunk of the 220's program had been constructed by the 220 itself.

The program's name was RUBICON, and for the last year its predictions had been chillingly accurate.

I wish we hadn't named it that, thought Dr. Joscelyn Petrie as she sat at the main control console waiting for the run to end. It was a little joke, then, when we started. Did we sense, even so far back, that if it worked we'd have crossed some kind of divide, to a place where the machines could judge the future better than we could? What was it Thorne had said just before he resigned?

"If this thing runs properly it'll be like crossing the Rubicon. We won't ever be able to go back."

"What?" asked Selfridge. He was one of the systems analysts, and knew nothing but systems analysis.

"Rubicon. Julius Caesar," Thorne had explained patiently. "There was a law in Rome that you couldn't bring your armies into Italy with you if you were a commanding general. The Italian boundary was the Rubicon River. If you brought your troops over it you had committed treason, and were under an automatic death sentence. So once you started you couldn't go back. Julius Caesar crossed it and the Roman government promptly capitulated. They hadn't remembered to keep any forces in Italy to protect themselves. Caesar made himself dictator."

"If it's that much of a bastard," Partington had said, "maybe we'd better call the program RUBICON instead of Project 8816. Just to remind ourselves."

There had been general amusement. But when they had finished the design and started generating the program, it had somehow assumed the name Rubicon.

The terminal beeped at her.

```
SYSTEM STATUS
DISKPACK G82
SECONDARY CONTROLLER CARD T16
POWER VOLTAGES 2% BELOW OPTIMUM
SHIFTING TO BACKUP
DO I CONTINUE THE RUN?
```

"Got it," said Butler at the maintenance console. "Tell the brute to go on."

Joscelyn typed YES on the keyboard. The screen immediately displayed:

```
THANK YOU. RUN CONTINUING.
```

"Damn G82 anyway," said Butler. "That's the second time this month."

"Yes," said Joscelyn. She leaned back in her chair and looked out the master-control room windows. Beyond them lay the 220.

The computer room had always reminded her of an aquarium. The white tiled floor like sand, the blue-and-white cabinets of the machine rising out of it, tall stones in the light shimmering down from the pale surfaces above. And the operators drifting in and out of the cabinets' shadows like fish in the ocean shallows in a California afternoon. And quiet, like the underside of the sea. All printers and terminals, for security reasons, were isolated from the computer room.

She looked back to the terminal.

```
OUTPUT AVAILABLE NOW. BEGIN OUTPUT?
```

She typed OK, and waited.

```
OUTPUT WILL REQUIRE 5 MINUTES. BEGINNING.
```

The high-speed printer began to whir. Reams of paper spilled into the output tray. Butler got up from the maintenance console and stretched. "You want to tell them it's coming through?"

Joscelyn picked up the internal phone and punched three numbers.

"Yes?"

"The run's starting to print. It'll need five minutes."

"Thanks. We'll be down shortly."

The printer continued to whisper. Occasionally it reversed its motion, drawing graphs. Joscelyn watched one of the graphs as it jerked into the paper tray. The sharp rise of the inked line made her scalp prickle.

Don't worry, she told herself. It's only a local simulation.

The printout thickened and then stopped coming off the machine. Butler had detached it and was laying it out on the long table behind the console when Richard Aubrey and Kenneth Partington entered the control room. Aubrey was general director of information processing for the Central Intelligence Statistics and Evaluation Center – called CISEC – and Partington, his second-in-command, was director of analysis and programming. Both were in their late forties. But where Aubrey presented the image of a successful oil company vice-president with silvering hair, a perfect tan and immaculate white shirts under precisely tailored suits, Partington was more like a down-at-heels professor of philosophy at some obscure midwestern university. He was approximately oval in shape, and almost totally bald. Thick spectacles – that was the word for them, "glasses" was not – sat uneasily on his nose and enlarged his already protuberant eyes. The eyes, however, were blue-green and very, very intelligent. He was far brighter than Aubrey, and both of them knew it. It did not, however, disturb their working relationship.

"Is the output file locked?" Aubrey asked Joscelyn unnecessarily. He knew it was, but preferred to ask anyway.

"Yes, it is," she said, brushing a strand of blond hair away from her forehead. Aubrey regarded her briefly as though wondering how Joscelyn Petrie had managed to stay unmarried for so long. She had the sort of high-cheekboned, exactly planed features that seemed intended more for looking into a fashion photographer's lens than into the green depths of a computer terminal's screen. Her figure and coloring matched the initial impression: bronze and gold, the prototypical California woman.

The eyes could belie the image. Aubrey had asked her once, in a jocular way, how she had avoided marrying, and the color of the eyes had changed from Big Sur sun-on-blue-water to the green of Atlantic rollers in March.

"Because I'm busy," she had said, and he had never brought the subject forward again. She had had the occasional liaison, of course, since her affair with Thorne had ended and he left the CIA, but they all had passed over her without visible marks. She was thirty-two.

"What's it look like?" asked Partington.

"I saw a couple of the graphs as they came off," said Joscelyn. "I don't think it's very good."

They flipped the printout open and began to read, all of them, very quickly. The parameters with which the 220 was modeling the world were given first; then there was a list of the modules that had been added. There were six of them.

MODULE 1: LIBYA PROVIDED WITH 5-10 DEVICES, ALCMS
           (AIR-LAUNCHED CRUISE MISSILES)
MODULE 2: LIBYA PROVIDED WITH 10+ DEVICES, ALCMS.
MODULE 3: SAME AS 1, EXCEPT SYRIA.
MODULE 4: SAME AS 2, EXCEPT SYRIA.
MODULE 5: SAME AS 1, BOTH LIBYA AND SYRIA.
MODULE 6: SAME AS 2, BOTH LIBYA AND SYRIA.

EACH MODULE CONSIDERED IN EACH OF THE FOLLOWING CASES:

CASE 1: NO CONVENTIONAL CONFLICT WITHIN 3 MONTHS.
CASE 2: MINOR CONVENTIONAL CONFLICT, RESOLVED.
CASE 3: MINOR CONVENTIONAL CONFLICT, NOT RESOLVED.
CASE 4: MAJOR CONVENTIONAL CONFLICT, RESOLVED.
CASE 5: MAJOR CONVENTIONAL CONFLICT, NOT RESOLVED.

CONVENTIONAL CONFLICT ASSUMED TO BE ISRAELI-SYRIAN GIVEN CURRENT WORLD MODEL AND AVAILABLE ISRAELI/ LIBYAN DELIVERY SYSTEMS.

Following this was a list of the other presumptions with which RUBICON was working, the major one being that Israel would not use nuclear weapons unless so attacked, or unless she were facing imminent defeat on the battlefield. Then the evaluation proper began: consideration of the diplomatic and leadership characteristics of any nations likely to be involved in the scenarios. Cases one through four resulted in no more than the usual mayhem and destruction. Case five was far more serious. The graph representing the likelihood of a nuclear exchange among Israel, Syria and Libya climbed steeply at the end of August.

"Shit," said Aubrey uncharacteristically. "There go Tel Aviv and Damascus."

"Damascus has been muttering about the Golan since March," said Partington. "This could be the one to watch. They want the Golan back. With a few warheads they might think they could use the mutually assured destruction ploy to get it."

"I'll move it up to the DCI," said Aubrey. "This is the worst one yet. I wish the Pakistanis hadn't been so damned successful with that cruise missile last week."

"There's one other part," said Joscelyn, "I put the condition in last night. That part of the run's still locked. I didn't want it out until we were all here."

The three men looked at her with some surprise.

"Drive that past me again?" said Aubrey.

Without answering she turned back to the last pages of the printout. The case-five graph displaying the likelihood of general rather than regional nuclear war humped at the end of August and then flattened out, suggesting that the superpowers would restrain themselves.

"That's not too ferocious if you're not Israeli or Arab," said Partington. "What else have you got?"

"It'll take a minute or two to output." She went to the main console and tapped briefly. The printer started up.

"Just what are you assuming?" asked Partington.

"Leschenko, as long as he'd been running the USSR, seems

to have been content to keep a lid on things. I put Boyarkin's profile in instead of his."

"You're assuming Boyarkin moves from KGB chairman to head of the Politburo?"

"Yes."

"That's very unlikely," said Aubrey. "He wouldn't be in line for anything like that. They'd put Gresko in. Or Distanov. Or another of the old guard. Nobody ever heard of Boyarkin until after Andropov died."

"Exactly," said Joscelyn. "That's what intrigued me. How did he get so far so fast?"

The printer stopped. She tore off the output and laid it on the table. Case five was exactly the same as before, except for Boyarkin's profile.

And the fact that the general-war plot, instead of leveling off after August, went almost straight up.

The White House
June 22

"IT SEEMS LIKE PRETTY THIN EVIDENCE for a prediction of Armageddon," said President Jason Law. "Suppose you substituted the profile of the director of the Omsk Cultural Institute for KGB Chairman Boyarkin's? If he were a real so-and-so, wouldn't you get similar results?"

"Possibly," admitted Cameron Harper. He was the director of Central Intelligence and he was sitting on a long sofa in the Oval Office. Beside him was Patrick Gellner, deputy director of defense for Intelligence. In armchairs sat Matthew Goodhand, deputy director of State, and Simon Parr, presidential assistant for national security. Together, excepting the president, they made up the CFI, the Committee on Foreign Intelligence. It was an advisory body designed to keep the president informed of critical developments in espionage, subversion, intelligence and the assorted devious maneuverings of international diplomacy. Cameron Harper was its chairman.

"Why possibly?" asked the president from behind his desk. He interlaced his fingers, rested his chin on them and stared at Harper.

"Because Boyarkin isn't the Omsk cultural director," said Harper. "He's chairman of the KGB. And we know there's a factional division in the Politburo at the moment. The defense minister, Kotsarev, after Andropov died, got the GRU out from under KGB control. It was a trade-off with General Secretary Leschenko so that Gresko – chairman of the Council of Ministers – and Kotsarev would support Leschenko's bid for general secretary of the Party and the leadership of the Politburo. Boyarkin's never forgiven Kotsarev and Gresko for reducing the KGB empire. He'd like both their heads. Gresko's position as chairman of the Council of Ministers gives him the number-two spot in the Politburo, but if Leschenko were replaced by Boyarkin both Defense Minister Kotsarev and Gresko would be out pretty damn quick."

"What has this to do with the RUBICON scenario?" asked the president.

"Defense Minister Kotsarev allied himself with Gresko, as I said. Gresko's the second most powerful member of the Politburo, and a moderate, at least for the Kremlin. So KGB Chairman Boyarkin's support has defaulted to the hard-liners and neo-Stalinists, the ones who got the Soviets into Afghanistan back when. Also, we've known for some time that Boyarkin was responsible for the big Chelyabinsk purges when he was district KGB chief there. There was a food riot and about ten thousand people went to the Gulags or disappeared. He wasn't in the Politburo during the Polish crises, but one of our residents reported that he got drunk one night in '81 and said he'd decapitate the Polish nation if he were in a position to do so. Our psychologists think he combines the worst traits of Stalin, Beria and Ivan the Terrible."

"Is he sane?" asked Goodhand.

"Opinions differ. He's good at his job, though. Every time there's a fuss in one of the Moslem republics in the south it's stopped short."

"And he can't stand Kotsarev, Gresko or the GRU," said the president.

"Pardon me, Mr. President," said Harper, "but that's an understatement." The DCI rubbed his nose gloomily. "He hates them."

"General Secretary Leschenko's still running things, though," said Parr.

"He's old," said Harper. "Chairman Gresko and Defense Minister Kotsarev have been able to control the Politburo because Leschenko has tended to back them. Not always, but mostly. It was likely Gresko's faction that was behind the condemnation of that Pakistani missile test last week. They don't like nuclear proliferation any more than we do. But what'll happen when General Secretary Leschenko goes is anybody's guess."

"What would Boyarkin's attitudes be on the proliferation question?" asked the president.

The DCI considered for a moment. "Look at it from the Soviet point of view. Our client states – West Germany, for example – have nuclear weapons on their soil – nominally under our control, of course. I suspect the KGB chairman doesn't see why the USSR can't have its own client states with the same capabilities, only using their own weapons, so the Soviets can't be accused of supporting the spread of nuclear weapons."

"Like Libya, for example."

"Like Libya, or Syria, or whoever."

"Surely he must realize what an explosive – pardon me – situation that would produce."

"I don't know if he realizes it," said Harper. "Or, if he does, whether he cares. He's never been much in touch with the west. He may have a distorted picture of our capabilities or our determination. That's what the RUBICON simulation assumed. A worst-case scenario."

"Tricky," said Parr.

The president leaned back in his chair and clasped his hands behind his head. He looked relaxed but was not. "He certainly doesn't sound like the kind of man we want running things over there."

Harper and Gellner looked at each other. Then Harper said, "Longstop?"

"No!" said Law. "Absolutely not." He leaned forward in his chair suddenly. "I will not countenance assassination. And if I ever hear that Longstop is even being considered as an option, there'll be blood all over the CIA and the State Department. And it won't be Boyarkin's.

"Yes, sir," said Harper and Gellner simultaneously.

The president straightened his tie. "What do you advise we do?"

Harper took a deep breath. Law's flashes of temper, partly because they were so rare and so intense, always unsettled him. "Several things have happened just recently. First, the RUBICON scenario we've discussed. Second, we know that Mossad is up to something having to do with those Pakistani bombs, but they haven't volunteered any information and at this stage we don't really want to know, anyway. But there's been an Israeli freighter docked at Durban for the past two weeks with engine trouble, waiting for parts from Scotland. It's taking an awfully long time to get those parts.

"Third, we're pretty sure the Libyans and the Pakistanis have struck a deal. Mossad agrees. We think Islamabad is going to lend Tripoli a number of the devices, with that cruise-missile delivery system, sometime next month. Our Islamabad station chief is sure the weapons are going by sea, so the Israelis can't shoot down the transport aircraft. I personally suspect the Israelis will try to stop the shipment on the high seas. It's very risky, but they may feel that it's less risky than the alternative."

"We are not to be involved," said Law.

"Certainly not," said the DCI. "I wouldn't let anyone on our payroll get anywhere near the operation." He emphasized the words carefully.

"On the other hand," said Parr, "we don't want those warheads in Tripoli, either."

Law ignored him, staring at Harper. "Exactly what do you mean?"

Harper shrugged. "It's always useful to have a man on the spot. A few days ago the Mossad station chief here approached one of our old employees. This man has been out of the CIA for four, nearly five years. He reported the approach. Mossad wants him to go along on the operation."

"That's a very odd request."

"At first glance. They want him to examine the weapons before they're disposed of to get an estimate of their capabilities. He's an expert at that sort of thing, that and computers. I wouldn't mind knowing more about the state of Pakistani weapons-technology myself." Harper added the last sentence with some trepidation.

"Why don't they use one of their own people?"

"Don't want to risk losing one, I'd guess. Also, the Mossad station chief knows him personally."

"And you want to let him go?"

"He's a private citizen, Mr. President," said Harper. "He

can do as he pleases. Naturally we'd be interested in what he found out on his . . . trip. We often ask people that sort of thing, after they've been overseas."

"You don't have to tell me that," snapped Law. He was clearly worried. "Suppose the thing went awry and he were picked up and killed or identified."

"There are soldiers of fortune all over the place these days, Mr. President," Harper pointed out.

"All right," said Law. "You're the DCI. We can help the Israelis out at least to that extent, since we're letting them do the work we can't diplomatically afford to do ourselves. I don't want those bombs in Libya, either. Pakistan's bad enough by herself. Now, if you'll excuse me. . . ."

The four CFI men got up to leave. Harper was the last to the Oval Office door.

"Cam," said the president as Harper was about to go through it.

"Yes, Mr. President?"

"How accurate is that RUBICON monster?"

"It's often inaccurate on details. But on the broad outlines, it's been right ninety percent of the time."

"I was afraid of that," said Law. "Keep me posted."

In the elevator on the way to the parking garage Goodhand said to Harper, "Is this guy of yours really that keen on cuddling up to a stack of Pakistani A-bombs?"

"I don't know," said Harper. "I haven't asked him yet."

Moscow
June 22

It HAD BEGUN TO RAIN over the Soviet Air Defense Command airbase at Kubinka when the twin-engined Antonov-26 transport dropped out of the overcast on its landing approach. Major Andreyev peered through the round porthole by his seat, past the starboard engine pod, towards the control and radar buildings edging the runway. The aircraft touched down lightly and began to slow. Through gusts of spray from the landing gear he could see MIG-21s and 23s tucked away in their revetments behind the taxiways. One 23 was running an engine test; the howl was audible even over the burr of the Antonov's propellers.

An army Moskvitch sedan drew up alongside the transport as it rolled to a stop. Major Andreyev got his kit, waited until the ground crew had lowered the steps, then got out of the air-craft. A man with colonel's shoulderboards was waiting by the open rear door of the car. He motioned Andreyev to get in. The driver started up immediately, heading for the airfield access road and the Mozajskoye Highway.

"Papers, please, major," said the colonel.

Andreyev handed over his pay book and documents. The colonel glanced through them carefully, and slipped them into his tunic. Andreyev opened his mouth to say something, thought better of it, and remained silent. The colonel looked at him, smiled faintly, and then turned to watch the countryside roll by.

Andreyev was frightened, a deep visceral fear that he had carefully partitioned off from his intellect ever since the tele-printer had required his presence in Moscow. Since the Dushanbe riot he had been at Thirteenth Military District headquarters in Alma-Ata waiting for the inquiry into the incident. Except for a cursory questioning, however, the district

GRU head had hardly bothered with him. Andreyev had asked to see the colonel of his regiment, once, and had been told brusquely to mind his own business and wait for orders. He didn't know what had happened to the battalion lieutenant-colonel.

He suddenly realized, with a start, that they were not on the new highway that drove almost straight from Kubinka to Moscow. They were taking the old road that passed through a series of small towns and then joined the Mozajskoye Highway on the outskirts of the capital. And the driver seemed to be constantly interested in the rearview mirror.

"Colonel, may I ask where we're going?" he ventured.

"General-staff headquarters. Don't worry. This is GRU business, not the brothers."

Andreyev relaxed slightly. Not KGB, then. Sometimes it was very hard to tell. "Why was I recalled?" he asked.

The colonel stiffened marginally. "You'll be told."

From the movement of the driver's ears, Andreyev guessed that the man was grinning. "Yes, colonel," said Andreyev.

The gray-green countryside passed. Even so close to Moscow the villages were made up largely of unpainted wooden cottages, the boards weathered to a silky gray. Some of the better frame houses had the ornate gingerbread of pre-revolution days, but there were very few of them. Most of this area had been burned over during the Great Patriotic War against the German fascists; the countryside was drenched in old blood.

They rejoined the highway a few kilometers from Kuntsevo and then reached the great Moscow Ring Motorway, the road circling the capital. At the ring the driver turned left, towards the new general-staff HQ that had been built to replace the aging and overcrowded quarters at Arbat and Frunze Streets.

The building was not yet finished. A great gray slab of concrete and glass, it humped sullenly in the drizzle. The Moskvitch was checked through into the underground parking garage and Andreyev and the colonel got out.

"In here," said the colonel. They went past two guards,

down a long corridor that smelled of lime and wet concrete and up two flights of stairs. A metal-sheathed door opened into another corridor, this one more or less finished; its walls were tiled in light blue and there was white linoleum on the floor. A few meters along it the colonel stopped and opened another door.

"You'll wait in here," he said.

Andreyev went into the room. There was a desk, vacant, with a chair behind it, and two more chairs of Scandinavian design facing the desk. The chairs were covered in a checked fabric. The walls were painted pale green and there was a portrait of Lenin on one of them. A lone gray filing cabinet stood in one corner. There were no windows.

The door clicked behind Andreyev. He waited twenty seconds, then tried the knob. It would not turn.

Andreyev thought about opening the filing cabinet, realized that he was almost certainly being observed and sat down in the right-hand chair. He began to wait.

Three floors up, in a paneled office, the anonymous colonel saluted and said, "General Yushenko, Major Andreyev is in the interview room. I apologize for the lateness. The aircraft was delayed by poor weather."

General Yushenko looked at his wall clock. It was three in the afternoon. "It doesn't matter. Did you ask if he'd eaten?"

"No, sir."

"Very well. Have the kitchen staff send something to the interview room within fifteen minutes. And no leftovers from lunch."

"Yes, general." A pause. "Vodka as well?"

"Yes, pepper vodka. We'll see what this Major Andreyev is made of."

The colonel smiled without much humor, said "Yes, sir," and departed. General Yushenko blew his nose, picked up Andreyev's file and headed for the interview room.

Andreyev recrossed his legs for the tenth time and tried to ignore the hunger pangs. He had not eaten since the previous evening and was feeling slightly faint and nauseated because of it. He put the sensations away at the back of his mind, with the fear. He had been taught the theory of this in the GRU school in Leningrad and had learned the practice in Afghanistan.

The door rattled softly. Andreyev stood up. A short, rotund man came into the room.

Andreyev had learned to read rank without consciously observing insignia. He was already saluting as General Yushenko walked to the desk and stood beside it. Andreyev stored the image in his memory automatically: thinning hair, rimless glasses perched on a fleshy nose, slightly overweight. Dark brown eyes, almost liquid. Incipient double chin, small ears. Immaculate uniform, salted with badges and decorations. A full general.

Yushenko, for his part, saw a young, rather frightened GRU major. Andreyev was thin, although the thinness was that of a steel cable. His face was angular, and even in these circumstances, his expression opaque. Unobtrusive chin, gray eyes, pale brown hair. A good neutral face, thought Yushenko. Just the one we want; it could be from anywhere. The nose was the only possible problem. It was straight and rather sharp, with a slight lift at eye level. Perhaps too memorable.

Well, thought General Yushenko, it couldn't be perfect. It never is, quite.

He returned the salute and said, "Sit down, major. I'm sorry to have kept you waiting."

This was a surprise. Senior officers did not apologize to juniors for anything. Andreyev sat down carefully, as though the chair were a land mine. The general flopped into the chair behind the desk and opened the file he had brought with him.

Major Nikolai Andreyevitch Andreyev, he read. Born 1956, Minsk. Excellent record in Young Pioneers, DOSAAF. Selected for Frunze Military Academy. Specialist in electronic engineering. Top marks in GRU training. Service in Afghanistan, 1982. Military attaché to our embassy in West Germany for two years. After that in the GRU section. One year in the US. For the past twelve months, on special assignment in the Thirteenth Military District, temporarily attached to the 368th

Motorized Regiment. Languages: fluent German, good English. Some Pushtu. Not married, but enjoys the company of women.

He paused, seeming to consider. Then he said: "This Dushanbe business was unfortunate. We thought you were better than that."

"General, I –"

"I did not ask for an opinion," snapped Yushenko. "The incident should not have happened. You were intimidated by the KGB local."

Andreyev straightened in his chair. "I request permission to make a partial report, sir."

Yushenko was pleased, though he hid it. "Do so."

"The battalion was moved to Dushanbe on twelve hours notice. My information system was still being developed. I could have requested an immediate presence in the city but felt that this would let the brothers know that there was another reporting network. There was also the possibility that the KGB had doubles among my sources. And my sources told me that there was no danger of a riot for at least seventy-two hours." He stopped.

"So what happened?" asked Yushenko.

"I think," said Andreyev, "that the KGB preempted us. I think they started the riot themselves, to prevent us from defusing it before it happened."

Yushenko stared at the major. "This is documented?"

Andreyev gestured at his kit on the floor. "It's in there. The GRU chief at Alma-Ata told me to keep it."

Yushenko closed his eyes for a moment. Then he opened them and said, "It is necessary for you to disappear for a while."

Andreyev felt his stomach collapse. "Yes, general."

"Not like that," said Yushenko irritably, noting the almost invisible wince. "I didn't say anything about penalties. Why are you so quick to jump to this conclusion? According to your dossier, you do not jump to conclusions."

"Yes, general. I try not to do so."

A tap on the door. "Food," said Yushenko. "You are at least as hungry as I am. I haven't had lunch, either. Come in."

A soldier wheeled a small metal table into the interview room. On it were slices of thick brown bread, deep-fried cheese, smoked salmon and cold Azov sturgeon; there was chicken salad and *pampushky*, doughnuts filled with jam. An iced carafe of mineral water stood next to a bottle of pepper vodka. General Yushenko grabbed an empty plate and began to serve himself. "Eat," he said. Andreyev followed suit hungrily.

"I often regret moving out here from Frunze Street," said Yushenko around a bite of sturgeon. "You can't eat at the Praga any more. The food here isn't bad, but it isn't up to the Praga."

The Praga was a restaurant around the corner from the old GHQ building in Frunze Street. It had been a favorite with the military before the move. Andreyev had never eaten at the Praga, although he agreed politely. General Yushenko poured vodka and they drank, washing the spirit down with gulps of icy mineral water. Andreyev began to feel considerably better.

"And now," said Yushenko, pushing away his plate, "what are we going to do with you?"

Andreyev immediately put the remainder of his meal aside although he had not quite finished one of the jellied doughnuts. "Begging your pardon, general, you said I was to disappear?"

"Hmn. You are a very astute young man. You say you believe the KGB arranged the riot?"

This was dangerous ground. "Sir, there is evidence in my report."

"It doesn't surprise me," said the general.

Andreyev barely prevented his mouth from dropping open. He had worried himself sick about reporting his suspicions, reasoning that such an accusation, if it ever got back to the KGB, would make life in the Soviet Union impossible for him. Even the GRU might not be able to protect him. And here was this general saying that he wasn't surprised.

"Sir?" he managed.

"You are likely aware," said Yushenko, "that there is considerable resentment in the KGB over the autonomy the GRU has achieved in the last few years. At the lower levels, the organizations cooperate well. But higher up, as I said, resentment. The higher up, the greater the resentment. You were put into the Dushanbe region to establish a monitoring system for the evaluation of Moslem dissidence and discontent. I had a long meeting with your military district commander when your assignment was made a year ago. We suspected that you might stumble across something like this. That is why you have been returned here on such short notice – because you did."

"General," said Andreyev, "I don't understand."

"There are certain factions that want the GRU to be brought back under KGB control," said Yushenko. "One way to do this is to discredit our supporters in the Politburo and elsewhere. Constant unrest in the Moslem republics would aid in doing so. I hope you understand. There have been incidents other than Dushanbe."

"Yes, sir."

"To return to your personal difficulty," said Yushenko. "The fact that the Dushanbe riot occurred before your unit could preempt it indicates that the local KGB believes we have penetrated their security. Which, in a way, we have, thanks to you. Now, there is little immediate danger to yourself, since your cover was not broken. Was it?"

"No, general," said Andreyev, hoping fervently that it hadn't been.

"Reassignment for officers such as you isn't unusual," said Yushenko. "There's no doubt the KGB knows you are a GRU man. However, there are enough GRU people floating about in the south that you won't be under any particular suspicion as the man who's discovered their nasty little secret. We're reshuffling a lot of GRU postings at the moment. The KGB won't be able to keep track of all of them. According to our records, you're being sent to the armor college at Kharkov for a refresher course in anti-armor techniques."

There was a pause. Andreyev waited.

"That's nonsense, of course," said General Yushenko. "That's not where you're going at all."

Moscow
1:13 A.M. to 7:00 A.M., June .

AT 1:13 A.M. ON JUNE TWENTY-SIXTH, Georgi Aksenov, personal cook to Konstantin T. Leschenko, general secretary of the Communist Party and chairman of the Presidium of the Supreme Soviet, prepared a late snack of caviar, toast and vodka for his employer. It was served to Leschenko in the study of his villa on Vorobyovskoye Way in the Lenin Hills, not far from Moscow University. Leschenko went to bed at 1:58 A.M. Aksenov conscientiously had the used dishes removed from the study by one of Leschenko's guards – Aksenov was not allowed in the study – washed them carefully and put them away. Then he went to bed himself.

At 6:11 A.M. on June twenty-sixth Leschenko had a heart attack. His wife, Yevdokia, sleeping next to him, woke to her husband's gasping and immediately called for the house guards. They rushed the general secretary to the ambulance stationed in the villa garages and sped him on his way to the Kremlin Hospital at 8 Kalinin Prospekt for emergency treatment. Several telephone calls were placed immediately, of which one was unauthorized.

Another unofficial contact was attempted, but without success. Nikolai Balakirev was Leschenko's personal chauffeur and lived in an apartment above the garages. He woke as soon as he heard the commotion below, saw a blanketed form being slid into an ambulance and went downstairs to see if he were needed. The KGB Ninth Directorate men told him to go back where he came from and not to return until he was told to do so. Balakirev obeyed immediately. The loyalty of Ninth Directorate personnel was closely monitored; no other KGB employees were allowed to carry loaded weapons in the presence of the leaders or their families. Balakirev had a healthy respect for the Ninth.

However, he did not return to his apartment. There was a back stair to the garage and he took that instead. No one stood at the rear door; the Ninth would be sealing off the perimeters of the grounds.

He followed the gravel path around to the service vestibule at the rear of the villa. There was a telephone there, used by the villa staff to place orders for supplies. Balakirev knew that it was monitored but guessed that in the confusion it would be hard for the monitors to know precisely who had used the instrument. He needed no more than thirty seconds.

The vestibule was unguarded. He picked up the receiver and began to dial.

He had just begun the last digit when a rifle butt smashed into his kidneys. He dropped the telephone and collapsed. The Ninth Directorate guard kicked him out of the way, hung up the receiver and shouted for assistance.

The successful unofficial call was from the cook, Aksenov, who had been awake all night. He waited until he heard the ambulance pull away, then went to the kitchen and sat at the table. A Ninth man put his head in, nodded and withdrew. Aksenov placed his call at the kitchen telephone. It was answered on the second ring.

"Kirov," said the cook.

The earpiece clicked as the receiver at the other end was hung up. Aksenov went to bed.

Moscow
8:30 A.M. to 2:30 P.M., June 26

IT WAS ALREADY FULL DAYLIGHT. On the Kutuzovskiy Prospekt, leading into the city, there was a little light traffic: bureaucrats and Party functionaries early on their way to their offices to prove their zeal. The sky was cloudless and the gray-stone neo-classical facades of the city looked nearly cheerful.

"Very sudden," said the chairman of the Council of Ministers, Viktor Gresko. He studied the gray city as it rolled past, trying to relax against the leather of the Zil's soundproof rear. The Zil limousine was one of the marks of Politburo or Secretariat membership; it was the equivalent, in the west, of a Mercedes or a Rolls or a Lincoln.

"Yes," said Defense Minister Fyodor Kotsarev. "There was no hint of it in the last medical report. But you can't always tell." He rubbed his nose, which was small, not much more than a button. He had an outsized round face, which made the nose look even smaller. His white hair was cropped short and he was marginally overweight. "Who called you?"

"Comrade KGB Chairman Boyarkin," said Gresko. The very thought made him feel queasy. As soon as the KGB chairman had telephoned Gresko had dressed hurriedly, shaved and called for the Zil. His curly gray hair felt unkempt, and the razor had missed a patch of whiskers at the center of his chin.

"What was the reaction of the other members when you called them?"

In a situation such as this it was normally Gresko's responsibility to contact the Politburo members to arrange any necessary emergency action.

"Boyarkin had already contacted everyone except you,"

said Gresko. "I was the second-last to know. I called you. You were the last."

"What was his excuse for leaving us till last?"

"That I was impossible to reach because of telephone difficulties. Then he asked me to call you."

"I had someone inside Leschenko's staff," said Kotsarev. "But he didn't make contact at all. The secretary's chauffeur."

"What happened to him?"

"Who knows?"

The Zil was rolling along Karl Marx Prospekt towards Manege Square, past the crenellated battlements of the Kremlin. The walls glowed a dark brown-red in the early sunlight, the color of old blood.

"The meeting isn't at Staraya Square?" asked Kotsarev.

Contrary to popular belief, most meetings of the Politburo are held not in the Kremlin but at 4 Staraya Square, the offices of the Central Committee of the Communist Party, just off Kuibyshev Street.

"No. Boyarkin said he was concerned about security."

"Thank you for the ride, by the way."

"We needed to talk," said Chairman Gresko. "This is not going to be good."

The Zil rounded the northern angle of the Kremlin, passed the Arsenal Tower on the corner and slowed for the Nikolsky Gate.

"The Ninth is everywhere," observed the defense minister. "Double or triple guards."

"I have a feeling," said Gresko, "that this government is going to be turned inside out in a few hours. We've left it too late."

The arrests began at 9:02 A.M. with the collection of twelve clerks in the Foreign Ministry offices. Normally the pickups would have been made by the Political Security Services of the KGB Second Directorate, but in this case they were handled by Ninth Directorate personnel. Over the previous twelve months the clerks had been observed in "unusual" contacts with non-Soviet citizens.

By 9:15 six department and sub-department heads of the Intourist travel bureau were also on their way to holding cells in the old KGB headquarters at the Lubianka Prison in Dzerzhinsky Square. More seriously, three records clerks and their supervisor at the Central Committee building at 4 Staraya Square were also arrested. This was a direct attack against Leschenko's personnel. A similar strike against Gresko was made by Ninth Directorate men, with detentions of six junior staff members of the Council of Ministers.

As a finishing touch for the early morning, the Ninth arrested a number of KGB personnel in its own armed-forces directorate, which was responsible for the monitoring of the loyalty of the navy, air forces and army. The men in question were suspected of being GRU plants. They were taken to the lowest level of the Lubianka and summarily shot as traitors to their KGB oath.

General Secretary Leschenko's unfortunate chauffeur, Balakirev, although he did not understand why, was among them.

The meeting was held in a nondescript room in the Kremlin's Old Arsenal, on the western side away from the central courtyard. Gresko and Kotsarev had been the last to join the meeting except for Zhigalin, Gresko's deputy chairman. Gresko tried not to look impatient as Zhigalin slipped into the high-backed chair beside him.

"What kept you?" he whispered in the deputy chairman's ear.

"I was at Uspenskoye. My apologies."

Deputy Chairman Zhigalin, like Gresko, Kotsarev and several others of the Politburo, owned a luxurious *dacha* near Uspenskoye, a small village some twenty kilometers outside Moscow. The country houses were among the perquisites of the ruling class.

Gresko looked around the table and tried to estimate his support. As chairman of the Council of Ministers, he was theoretically the dominant member of the Politburo if the general secretary were indisposed. The third key position, after that of the general secretary and his own, was chairman of the Presidium of the Supreme Soviet. Leschenko had followed precedent and held both the general secretaryship and the chairmanship of the Presidium. This reduced factionalism, but concentrated a great deal of power in one man. Gresko had always considered this dangerous.

"Now that everyone is here," he said, jumping in before Boyarkin could, "we may begin." He glanced around the faces again; all were suitably opaque. In General Secretary Leschenko's absence, there were fourteen members: the four secretaries of the Central Committee; the secretaries for Moscow, Leningrad, the Ukraine and Kazakhstan; the chairman of the Control Commission; the minister of foreign affairs; and, all at the table's end, Deputy Chairman Zhigalin, Defense Minister Kotsarev and Gresko himself. And fourteenth: Boyarkin, chairman of the KGB. His head, which seemed to droop because of its unusually long neck, was very thinly fleshed, exaggerating the high Mongolian cheekbones and the triangular chin. His eyes were deepset and intelligent; his hair thin, still dark and straight. And as always, there was an internal tension about him, like that of a drawn wire.

Gresko decided to go over to the attack.

"We are here to consider the problem of the general secretary's illness," he said. "Comrade KGB Chairman Boyarkin, perhaps you have a recent report on his condition, since you have been careful to be close to the situation since it began."

He had intended it as a rebuke, but Boyarkin seemed to accept the remark as a gesture of confidence in his handling of events. "The general secretary is extremely ill," said the KGB chairman in his light, timbreless voice. "But there is reason for hope, according to the doctors. I have given orders for any change in his condition to be reported here immediately."

"This is quite unexpected," said Andrei Zaseda, first secretary for Kazakhstan. "There was no hint of this . . . collapse before. There was difficulties with the secretary's health, to be sure, but –"

"That is not the point at issue," snapped Gresko. First Secretary Zaseda was one of his supporters, but Gresko had to keep the meeting on track. If Boyarkin were allowed to delay a decision on the succession, there was no judging how far he could extend KGB control. Gresko already sensed power slipping from his grasp. Several members who might normally side with him appeared uncertain where the real power lay. Gresko knew the signs: body movements and hints of expressions that were impossible to control. If he were aware of it, then so was Boyarkin.

"I don't think," said Aleksandr Morosov, first secretary of the Central Committee, "that this is the time to be discussing the secretary's death. Such a discussion might well be premature."

Ah, Morosov, thought Gresko. Now I know where you are. With Boyarkin, the easterner.

"Then why are we here?" snapped Defense Minister Kotsarev, speaking for the first time. He had always disliked Morosov.

"To make sure that the Party's obligations are carried out while the secretary is unwell," said Morosov, with apparent surprise.

"There was to be a meeting later today in any case," said Boyarkin, "to deal with various matters of internal security. Perhaps we ought to proceed with that until further medical information is available. Would Chairman of the Council of Ministers Gresko agree to a vote on that?"

"No," said Gresko. "If the general secretary dies, we will be caught at even shorter notice than we are now. We must agree at least on an interim general secretary until –" he paused, "various loyalties are sorted out."

There was a loud knock at the conference room door.

"This may be regarding General Secretary Leschenko," said Boyarkin. Without Gresko's permission, he called, "Come in."

A Ninth Directorate captain entered, handed Boyarkin a note and departed. The KGB chairman unfolded the paper.

"The secretary?" prompted Kotsarev after a moment.

"This is not regarding the secretary," said Boyarkin shortly, and continued to read.

"Perhaps your departmental correspondence could be dealt with at Dzerzhinsky Square," suggested Gresko, letting his anger show at last.

Boyarkin placed the sheet of paper facedown in front of him and said, "This is a Ninth Directorate report." He paused so that his words would sink in. "Given the peculiarity of the situation, I have had a number of security measures taken. There have been several arrests, made on the authority that General Secretary Leschenko provided me two months ago. I –"

"There is no present proof of this authority," snapped Gresko. "You had better furnish it now."

"No," said Boyarkin. "While the general secretary is alive – and he is – that is a matter between himself and the KGB."

The sword had never been so nakedly drawn. Dear God, Gresko thought, in a way that he had avoided since his eighteenth year, how sure he must be of himself. Or is this certainty a mask for weakness, only to confuse or convince others?

"I'm needed at Dzerzhinsky Square," said Boyarkin after another moment. "May I propose that the meeting be adjourned until one o'clock?"

"No," said Gresko. "We must not leave the situation uncontained."

Boyarkin leaned across the table. "Uncontained? I have just been given this message –" he gestured at the note without looking down, "which says that, in addition to what I just told you, there was large-scale rioting last night in Baysun, not two hundred kilometers from Dushanbe. And the Dushanbe incident was only two weeks ago. The situation is already uncontained. And it is you, Chairman Gresko, and others, who have misdirected Secretary Leschenko into ignoring the disastrous state of loyalty of the southern Union republics. I request adjournment now. I have to act in the Baysun matter."

"Vote," said Morosov.

There were other nods around the table. Gresko, defeated, allowed it. The adjournment was decided.

As the other members of the Politburo stood up to leave, Boyarkin, still seated, said, "Please don't be alarmed if there is some concern in your organizations when you contact them. We have had to take a number of security precautions. The situation will be normal before very long."

Gresko, standing, looked at the chairman of the KGB. Boyarkin's expression, unguarded for a moment, reminded him of one he had seen, only once, a long time ago. He had to rummage in his memory before he found its predecessor. It was in November 1942, when the Red Army pincers had met at the forlorn village of Kalach, and surrounded the German Sixth Army at Stalingrad. Gresko had been eighteen, a signaler at General Romanenko's headquarters, when the news came in.

The expression on Boyarkin's face was exactly that which had been on Romanenko's: the toothed grin of a wolf at the beginning of the kill.

By one o'clock in the afternoon more than two hundred known dissidents and unapproved writers, painters and musicians had been rounded up. The Lubianka cells were full and the last detainees were sent far outside the city to a transshipment camp near Podolsk. There had been a few other arrests in various industrial ministries, primarily on charges – which were usually justified – of graft and corruption. The Security Services had been used for the last of these, since they were economic crimes rather than treason. The news had been getting around; when Gresko returned to the Kremlin from his office, which was trying, despite extreme agitation, to carry on a normal day, the streets were nearly deserted.

At 1:10 P.M. Konstantin T. Leschenko, general secretary of the Communist Party of the Soviet Union and chairman of the Presidium of the Supreme Soviet, died in the Kremlin Hospital. This news was transmitted to the Politburo conference room at 1:26 P.M., accompanied by six guards of the Ninth Directorate. The guards, against all precedent, did not leave the room. In the vote that followed, Vitaly A. Boyarkin, hitherto chairman of the KGB, was chosen general secretary of the Communist Party of the Soviet Union and chairman of the Presidium of the Supreme Soviet. Aleksandr D. Morosov assumed the KGB chairmanship. Alexei S. Blinov, minister of internal affairs, took over Morosov's position, being moved up from his lower position in the Central Committee. The meeting was adjourned at 3:10 in the afternoon, after making basic preparations for Leschenko's funeral.

In the Zil outside the Nikolsky Gate, Gresko said, "This could be disaster."

"Yes," answered Kotsarev. "But not yet. Not yet."

Moscow
July 3

AT TEN IN THE MORNING, Nasir Rashidi, Pakistan's ambassador to the USSR, quietly left his embassy at 17 Sudovo-Kudrinskaya to pay a visit to Boris N. Distanov, Soviet minister of foreign affairs. When he left the Foreign Ministry building after an hour's convivial discussion, Rashidi took with him a rather unusual document. Most of it was characteristically Russian and obtuse, but three points stood out clearly:

1) The new Soviet leadership has no serious reservations about defensive measures taken by sovereign states, either in their own interest or in support of their allies, provided such measures are not directed to imperialist ends, as is the case with the United States and Israel.

2) The Union of Soviet Socialist Republics will extend both friendship and material aid to those nations who resent the manipulative assistance campaigns foisted on them by the imperialist west, particularly those of the United States.

3) Such friendship and aid is, of course, contingent on the willingness of such nations to refuse to be channels of western subversive intervention in the affairs of Socialist states or their allies.

The ambassador was no fool. Most of the document was the standard Russian move when relations between a Third World nation and the United States began to deteriorate. But the point about defensive measures startled him. The late General Secretary Leschenko's policy had been firmly set against nuclear proliferation. This looked like a complete reversal.

He would send the note home to Islamabad in the afternoon diplomatic bag. At the very least it would serve as a stick with which to beat Washington.

Uspenskoye
July 4

DEFENSE MINISTER FYODOR KOTSAREV ladled the brown beans into the American coffee mill. Between spoonsful he watched the zigzag flight of a butterfly along the fringe of lawn that separated the *dacha*'s sunroom from the birch wood. The thick masses of greenery beyond the room's expanse of glass seemed almost part of the decor. No leaves stirred; even here, twenty kilometers from Moscow, the heat was oppressive. Only the West German air conditioning made the sunroom habitable.

"Is it more or less what you remember him saying?" asked Kotsarev.

"Not quite finished," grunted the chairman of the Council of Ministers from his seat at the broad elm table. The document Gresko was reading had been reconstructed from his and Kotsarev's recollections of the Politburo meeting of two days ago, when General Secretary Boyarkin had outlined, among other things, his plans for an approach to Islamabad. This document represented one of the other things. Each Politburo member had received a copy and when the meeting was over the copies had been collected. Boyarkin had allowed no note-taking. Consequently Gresko and Kotsarev had pooled the resources of their highly trained memories and produced an accurate facsimile:

A. The west's fear of nuclear war in or near its sources of oil will cause the west to make great concessions to prevent such a conflict.

B. The result of this, in the immediate future, will be that US allies and dependents (Japan, for example) will try to prevent provocative American actions in the mid-east, should pro-Soviet or presently nonaligned nations there acquire a military nuclear capability. This presents many opportunities for causing dissension in the capitalist camp.

Here Gresko had added in the margin: *e.g. Why should Tokyo risk being bombed because the US overreacts to a perceived threat?*

C. Such divisions between the west and its allies could be produced, for example, if certain Arab states, under Soviet guidance, were to imply that the use of nuclear weapons was not beyond possibility. Given the conditions of A and B above, this would force the west to comply, to some degree, with Arab and therefore Soviet wishes.

D. It is also highly significant that the west is hardly in a position to use nuclear weapons on its major sources of oil. This is less the case with Libya, but an American attack on that nation would likely cause Saudi sources, for example, to be cut off in retaliation.

E. A useful offshoot of this situation is that the US will have to restrain Israel from any adventurism that might cause a local nuclear exchange. This will increase Arab, and eventually Soviet, freedom of action in the area. Also, the apparent powerlessness of the United States to protect one ally will have repercussions among her other friends.

F. The <u>eventual goal</u> [this had been underlined in the original as well] is our hidden but complete domination of mid-east oil and the slow but inevitable crippling of the capitalist economies. This strategy has been followed for twenty years, and it is now time to bring it towards fruition.

G. The implication of the above is that this body should no longer oppose the spread of nuclear weapons to selected nations. Covert assistance in the acquisition of nuclear devices may also be considered in the appropriate situations.

The coffee mill buzzed furiously for twenty seconds. Kotsarev poured the grind into the coffee maker and started it. Gresko finished reading.

"My apologies for the typing," said Kotsarev, "but I thought I'd better do it myself." His voice was wry.

"What do you think of it?" asked Gresko.

"It's horribly dangerous," said the defense minister. "It's one thing to risk war with the west – we've contemplated it on more than one occasion – but it's another to place ourselves in a position where we could get dragged in like drunks to the detoxification cells. If we're going to have a war, we should begin it ourselves, at the best time and in the best way – not let someone else arrange things so that neither we nor the United States can avoid it."

Gresko looked momentarily thoughtful. "Has this room been swept?"

"HQ team went over it an hour before you came. They didn't find any bugs."

"We shouldn't sit facing the window, anyway," said Gresko.

They made sure they were not. The coffee maker hissed jubilantly and clicked, and coffee began to dribble into the urn. Kotsarev ignored it.

"You know what's going to happen," Gresko said. "He's going to do to us what the Politburo did to Khrushchev because of that fiasco in Cuba. Force us to resign, to become nobodies. He doesn't dare yet, because that kind of behavior might swing some of the less committed members against him. But it's only a matter of time."

"Not even that bothers me so much," said the minister of defense gloomily. "It's the possibility that they go even farther and have us shot – as Khrushchev and Malenkov did to Beria."

"That's also not unlikely, given time," said Gresko. He paused. "Do you think General Secretary Leschenko died naturally?"

"The autopsy report said he did."

"It would, if the writers had Ninth Directorate men hanging over them. Have you had any hint of anything at all?"

"We've checked on Leschenko's house staff as far as we could without arousing KGB interest. The chauffeur, the man we had inside, has disappeared. General Yushenko hasn't been able to trace him. Everyone else is still around."

"Curious," said Gresko. "It's unlike Boyarkin not to clean up afterward – if there was anything out of order."

"This isn't solving our immediate problem." Kotsarev got up, poured coffee and sat down again. "Are we going to wait like two steers in an abatoir?"

Gresko studied the minister of defense closely. He had known Kotsarev for thirty years and had worked near or with him for ten. He was almost certain he could trust him. Almost.

I have no choice just now, thought Gresko. Kotsarev has the GRU and I cannot fight Boyarkin and his KGB with my own Council of Ministers.

"We should consider some preliminary action, I think," he said. "You said something interesting in the car on the afternoon of Leschenko's death. I am still wondering precisely what you meant."

Kotsarev rotated his coffee cup slowly on the table's smooth grain. "If this goes to the wrong people, it will cause many deaths, mine among the first. It will also give you a way of allying yourself with Boyarkin, by betraying what I tell you."

"It wouldn't save me indefinitely," Gresko pointed out. "Anyway, I wouldn't do it, Fyodor."

"All right. Remember, though, even knowing this is extremely dangerous."

"A very small part of the GRU counterespionage section has studied measures we might take if the KGB attempted to reassert its old control. A subsidiary study considered options if the KGB tried to fill the Politburo entirely with its own person-nel. No one wants another Beria. We depend, somewhat like the Americans, on a balance of power at the top of the pyramid. This study had very frightening implications."

"What?" asked Gresko. He had no idea that Kotsarev had already gone so far.

"It suggested an army coup against a KGB-packed Politburo, exactly the sort of thing KGB domination of the GRU was intended to prevent. The very existence of the study was reason enough to turn control of the GRU back over to the KGB. I had it destroyed."

"And the authors?"

"They were promoted. General Yushenko and I considered it the best way to ensure their silence."

Gresko smiled. "Hardly Boyarkin's methods."

"Hardly," said Kotsarev. He drank half his coffee at a gulp. "But there was more. The study also examined possible American reactions to the confusion that would accompany such a coup. If it happened at a period of extreme tension, the probability was high that the Americans would launch a first strike."

"Why?" asked Gresko.

"First, because they would fear irrational acts by our leadership in such a crisis, especially if the coup were failing and American complicity were suspected. Second, and following from that, is that they would have a good chance of destroying our counter-strike forces while our reactions were confused and delayed. That scenario presupposed that the Americans were unaware of the imminence of the coup."

"Go on," said Gresko. He was aware of a sudden tension in the back of his neck.

"There was an alternative scenario. This was to inform the Americans shortly before the fact and to keep them informed while the . . . process went on. This substantially reduced the risk of American panic. It did not, however, preclude their taking advantage of us during a momentary weakness. Much depended upon the character of the American president at the time."

"I see why you don't want Boyarkin to know," said Gresko dryly. "The very existence of such a study is treason."

"Yes."

"On the other hand," Gresko said in a measured way, "if Boyarkin's policies are inevitably going to lead to accidental war with the west, he must be removed – regardless of the question of our own personal futures. Given his control of the KGB through KGB Chairman Morosov, the only swift way of doing so would be by using the GRU and the army. It would have to be very carefully planned. But you tell me that the skeleton of such a plan exists – has existed. Would it be possible to explore the subject further?"

"It would be. But it is very dangerous."

"What about the Americans?" asked Gresko.

"If Boyarkin is leading us to an uncontrolled outbreak of war, and the only way to stop him is by force, then the safest way to do so is to hint to the Americans what is going on. They'd like a power struggle here, if they were reasonably sure it wouldn't mean war. It would weaken us somewhat."

"It is better than war," said Gresko, remembering Stalingrad. "Almost anything is better than war."

"The situation needs more study," said Kotsarev. "Let me see what General Yushenko's reaction is."

"The GRU head," said Gresko, wishing to be quite sure.

"Yes. He was one of the original study group. There was also myself. And two others."

"Good," said Gresko. He turned and looked out the window. The butterfly had long departed from the fringe of the lawn. The birch wood looked cool and refreshing.

"I hope we won't ever need to go through with it," he said.

At 11:36 that night, a hit-and-run victim was brought to the emergency entrance of the Botkin Hospital. Despite the efforts of the admission team, he died twelve minutes later of severe internal injuries and a dreadfully broken skull. There was a high percentage of alcohol in his bloodstream.

His identity papers showed him to be Georgi Y. Aksenov, a cook on the Leschenko household staff; his death was treated as a routine traffic mishap. By eight o'clock the following morning, the investigation file on the accident had disappeared as though it had never existed. Boyarkin had finally gotten around to tidying up.

Islamabad, Pakistan
July 10

THE HEAT, EVEN AT EIGHT O'CLOCK in the evening, was intense. The moon bulked huge and orange on the eastern horizon, shimmering a little in the wavering air. Under its light Islamabad lay pale and rectilinear, its great unpopulated avenues picked out by sparse streetlights. To the north and east heaved the black humps of the Margala Hills, the first low ranges of the Pir Panjal Mountains beyond.

Many more lights had been planned in the city than were burning; electricity had been severely rationed for two years. At the diplomatic enclave at Ramna 4, however, the rationing had had little apparent effect. The Soviet Embassy was well lit, perhaps even more so than usual, for Ambassador Viktor I. Petrunin was holding a large reception in honor of the new Saudi ambassador.

"They look thirsty, don't they," said Vasili Obukhov, surveying the multicolored diplomatic spectrum in the reception hall. "The Germans especially. We should all receive hazard pay for serving in a strict Moslem country. No alcohol at diplomatic functions, and hardly anywhere else. Barbaric."

Major Vladislav Kochin glanced at the first cultural secretary, not sure whether to respond. "It makes tongues less likely to wag," he said noncommittally. He had been posted from the Karachi consulate three months previously, and was still finding his way around his superior's astringent brand of humor. Kochin was supposedly in charge of supplies for the embassy. Actually, he was the KGB deputy station chief, holding major's rank. Obukhov was in charge of the station, and was a colonel.

"Should we ask the American ambassador upstairs for a

glass of Stolichnaya?" asked Colonel Obukhov. "It might do wonders for the cause of world peace."

"It probably would," said Major Kochin. "But I don't think he'd come."

"No, he wouldn't. We'll have to settle for our other guest. Did you get rid of the little brothers?"

The phrase "little brothers," once used exclusively for the intelligence services of the non-Russian Warsaw Pact nations, had over the last two years been extended by KGB personnel to include members of the GRU. There were two of the military intelligence people at the Islamabad embassy.

"Yes. I set them up with some of the Czech industrial delegation."

"You're a cruel man, Vladislav Alexeyevich. They'll both have reeking heads tomorrow."

"He's here," said Major Kochin. "Over there by the punch bowl. Talking to the Swedish military attaché."

The man, a tall Pakistani in a finely cut suit, was pouring himself a glass of punch. He drank three times, in abrupt sips, and then put the glass down.

"He's clean," said Colonel Obukhov, noting the movements. "Ten minutes from now. You'd better go on up. Don't offer him anything to drink. He's very strict."

Major Kochin left the brilliant room with its geometric designs and bright swirl of nationalities and went up the back stairway to Obukhov's office. There was a small bar in one corner of the room. He poured an ounce of Scotch whiskey and drank it straight down. To his disgust, he found that his palms were damp. He had never operated at this level before. The man by the punch bowl had been Riaz Hasan, Pakistan's chief of intelligence and counterespionage, and a close associate of President and Head of State Mohammed Zia ul'Haq.

Kochin thought about another Scotch and decided against it. Sixty percent of Soviet diplomatic personnel overseas were alcoholics to one degree or another, and Kochin had no intention of joining the majority. In his position, it was much too dangerous.

The door bumped softly behind Colonel Obukhov. "He'll

be here in a couple of minutes," he said, sitting behind the desk. "We have up to a quarter of an hour with him. Then he'll have to go."

"Yes, secretary."

"I hope you realize the level of responsibility I'm giving you," said Obukhov. "The directions from Moscow Center have changed since the new leadership came in. In some ways we are reversing ourselves on certain matters. It's no secret – in here, anyway – that the Libyans have been requesting military assistance of a nuclear nature from Pakistan. We are to expedite it, to the best of our ability." He paused. "No, not to the best of our ability. We are to expedite it. Period."

Kochin tried to swallow his shock. "What?"

"You heard me. I'm delegating you to cooperate with Riaz Hasan. Whatever he needs to move his . . . equipment, you provide it."

Major Kochin brought himself back under control. "Yes, colonel."

"Don't call me colonel. You might do it by accident at a bad time."

There was a soft tap on the door. Colonel Obukhov answered it and ushered Hasan in. The Pakistani intelligence chief paused when he saw Kochin, who had stood up politely.

"It's all right," said Obukhov in English. "Major Kochin works very closely with me."

All three sat down and the maneuvering began. It would have been very bad manners for Obukhov to come straight to the point, and he was careful not to do so. Kochin, not for the first time, admired his superior's skill in adapting his approach to Islamic etiquette; it took a full seven minutes for the conversational preliminaries to be cleared out of the way. Even this was hurrying the situation to its limit. Kochin noticed Hasan's eyes flick towards him periodically, as though to make sure he were still there. The intelligence chief's face was gaunt and lined; the addition of a hook of a nose made him resemble a peregrine falcon.

Finally Riaz Hasan said, "There was a small matter the head of state wished me to discuss with you. It is in connection with the note that was dispatched here by our ambassador in Moscow. General Zia found it extremely interesting."

Obukhov made a deprecatory gesture. "We are glad to cooperate. I believe a new perspective on Soviet-Pakistan relations might be near at hand."

"Perhaps," said Hasan. "There is one specific area in which we might be glad of your assistance."

"Ah," said Obukhov. "Perhaps you would be so good as to elaborate."

"The Libyan government is suggesting that we respond to the help they have provided over the past fifteen years. General Zia is most anxious to discharge our debts. However, certain difficulties have arisen." Hasan paused and studied Major Kochin for a moment. "I'm sure you will understand what I mean."

Kochin nodded. Hasan went on.

"One particular method of repayment is decidedly unpopular with Israel, and accordingly with the United States. We believe that our plans of shipping a number of nuclear warheads and delivery systems to a sister Islamic nation have been compromised by the Central Intelligence Agency and Mossad. As their resources are rather greater than ours, an ally would be very appreciated."

Obukhov nodded thoughtfully. "By what means had you intended to send the devices?" He already knew, but it was necessary to preserve the other man's face.

"By ship. A small freighter, very secretly, with false manifests and a security detachment on board. We no longer believe this to be a safe method. An Israeli vessel has been in Durban harbor in South Africa for more than two weeks. We had intended to send our ship that way, as a transit through the Suez Canal is too close to Israel. We think the Israeli ship is intended to intercept ours."

"What is your alternative?"

"An air shipment. We had intended this first of all, but rejected it as being too vulnerable to Israeli interference. We do not wish to lose these weapons as Iraq lost its reactor in 1981.

We are now considering the use of the ship as a blind, a distraction, but are concerned about penetration of this as well."

"A very realistic worry," said Colonel Obukhov. "Both CIA and Mossad are very clever, very tenacious." The KGB colonel rubbed his nose pensively.

Hasan said, "You have information about the agents both of these organizations have in our country, information you have not passed on to us. It would be delightful, for the new perspective you mentioned, if enough such information were provided to ensure the operation's success."

Major Kochin realized suddenly that Hasan was hating this encounter. The Pakistani was barely concealing the injury to his pride that must have come when Zia ordered him to request KGB help. Obukhov would have to deal with the man very carefully.

"Your intelligence service is among the world's best," said Obukhov smoothly, "but in this case you are dealing with rich nations that have services almost as effective. It's natural to need assistance." He folded his hands neatly on the desk. "We will provide you tomorrow morning with all the information you need to make the Israelis and the Americans think the devices have gone by sea. Additionally, we'll put certain of our facilities at your disposal for the real shipment."

"Thank you," said Hasan. "This will relieve General Zia's mind very greatly, as well as the minds of our ally." He stood up. So did the two Russians.

"Call me tomorrow at ten," said the KGB colonel. He saw Hasan through the door and then turned to Kochin. "You heard what he needs," he said. "We had better start now. I want that data ready for him by 10:00 A.M. Anything he can use to hide his tracks. If they don't succeed in making this shipment, we can look forward to an interview with the new secretary of the Party." He looked pensive. "I've met him. You wouldn't like it."

The Red Sea
July 13

IT WAS SO HOT THAT THE WAVES seemed to have been bleached of their color. Here, twelve hundred miles south of the southernmost Israeli port of Eilat, the very horizon lay blurred and uncertain in the distance. *Reshef* and her sister ships cruised at the center of a circle whose boundaries were formed by a haze of superheated air.

There were four of the vessels: Israeli fast-attack boats, three of them armed with twin 76-mm cannon, four machine guns and six Gabriel anti-ship missiles each. The fourth, *Kidon,* carried a reduced weapon load; the weapons had been replaced by an extensive electronic-countermeasures and surveillance installation. Two hundred feet long, the ships had a range of twenty-four hundred miles at twenty knots, and would need both the range and speed. They were ostensibly on long-duration cruising exercises; a small Israeli tanker kept distant company, for refuelling.

Thorne stood by *Reshef's* fore turret watching two sailors tighten the weather seal around the barrel of the gun. The turret's steel was almost too hot to touch, and the men cursed intermittently when they burned their fingers. Above and behind Thorne, *Reshef's* captain observed the work from the wheelhouse windows. The attack boat was making about six knots, just enough to provide a light breeze over the deck without causing too much pitch. The breeze, if anything, made Thorne feel hotter.

The last two-and-a-half weeks seemed as blurred as the horizon. Thorne had reported Stein's approach, then waited. Nothing happened for three days, except for a phone call indicating that the matter was under consideration. He had tried to work on the book, but it seemed flat and tasteless. His monthly call to Los Angeles had left him even more out of sorts; the children were fine, his ex-wife told him, and she had let him speak briefly with the two girls. They seemed, as they did with each contact, a little more distant, which was not surprising considering that he had seen them barely a dozen times since Alison remarried and moved to the west coast. That had been three years ago, a year after the divorce, six months before he and Joscelyn put an end to their relationship, six months before he resigned from the CIA to get away from weapons and the technology of murder.

On the morning of the fourth day after Stein's visit, Cameron Harper called him. On June twenty-sixth he found himself, once again, in the "miscellaneous projects" office in Langley.

The office resembled a hunting lodge; a slanting, beamed ceiling rose a full twenty feet at one end. A large desk, several leather chairs and a fireplace enhanced the illusion. There were hunting lithographs, good ones, on the walls.

Two of the armchairs were occupied. In one of them sat Richard Aubrey, in the other, Adrian Northrop, deputy director of Special Operations. Thorne had not expected to see Northrop. As one of the special-research-and-evaluation staff, with his fieldwork long past, Thorne had had little to do with Special Operations except for providing requested data and projections.

Harper came in seconds later and they got down to business, going over the substance of Stein's request. Harper wanted to know whether Thorne was going to accept the Israeli's offer. Thorne said he hadn't decided. After a moment of silence, Harper said:

"Let's go over to the Statistics and Evaluation Center. There's some information there you ought to have."

They walked through a maze of tunnels to a guarded door. Inside. . . .

Inside, Joscelyn Petrie looked up from a stack of printouts.

He saw momentary shock on her face; he knew it was mirrored in his own. The introductions were faintly awkward.

Thorne had a sudden sense of being manipulated, which receded slowly as they read through the printouts. The RUBICON projections were dismal. They assumed that General Secretary Leschenko was replaced by KGB Chairman Boyarkin, and that both sides in the Arab-Israeli dispute had nuclear weapons. There would be general war within a year unless one of those two events failed to occur.

At 5:10 Harper was informed that General Secretary Leschenko had died of an apparent heart attack and that there was every indication that Boyarkin was assuming control.

Thorne, not looking at Joscelyn, had said, "Call Stein. I'll do what he asked."

He had flown out of Washington on July 8 on a direct flight to Israel. At Lod Airport an anonymous Israeli captain had collected him and had him flown to Eilat in an Israeli Air Force liaison plane. As Northrop had told him he would be, he was met at the Eilat IAF base by a major in Israeli intelligence. Northrop had seemed angry about something during Thorne's last briefing at Langley, but Thorne hadn't found out why until he was sitting in Sha'ul Gefen's operational command post in a nondescript building overlooking Eilat harbor.

"I thought I was going to South Africa," Thorne had said to Gefen.

"Ah." Gefen rubbed his sunburned hook of a nose. He had curly black hair and blue eyes. "Probably we should have been more forthright with your people, but we've changed the plan for security reasons. You're referring to the freighter we placed in Durban harbor."

"That's the one."

"We put it there on purpose. Expensive, but it's distracted attention from what we're actually intending. The ship is positioned to intercept a freighter coming down the Mozambique Channel, so that's what interested parties assume we're going to do. Including your people, apparently."

"Apparently. What's actually going on?"

Gefen stood up and unrolled a large wall chart. It covered Israel and the Red and Arabian Seas south of the Horn of Africa. "We've been doing exercises with two Saar-III class boats and a tanker out of Eilat for the past month," he said. "They're ostensibly to develop our long-range naval capabilities and to show the flag down to the Horn. There have been a couple of short excursions as far as the Horn, right out of the Red Sea. Two of the boats are down there now. *Reshef* and *Kidon* are sailing to meet them. We think the target freighter is going to sail from Karachi Harbour within four days, although there's been some trouble with our information services in Pakistan. It appears that the KGB is giving the Pakistani intelligence services some help. Anyway, as soon as the freighter sails, two of the boats are going to refuel and run for the interception area out here." Gefen's finger stabbed into the blue of the Arabian Sea. "They can reach it in one to two-and-a half days, depending on the course the target decides to follow."

"How are you tracking her?"

"Combination of satellite surveillance and air reconnaissance. If aircraft from your carrier task force in the Indian Ocean happen to spot her on routine missions, we'll be quietly informed. As well, she may not maintain radio silence. Her orders may be to check in periodically to let Islamabad and Tripoli know she's all right."

"Assuming the Libyans and the Pakistanis know about your freighter in Durban, why would they go ahead?"

"A pair of Russian frigates turned up in Beira Harbour in Mozambique two days ago, presumably for revictualling. They'd likely be very obviously present until the target freighter got out of range of our vessel."

"I see," Thorne said. "Good enough. When you make the intercept, what then?"

Gefen looked at his watch. "I'll tell you on the way to the docks. The tools and instruments you brought should be on board *Reshef* by now. Your name, by the way, is Mr. Gold. You sail in an hour."

Sixty minutes later, *Reshef* and *Kidon* had hauled in their mooring lines and were running for the open sea.

I wonder what Joscelyn is doing now, Thorne asked himself as the sailors finished and began to clear away their tools. He had seen her only once since the meeting in the secure output room. The day after that meeting he had called her from his hotel in central Washington and had asked her out to supper. She had agreed with neither enthusiasm nor reluctance. Somehow, although the evening was superficially pleasant enough, it was not a success; there were too many ghosts at the table. She had dropped him off at his hotel near midnight and he had momentarily considered asking her to come upstairs with him, but rejected the idea almost immediately. There was a fragment left of the old relationship and he didn't want to jeopardize it.

He still wasn't sure whether he wanted to see her again, and she had been quite opaque about her own feelings.

"Mr. Gold," said one of the ratings in accented English, "We're finished."

Thorne recollected himself and followed them into the lower level of the bridge. The temperature immediately fell thirty degrees; the attack boats were air-conditioned, as they had to be for service in these waters. He was about to continue below to the mess deck when a crewman with a message flimsy in one hand hurried past and scuttled up the companionway to the bridge. Thorne waited.

A moment later the sailor came back down, said "Captain Levin would like to see you," and disappeared hastily in the direction of the radio room. Thorne, ducking his head to avoid painful encounters with the ventilation trunks, clambered up the steep ladder to the bridge.

Captain Levin was standing beside the central fire-control console, talking quietly to the chief weapons officer. Abramov, who was the leader of the freighter assault team, was bent over the chart table, marking arcane symbols on a sheet of blue paper – a plan of the target ship, Thorne realized. Around them the bridge was jammed with navigation, electronic-warfare and miscellaneous combat equipment. Outside, in the hot blue glare of the sea, the three other attack ships were echeloned on *Reshef's* starboard beam.

Levin glanced up as Thorne came onto the bridge, nodded at him, and then turned to the helmsman and gave an order in Hebrew. The helmsman slid a pair of levers forward. *Reshef* grumbled in her belly and began to pick up speed. To starboard, beyond the rectangular bridge windows, the three other craft followed suit.

"Mr. Gold," said Levin. His English was very good. "We've just been contacted. The target ship left Karachi Harbor four hours ago. She's a Libyan freighter called *Al-Mansour*, four thousand tons. Cruises at about eleven knots. That puts us in contact with her in three to four days, depending on her course."

"Are the weapons on board?" Thorne asked.

"They were flown into Karachi Airbase last night from somewhere else, I don't know where." *Reshef*'s deck was taking on a pronounced slant as she gained speed. "We're going to refuel now and then lay a course for the interception area."

The outlines of the Israeli tanker were hardening in the haze beyond *Reshef*'s bows. Thorne hoped he wouldn't get seasick.

Central Intelligence Statistics
and Evaluation Center
Langley, Virginia
July 15

*T*HE FOURTH LEVEL WAS NEARLY DESERTED. In the pale fluorescent-lit corridors the only sound, other than the hiss of air conditioning, was the clack of Joscelyn Petrie's sandals on the tiled floor. It was eleven o'clock in the evening.

At the security desk outside the computer area the two guards sat in front of a bank of closed-circuit-television monitors. As always, they were thoroughly alert. The older one palm-printed and voice-checked her, logged her in on his terminal and then tapped a key sequence to unlock the access doors. Security had been tightened since Thorne's visit; it was one of the things that was worrying her.

Her office was along a cross corridor a hundred feet from the main computer room. She unlocked the office door, entered and locked it again. It was unnecessary to turn on the lights; they were never extinguished down here. Throwing her light-blue cardigan onto the top of the bookcase next to the philodendron, the only plant that would grow under the fluorescents in the twice-conditioned air, she sat down at her desk and switched on her remote terminal. It hummed faintly and a small green rectangle began to blink at her.

She leaned back in her chair for a moment, staring at the cream of the office walls. The only splash of color in it was a wall hanging from – she thought – Tashkent: red, blue, pale yellow, black. A stark black and white calendar hung beside it.

She sighed and began to tap on the terminal, idly calling up files she had been working with earlier in the day. She had not really admitted to herself what she was about to do. After displaying the last half-dozen sectors of the afternoon's RUBICON output, she typed:

SECURITY KERNEL STATUS/RUBICON

AUTHORIZATION, said the 220 from its lair in the computer room.

She typed the day's password. The 220 responded with AUTHORIZED ACCESS: AUBREY, HARPER, NORTHROP, PARTINGTON, PETRIE

Well, I'm in exalted company, she thought. She typed STATUS, DISKPACK G82

DISKPACK G82 ON STANDBY, said the 220. AVAILABLE AS EMERGENCY BACKUP ONLY

Joscelyn typed MONITOR ACCESS TO DISKPACK G82

The 220 considered this for a moment. Then it responded.

ACCESS PERMITTED   +++

M668200-668300, typed Joscelyn. The 220 displayed a series of numbers. Joscelyn began to change them one by one, inserting a program she had been quietly developing for the past two days. It was short program, but not simple. It was intended to breach the 220's inner security kernel, to which only Aubrey, Partington and Ramsden, the security coordinator, held access codes.

The meeting with Thorne and the others in the secure output room had disturbed her more than she had admitted to herself at first. During it she had had the sensation of acting in some obscure stage production whose intent and script were known only to the director – who must have been Harper, of course. It had been an unpleasant script, and Thorne had been at the center of it: they wanted him to do something without knowing why he was doing it, or *that* he was doing it. She was sure there was more involved than his work with the Israelis, yet she hadn't dared say anything about her suspicions during their supper, which was why the evening had been so . . . neutral? Was that the word for it? He had been about to ask her to come into the hotel, but hadn't. She didn't know whether she would have gone.

What she did know, however, was that she disliked what someone – Harper? – was trying to do to Thorne. It had something to do with helping the Israelis stop the weapons shipment to Libya, but she had an intense, perhaps irrational conviction that something else was mixed into the situation somehow.

Such as RUBICON ONE. Whatever that was.

Partington had been very secretive about what he was doing in the central control room the evening after the meeting, but she had simply gone to her office and called up the listing of the print queue. The only thing in it at a really high security level had been a run called RUBICON ONE. Another potential security leak, that queue listing, thought Joscelyn. No matter how you tried to make the machine watertight, it always dribbled at its software seams.

She rather suspected that the RUBICON ONE printout had gone to Harper.

Why?

She had decided to find out. What her motivations were, she did not entirely understand. She was about to commit an unpardonable security breach. Criminal, in fact, although she would never be found out. She had enough confidence in her knowledge of the 220's protection systems to feel secure in that, at least. But the spectacle of David reacting as Harper wanted, with her as a dragooned participant, had revolted her in some obscure fashion.

Face it, she instructed herself. You want to protect him, or at least find out whether it's necessary to do so.

Because of an affair that was over four years ago? a sardonic voice snapped at her from the back of her mind.

It didn't end, she told the voice. It's still here, damn it. That was clear enough at supper. I can't even remember what I ate. What are they trying to do to him, anyway? And why hasn't he contacted me? It's been more than two weeks.

I'll call him tomorrow. Saturday would be good, she told herself.

She grimaced. She had made a mistake in the code. Jesus, that would have been disaster if it slipped through, she reflected as she corrected it. I'd better stop woolgathering. This may be a long job.

By midnight she had got from the lower levels of the operating system into the supervisory program, the one that managed the 220's activities and contained the security kernel. The kernel was heavily protected but she had found an obscure flaw in the supervisor which, if manipulated correctly, would give her access to the highest privilege levels of the computer. She had checked back over the system documentation and the Confidential Monitor Change Orders for the past two years; the flaw had always been there. Apparently she was the only one who had ever noticed it.

She keyed in the last of her subversive code, checked it minutely, took a deep breath, and typed:

EXECUTE

A long pause. It grew longer. She looked distractedly at her watch. Ten seconds. Twelve.

It shouldn't be taking this long, she thought. Christ, what have I done? I could spend a long time in jail for this. Or worse.

She had provided herself with an escape route, coding that would cause the 220 to shut down in an apparently routine systems crash and simultaneously remove all records of her illegal access. She started to type the execute instruction for the code.

The terminal screen cleared, erasing what she had typed. A system-command menu printed itself in green phosphorescent letters. The last said simply CORE SECURITY. She was in.

Joscelyn exhaled slowly and called up one of her own files. It displayed perfectly.

All right, she thought. Let's get it over with. She typed:

CATALOG RUBICON/

The screen began to list all file titles containing the word RUBICON. Several she had never seen: they did not display at her normal access level. Fourth from the last was RUBICON ONE. She raised her eyebrows at the listing: the file had a protection code she hadn't known existed.

Does any one person know everything that's in this monster of a machine? she wondered. I doubt it. Are there things in there that *nobody* knows about? The thought chilled her. Normally she viewed the 220 as an extension of her own intellect, but tonight the computer had taken on a baleful indentity of its own.

She worked at the unlock sequence until she was sure she had it right, then tapped the keyboard. The screen cleared again and the green text began to fly across it. Unlike the system commands, this was in upper- and lower-case letters, like normal printing.

RUBICON ONE
Version 6.8:21
July 12/86

That's a recent update, she thought. They've done something to it since Partington printed it out. She read on.

This simulation is security-coded alpha one. Unauthorized access is punishable by a prison term of not less than five years. If you are not authorized, call security immediately, local 3435. If you are authorized, you may continue the display by typing the escape key.

Here the text stopped. Joscelyn bit her lower lip and tapped the key. The screen cleared.

RUBICON ONE is a scenario providing a method for destablizing the Soviet government. This scenario uses the personality profiles and political/military/economic data of the RUBICON main program. Execution of the specifics of this scenario should be considered if and only if the worst-case scenarios of the RUBICON main program are objectively and realistically true. The essential prerequisite for the real-life execution of the scenario is

The text stopped, although the screen was only half full. Joscelyn stared at it for a moment. Nothing happened. She tapped the ESCAPE key. Still nothing. She sat back in her chair, frowning.

There were footsteps in the corridor, more than one set. A key rattled in the lock of her office door. Joscelyn felt the blood drain from the capillaries beneath the skin of her forehead.

The door opened abruptly. Ramsden stood there, flanked by two security guards. "Please sit quite still, Dr. Petrie," he said. "And don't touch the terminal. It's locked from the security office, anyway."

She did as she was told, feeling as though she were hanging in midair, as though her office were not a real place. Ramsden came around her desk and looked at the terminal, then nodded to one of the guards, who was carrying a camera. The guard photographed the screen several times and then stepped back. Ramsden sat down in the vinyl-covered chair in front of Joscelyn's desk. She stared at him blankly.

The security coordinator rubbed his mustache. It made a faint, dry, bristly sound. "You got in through that flaw in the supervisor," he said. "Didn't you? It's been there for a long time. On purpose. A security trapdoor, in fact, programmed to call for help if anybody fell through it. I'm afraid you've fallen through."

Joscelyn nodded, fighting to regain her composure. She wanted to say: God *damn* Thorne.

"What next?" she asked, throat constricted.

Ramsden was spared replying by more footsteps in the corridor. Partington appeared in the doorway, dishevelled, obviously just aroused from sleep.

"God damn it, Joscelyn," he said, looking at her, distraught. "What are we going to do with you *now*?"

The Indian Ocean
July 17

THE CLOUDBANK ON THE SOUTHWEST HORIZON was a swollen-bruise purple. The four-foot swell rolling from beneath it did not break at all at its crests, as though it were overlain by a skin of oil. The water looked sullen and metallic.

Captain Levin studied the sky worriedly from *Reshef*'s forward gun position, bracing himself against the ship's roll and yaw. Major Abramov, leader of the commando assault team, stood beside him, waiting.

"What do you think?" Abramov asked finally.

Levin lifted his shoulders slightly. "According to the radar we have four hours, maybe three, if we stay here and if the wind freshens. But once that stormline gets inside three hours, we'll have to delay until it's gone. A day, at least."

"Anything could happen in a day," said Abramov.

Levin's black eyebrows flexed in irritation, although not at the man beside him. *Reshef* and *Kidon* lay ten kilometers off the Libyan freighter's track as it had been projected by Eilat Control at four that afternoon. A day and a half earlier, *Al-Mansour* had swung far east of the normal shipping lanes, obviously hoping that she would escape unwelcome attention in the wastes of the Indian Ocean. She had subverted her attempt, however, by transmitting a brief situation report every six hours. The transmissions had been compressed to less than a second's length, but the sophisticated monitors of the US Seventh Fleet vessels down by Ceylon, assisted by triangulation by jets from the carrier *Nimitz*, had established the freighter's exact position without difficulty. She lay sixty kilometers northeast of *Reshef* and *Kidon* and was steaming southwest at a stolid eleven knots. The Israeli attack boats had intended to make the interception two hours before dusk, but the approaching storm had upset the timetable. Satellite tracking had put its arrival in the area at about 10:00 P.M. but an hour ago it had abruptly altered course.

These are Arab waters, remember, Levin reminded himself without humor.

"We'll have to move towards them," he said. "Damn." The freighter's radar would pick them up as fast-moving traces and the crew would be alerted. *Kidon* would have to start radio and radar jamming as soon as the Israelis came within visual range.

Levin looked at his watch. *Al-Mansour*'s next position report was due in half an hour; they couldn't afford to be detected before that. He wished momentarily for a contact with Eilat Control but the two boats had been observing radio silence for the last twenty-four hours. They'd be biting their nails in Eilat and Jerusalem.

"Let's get on with it," he said and started for the bridge. Abramov followed him. "Where's our friend?" the major asked as they stepped over the doorway coaming.

"The mess. Checking his gear, when I last saw him. I wouldn't like to be wearing his hat."

"It won't matter if he makes a mistake," said Abramov. "The hat's big enough for all of us."

The possibility of anti-tampering devices fitted to the warheads was one they thought about but rarely mentioned. The American had been brusque on the subject.

He was not in the mess, however. He was at the bottom of the companionway leading to the bridge. Levin had come to know a little of the American in the past two-and-a-half days; Abramov and he had outlined the assault plan to "Mr. Gold" in considerable detail, on the principle that Gold's knowledge of weapons might be useful in an emergency. Levin had half-expected the American to be a narrowly trained specialist and was pleased at the man's quick recognition of the tactical difficulties of the situation in which they had been placed. There would be only two hours in which to examine the weapons, remove the warheads from the missiles and dispose of them in the depths of the sea. One would be defused and taken home to Eilat for more extensive dissection.

Levin didn't envy the American his job. He nodded at Gold and said, "Ready to go?"

Momentary relief on the other's face; a nod. "Come on up," said Levin. "We're getting under way."

Two minutes later *Reshef* and *Kidon* were accelerating towards thirty knots into the northeast, razor bows slicing through the swell, transoms sunk deep in white water. Away astern the rampart of cloud, flecked with lightning, loomed onward above the horizon.

"Weather ahead," said Captain Mustafa Khleif. He studied the darkening horizon's rim beyond *Al-Mansour*'s forepeak, past the peeling buff standards of the forward cargo booms. "How long until we reach it?"

"Radar says three-and-a-half hours," said the first officer. "It's still well over the horizon. We're just picking up the tops of the clouds."

"Has the position report gone out?" asked Khleif, nervously. The presence of the armed guard on the bridge still made him uncomfortable, even after four days. The guard and his twenty-nine compatriots were aboard not only to watch over the ten long, narrow crates in the number-one hold, but also to make sure that Colonel Qadhafi's shipment – whatever it was – was not endangered by inefficiency or counterrevolutionary behavior by the crew. A failure on the part of any sailor could easily – likely – mean the wall and a dozen bullets for Khleif.

He should have watched the position report go out himself.

The interphone buzzed. The first officer picked it up, listened and frowned. "Captain," he said, replacing the receiver, "radar has two blips at 210 degrees; heading 045; 6 knots."

Khleif felt his bowels contract. They were well off any regular shipping lanes. At that speed the blips could be small feluccas bound from the Horn of Africa making a direct crossing to the Indian coast, running before the storm. Gold smugglers, he thought hopefully.

"How big?" he asked.

"Not very big. But radar says the echoes are very hard. They're not wooden ships."

The first officer had obviously been thinking the same things as Khleif.

Metal ships, then, thought Khleif. Dogshit Americans. Or Israelis. He settled his cap more firmly on his head and said to the officer, "Take the bridge. Get a lookout into the foremast position. I'm going to the radar room."

Al-Mansour's navigation and radar installation was directly below the bridge. The compartment was bathed in a reddish glow relieved only slightly by the yellow glimmer of the incandescent bulb over the radio console and the green, circling trace of the big radar scope. Most of the equipment was the newest obtainable, installed just before this voyage. Unfortunately, none of the radio or radar operators was very good at using it.

The radar man looked up nervously as Khleif entered. The captain rarely visited the compartment; he did not quite trust the electronic tools at his disposal. The radio operator, headset clamped firmly over his ears, was edgily twiddling dials.

"What is it?" asked Khleif brusquely. Images of bullet-pocked walls jittered in the back of his head.

"Sir, they're small. They'll pass us going the other way, if they hold their course and speed."

"They're not warcraft?"

"I don't know, sir. I don't know very much about this equipment. But I don't think they're made of wood. The echo is too strong."

Khleif studied the radar plot for perhaps a minute. The two echoes crept steadily towards *Al-Mansour*. They were still just barely inside the radar horizon.

Khleif picked up the interphone and called the bridge. "Anything from the lookout?"

"It's getting very dark over there," said the first officer in his ear. "It's hard to pick anything out." A pause. "Wait, please, captain." Another pause. Khleif's neck began to itch. "Well?" he asked after a moment.

"The lookout's seen something. Two very small ships, low, gray. No cargo masts."

O Allah protect me now, thought Khleif. "Radio," he snapped. "Encode this message and send it on our reporting frequency. Quickly!"

The radio operator scrambled for his encoding pad. Khleif waited, fury rising. "Start. Call sign," he said as the operator found the pad. "Possible enemy –"

The pale glow from the radar scope blossomed into bright green. The radio operator, who had pulled one earphone back to listen to Khleif, tore the headset off and threw it on the deck plating, his hands over his ears. Even from the other side of the compartment, Khleif could hear the shrilling from the headset.

Their transmitter and radar were being jammed, across all the frequencies.

Thorne was on *Reshef*'s bridge when Levin gave the order to start jamming. Instantly, both *Reshef* and *Kidon* swung to starboard and accelerated, driving towards the distant silhouette of the Libyan freighter. On both vessels' foredecks the 76-mm cannon were manned. Spray beat back over the turrets as the attack boats worked up to combat speed. The vibrations of the heavy engines drummed up through the soles of Thorne's seaboots.

"She's swinging away," said Levin. He was watching *Al-Mansour* through a large pair of binoculars. Thorne saw a plume of smoke issue from the Libyan's single funnel. The freighter, hopelessly, was cracking on speed. She could make barely eighteen knots, at the best.

Twenty minutes passed while *Al-Mansour*'s upperworks grew more and more distinct in the early evening light. *Reshef* and *Kidon* drew away from each other and began to move up on the freighter's port and starboard flanks, two kilometers off, preventing the Libyan from turning away from her pursuers.

They were about six kilometers astern of her now. Thorne spared a glance for the southwest horizon. The cloud bank had edged perceptibly closer and the swell was steepening.

Levin said something urgent in Hebrew. Two hundred

meters ahead of them a waterspout heaved itself into the air and fell lazily back.

"Wire-guided missile," said Thorne. "He doesn't quite have the range."

A spurt of flame lanced from *Al-Mansour*'s stern. Thorne watched the black-tipped spark as it hurtled nearer and nearer. *Reshef*'s deck tilted suddenly as she swerved. The missile struck the waves fifteen meters off her port bow and detonated with a roar. Tracers began to arch from the Israeli vessel's bridge machine guns towards the freighter. *Kidon* was firing as well.

"We'll have to put a shell into the bridge if she won't stop," said Levin. He gave an order and the fore turret swung to port. Thorne watched *Al-Mansour*'s taffrail as the machine guns stopped. There were no more lances of flame.

Reshef was now weaving to and fro a kilometer and a half from the Libyan freighter, which had worked up to full speed, smoke billowing from her stack. Thorne took his first good look at her. She was old, dirty and not very large, with ungainly superstructures at bow and stern and a high bridge and deckhouse amidships. A three-islander, probably laid down at Tyneside a good thirty years before. Yellowing cargo hoists stood in the well decks fore and aft of the midships superstructure, which was a grimy buff above a rust-pitted black hull. There was no fixed armament that Thorne could see. White water, piled up by her speed, creamed around the Libyan's bows.

"She's going to blow a gasket if she keeps that up," said Levin conversationally, swaying to the twists and turns of *Reshef*'s course. "We'll put a shot across her bows anyway." He spoke to the fire-control officer in Hebrew. The forward gun banged, a dry, flat crack. A plume of white water sprouted two hundred meters from *Al-Mansour*'s stem.

"She's slowing," said the first officer.

She was, the mound of foam around her bows diminishing. Thorne studied her bridge. "There's something going on in the wheelhouse," he said.

Levin turned the binoculars on it.

The starboard bridge door opened and two men came out

onto the partly enclosed bridge wing. They seemed encumbered, as though they were dragging something. One of them flopped the top of their burden over the wing rail and the other disappeared for a moment, as though he were pushing from below. Then a bundle about the size of a man tumbled over the rail and into the sea.

Levin whistled quietly between his teeth. "There must be a security detachment aboard. They don't want to stop."

Al-Mansour was speeding up again.

"Shit," said Levin. "I was hoping we wouldn't have to do this." He shifted into Hebrew again. Expressionlessly, the fire-control officer relayed the order. The forward gun cracked.

The after third of *Al-Mansour*'s wheelhouse disintegrated. Flame and smoke shot into the air. A chunk of debris sailed towards *Reshef* and dropped heavily into the water between her and the Libyan. Fires sprang out of nothing on the freighter's bridge. A man ran out onto the bridge wing and started down the ladder to the main deck.

"She's still maintaining speed," said the first officer.

Levin shrugged and nodded to the fire-control officer. The gun decreased its elevation and banged again. A hole split open in *Al-Mansour*'s hull beneath the after part of the bridge, about a meter above the waterline, where the upper part of the engine room lay. The Libyan's funnel hiccuped a huge gout of blackish-brown smoke and the ship began to lose way. *Reshef* nosed towards her. *Kidon* was out of sight on *Al-Mansour*'s other beam but would be moving closer as well. Her assault team was to take the after well deck and secure the ship's stern; *Reshef*'s commandos were to deal with the bridge and the fore section.

The black cliff of the freighter's hull slid nearer and nearer. Two men appeared, crouching, at the rail next to the starboard lifeboat. With whiplike cracks, the armor glass of *Reshef*'s wheelhouse windows starred in half a dozen places. The bridge machine guns opened fire and the two men collapsed tiredly, like broken puppets. A submachine gun tumbled into the sea. There was more firing from the Libyan ship. Thorne couldn't see where it was coming from.

"They're using the freeing ports," said the fire-control officer.

Bright disks of metal, like coins, appeared around the oval openings in the main-deck bulwarks under *Al-Mansour*'s bridge: strikes from *Reshef*'s machine guns. Some of the bullets must have gone through the ports to find whoever was behind them, because the shooting ceased.

"Keep their heads down," said Levin. The fire-control officer nodded. Levin snapped an order into the interphone. Over the rumble of the attack boat's engines, Thorne could hear the slamming of metal doors. Ten commandos ran out onto the foredeck, carrying coils of rope fixed to grappling irons. *Reshef* was now rising and falling about a meter and a half with respect to the freighter, which was not as affected by the waves. The Israeli's hull would take a pounding if Levin didn't con her very well.

The engines reversed with *Reshef*'s port bows six meters away from the Libyan's pocked steel. She slowed to a crawl a dozen feet off, just keeping up with the freighter, whose speed was now only five knots and still dropping. The swell pressed *Reshef* to within half a meter of *Al-Mansour*'s hull and then began to drag her away. At the nearest approach, grappling irons arched up and clanked over the freighter's fore well-deck railings. On the next inward swing, the five commandos of the advance party began to swarm up the knotted ropes. The bridge machine guns racketed twice and stopped.

The next five commandos clambered out of sight over the freighter's rail. *Reshef* drew away to a safer distance. *Al-Mansour* lay nearly stopped, lifting and falling sluggishly in the deepening swell. Thorne looked southwest. The storm line appeared somewhat nearer, although in their run to intercept the freighter they had given themselves another half hour. There would be just enough time.

If nothing went wrong aboard the freighter.

A rattle of shots, muffled by distance and *Al-Mansour*'s superstructure. They seemed mostly the flat, staccato snap of the Israeli Uzis, with the occasional heavier accompaniment of a Soviet AK47 assault rifle.

A man in uniform appeared on the bridge wing above them. He was swinging something bulky up to his shoulder.

He's not going to miss at this range, Thorne realized. There was no room on the cramped bridge to take cover, either.

The Libyan soldier had the weapon positioned. A Strela short-range missile, Thorne observed with detachment. Damn. I'm not going to get out of this one.

The bridge machine guns thumped. The stream of bullets caught the soldier in the chest, hurling him back against the wheelhouse. At least one bullet struck the Strela's warhead. The bridge wing and the unfortunate soldier dissolved in an expanding bubble of orange flame. Bits of indescribable wreckage spattered *Reshef*'s armored windows.

There was still heavy firing from the Libyan's forecastle. The fire-control officer spoke to Levin who nodded and gave orders. *Reshef* began to pull away from the freighter, whose bridge was aflame in several places.

"They're meeting some resistance from the forecastle," explained Levin. "We're going to lie off and give them fire support."

Thorne nodded. The leader of the assault team was in direct communication with fire control through *Reshef*'s radio room.

The Israeli vessel slowed three hundred meters from the burning freighter. The gun turret tracked to port. Again the flat, dry crack. Fragments of debris mixed with smoke and flame rose from *Al-Mansour*'s forepeak. Thorne could see hunched figures racing along the well deck from the midships deckhouse towards the bows. Two minutes passed. The fire-control officer spoke to Levin.

"They've secured the forward half," said the captain. "You'd better prepare to get aboard. We haven't much time."

"Can you get my tool kit up there while I search for the weapons?" Thorne said. "It's too heavy to drag all over while we look for them."

"All right," said Levin. "How do you feel about those ropes?"

Thorne dubiously studied the knotted lines snaking up the

freighter's hull. "I can walk up the side if somebody above will do the pulling."

"Good," said Levin. "You'd better get on deck."

Five minutes later Thorne scrambled, arms aching, over the freighter's rail. Abramov steadied him as he dropped into the well deck. The Israeli major had a great livid bruise on one cheekbone and there was blood on his combat jacket. Thorne looked at him with an unvoiced question.

"We lost two," said Abramov. "The crew all dived into the hold. What's left of the security detachment we've locked up in the aftercastle. They killed the first mate," he added conversationally. "That was the body we saw them pitch overboard." He passed a hand over his cheek and winced slightly. "Start the search amidships and work forward?"

"Okay," said Thorne. It was a long time since he had been near or in combat, not since Vietnam and its dreadful aftermath in Cambodia, and it still made him feel light-headed. The air, despite the freshening wind, reeked of gunfire and explosives and the fire on the bridge roared and crackled above them. Thorne looked up at it.

"We'll try to put it out before we go," said Abramov. "We're persuading some of the crew to start the emergency power plant to drive the fire hoses. Don't worry, we won't let you bake in the hold."

They entered the midships deckhouse and descended a series of companionways. Abramov undogged an oval metal door in a bulkhead and they stepped through it into the number two hold. The Israeli major snapped a switch beside the door and the compartment was dimly lit by low-wattage bulbs in wire cages. The hold was piled with wooden crates bearing enigmatic stencils and international this-side-up symbols.

"They likely haven't piled anything on top," Thorne said, "I don't think. Thank God this isn't a twenty-thousand tonner."

They were searching for ten or a dozen long, slender crates. Nothing in number two hold resembled what they wanted. They went forward, through another oval door, into number one. It was much dimmer in here; some of the lighting had burned out. Abramov switched on a battle lantern and began to play its beam over the crates in a kind of square search.

"There," said Thorne.

They were right up forward, where the hull tapered inwards to the forepeak and the freighter's stem. Ten five-meter-long crates without markings were laid along the centerline of the ship. Thorne stopped in front of the nearest and studied it.

"What's wrong?" asked Abramov.

"It's a bit odd, that's all. In heavy weather the weapons would be more likely to get bounced around up here. I wonder why they didn't load them in the after section of number two, nearer the center of the ship."

"I'll have your tool kit sent down," said Abramov. He thumbed the side of a fist-sized black box and spoke into it.

Thorne suddenly felt very isolated in the depths of the hold. The crates humped enigmatic and uncaring in the shadows. *Al-Mansour* lifted and fell in the southwest rollers. Somewhere a plate or girder creaked.

He walked across the oily deck plates to the nearest crate and squatted to examine it. It was constructed of a roughly planed pale wood, likely fir. The top was tightly secured by spikes.

Suddenly Thorne didn't like the look of the crate's lid. He would have expected a more careful method of packing the weapons. These containers were no different from those that might be used to ship machine parts.

Unless, he reminded himself, this is just an outer shell and the main packing is inside. That must be it. But why were the damned things up here, in the most vulnerable part of the vessel?

He was suddenly convinced that he shouldn't open the tops of any of those crates.

There were footsteps behind him as two commandos carried the tool kit into the hold. It contained rather unusual devices that Thorne and two other weapons technologists had selected in Washington. The soldiers put the kit down and hurried away.

"What do you think?" asked Abramov.

"I think they're booby-trapped," said Thorne.

"Ah," said the Israeli major. He didn't seem surprised. "Why do you think that?"

Thorne told him. Abramov eyed the crates. "We considered that possibility," he said. "I've done some disposal work. We really ought to go in from the bottom."

"It would be safer to sink the ship," Thorne said.

"We can't – we need to look at those weapons," Abramov told him. "In case we can't get one out before we have to leave. Look. It would have to be a small antipersonnel charge if they weren't going to risk blowing the bottom of the ship out by detonating the charges in the other crates sympathetically. I'll try to get in. We don't have the equipment to lift them so I can get at the bottom – I'll try to get in from the side. You go back into the number two hold. Stay out of line of the doors in case something goes wrong. I'll call to you what I'm doing and leave my transmitter switched on so *Reshef* can monitor what's being done. If I make a mistake, you'll probably have found out enough to get into another crate safely. Captain Barak's done disposal work as well, so he could finish the job off if necessary."

Thorne looked at the Israeli. "I'll stay put," he said, knowing it was foolish.

"No, you won't," said Abramov patiently. "We only have one nuclear-explosives expert. And we also haven't much time. Do you have a saw in that magic box of yours?"

Thorne did. It was a small power saw, courtesy of the CIA. Thorne showed him how it worked and retired to the other hold.

"Starting now," called Abramov. "I'm taking out a ten-centimeter square at the forward inboard bottom edge of the crate."

The saw whined. It stopped and then repeated itself three times.

"The section's cut," called the Israeli. His voice echoed metallically in the shadows. "I'm removing it now." A pause. "There doesn't seem to be any packing. But there's a kind of cradle. There's something in it, I can't see what. Taking out another square above the first."

Again the whine. Thorne looked at his watch. He was going to have an hour with the weapons at best unless he wanted to risk being caught on *Al-Mansour* during the storm. His shirt collar was clammy with sweat.

"Next section out," called Abramov. "There's a cylindrical thing inside. I'm looking up at the inside of the lid now. Yes. There's an antipersonnel grenade arranged to explode if the lid's raised. There's probably one at the other end as well. It's rudimentary – like an afterthought. I'm going to take out a big section of the side now."

The saw's rasp vibrated in Thorne's teeth.

"You can have a look now," called Abramov. "Then I'll pull the grenades and you can get back to work."

Thorne started towards the number-one hold. "Shit," said Abramov.

Thorne stopped. "What's the matter?"

"Come and look."

Thorne hurried into number-one hold and squatted beside Abramov. Inside the crate was a long tubular metal object. It had streaks of rust on it. Thorne selected a non-magnetic screwdriver from the tool kit and tapped the metal. It should have given a light *tink*, the sound of an aircraft's alloy skin. Instead there was a solid *bong*. Thorne had to ransack his memory before he recognized the sound.

"Jesus Christ," he said. "It's a fucking water tank."

Six hours later, at Okba bin Nafi Airbase in Libya, an Antonov transport plane bearing the colors of the Libyan Air Force taxied up to a group of waiting trucks. In the Antonov's hold, packed in green fiberglass containers, were ten nuclear-tipped cruise missiles.

Rᴀᴍsᴅᴇɴ ᴄᴀᴍᴇ ꜰᴏʀ ʜᴇʀ at eight in the morning.

She had spent a dreadful day and a half locked in a room that contained only a cot and a chair. The room was in the Center, but she was uncertain of the exact location. A guard at the door had provided coffee when she asked for it. There had been food, too, but she had eaten hardly any. They had taken her directly from the computer room to this one; she hadn't bothered to ask for legal help, knowing it was futile.

She looked up at Ramsden silently as he stood in the open doorway.

"Come with me, please, Dr. Petrie."

She walked beside him until they reached a large room fitted out like a hunting lodge, which she took to be Northrop's office, since he was sitting behind the desk. Harper was in a leather armchair beside it. The two men remained silent until Ramsden left, closing the door softly behind him. The quiet thud sounded unpleasantly final.

"Dr. Petrie," the deputy director of operations said, "why did you break into the RUBICON ONE simulation?"

There was no point in prevaricating. "I thought Dr. Thorne was being manipulated in some manner, and that I was being used to help do so. I knew RUBICON ONE existed and that it was accessed shortly after Dav – Dr. Thorne was at the Center. I also knew he worked on the program several years ago. I wanted to see if the file would tell me what you wanted him to do."

"What were you going to do if the file had told you that?"

"I hadn't thought that far."

"Do you still think we were manipulating the two of you?"

"Yes." Defiantly.

The DCI steepled his fingers and spoke for the first time. "You must realize the extent of your security breach. The precise nature of that file is supposed to be known only to four people: myself, Deputy Director Northrop, Dr. Aubrey and Dr. Partington. Even the programmers and analysts who helped write it constructed their modules in isolation and do not know how the modules are integrated. We did not want a fifth knowledgeable person. Now, however, we have one."

"The question remains," said Northrop, "of what to do with you."

A silence. For the first time Joscelyn thought that they might kill her. Northrop was staring at her with flat green executioner's eyes.

Her voice trembled when she spoke. "Fire me, then. It's certainly in the contract."

"I don't think we're going to do that," said Northrop.

"We could, you're quite right," said Harper. "However, it would mean losing a valuable member of the RUBICON team. Not to mention the fact that your knowledge makes you a risk should you happen to fall, ah, into the wrong hands."

"What, then?" asked Joscelyn in a small voice.

"I believe it's referred to as co-optation. You become part of the project. We would have required an additional person in any case. You have happened to be in the right – or wrong – place at the right – or wrong – time."

"But I'm not an operative," exclaimed Joscelyn, aghast.

"You don't need to be," said Northrop. "You would only be a communications link."

"You *do* have the option of refusing," said Harper. "We would then have to release you from your contract. There would be no other punishment. Except that you would never be able to work in a government installation again, because you would never receive any kind of security clearance. Nor would you be permitted in industrial or university work associated with federal or state funds."

"It rather narrows the field," said Northrop dryly. "Especially for someone of your ability."

"You're saying I can walk out of here and go home."

"Oh, absolutely," Harper said. "Provided you're willing to suffer the consequences. You'd be under surveillance, of course. For a long time."

"What do you want me to do?" asked Joscelyn, defeated.

"Not now," Northrop said. "You'll be informed."

Washington
July 25

NORTHROP HAD RENTED THE ROOM in the Hotel Trevanion half an hour before the meeting, registering under a false name. He had refused the first room offered and requested another two floors above and several dozen yards away. Even so, he spent a good fifteen minutes with the curtains closed, minutely checking the walls and furniture with a bug sweep. He did find a microphone-transmitter on the back of a desk drawer but the device was covered with cobwebs and of a design two years out of date. He removed its battery anyway.

Harper, Thorne in tow, arrived as he was finishing. They had met in a crowded shopping mall on the outskirts of Washington and had spent two hours dusting off any possibility of surveillance. There hadn't been any obvious watchers. Thorne was black-eyed from lack of sleep; he had gotten into Bolling Air Force Base only sixteen hours previously.

"Stein?" asked Northrop.

"He'll be here at two," said Harper. He sat down on the bed and loosened his tie. "God, it's hot out there. The room okay?" He already knew it was or the deputy director for operations wouldn't have mentioned Stein.

"Okay. There was a fossil bug but it's out of service now."

"Washington," said Harper. "Where even the rooms nobody cares about have bugs. Where even the bugs have bugs. Upon their back to bite 'em."

"Mm," said Northrop. He pulled out the desk chair and sat on it. Thorne was still standing. "Sit down, Dr. Thorne," he said, not unkindly. "You look pretty beat."

Thorne sat on the bed beside Harper. What he really wanted to do was lie down on it and go to sleep. The past week had become a jumble of semi-connected events; he needed time and rest to unravel them. After searching the remainder of *Al-Mansour* for the weapons without success, he and the Israelis had reboarded the missile boats, leaving the freighter's crew to deal with the remnants of the bridge fire. All of the Libyan's radio equipment had been smashed. Then they had sailed for the Horn of Africa and the waiting tanker at their most economical cruising speed. Because of the storm, they had reached the tanker with only enough fuel in their tanks to boil, perhaps, a teakettle. Then there was the nerve-wrenching run up the Red Sea to Eilat, constantly expecting attack by outraged Libyan or Pakistani aircraft using Iraqui and Saudi runways. After landing at Eilat, Thorne was given a cursory debriefing by Gefen and was then bundled off to Hazor where he caught a MAC flight to Lajes in the Azores and from there went on to Bolling. Even now he couldn't understand why they hadn't been attacked in the Red Sea. It was as though no one had noticed the operation. *Al-Mansour*, Harper had told him in the car, limped into Mogadiscio Harbour in Somalia the morning Thorne returned to the United States. There had been no diplomatic repercussions whatsoever.

There was a knock on the door and Northrop let Stein into the room. The Israeli looked much older and more tired than he had the day Thorne last saw him, at Round Lake. Even in the dim room his face was pouchy and haggard.

"Hello, Isser," Thorne said.

"Hello, David. I'm glad to see you back healthy." A chair of Scandinavian design sat next to the window. Stein planted himself heavily in it. "I have less than an hour," he said. "It's very thick over at the department just now. Also everyone and his aunt wants to keep an eye on me. It took an hour and a half to clean myself off." He turned to Thorne. "What happened? I had an account from home but I need your perception of it, too."

Thorne told him. When he finished, Northrop asked, "Mr. Stein, is it possible the weapons aren't in Libya? That they're still to be sent?"

"They're there." Stein looked furious for a moment. "Two days ago a Libyan intelligence man in Algiers thoughtfully informed his Egyptian opposite number that the things arrived safely on the morning of the eighteenth. They knew the Egyptians would pass it on to us – laughing up their sleeves." He went on bitterly, "We haven't been outmanuevered like this since the Yom Kippur War."

"Bluff?" suggested Harper.

"No. We have a man who saw the transport plane come into Okba bin Nafi. Our man didn't see the plane unloaded but we're sure in hindsight that it was the shipment."

"Why no reactions to the attack on the freighter?" Thorne asked.

Stein looked at Harper. "What do your people think?"

The DCI thoughtfully lit a cigarette. "That Libya and Pakistan have bigger fish to fry, or that someone else does. When you told us the weapons weren't on that ship we immediately suspected a leak, at your end or ours. Looking over the situation during the past week, though, we think the change in the transport method was a somewhat unusual KGB insurance policy. The change was very carefully handled. Neither the Libyans nor the Pakistanis could have managed it without Russian help. Hasan, the Pakistani intelligence head, pulled in a lot of our people just before that ship sailed. It's good odds they got the information they needed from the KGB station chief in Islamabad." The cigarette was nearly out and Harper puffed on it furiously. "We think the lack of diplomatic reaction indicates that Moscow is working on something much bigger than a diplomatic incident and that they don't want Tripoli or Islamabad to stir things around before Mother Russia's ready to let them. Which says uncomfortable things about a warmer trend in Pakistani-Soviet relations. State says they think Pakistan's about to opt out of our aid programs. So they must have a compensatory promise from Moscow, with all that that implies."

"What's their hold over Libya?" Thorne asked. "I didn't think Qadhafi would ignore, um, Israeli countermeasures just because the Kremlin said he should."

"That's one reason we're worried," muttered Stein. "The Russians must have offered him a secure passage for the weapons in return for his silence about our attack, which means they want the Libyans to have the weapons. It's a complete reversal of their old policies."

"It's very dangerous," agreed Harper. "Not that I need to belabor that point. It bears out a number of predictions we made several weeks ago about probable courses of Soviet action under Boyarkin. So far he's running true to form."

"Mr. Stein," asked Northrop, "what cooperation do your people need?"

Stein looked uneasy for a moment. "There's a conflict of opinion on that back home. There's a worry that the shipment got through because of a security problem at your end. In short, we're happy to provide information about the opposition's behavior, but for the moment, anyway, we'd prefer to take any sensitive measures on a unilateral basis."

"Short of a first strike, I trust," said Harper.

"We will never be the first to use nuclear weapons," said Stein.

"Mr. Stein," said Northrop, "pardon me, but I think that's a crock. With a country the size of Israel, you can't afford the luxury of a second strike. If it looks as though Libya is going to hit you with a dozen nuclear devices, you have to move first. If you don't, you risk losing not only a third of your population and most of your industry, but also your capacity for retaliation. I know what you politicians say. What's the story according to your general staff?"

Stein made a chopping motion with his hands. "I don't make policy, Mr. Northrop." His voice was rough. For a moment Thorne glimpsed the young man who had fought for Israel against the Arabs in 1948.

Harper studied the smoke drifting from his cigarette. Then Stein said levelly, "I'm asking only for myself, not in any official capacity. What would be the US reaction to a justified first strike? Has it been considered?"

"Not in any detail," Harper said smoothly. "But as you can understand, it wouldn't be very favorable, particularly as matters now stand with the Kremlin. We'd argue against it if we were consulted, I'm sure. I'm speaking unofficially, of course."

"And when you had persuaded us to let Libyan bombs fall on Tel Aviv and Haifa?" asked Stein. "What then? Would you permit us to counterattack at that point? Or would you say that there was no point in continuing the destruction? That you would send aid to help us rebuild? Would you then send troops to stop the Syrian tanks rolling into what was left of our cities? When would you do that? What will your country do, Mr. Harper?"

There was an embarassed silence. Then Stein said, "I am sorry. But there has never been a threat like this since the State of Israel was founded. This is why we are less in favor of active cooperation than we were." He looked at his watch. "I must go. We will share as much with you as we possibly can." He stood up. "Good-bye, David. We appreciate all you've done for us. I may not see you again for a while; I've been recalled to Jerusalem."

And he was gone.

Northrop let his breath out slowly. "For a second I thought he was going to clout you one."

"I wouldn't blame him if he had," said Harper dryly. "David, you can go back to your hotel now if you want. Call me at seven this evening and we'll make arrangements about what you could help us with next, if you feel you want to go on."

"I'd like to see the end of it," Thorne said, "one way or the other."

"Don't be so pessimistic," said Harper. "We'll weather it."

When the door had closed behind him, Northrop said, "Well?"

Harper looked at his cigarette. It had burned down to the filter and a tube of whitish ash was all that remained. He stubbed out the filter and said, "We have to move to the next step. I'd hoped the raid would make it unnecessary, but. . . ."

"This business is full of buts," said Northrop. "Have we got to the point, really, where you think we should execute RUBICON ONE?"

"We needn't carry out the final phases if it turns out to be unnecessary," said Harper. "That's the beauty of the scenario.

We can put it all in place and only move if the GRU and KGB start for each others' throats."

"Will they?"

"I'm expecting something any day. The difficult thing is convincing the president. In a way, we're talking about our own equivalent of an Israeli first strike."

"Yes," said Northrop. He shivered involuntarily. "So much of it depends on Thorne."

"And on Joscelyn Petrie."

"Will she cooperate?"

"No choice, there." Harper ruminated for a moment, then looked at his watch. "I have to go to the White House for the foreign intelligence briefing. Make sure Thorne stays under wraps."

Alone in the room, Northrop replaced the battery in the fossil bug and tucked it into its old position at the back of the drawer. He mussed the bed carefully and lathered the soap in the bathroom before leaving. Northrop was a careful man.

Except that President Jason Law was slouched on one of the settees by the marble-topped fireplace of the Oval Office, the meeting of the Committee on Foreign Intelligence closely resembled that of June twenty-second. Harper watched Law turn to the last page of the president's daily brief – the digest of significant intelligence matters supplied each morning by the National Foreign Assessment Center – and begin to reread the special-intelligence estimate Harper had brought with him.

Harper shifted uncomfortably in his leather armchair. Law glanced up. "Oh. Sorry, Cam, Simon. Go ahead and smoke. I'll be done in a moment."

Gratefully, Harper and Parr lit, respectively, a cigarette and a malodorous pipe. Law flipped the report's last page over, straightened and put the document on the coffee table.

"I wish I'd been more receptive when you warned me about Boyarkin in June," he said. "I don't know what we could have done about it, but your computer forecasts have been very close to the mark. Do you think the new general secretary's hell-bent on war? Pat?"

Gellner chewed his lower lip. "There haven't been any unusual Warsaw Pact movements since the Pakistani weapons reached Libya. However, they've sent a helicopter carrier, the *Kiev*, and a support group of missile cruisers, frigates and support ships into the Central Atlantic. The task force was steaming for Gibraltar at eight this morning, our time. But their missile subs are only normally active, the usual number in port and so on. It's a confusing picture, but it doesn't appear that they're gearing up for an adventure. The details are in the national intelligence daily report."

"I've read it," said Law. "But Cam's people don't think the Libyans got past the Israelis without some powerful help. Cam?"

"I'm afraid I have to differ with defense intelligence," said Harper. "I think the Soviets are ready to move if a crisis occurs, but I think they're estimating that a critical situation is some weeks away. The worst of the situation – the immediate one, anyway – is that we don't know where those devices went after they reached Libya. There's been interference with our reporting functions there, probably courtesy of the KGB. It's the same pattern we saw in Pakistan."

"What do you think Boyarkin's going to do?" asked Law. "Simon?"

Parr took his pipe out of his mouth. "I think he's going to try to maneuver us into an untenable position vis-à-vis Israel – " the assistant for national security drummed his fingertips on the arm of his chair " – on the principle that we'll go to any lengths to avoid a nuclear war in the mideast. The RUBICON scenarios of last week outlined it. If there's a nuclear war there, and Israel loses, we'll have lost our major dependable ally and the Soviet Union will gain a lot from having helped Libya obtain the means of an Israeli defeat. Contrariwise, if Israel wins, we'll be perceived to have helped her devastate her neighbors. The Arab nations will be only too happy to get any Soviet aid they can, to circumvent the nuclear capabilities of the Israelis. Either way, we lose our oil and our strategic position. And if we don't react in the strongest way, NATO may collapse. It's a question of credibility."

"And if we do react in the strongest way?" Law asked.

"We risk a thermonuclear war. The problem is, given Boyarkin's temperament and political position, he can't afford to back down on an operation of this scale. It would do the same thing to him the Cuban missile crisis did to Khrushchev. A retreat from the strong position he'd have after a mideast war would be just as hard on his government's credibility as an Israeli defeat would be on our own. He couldn't back down."

"So," said Law. "We're playing a game of chicken – like a pair of drunks with fast cars and a stretch of straight road. If neither's willing to lose face by giving way, you have two dead drunks. Is it that bad, Cam?"

"It's bad, Mr. President. For comparison we ran the Cuban missile crisis through the RUBICON programs. We gave them what Kennedy knew then, plus profiles of the 1962 Soviet leadership. The simulation resulted in major war sixty times out of a hundred."

"What are the projections in this situation?"

"Eighty out of a hundred. Not local war: major, thermonuclear. The local rate is ninety-five out of a hundred."

"And it's Boyarkin who's at the center of it?"

"Yes."

"I hesitate to mention this," said Law, "given my reaction in June. But what about Longstop?"

"We've studied it," said Harper. "But it gives results as bad as anything else. Boyarkin's taken such extensive control that his outright elimination would cause chaos at the top. Without some form of organized government, the possibilities of a spasm nuclear strike against us are very high. What we need," he said carefully, without looking at any of the others, "is a way to remove Boyarkin and still retain an organized Soviet leadership."

"I hardly need ask," said Law, "whether you've made a study of that, too."

"Well, yes, we have," said the DCI. "It goes back several years. We elaborated a section of the RUBICON program to produce a scenario for the destabilization of the Soviet government. It was so successful – under one set of circumstances – that we held onto it and developed it quite extensively."

"What were the circumstances under which it was successful?"

"There had to be a split between the Communist Party and the military. There wasn't any likelihood of that before Andropov died so we didn't consider it seriously. But when General Secretary Leschenko took over the GRU got its freedom back, much to the KGB's disgust. They've been trying to reassert their control ever since. We intensified work on the study – it's called RUBICON ONE – at that time."

"And the KGB-GRU rivalry is the thin edge of our wedge," suggested Law.

"Exactly. The scenario proposed that we avoid interfering with the GRU as long as they were causing trouble for the KGB. To strenghten the GRU's position in the Politburo, GRU operations, as long as they weren't exceedingly dangerous, would be monitored but not interfered with. Being military intelligence, the GRU tends to see political and military realities more clearly than the KGB. By and large, the Soviet general staff doesn't want war on any but their terms." Harper lit another cigarette, coughed and went on. "Boyarkin's policy is moving us all towards a critical period. We think that we might have a chance of, ah, you might say, recruiting the GRU to prevent the situation from going too far. If we persuade them that Boyarkin's methods will put them into a war they haven't had time to prepare as well as they'd like, the general staff might be encouraged to remove Boyarkin and the KGB from the influence they now enjoy in the Politburo."

The deputy director of state took a deep breath. "Do you realize what you're saying? It's one thing to frig about with South American or African internal politics, but this? It's a direct attack on the major foreign power."

"We may have no choice," said Harper. "If Boyarkin's policies get out of hand, we have to subvert them. It's as simple as that."

The president stared at Harper for a long moment. "No one could ever accuse you of thinking small, Cam," he said.

"How would you propose to go about this . . . project? I assume that the execution is more complicated than the theory, as usual."

"Well, yes. The first step is to convince the GRU that we won't interfere with their actions or attack the USSR if the government is, um, disorganized for a few hours. Consequently we need to make contact with a reasonably exalted member of that organization, the GRU. It would be much preferable if one of them contacted us. There are ways to make that happen."

"Go on," said Law. Gellner had let his pipe go out.

"At that point we would arrange a secure link between ourselves and the GRU central office in Moscow. A direct one, not through their embassy here, but through ours over there. We would also put another link into the chain of communication, again in our Moscow embassy, handled directly by myself and the deputy director for operations. Our operative would liaise with the GRU on the outside, and the inside link would deal with the housekeeping and data traffic. We can't let one of the embassy case officers handle the outside man; the security risks are too great. The inside link could not be allowed to leave the embassy perimeter, or have anything to do with the CIA resident or the case officers."

"I hope these two are good at their work,". said Parr. "I for one wouldn't like playing footsie with the GRU while there was a KGB heavy on every street corner."

"The interior link won't be exposed," said the DCI. "The one we've selected for the outside link is very experienced."

"Suppose the KGB collects him anyway?" asked Gellner. "I can't think of anything more likely than this project to make Boyarkin go over the edge."

"The outside link won't know anything except what he's been told to tell the GRU," said Harper.

"And what's that?"

"Whatever will encourage the GRU to go ahead," said the DCI.

"Which may or may not be true?" asked Law.

"That's the essence of RUBICON ONE," said Harper.

"Whatever will produce the removal of Boyarkin's clique is what we tell the GRU."

"Including assurances that we wouldn't take advantage of them at a weak point," said Gellner.

"That would be uppermost in their minds, yes."

"But these assurances might be ones we wouldn't necessarily keep."

Harper lit another cigarette, noting with detached clarity that his hands were trembling slightly. "That was a sub-option of RUBICON ONE, not a necessary option. It predicted a very successful first strike against them, with minimal casualties in the west, if we took advantage of them."

"Jesus Christ," said Gellner, despite himself. The president stared at the DCI.

Harper looked down at the cigarette. The faint stripes of its paper seemed very clear. "I'm one of the last to propose such an act," he said. "It would be genocidal and reprehensible and its memory would haunt this nation for centuries." He paused for what seemed a long time. "It would also be preferable to a full-scale exchange of thermonuclear weapons."

He let that hang in the air for a moment, then said, "Our options have been diminishing ever since the day the Soviet Union decided to achieve parity or superiority in strategic weapons. The decision tracks are becoming fewer and fewer. The situation in the mideast, if it isn't reversed, is probably going to lead to nuclear war there. Simon put it very clearly a few minutes ago when he said that we were damned if Israel lost and damned if she won. We have *got* to stop Boyarkin. Because if there's an Arab-Israeli nuclear war, we will have to threaten either a full-scale attack – which likely will provoke one by the Russians – or resign ourselve to military, diplomatic and economic isolation by the end of the century. But if the Soviet military succeeds in getting rid of Boyarkin, we'll be able to deal with a confused and disorganized government, or at least a saner one. If it appears their coup is failing, then in the confusion we could. . . ." He stopped.

"Could have the option of a first strike," supplied the president.

There was an interminable silence.

"Cam," asked the president tiredly, "how much of a juggernaut is this project? Does it have to go to completion once it's begun?"

"No, sir. We can't persuade the Russian military to overthrow Boyarkin. They have to decide to do that themselves. All we can do is provide an environment in which they'd feel secure enough to act. That's what our link to the GRU would be for, to reassure them of our good intentions and to keep us informed of, well, I suppose you might call it the insurrection. We have to know what they're doing. Otherwise we can't afford to risk supporting them."

"We have no guarantee that they'd tell us the truth."

"No more than they have of us. For once it's going to have to be a two-way street, as far as trust is concerned. Up to a point."

"This would have to go before the House and Senate intelligence committees," Matthew Goodhand pointed out. "It would have to be presented in a very delicate way."

"Tell them," said Harper, "that it's only an information-gathering operation. It's not direct involvement in the internal affairs of another country."

"What would be the next step?" asked Law. "Before it went to the committees?"

"A contact with the GRU."

"All right," said the president. "Go as far as that. But we must be prepared to stop at any time. There must be no pos-sibility of this getting out of hand." He paused. "Wait. If your outside link were caught, and Boyarkin felt we were trying to get rid of him, would that cause him to start pushing red buttons?"

"I haven't quite finished," said Harper. "Please bear with me while I elaborate. RUBICON ONE has four scenarios associated with it. In the first, we do not execute RUBICON ONE, in which case the projections of the main RUBICON program remain valid: war, sooner than later. In the second, the GRU plot is discovered at an early stage and we perhaps are implicated. But we would make sure that it looked only like the usual attempt to stir up trouble in the opposition's security forces. Both sides are used to that. In any case, Boyarkin would be so happy to use that situation to break the GRU that he wouldn't bother with a confrontation. But we are still looking at a war somewhere down the road, because he's still firmly in the saddle.

"In the third scenario, Boyarkin is eliminated and a more or less sensible army regime takes over. We get no war but a strong Kremlin.

"The fourth option is, from our point of view, the most attractive. In this, the GRU plot is discovered at an advanced stage, preferably just before it's carried out or even just after it starts. It's suppressed. In this case it doesn't matter if Boyarkin survives or not, although we'd prefer it if he didn't, obviously. The result is that the Soviet officer corps is purged, perhaps even wiped out, by the KGB. With their military-command structure wrecked, and with the morale problems that would cause, the Russians would have far too much on their plate to go on interfering in the mideast. Even Boyarkin, if he survived, would have to keep his attention focussed at home. He'd never be sure he could trust the army to carry out his orders. And it would take them years to rebuild their officer corps. We would have a relatively free hand for as long as that took."

"And how," asked Law with an ironic lift in his tone, "would we explain to Secretary Boyarkin why we were supporting the GRU and the army? He might decide to fight first and purge afterwards."

"Ah," said Harper, "that's the elegant part of the fourth option." He looked down at the floor. "We're the good guys. Just before the GRU and the army start to move, we blow them to the KGB."

Jerusalem
July 28

*E*VENING. Cold mauve-grays under the hill crests. On the crests, walls in great orange planes, gray-white at noon, radiating now an ancient warmth. Domes, old gravestones sliding decade by decade under the dust. In the streets: Arabic and Hebrew script in neon, gold leaf, stainless steel, mosaic; smooth desert forms repeated in the stone of the Shrine of the Book. Men in dirty robes carrying crates of oranges and chickens down streets as wide as the stretch of two arms. Quarter-tone Arabic melodies sifting through slatted doors, scents of coffee, tobacco, charcoal, diesel exhaust, ancient mortar and new concrete.

And weapons. Soldiers in Zion Square, the glint of fading sunlight on the barrel of a submachine gun, patrols in the Old City alleys. Farther out, in the revetments and shelters of the airbases, the jagged outlines of Skyhawks, Phantoms, F-15s and 16s, Kfirs; and in the armor parks the tanks, the personnel carriers, the guns under nets; base after base, north by Ramat David, Haifa, Mahanayim; south to Herzliya, Yafa, Hazor, Sedom, to the squat, forbidden reactor complex of Dimona. And over all the listening ears, the radar complexes, from Eilat to Mount Hermon, all falling now into the dark, into the long shadows cast by the sun descending in the west.

The shadows lay particularly long in the executive offices of the Knesset, the parliament of Israel. Haim Choresh, head of Mossad, paused at the door of the Cabinet Room, feeling the drag of his briefcase in his wrist tendons. It carried a terrible weight; never in the existence of Israel had the burden been so heavy. Not even at Yom Kippur in 1973; perhaps not even at the beginning of the Diaspora two thousand years before.

He knocked and was admitted. There were three men in the room: Chaim Reisman, prime minister of Israel, Mordecai Seri, minister of defense and Avshalom Eldad, minister of foreign affairs. They remained silent as Choresh sat in one of the chairs at the conference table and opened the briefcase. He drew a file from the case, placed it carefully on the table and waited. Mossad's failure in the *Al-Mansour* catastrophe hung blackly over the gathering.

"Please give us your report," said Reisman. His voice was neither accusing nor conciliatory, merely neutral.

Choresh didn't bother to open the file. Its contents were burned into his memory.

"Sir. The Libyan government is now in possession of ten nuclear weapons of ten to twenty kilotons each. With each warhead they have a delivery vehicle, a standoff cruise missile of approximately one thousand kilometers' range. These missiles can be transported by their Mig-27 aircraft – the Pakistanis modified the missile to mate with the Mig-27 – and the Migs can easily reach an offshore attack position from their El Adem base. A likely mission profile would be to launch the weapons from about four hundred kilometers off our coast. The guidance system would be primitive by our standards but quite adequate to achieve a low airburst over Haifa or Tel Aviv. Jerusalem would be much more difficult to target but because of its religious and political significance we think it unlikely that such an attack would be mounted."

"Where are those weapons now?"

Choresh mentally drew a deep breath. "They are not all in Libya. We thought all ten were sent to the El Adem Airbase. But there has been a great deal of interference with our people in Libya since the *Al-Mansour* affair. We believe it's because of KGB counter-operations through Libyan security forces. The Americans have been experiencing the same thing. We haven't been severely damaged, but a number of our sources have dried up or gone silent. Consequently our information comes in bits and pieces."

"You said not all the weapons are in Libya," said Seri.

"Yes. As I said, our information comes erratically. But as of this midafternoon it was quite certain that only five of the crates that arrived at Okba bin Nafi on the eighteenth have gone to El Adem. The other five were loaded onto a Russian freighter, the *Vatutino*, in Tripoli Harbor, on the same day."

"Where is that freighter bound?" asked Reisman.

"There is no definite information. But for myself, I would estimate Latakia, in Syria. She sailed on the twenty-fifth."

There was a silence that went on and on. Choresh watched a last bar of sunlight on the wall, which did not apparently move but shifted ever so slowly towards the ceiling anyway.

"We can deal with standoff missiles launched from out at sea," the minister of defense said at last. "There's time. But if the Syrians can strike from Homs or Es Suweidīya we'll have next to no warning. Any air attack could be a nuclear one. We'd have to assume the worst at every incursion."

"And they're still moving tanks up towards the Golan from Damascus," said Avshalom Eldad. "And artillery. They've done that before, over the last two years, and then withdrawn. But they didn't have the support of the weapons they may be receiving now." He rubbed his forehead tiredly.

"What are the Americans going to do?" asked Seri of the foreign minister.

"There is not a great deal they can do publicly. Their ambassador in Tel Aviv has informed me that the secretary of defense has told the senior Russian military attaché in Washington that Soviet involvement in this affair could result in severe economic reprisals."

"Like Carter over Afghanistan?" asked Reisman snappishly. "What happened then?"

"The Russians didn't bother to reply."

Reisman turned to the minister of defense. "Is there nothing we can do about the *Vatutino?*"

"A Libyan freighter is one matter," said Eldad. "A vessel under the Russian flag is quite another. I do not see how we can touch the *Vatutino*."

"An air raid on Latakia while she's off-loading?"

"No. If it failed, we'd be worse off, and if we hit the weapons we'd risk blowing the fissionable materials all over the port. Even our closest friends couldn't stomach that."

"There might be other options," said Eldad.

Seri spread his palms. "A raid on the storage location might be possible, if we could find it. But it's likely they'll disperse the weapons from the moment they're off the *Vatutino*. We'd never be certain we got all of them – although we could try."

"The genie's out of the bottle, anyway," commented Eldad morosely. "They can always obtain more weapons. And we cannot possibly deal successfully with their source in Pakistan. Somehow we must defuse this thing diplomatically. There were ways of doing that, before. But with this new group in the Kremlin. . . ." He trailed off.

Reisman, elbows on the table, set his fingertips together and rested his forehead on them. "We must arm ourselves," he said. "We have no choice."

"And the Americans?"

"We must not tell them."

The last bar of light faded from the ceiling as the sun fell below the horizon. Haim Choresh, silent among his silent colleagues, felt not that their time was running out, but that it was irrevocably and utterly gone.

"BOYARKIN'S GOING TO CAUSE DISASTER with this crackdown on the intellectuals," complained Gresko. "Have you seen the digests of the last two days of western newspapers? You'd think we'd invaded Afghanistan all over again. And he's been pushing Morosov at the KGB to clean out some of the more liberal members of the Party, at the lower levels, where they can't defend themselves. Morosov seems to think the KGB is his new toy. My office staff are hopping about like fleas on a griddle, they're too nervous to get any work done."

"I know," said Kotsarev. They were sitting in the high-ceilinged study of Gresko's twelve-room flat on the Kutuzovsky Prospekt. The flat had been freshly checked for listening devices two hours ago.

"It wouldn't be so bad," went on Kotsarev, "if Boyarkin and Morosov's thugs in the KGB were just collecting the dissidents and the intellectuals. But they're starting to rummage around in the army. So far just the units with a lot of ethnic minorities have been affected, but it's bound to spread."

"Morosov," ruminated Gresko. "I wonder what he promised Boyarkin to get the KGB chairmanship?"

"Morosov was always a snoop," said Kotsarev. "I suppose he promised to confine his snooping to people other than Boyarkin. I wouldn't trust dear Aleksandr Morosov very far, myself."

"Boyarkin doesn't," said Gresko. "He's never trusted anybody."

There were two carafes on the inlaid table at Gresko's elbow, one of Stolichnaya vodka and another of mineral water. Gresko poured two glasses of the spirit and handed one to the minister of defense. They drank. Kotsarev's went down the wrong way and he coughed violently. Gresko gave him some mineral water.

"That was almost as hard to swallow as the Syrian business," Kotsarev said after a moment, scrubbing a tear from the corner of one eye. "Handing that crazy Libyan the bombs wasn't good enough. Oh, no. Now he has to help pass some on to those berserkers in Damascus. The Americans are very angry."

"It indicates how well Boyarkin's consolidated his position in the last weeks," observed Gresko. He was referring to the Politburo meeting in which the new general secretary had raised the question of shipping the weapons to Syria in a Soviet vessel; the decision had been passed with only Gresko, Kotsarev and Zhigalin dissenting. "Leschenko never would have tried to reverse policy over so short a time."

"He's gained a lot of credit because of the understanding with Pakistan," said Kotsarev. "Foreign Minister Distanov's as happy as a *kulak* with six cows. Needless to say, the Indians won't like it, but with the support we've given them in the past, there's not a lot they can actually do except complain."

"The Americans will like it even less when they find out about it," warned Gresko. "If they don't know already. Will Zia break off relations with them entirely?"

"Not likely. He'll try to play both ends against the middle, as usual."

Gresko ruminated. Drawing Pakistan into the status of a client state made very good sense. And there was always the possibility of Pakistan's discontented province of Baluchistan acquiring independence as an Islamic socialist state, given the proper manipulation of Islamabad and Zia. Then the Soviet Union would have an ally on the Indian Ocean, one that could be reached by land through Afghanistan. That dream went all the way back to the czars. And Boyarkin was spitting distance from achieving it.

If only it weren't for the Americans, Gresko thought. They'll be furious over the Pakistan rapprochement. And the

Syrian business would already have their hackles up. It was all too fast.

"I'm very glad the Americans don't have their first-strike capability completely built up yet," said Kotsarev, reading the other's throughts. "That would make the situation hyper-critical."

"Instead of only critical."

"Yes."

"Boyarkin has to go," said Gresko. "Your days are numbered, and so are mine. He knows we're not going to fall into line. I'm not as important in that respect as you are. He needs a defense minister who won't oppose him. Also, he's very likely to get us into a war we can't be sure of winning. Have you considered any possible ways out of the problem?"

Kotsarev motioned at the carafe of Stolichnaya. Gresko poured again, fuller glasses than before. The minister of defense got his vodka down the right way this time and set the glass carefully on the arm of his chair.

"There are two elements to the . . . proposal," he said. "First, we need a link to the Americans, as we discussed a few weeks ago. I have already established the prerequisites for this. One of General Yushenko's people, a Major Andreyev, who was keeping an eye on KGB activities in the south, was pulled out just before Leschenko died. We were going to post him to Warsaw after a debriefing period out east. But following the conversation you and I had at Uspenskoye I ordered General Yushenko to delay the posting. Major Andreyev's being groomed to go to the west. We have to insert him directly from home; going through the GRU station staff in Washington would be too dangerous. All we're going to have the GRU station do is link the operative to the US intelligence people. The Washington GRU station chief is close to General Yushenko."

"Can we trust Yushenko?" asked Gresko. He poured more vodka. The conversation was frightening him. He had to remind himself that they were only trying to keep the Americans sitting on their hands while an internal threat to the Soviet

Union was disposed of. That wasn't treason. Boyarkin, really, was the traitor, with his mad policies.

Kotsarev laughed, a short bark with no humor in it. "Absolutely. He did the initial study for this kind of thing. His interests coincide exactly with ours."

"I presume the link to the Americans is the first element of the proposal," said Gresko. "What after that?"

"This is somewhat more difficult," said the defense Minister. "It's an old idea, really. The Germans tried to use it to overthrow Hitler in 1944, only they panicked at the last moment and didn't have the nerve or the organization to follow through. They prepared the coup under cover of an existing army plan named Valkyrie. That was a routine exercise developed against possible revolts in Germany or the occupied territories. Except the targets in 1944 were the SS and the top Nazis. The SS in Berlin was to be disarmed and Goebbels, Himmler, Hitler and Goering were to be arrested. The army buggered it up, obviously."

"Obviously. And no doubt similar contingency plans exist here – for internal revolt, of course. And better organized."

"Of course. The awkward part is that we need a full-scale international crisis to make that kind of troop movement in Moscow look reasonable to the KGB. The timing would have to be very precise. There's a short span of time, just short of the critical point of war, during which we could both deal with the KGB and have a chance to defuse the crisis. Too soon or too late and everything's lost. We would have to be absolutely certain of collecting Boyarkin, Morosov and all the KGB department heads and deputies. At that point you'd become interim general secretary and start a thorough housecleaning, with army help, while dealing with the Americans. Not a small order. But the KGB Moscow apparatus must be left headless. The regional chiefs won't try anything by themselves, at least not before the military district headquarters are told to deal with them."

"The operation would be confined to Moscow, then."

"It has to be. Anything involving more than a few army units would certainly be penetrated."

Gresko thought about more vodka and decided against it. "How are you going to keep the unit political officers unaware of the situation? They're supposed to verify all orders and movements."

"That will not be easy. But we've made a start by replacing unit GRU people who might have, ah, KGB sympathies with those we know are clean. And the regimental commanders will be told to arrest their political officers as soon as the so-called routine maneuvers begin. The commanders will be given their orders from general staff HQ, so that officers above regiment level won't be able to interfere quickly, even if their political counterparts try to get them to do so. In fact we'll try to neutralize all political officers in the Moscow units if we can. The last thing we want is army units not in the planned exercise ordered to attack those that are."

Gresko clicked his teeth nervously. He could see a number of difficulties for himself in the proposed action. Kotsarev, with the KGB beheaded and the army in control, might decide that Gresko was redundant, assuming the coup succeeded. He would have to take some precautions, despite his regard for the minister of defense.

"Another thing," said Kotsarev. "The KGB's started chipping away at the GRU. We had turned the KGB deputy station chief in Islamabad. He's dead, apparently suicide. General Yushenko doesn't think so. He thinks it was a warning."

Gresko recollected himself with an effort. "How serious is KGB penetration of the GRU?"

"We can't prevent it completely. But Yushenko assures me it's under control at the higher levels."

"All right. We have to go ahead. I'll do what I can to head off Boyarkin's worst excesses while you put the finishing touches on the operation. How long do you need?"

"Two weeks."

"And then we can wait for an international crisis."

"We won't have to wait long," said Kotsarev grimly. "Not with Boyarkin in the general secretary's seat. Pass the Stolichnaya."

Tactical Training School 119
Amur Military District
July 29

*F*LAT GRAY-GREEN STEPPE. Stone-smooth sky, low and gray. It was raining for the first time in two weeks, the clouds piling in on the west wind, out of the distance upon distance of Asian Russia. It was a fine rain, really not much more than a mist, and it beaded slowly on the windows of the long rows of huts, trickled from the corners of their rough shingled roofs, turned the raw earth at the guard posts into blackish mud that squelched around the sentries' boots whenever they moved.

It was bleak beyond belief, even to someone who was born to it, and Major Andreyev was not. Near Smolensk, where he grew up, the country was also flat and gray-green, but there were villages and towns always just over the horizon, a sense of a land inhabited. Here, a hundred and thirty kilometers north of Khabarovsk across the Amur River, there was no such perception. It was as though one lived on the back of some colossal sleeping animal and had no more importance to it than the clouds of midges that bred in the marshes along the Amur's flats.

Andreyev turned away from the hut window and sat at the splintery wooden table that served as a desk. The conditions at the training school were Spartan; only the excellent food betrayed the fact that the men trained here were officers of the GRU.

Tactical School 119 was not really a tactical school. It was a postgraduate institution and retraining establishment for the most talented of the GRU's military-intelligence specialists. Andreyev had spent four months there before leaving for Afghanistan. His ability had surprised even his instructors, which was why he had been selected for the anti-KGB operations in the south.

Now he was back again, although he did not know exactly why. During the first five days he had been intensely debriefed regarding the KGB's agent-provocateur activities in the Moslem republics. The next five had been spent on the current Polish situation, from which he understood that he would be posted to Warsaw. Then there was an abrupt change. He had been removed from the Pact Section and was given an individual instructor, Colonel Aistov, who specialized in American intelligence operations. Colonel Aistov taught a regular section as well, but had been relieved of that to spend his time with Andreyev. Simultaneously, Andreyev had been isolated from the other students. He ate and exercised with Aistov.

His training covered three areas. First, the political situation in the United States and the methods and organization of the CIA and its sister security services. Next, a detailed analysis of Arab-Israeli relations. Finally, the construction of an identity as a Swiss-German businessman who owned a small machine-tool fabrication plant near Geneva. He was purportedly interested in American microprocessor-control technology for his operation.

The identity worried Andreyev. It was not possible to develop a solid cover in the time Colonel Aistov had spent on it. It appeared that whatever he was expected to do would be quick and unsophisticated, the cover intended to hold only for a short time.

There had also been many hours of English lessons. Andreyev thought it likely that he was to be sent to the United States. The prospect excited even while – because of the poor cover – it frightened him. The time he had passed in Washington two years previously had been an education. At first he believed that the opulence of the American capital existed only there, that its residents were the favored minority of the decaying west.

"Don't be an ass," the GRU station chief had told him when he ventured this opinion after a stay of ten days. "Take a bus trip for a week – it doesn't matter where. Most of the country lives like this, or close to it, by our standards. The only places there are problems are in the inner slums of the big cities, and even there the people are no worse off than the peasants in most of the Union." The station chief had paused for a moment, as though he realized he might be praising the west overmuch. "It all depends on plundering the rest of the world, of course. But go and see. You'll understand better what we have to cope with."

Andreyev had, and did. Even the memory of the wealth he had seen left him, figuratively speaking, open-mouthed.

He had learned a lot of English in those months. Andreyev had a gift for languages, among other things.

He penciled a series of squares and curlicues on the scratchy pad of paper he used to take notes during Colonel Aistov's briefings. The squiggles began to take on the shape of a woman's breasts. Andreyev shaded in the curves underneath. The compound outside was quiet; the previous class of students had been assigned out the previous day and the new draft had not yet arrived.

Andreyev felt very lonely. He stopped penciling and listened to the hiss of the rain. It sounded older here than it ever had in Smolensk, as though it had been falling for centuries instead of one day.

Another sound under the sound of falling water: an engine. Andreyev straightened. Then he went to the window and looked out. Around its frame he could just see the school's barbed-wire main gate. As he waited, the sound of the engine grew louder, its note rising and falling as the vehicle slithered through the access road's mud. A BRDM drew up to the gate and stopped. Andreyev went back to his desk. The BRDM belonged to the camp and was used to reach Khabarovsk Airport when the roads were bad, which they normally were.

He was adding a face above the breasts when he heard boots thudding in the corridor. A knock, and Colonel Aistov said outside, "Major?"

"Sir." Andreyev got up and opened the door. Aistov, mud

on his boots, stood there, wearing a worried expression. "He's here," he told Andreyev.

"Sir? Who?"

"Your case officer. Or I think he is. You've been a good student. Don't let me down."

"No, Colonel Aistov. Of course not." Andreyev felt a resurgence of the fear that had been in him since he had been summoned from Alma-Ata to the Kubinka Airfield. Something very peculiar is going on, he told himself. I hope it's not going to be the death of me.

"He came in the BRDM," said Aistove, entering the room and straightening his tunic. "He'll be here any moment."

More footsteps in the corridor, less certain than Aistov's. Then a tall, lean man with Mongol cheekbones was standing in the doorway. Andreyev and Aistov snapped to attention.

The man returned the salute precisely. Although the toes of his boots were muddy the uppers shone like glass, beaded with rain. "Comrades," he said. "Good morning. I am Colonel Lukashin."

I don't believe that, thought Andreyev. If this operation is the weird one I believe it is, that's not your name.

"Sit," said Colonel Lukashin. "Let's be comfortable."

They did, Andreyev and Colonel Aistov on the bed, Colonel Lukashin on the chair at the splintery table. Lukashin surveyed them intently. "I'm tired and very irritable," he said. "I left Moscow twelve hours ago. Please forgive me if I'm abrupt."

The two on the bed nodded.

"Major Andreyev," said Colonel Lukashin. "You are to go to the United States." He drew a thick envelope from his tunic. "Here are your movement instructions and travel documents. Colonel Aistov will review them with you. There will be security en route, so you won't be alone." He paused and scratched at a patch of mud on the knee of his trousers. Then he said, "This is much more difficult, what I have to tell you. To be precise, Major Andreyev, you are to go to New York. There you will be contacted by the GRU station chief. It is absolutely essential that the KGB resident be unware of your arrival. At the moment, why this is so is none of your business. But it must be so. Do you understand?"

"Yes, Colonel," said Aistov and Andreyev simultaneously. Andreyev thought: This is worse than I could have imagined. Whatever else the KGB is, it's loyal to Russia. This has to be treason.

"Is Major Andreyev well prepared?" asked Colonel Lukashin.

"Yes, sir," said Aistov. "Very."

The Mongol eyes narrowed. "He had better be. Major Andreyev has found that the KGB itself is subverting socialist accord in the southern republics. This is against all of the precepts of Lenin. All peoples of the Union must be free to preserve their traditions within the Soviet framework. To attack this right is treason."

Colonel Lukashin paused and looked out at the rain. Then he said, "If Major Andreyev's activities are ever found out by the KGB, and it is known that we suppressed the information, our lives will be very short. And painful."

"Permission to query," said Andreyev.

"Go ahead," said Colonel Lukashin.

"What am I to do in America?"

Lukashin smiled briefly, a smile that did not reach his eyes. "You will be told that when you arrive."

"I do not trust my cover," said Andreyev, greatly daring.

"It is not intended to hide you from the Americans," said Colonel Luskashin, and then frowned. "I have said too much already. Forget it." He looked out the window again at the falling rain. "I have to go. You will follow your orders precisely. After you leave this place you will be controlled directly from. . . ." He hesitated. "Moscow. Colonel Aistov, I don't want any errors in his preparation."

"There won't be any."

"Fine," said Lukashin. "Major Andreyev, good luck." He turned his collar up and left the room.

When they heard the BRDM pull away, Aistov said, "You heard what he wants. Let's get started."

Washington
July 29 & 30

THERE WERE TWO MEN in a bar on M Street. One of the two, fair and thickset and in his late thirties, had been watching the other for an hour. The man who was being watched had been aware of the surveillance for almost as long. He was used to it; it came, as they said, with the territory. He was one of the department assistants to the director of central intelligence.

He finished his whiskey, left his stool and walked to the booth where the fair, thickset man was fiddling with a glass of beer. He sat down. The other glanced at him uncertainly.

"It's a nothing night," said the American, "except for you. What do you want?"

"You haven't seen me before," said the fair man in accented English.

"I know a Slav when I see one. I picked this bar because nobody's ever followed me into it before. Why you?"

"Unofficial contacts are often better in out-of-the-way places."

The American considered this for a moment. There was a stream of information that flowed between intelligence operatives of both sides, on the principle that – for some purposes – it was better to let your opponent know where you stood. In some ways the stream was above national loyalties: it was rather like establishing the rules of a game. In some cases, it also provided a form of life insurance – in the literal sense of the word.

"True," said the American. "How are things over your way?"

"Interesting," said the fair man. "By the way, I'm not KGB."

"Oh?" Polite lack of interest.

"GRU."

"Oh, that's where I've seen your face. An interested observer on a public Pentagon tour. They photograph everything, don't they?"

"Yes," said the Russian. He had begun to look nervous. "Listen to me for a moment. There is someone who wants to see Harper. Badly. I can't tell you how badly."

"Oh?"

"It is essential to arrange a meeting."

"With the GRU?"

"Yes. No one else."

"Not even your, ah, brothers?"

"Particularly not them."

'Why not?"

'I can't tell you."

The American began to feel a certain interest. There were fine beads of perspiration in his armpits despite the bar's air-conditioning. "The DCI doesn't make a habit of meeting with members of your establishment," he said. "I can't imagine why he'd want to start now."

The Russian squeezed his glass very tightly in one fist. The American realized suddenly that the man was frightened.

"The KGB thinks I'm trying to recruit you," the GRU man said. "Don't make pigshit of my cover, or I'm dead. Listen. Your DCI has to meet someone. Tell him it concerns an arms shipment to Libya. And Syria. He'll come."

The American raised his eyebrows. "People are always shipping arms to Libya and Syria. I don't see why that should interest him more than ordinarily."

"They aren't ordinary weapons," said the Russian. He stood up. "They are like the ones your Israeli friends have been hiding for years." He looked down at his companion.

"Oh," said the American. "They finally got some, did they?" He was on the Latin American desk; in the tightly compartmented world of the CIA he was not permitted access to information outside the interests of his department, except in unusual circumstances.

This situation, clearly, was unusual.

"Yes," muttered the Russian. "If he'll come, you be here at ten tomorrow evening. Do not talk to me. I'll make the drop behind the toilet tank third from the left as you enter the washroom. Fallback is to Blake's on K Street two hours later. Second tank from the right."

"We'll need some bona fides."

"They'll be with the other information. I'm out of time."

And he was gone.

The American exhaled slowly. He waited forty minutes, then walked six blocks to a pay telephone.

He *would* specify a meeting in the Watergate, Harper thought as he walked along the empty corridor towards the safe room. He's always had a peculiarly Russian, oblique brand of humor. I wonder how he managed to get here without being watched. The KGB is nervous these days, as they should be, with that madman in the Kremlin. Boyarkin. What does the GRU want to do about Comrade General Secretary Boyarkin?

He reached the door and fumbled in his pocket for the key. The key's original was now at the hotel desk, left there an hour earlier by an anonymous CIA employee. Copying keys in a hurry was not difficult, even if the blanks were restricted, if you had the technology.

Technology: that we have, thought Harper, inserting the key into the lock. And we have RUBICON, and RUBICON ONE because of it. Humanity, ah, there's another thing.

Perhaps I'm getting old.

He opened the door and stepped inside. GRU Colonel Pyotr Karelin sat in a chair by the window. The curtains were drawn. Harper closed the door.

"Hello, Cameron," said the Russian. He had a wide, flat face and thin eyebrows. "We haven't had a private talk in a long time."

"You requested it," said Harper. "You're satisfied with the place?"

Because of the KGB, Karelin had more to lose from eavesdropping than Harper did: accordingly, the Russian had been given half an hour to inspect the room before Harper arrived.

"I'm not terribly skilled," said Colonel Karelin. His accent was an odd mixture of Russian and British. "But with these devices – " he nodded at a small bag inside the desk, "I think we're not overheard by anyone. At least we shouldn't be. All my detection devices are your capitalist technology's. I might say you're very good at them."

"Thank you," said Harper dryly. "Open-market technology won't detect everything, but I guarantee that we haven't planted anything."

"That improves my mood greatly," said Karelin. "Would you like a drink?"

Harper wanted one very much. "No, thank you."

"You can't do business with Russians without a drink."

"Is this business?"

Colonel Karelin raised his eyebrows. "Do you think I've avoided the attentions of the KGB for two hours to discuss methods of listening to other people's conversations?"

"No," said Harper. "All right, let's have a drink. Then get to the point."

There was a leather briefcase beside Karelin's chair. The Russian opened it and took out a thermos and two shot glasses. "It should still be cold," he said, and poured colorless liquid. "Would you prefer me to drink first?"

Harper took the proferred glass. "I don't think your department goes in for that sort of thing – at least not in these circumstances."

"We certainly don't employ some of the more gruesome tactics of the KGB's infamous Department V," said Karelin. "Nevertheless." He drank the vodka down and rested the glass on his knee.

Harper sampled the spirit. It was icy and clean. "What else is in your briefcase?"

"Nothing," said the GRU station chief. "What I have to discusss isn't for paper."

He looks uncomfortable, Harper thought. The DCI waited.

"You're certainly aware that the Libyans have acquired nuclear weapons and have passed a number along to Syria."

"Yes. With a little help from your merchant marine."

'What is your government's reaction to that?'

"We're not happy."

"Nor your military?"

Harper shrugged. "Judge for yourself."

The Russian put his glass on the desk and took a cigarette from a crumpled packet. He tossed the packet to Harper, who extracted one and passed the remainder back. Karelin hunted through his pockets. "Shit. I haven't any matches."

"I have a lighter."

What a bloody dance, thought Harper as he lit the Russian's cigarette. Why won't he come to the point?

"The point is," said Colonel Karelin, settling back into his chair, "that some of our own people are very worried about the situation as well. Unfortunately, there are other factions in our government who don't share their concern. Given American tendencies to shoot first and ask questions later, the situation could become lethal under the wrong circumstances."

"That tendency isn't restricted to the United States," Harper observed. "What circumstances are you referring to?"

"A nuclear war in the Middle East. Israel has a nuclear capability, we've known that for some time. I'm sure Mossad's informed Jersualem about the Syrian and Libyan acquisitions. The Israelis are assembling their warheads right now, if they haven't already done so."

"Would you blame them?"

"No. We would do – have done – the same. The fact remains that a nuclear war between the Arabs and Israelis is far more likely now than it was a few months ago."

"Particularly since Boyarkin has made himself general secretary."

Karelin looked away.

"Is that what you're here about?" asked Harper, feeling apprehension and excitment rise simultaneously within him. "Because the GRU doesn't like what Boyarkin's doing?"

The Russian's face was stony. "That's not for me to

indicate. I am saying to you exactly what I was told to say, no less and no more."

"All right. I understand."

"Some of us do not like to risk being dragged into general war because of a flare-up in the Middle East. If there were to be a war, we'd rather pick the time and circumstances ourselves – as you would. It is an old principle."

Harper nodded.

"The same people," Colonel Karelin went on, licking his lips as though they had gone dry, "would like to arrange a very unofficial channel to reduce misunderstandings if the worst should happen in the Middle East."

"Who?" queried Harper. "The KGB? The GRU? The general staff?"

"You don't really think it's the KGB. It's too close to Boyarkin."

"No. Otherwise I'd be talking to Colonel Antipov, not you."

"The KGB must not know of this," said Karelin running his tongue over his lips again. "You or your staff may be tempted to cause trouble in our Washington station by blowing this conversation to Antipov. I warn you, doing so is in your worst interests."

"Not to mention yours."

Karelin shrugged. "Naturally."

"Between what parties would this unofficial channel communicate? Myself and who else?"

The Russian put another cigarette between his lips. Harper lit it for him.

"He has a code name. Larch."

"Come on, Pyotr. You know I have to have more than that."

Karelin took a deep breath. "General Yushenko."

Harper stared at him. "I beg your pardon?"

"You heard me."

"What's led the chief of the GRU to this?"

"I don't know."

But I do, thought Harper. Likely better than you, Pyotr.

Yushenko's in something with Kotsarev and probably Gresko as well. Even if he is head of the GRU he wouldn't go sailing off on his own. How did that bloody computer know what the Russians would do before they knew it themselves? Or is it coincidence? Is Karelin setting up a gigantic deception for the KGB? Maybe Boyarkin and the Gresko-Kotsarev-GRU mob aren't really at each other's throats at all.

We have to find out.

"General Yushenko's not doing this all by himself," he told Karelin. "Who's backing him? He'll end up in the Gulag if he's not well protected and if any of this gets to Boyarkin and the KGB."

"He has powerful support."

It might be true. "Exactly what do you want of us?" Harper asked.

"I told you, a link." Karelin looked at his watch. "We have wasted time. We want a link so that the more . . . cautious influences in our government can tell your people of measures they are taking to avoid a general war if there is an Arab-Israeli nuclear exchange."

A silence.

He really did say it, thought Harper in the stillness. They're thinking about a coup and they don't want us to interfere but they don't dare leave us in the dark, either.

"Who did you have in mind? For the link?"

"A man we carefully selected some time ago. He'll be in the country soon. He's not part of our station staff." Karelin grinned. "He's an illegal."

"It's still that easy, is it?"

Karelin shrugged again. "We can't use any of our staff; they don't have freedom of movement because of the KGB and your surveillance. The link would report to Moscow by radio while in this country. But for the bulk of the work we'd want him in Moscow. Communications to you would be quicker if he were. That might be very important."

"He's just supposed to walk up to our embassy gate, knock and say, 'I've got some information from the GRU for the CIA'?"

"Don't be ridiculous," snapped Karelin. "You'll have to have someone there who can move freely, someone connected with the embassy. We'd take care of the contacts outside."

"Why are you bringing your end of the link to the United States?"

"We want your man to know him. Procedures have to be established. It would be easier here than back home."

"What decision are you hoping for today?"

"That you'll consider the arrangement. If you accept it, we'll arrange a meeting between our operative and whoever you select."

"When?"

"As soon as possible."

"That doesn't give us much time."

"I am reliably informed," said Karelin, "that there is not much time to be had."

"This has to go before the Committee on Foreign Intelligence and the president. I can't promise anything at all."

Karelin gestured impatiently. "You know what you're being offered. You will have to choose."

"We'll consider it. Can you meet me here at 5:00 P.M. on the first of August?"

"Once more is safe."

"All right. I'll let you know the answer then." Harper stood up to leave.

"Another thing," said Karelin. He stubbed out his cigarette. Harper waited.

"There is one particularly important message. If the United States tries to take advantage of Soviet domestic problems, the United States will bear full responsibility for the risk of war. Is that understood?"

Harper nodded somberly. "Yes," he said. "We understand it very well indeed."

Selznevo — Helsinki — Zurich
July 31

THERE IS A SOVIET AIR DEFENSE COMMAND airbase near Selznevo, some one-hundred-fifty kilometers northwest of Leningrad, near the Finnish border. At about nine o'clock on the morning of July thirty-first, an aging Ilyushin-14 transport aircraft touched down at the eastern edge of the airstrip, taxied to the control tower and delivered itself of three army officers. Of these, two were returning from leave to their regiments up along the Russo-Finnish border. The third was Andreyev, although this was not what his identity papers indicated.

An army truck was waiting behind the control tower. Andreyev said a brief good-bye to his traveling companions – he had boarded the Ilyushin only three hours previously, at Serpukhov Airbase –and got into the truck.

"He could at least have offered us a ride," said one of the two officers as the truck pulled away. He was sweating in the early heat.

"One of the *nachalstvo*," said the other. "Father's probably a general or whatever." He lit a cigarette and coughed once. "Cheer up. We might have had to take the train. That's the first time I was ever shipped back to the regiment by air."

The other agreed. By the time they arranged transport to their units, they had forgotten what Andreyev looked like, not to mention what they had thought was his name.

In the truck's jolting cab, Andreyev studied the driver obliquely. The man was young and not at all Slavic in appearance. He wore corporal's insignia but looked too old for the rank. A GRU lieutenant or captain, then, Andreyev thought. He relaxed slightly.

The road to the Finnish border was not very good; the asphalt had broken up in the spring thaw and had been sloppily repaired. The larch, pine and birch groves hedged it closely on both sides, green and peaceful in the morning light. There was no wind and the birch leaves hung straight down.

Some fifteen kilometers from the airbase the driver began looking frequently in his side mirror. He had been driving rather slowly and now he slowed even more. Andreyev watched the mirror outside his own window. Several hundred meters behind was another truck. Civilian, nondescript. Andreyev tensed. "We're being followed."

"Yes," said the driver. He had a slight lisp. "It's the change-over vehicle. Get ready to leave." He wheeled the truck onto the road's shoulder, got out and opened the hood. Andreyev opened his door and dragged his kit bag after him onto the treeward side of the truck. He went around to the opened hood.

The civilian truck drew up behind them. There were two men in the cab. The passenger got out and walked over to Andreyev's driver, who was muttering at the engine.

"Buggered," said the driver. "Can you give my passenger a lift?"

"It's very close to the border," said the man from the other truck. He wore rough laborer's clothes.

"People worry too much," said the driver and nodded at Andreyev.

"There's room in the back," the civilian told Andreyev. "Too crowded up front with three."

Andreyev nodded, went around to the rear of the other truck and clambered in over the muddy tailgate. The civilian followed him. The truck's engine, which had been left idling, roared and they lurched onto the road. The civilian dragged a canvas sheet three-quarters across the open rear of the truck, plunging the interior into gloom. Taking a large jacknife from his pocket, he began to pry at the floor. A section of boarding lifted up, revealing a shallow compartment. In it were two bundles of clothing, a small suitcase of good leather, a thin briefcase and a half-liter bottle of vodka. The civilian handed Andreyev one of the bundles.

"Put these on. Your papers are in the jacket."

They were coarse working clothes: jacket, flannel shirt, baggy trousers, thin cotton socks. The boots were heavy, well-used and thick-soled. Andreyev put the clothes on and the civilian tucked the discarded uniform into the cache and sealed it up. The access panel was quite invisible.

"You don't speak Finnish."

"No," said Andreyev. He wiggled his toes. The boots fit badly.

"Study your papers. We're doing an electrical installation in Vyborg. It's Finnish equipment and we're part of the installation team. So are you."

"You're Finns?" Andreyev was taken aback.

The man gestured impatiently. "Does it matter? Since you don't speak the language, you'll have to look drunk when we go through the frontier checkpoint. And I mean blind drunk, stinking. Spill some of the vodka on your jacket when I bang on the back of the cab. And drink a good gulp, too. Rap back so I know you've heard me and lie down on the floor. Not neatly. Make sure the bottle's empty. I'll come back here when they do the identity check and show them your papers. Snore or something if you can make it sound good. Don't talk, whatever you do. On the other side you can get into your travel cover. You know what to do after that. Understand everything?"

Andreyev nodded. The man rapped sharply on the partition between the cab and the truck's cargo bed and the vehicle slowed. The Finn swung himself over the tailgate. A few seconds later the cab door slammed and they began to pick up speed.

Andreyev sat down at the front of the cargo box, his back against the partition. Through the ten-centimeter gap between the canvas curtain and the side of the truck he could see the stands of larches and birch slipping by.

The Finn had to be a GRU man, likely slipped into Finnish industry in the early fifties. There would have been three men in the truck when it entered Russia; Andreyev was replacing one of them, as the count of border crossers was carefully monitored. He wondered how they were going to extract the one he had substituted for.

Well, there was more than one way to get over a border. This was one he hadn't tried yet. He hoped it would work.

Despite his nervousness he began to drift off to sleep. He had slept very little since leaving the training school. Lukashin had been long gone when Andreyev departed.

His head lolled. A splinter dug into his left buttock. He swore briefly and shifted position. The vodka bottle caught his eye. No harm in getting into the part to some degree. He took off the jacket, wadded it into a pillow and opened the bottle. After swallowing an ounce and a half he recapped the bottle and lay down, head on the jacket.

Four minutes later he was asleep.

He awoke to a furious pounding on the partition. Shaking his head, Andreyev sat up and rapped back. The pounding stopped.

Shit, he thought. What a way to begin. Where the devil was the bottle? There. He opened it, poured half the contents over his shirt and drank half the rest. The remainder went onto his jacket. Andreyev arranged himself loosely on the splintery floor and breathed noisily through his mouth.

The truck lurched onwards for perhaps ten minutes. Andreyev's tongue began to dry out. He closed his mouth and breathed through his nose instead. The alcohol was beginning to steal warmly through his brain. It will be very smooth, he told himself, this won't be any trouble at all.

The truck slowed, gears scraping and grinding. They stopped. Four or five minutes passed. Andreyev began to worry despite the vodka.

There were voices from the cab, then a third voice; all were speaking Russian.

"Coming back? Where from?"

"Vyborg. Here are the transit passes."

A silence.

"Where's the third one?"

"In back. He's drunk."

"Let me see him."

"All right. But he's drunk as a pig."

A door slammed; there was the crunch of gravel and the sound of heavy boots over the tailgate.

"He's a pig," said the civilian's voice above him. "He must have had that other bottle in his shirt. He hasn't been worth a fuck since we started the job."

"Give me his papers," said the border guard.

Andreyev felt the jacket pulled roughly from beneath his head. He kept his neck muscles slack as his head dropped to the floor.

"Here they are." Riffling of pages.

"All right. Here. Keep them until he's woken up. Somebody might steal them."

"Whatever you say."

There was a tension in the guard's voice that unnerved Andreyev. He forced himself to relax. The vodka's effect seemed to have disappeared.

Something hard and blunt smashed into his upper right arm. The blow was heavy enough to drive his shoulder blades three or four centimeters across the floor.

His training took over before the pain took hold. He snorted loudly through his mouth, hacked and was still. Fire ran through his arm and shoulder.

The guard laughed. "He's drunk, all right."

The civilian spat. "I'll tell him he fell out of the truck. Maybe it'll take his mind off his headache."

"Go on across," said the guard. "Better keep him out of the vodka next time."

"He can kill himself with it," Andreyev heard the Finn say, voice receding over the tailgate. "And the sooner the better."

The procedure through the Finnish checkpoint was much the same, except that the guard there didn't kick him.

The suit fit well, although the label at the back of the undershorts scratched the small of his back just above the tailbone. It was a Swiss label. Andreyev tried to ignore the ache in his arm and scanned the occupants of the boarding lounge. Outside the lounge windows the midafternoon sun lit Helsinki's Seutula Airport with a clear, bright glare. The distant hills, heavily forested, rolled cold green towards the horizon line.

There was no one paying any particular attention to him. But, then, a professional would not. Andreyev was looking for telltale movements, a shift in the eyes, a positioning of the feet. Apart from the obvious airport security staff, there was no sign of a watcher.

Half-consciously he moved to rub his shoulder, then scratched his nose instead. If there were anyone looking for a Swiss businessman with an aching arm, it would be preferable not to advertise the condition.

At first, after the truck reached the drop-off point, he thought the arm would be useless, it had stiffened so. But the Finn, surprisingly gently, had massaged it and helped Andreyev into the pin-striped business suit.

"I'll give you a hand out of the truck," he said. "The public transit stop's around the corner to the left. Use your left hand for the suitcase. It's lighter than the briefcase."

At least somebody's on my side, Andreyev thought. Now if the plane's only on time.

He looked at his watch – 4:10. Ten minutes until boarding . . . assuming that no KGB influences had been exerted at the airport control level.

Time passed. A small blond girl trotted up and asked him something in German, but her lisp made the words unintelligible. Andreyev smiled at her and muttered a few phrases back. Apparently disappointed, the child trundled off to her equally blond mother on the other side of the lounge. The woman smiled vaguely at Andreyev. Andreyev smiled back.

An incomprehensible statement from the public-address system, repeated in German, French and English. Boarding to begin in five minutes. People began to line up at the access doors. Andreyev joined them.

He had still seen no evidence of a follower by the time he was installed in the aisle seat of Row G of the Swissair 737. A minute later the mother with the small girl took the seats across the aisle from him. Andreyev smiled at the child again, then put his head back against the headrest. It was much more comfortable than the truck partition. He was very tired.

"*M'sieur? Excusez-moi, s'il vous plaît.*"

He understood that much French and got up. A pair of middle-aged women with sharp, rodent-like noses scrunched past him and took the two window seats. They began to gabble softly, not much above whispering.

Not likely KGB, Andreyev thought. He closed his eyes again. The brothers would sit farther back, anyway, where they could see him if he left his seat.

After a while the warnings signs came on and the plane began to move. The stewardess provided the obligatory emergency instructions and then disappeared.

Andreyev was asleep before the 737 reached cruising altitude. The stewardesses passed him by with their pillows and magazines and not even the tinkle of the liquor cart at his elbow disturbed him.

He was dreaming that Lukashin stood above him, shouting in German, over and over, but Andreyev could not understand the words. The colonel became angrier and angrier, frightening Andreyev more and more. The GRU man shot out a hand and began pulling at Andreyev's left arm.

Lukashin went away but the tugging continued. Andreyev realized that he was no longer asleep. He started up in his seat. The blond child was standing in the aisle beside him, one small pink paw holding his cuff. She let it go and backed away, uncertain. Andreyev looked at her blearily.

"Are you asleep?" she asked in lisping German.

This time he understood her. "No. Not now." He ran his tongue over his lips. They felt dry and tasted salty.

"Did I wake you up?"

"Brigitte!"

The child's mother had also obviously just woken up. Flushing with embarrassment, she looked across the aisle at the Russian. "I'm terribly sorry. She *will* speak to strangers. Did she wake you?"

"Well, yes," said Andreyev. "But it doesn't matter." He didn't want to talk. His German accent was indeterminate in origin, but he had planned to use the language as little as possible while among Germans, Swiss or otherwise. Filthy luck that the woman was probably Swiss German.

She was rather pretty in a solid way. He searched his memory. Buxom, that was the word.

"I'm terribly sorry," she said again.

"I don't mind," said Andreyev. "Will we be landing soon?"

"In about forty-five minutes," she said, looking at her watch.

"I should have been waking up anyway."

"You look like my papa," said the child.

Andreyev liked children. But an instant after she said this he stopped thinking of her as a child and began to consider how she and her mother could be used to cover his vulnerability as he went through customs, until he could lose himself in the Zurich airport terminal.

It was this opportunism that made him such a good intelligence operative.

He smiled and said, "Where is your papa?"

"At home."

"Oh? Where's that?"

"Home." Utter seriousness.

"She's only three-and-a-half," said her mother. "She doesn't really know where home is."

"Have you been on vacation?"

"Yes. In Finland." She smiled. "I suppose that's obvious. My husband had to return a week early. Business, you know." The smile faded.

"Yes, business," said Andreyev. He searched for something to say. "Do you live in Zurich?"

"Geneva. But we're going to visit Brigitte's grandmother in Zurich before we go home. Aren't we, dumpling?"

The child nodded solemnly.

"Her words dry up if I'm around," said her mother.

A stewardess appeared from aft. "Fasten your seatbelts, please. We will begin our descent soon and it may be a little bit bumpy."

Brigitte's mother began to fuss with the child. Andreyev tightened his seatbelt, thinking hard.

They had to stack in the airport approach for twenty minutes. Andreyev watched Zurich slide below, long-shadowed in the early evening sun, as they banked in their circling. Brigitte's mother sat bolt upright beside her daughter, obviously worried by the delay. Brigitte herself fiddled with the lid of the ashtray in the arm of her seat. By the time the airliner's tires were squealing on the runway the fingers of her right hand were mottled an ashy black and gray.

Her mother didn't notice until the exit ramps were being clamped to the aircraft.

"Brigitte. You little wretch. Your grandmother is meeting us and you're filthy." She began to rummage in her purse for a tissue.

Other passengers were filling the aisle. Andreyev remembered the linen handkerchief in his breast pocket. He whipped it out. "Here."

Brigitte's mother looked up. "Oh, no, you can't. It will get filthy."

Andreyev had no intention of getting off the aircraft without the child and the woman. He reached between two aisle standers, took Brigitte's hand and began to dust off the ashes. Her mother, too late, found a crumple of tissues and looked on helplessly while Andreyev mopped. The child regarded him thoughtfully.

He finally had to stop to let people get by. He handed the soiled cloth to Brigitte's mother and the gap closed.

He waited. The two Frenchwomen climbed over him and joined the line. A snivel and then a wail erupted from the other side of the aircraft, followed by a sharp smack. The wailing redoubled and then subsided.

Andreyev waited some more. The line thinned out.

Brigitte's head was buried in her parent's lap. The small shoulders heaved rhythmically. Her mother looked at Andreyev with helpless exasperation.

The end of the line passed. "Let me help you," Andreyev said, standing up. "She's tired. I'll carry her."

Brigitte's mother studied him, wondering whether to trust her child to this stranger outside the aircraft.

She decided. "Thank you. We're both tired. But have you nothing to carry?"

An oversight in his camouflage. A real businessman would have brought the attaché case into the cabin. "No. I decided to leave work out of my sight for a few hours."

"Very wise. Not everyone does." She looked at him, for the first time, as a man rather than a fellow passenger, a momentary lock of the eyes. It went on a fraction too long and Andreyev looked away.

"We have to go now, dumpling," she said to Brigitte. "Mr. . . ."

"Leuteritz," said Andreyev easily. "Heinz Leuteritz." He momentarily cursed himself for leaving even his cover name behind him.

"Mr. Leuteritz will carry you," she said to the child. "Mutti's too tired." She paused. "I'm Lise Wegman."

"My pleasure," said Andreyev. Brigitte scrambled off the seat and Andreyev picked her up. She was very light, like a bird.

"Her nose is running," her mother said and mopped it. The three of them went up the aisle towards the impatient stewardess by the exit door.

Andreyev still had the child in his arms when he detected the surveillance as he was going through customs. He had been unobtrusively but minutely observing the clumps of relatives and hangers-on beyond the glass partition separating Switzerland from the no-man's-land of the customs area. There was nothing disturbing until a large, heavy-set man with black-rimmed glasses prodded his way into sight at the left exit door. The man had "surveillance team" written all over him, in his ill-fitting clothes and his walk.

Where there's one there're two, Andreyev thought. Are they just here as the routine observers or do they have something more concrete to do? Like collect me?

"Sir?"

The customs officer was waiting for him. Andreyev put Brigitte down and lifted his bags onto the table.

"Anything to declare?"

"No."

"Business trip?"

"Yes."

"A beautiful child. How old is she?"

"About three. I'm not certain. I'm just giving her mother some help."

"Oh, I thought you were her father. How long have you been out of Switzerland?"

The catechism went on. Eventually, satisfied, the officer chalked his luggage. Andreyev went on through the check, then stood with his back to the glass partition while Brigitte and her mother were passed through. He didn't think the watcher had picked him out of the transients but he didn't want to negotiate the doors until he was carrying Brigitte. He had ninety minutes before the Pan American flight to Washington began to load.

A porter trotted up. Andreyev motioned him to the stack of luggage next to the child and picked her up. Her mother was anxiously scanning the crowd outside customs.

"You don't see her?" Andreyev carefully interposed Brigitte's face between his own and the watcher.

"No. She must be late."

"Where's grandma?" asked the child.

"She's coming."

They followed the porter and their luggage through the glass doors. The man with the black-rimmed glasses stood off to Andreyev's left somewhere. Andreyev risked a look around Brigitte's curls. Glasses was still engrossed in the passengers remaining in customs.

Where the devil was the other one? They always worked in pairs.

"There's grandma!" Brigitte squeaked in Andreyev's ear.

She squirmed out of his arms and raced away towards a middle-aged woman with rimless spectacles and tired brown hair. Lise hurried after her.

Shit. The child's squeal was certain to attract attention. The porter turned and grinned happily, displaying a family man's warmth in the hopes of a larger tip. Andreyev pushed a handful of change at him, grabbed his two cases and began to move off. He sensed the KGB man's attention swinging in his direction.

"Oh, Mr. Leuteritz!" Lise was waving and smiling, collapsing Andreyev's strategy around his ears. Cursing silently, he walked over to the three, placing as much of the crowd as he could between himself and Glasses.

"Mr. Leuteritz," Lise said. "This is my mother. Mr. Leuteritz helped me with Brigitte and the luggage. I'm very grateful."

The mother smiled suspiciously.

"You're welcome," said Andreyev desperately, looking at his watch without seeing it. "It's been very pleasant. If you'll excuse me, I have some urgent telephone calls to make. Perhaps we'll meet again." He knew he was being brusque, but he couldn't rid himself of the conviction that two highly professional eyes were fixed on the back of his head.

Lise's smile faded slightly. "Good-bye, then."

"Good-bye," said Andreyev and hurried away, trying to reconstruct the terminal's layout from the map he had studied at the training school. He needed somewhere to go to ground, somewhere complicated with lots of exits.

If he were oriented correctly, there was a service corridor off the left of the concourse ahead with stairs going up and down next to its entrance. The down staircase led to a set of garages and vehicle parks. He couldn't remember where the up one went.

He'd risk it. The worst the airport staff could do was redirect a lost traveler.

A row of shops edged the concourse. One had an angled wall of glass beside its entrance, providing a good reflected image of the concourse behind him. Andreyev paused, looking into the window, and waited.

There was Glasses, not twenty meters back, taking no precautions at all. When he saw Andreyev at the window he stopped, knelt and began to retie his shoelace.

Andreyev thought, if he's no better than that I should be able to walk away from him without any trouble.

He went on. There was the service door, in an alcove ahead. Andreyev went through it quickly, not caring whether Glasses saw him. He hurried for the down staircase, but his luggage hindered him. Out of breath, he stopped on the first landing and listened. The service door banged above.

He had miscalculated. He could not possibly lose Glasses while carrying the luggage, and he could not possibly leave it behind. Its false walls contained too many essential documents.

Down the next flight. Another corridor, walls of rough concrete, floors of the same material but smoother. He needed a closet, a room. There would have to be a utility space in a service corridor.

There was one, ideally placed, around the next corner. Its door was unlocked. Inside were a sink, a mop and pail and a can of detergent. There was enough room for a man and the door could be locked.

Andreyev put his luggage down three meters beyond the door, went back to the corner and waited. Footsteps approached, slowed uncertainly, then stopped.

He could hear the man's hurried breathing. Andreyev's diaphragm strained with the effort of moderating his own breath.

Where was Glasses' henchman?

A tentative step. Another.

Glasses came around the corner. Andreyev's right hand, tensed into a flat blade of flesh and bone, sliced toward where Glasses' carotid artery ought to be.

It wasn't there. Glasses had rounded the corner in a crouch.

Andreyev managed to change the angle of the blow but much of its force was lost. Still, it was sufficient to knock

Glasses off his feet as it hit the right corner of his mouth. He tumbled over, cracked his head on the floor and lay stunned.

Andreyev's thumbs were at the man's carotid in an instant, cutting off the blood to the brain.

Glasses was not quite as stunned as he had seemed. His right hand arched up and smashed into Andreyev's left bicep. The arm went numb and his thumb slipped away from the other's throat. Glasses brought his knee up and knocked the off-balance Andreyev onto his haunches. Andreyev, momentarily, had lost control of the situation.

Glasses didn't take advantage of it. "For fuck's sake," he croaked. Blood was trickling from the corner of his mouth. His glasses had been knocked askew. Pushing them back into place, he sat up shakily. "For fuck's sake," he said again. "What are you trying to do? What do you think I am? A CIA thug?"

Andreyev stared at him.

"Oh, KGB, is that it?" said Glasses. He dabbed at the blood. "I've got something for you in my coat. Can I open it?"

"With your left hand. Slowly."

There was nothing in the inner jacket pocket but a ticket folder. The man tossed it to Andreyev. "I was told to get this to you. I didn't have a photograph. You were very careful. The girl made me think it wasn't you."

"Why wasn't I informed?"

"How should I know? Would you like to come and ask the GRU resident?"

Andreyev ignored him and opened the folder. It contained a ticket for a flight an hour earlier than planned. A normal procedure. But the delivery had been abnormal. It should have been a dead drop. Andreyev said so, irritably.

"I don't think there was time. It was very quickly set up."

"Were you followed?"

"No."

"How would you know, if you usually slow yourself down with a loose shoelace? I've never seen anything so sloppy."

The man grimaced. "I wasn't really tailing you, remember.

I wanted to make sure you were you. Give me some identification."

Andreyev showed him the Leuteritz passport. "Why did they change things so fast?"

"I don't know."

Andreyev thought he did. Someone higher up, Lukashin maybe, was worried about his security. On the other hand . . . . . He studied the GRU agent for a moment. But there was no quick way of finding out whether he was in fact GRU, or something else.

"All right," he said. "Get lost. If I see you once more, I'll break your head."

Andreyev flew out of Zurich an hour later, but it was not by Pan American. He used a large chunk of his ready cash to book a flight on JAL; the accounts office would just have to put up with it.

Washington
July 31

THORNE STRUGGLED AWAKE, for a moment unsure of where he was, and found himself sitting bolt upright in bed with brilliant morning light flooding in through the bedroom's bay windows. He was tacky with sweat. There had been a dream, a bad one, of missiles climbing into blue sky.

He lay down again, kicked off the blanket, and closed his eyes. He could barely hear the distant hum of the Georgetown traffic. Joscelyn was moving around downstairs, and all around him – from the sheets, his hair, his hands – he began to breathe in the provocative scent of her perfume and sex.

Images of Round Lake formed, dissolved, formed again; Joscelyn floating on her back in the water by the swimming raft, Joscelyn sitting on the porch in the evening light. She had turned up unexpectedly four days ago at the lake. They had swum, eaten and she had spent the night, almost as if the four years of separation had not occurred at all.

Thorne still was puzzled by her behaviour, which was unlike that of the Joscelyn he had known; but then, four years could have changed her more than even he might have guessed.

"Good morning. Are you awake yet? I brought some breakfast." The smell of coffee spread through the room. As Joscelyn set a tray on the bedside table, he could also pick out the rich scent of her shampoo.

Thorne rubbed at his eyes.

"Headache?"

"Bad dream."

"Oh." She sat on the bed beside him. The light from the window behind her set her pale hair aflame. "What about?"

"War."

She smoothed the bedclothes absently. "I've had some of those, too. How did we ever come to this?"

"Foolishness and greed," said Thorne, his voice a curious mixture of resignation and anger. "And fear."

He paused to collect himself.

"I keep wondering whether I should warn Alison. Because of the children. They're in Los Angeles. It'd be one of the first cities to go if they went beyond a counterforce strike."

He had rarely mentioned his wife or children to her. "I understand how you feel," she said somberly. "But apart from the security breach, it's not that desperate a situation just yet. Nobody's threatened to use the damn things so far."

"So far."

"Are we going to get out of it?"

He didn't answer. And Joscelyn, sensing from his silence that it was best not to push him further, began arranging the food.

"We'd better eat. The toast is getting cold."

As they were finishing the coffee, she asked, "Are you coming to the center this morning?"

Aubrey had given Thorne a temporary office on the fourth level of the evaluation center, not very far from Joscelyn's. Since the fiasco over the *Al-Mansour* a crisis-management team had been formed and, with the help of RUBICON, was working around the clock to find ways of heading off disaster. Two days after Joscelyn's visit to Round Lake, Aubrey had asked Thorne to join the team. He had accepted.

Not the least because of Joscelyn. On his arrival in Washington he had booked into a housekeeping unit in a suburban motel, but after two days this didn't make any sense because he never used it. On the third day Joscelyn had suggested that he take up residence in her Georgetown row house "until we get tired of each other or for the duration of the crisis," as she put it.

The crisis wasn't very evident. Neither the Syrians nor

the Libyans had opened their collective mouths about their new weapons or about *Al-Mansour*. None of the media had picked up any rumors. The world seemed to be stumbling along much as usual.

It was an illusion.

"Well? Are you coming?" Joscelyn got up from the bed and removed her robe. Her slip was of the lightest blue, the color of clear water. He caught at her hand.

Looking at the clock, she said, "We really ought to go if we're going. The contingency-review committee meets at 9:30. They wouldn't want us to miss it."

"There's lots of time yet," said Thorne, drawing her gently back to him. In a slow circular motion he moved his hand up the inside of her thigh until the pale blue silk of her panties came into view. She let go a short, catching gasp.

He was right. There was plenty of time.

In fact, the contingency committee had little new to discuss. The scanty information about Syrian, Libyan, Soviet and Israeli intentions made it impossible to develop scenarios beyond a certain point. After that the RUBICON output became repetitious. Aubrey was beginning to receive pressure from the state and defense departments because of this.

There's one thing missing from the simulations, though, Joscelyn thought as she approached her office after the meeting dispersed. That hidden program I broke into, RUBICON ONE. Why hasn't that possibility been considered?

Too sensitive, she told herself, and felt a chill, remembering the session in Northrop's office after they caught her. But perhaps they've decided to drop the idea. And forget about me, too, I hope.

She opened her office door. Northrop was sitting in the chair in front of her desk.

"Good morning, Dr. Petrie," he said. "I hope you're ready to start work."

The Watergate
August 1

*H*ARPER MET KARELIN AT 5:00 P.M. The Russian looked dissipated. "Well?" he asked, as soon as Harper had closed the room's door.

"We're prepared to go this far. Keep us informed of the progress of your operation. Obviously we don't expect very many names or details. But we have to know when or if to expect an upheaval. If you decide to close the operation down, you tell us. We guarantee we'll remain observers as long as we know what to expect."

"Against all temptation?"

"Yes. No matter how good a first strike we launched, we couldn't get all your submarine-based missiles. It's not worth the price."

"I'm glad we agree on that."

"So am I," said Harper. "When can we arrange a meeting between your end of the link and ours? There are logistics to be settled."

"I don't like the idea of the two knowing each other," said Karelin. "It's a dangerous violation of procedure."

"Why did your people bother to send him here, then?"

"It's set up in an unusual fashion," said the Russian. "Once I've put him into contact with you, you take him over completely until he has to return to Moscow. He establishes with you the communications protocols you want to use. On his return he tells his control, who puts the GRU end into place. It cuts out any need for contact between his control and your man's."

"Sensible. When does he have to be back in Moscow?"

"Not later than August eleventh. He must leave here on the ninth to be certain of that."

"We can't be responsible for getting him back."

"You're not. He has instructions. I will inform Moscow of your decision. From now on I'm to be contacted only in an extreme emergency."

"Okay," said Harper. "When and how do we collect him?"

At about this time, Vladimir Antipov, the Washington KGB resident, was finishing a meeting with the head of the residency's Operational Section Two, which dealt with – among other things – the loyalty of the embassy staff and other Soviet citizens in the United States. It had been a long meeting and Antipov was impatient to get away from his desk. "Anything else?" he said at last, cutting off the section head in mid-sentence.

"No, that's all. Well, except for one minor item. We don't make a habit of watching all Colonel Karelin's movements, but during a routine check he *did* drop out of sight for an hour and a half. On the thirtieth, in the morning."

"Where was he?"

"We don't know. He has a mistress, as you're aware, but he wasn't at her apartment."

"Write it up," said Antipov, who loathed Karelin. "I'll put it in the weekly report to Center. And watch him more closely. Ever since they got loose from us, the GRU people have been getting too big for their breeches." He paused. "Wait. Wasn't there a Moscow Center directive last week about watching for GRU assets being run outside embassy cover?"

"Yes. Shall I find it?"

"Tomorrow. For now, just do as I told you. This may be the kind of thing Center's worried about."

Kirov Maneuver Area
August 1

*T*HE PLAIN LAY DRY and yellow in the heat. At the horizon the air danced, shimmering faintly against the dusty haze of the eastern sky. Overhead a meager dapple of cirrus: no rain for two weeks.

"They'll be very dusty by the time they move out of the landing zone," said Lieutenant-Colonel Ivan Dushkin conversationally to hide his nervousness. He was responsible for the success of the air-landing exercises, and they were being executed in full view of several exalted functionaries from Moscow. Including, heaven help him, the minister of defense and the chairman of ministers, Viktor Gresko, not to mention General of the Army Pavel Travkin, chief of the general staff.

"Don't worry," said Kotsarev. "I have every confidence in your regiment's ability. If the Americans could do it in Vietnam, so can we elsewhere. And better."

Dushkin looked marginally reassured. Gresko studied him obliquely. The lieutenant-colonel was a tall, spare man of about forty with thinning blond hair and a prominent chin. He gave an impression of intense energy coupled with equal competence. I hope he's as good ..s Kotsarev says he is, thought Gresko. This is the unit Yushenko has selected for the center of things. Dushkin and his troops will be back at their Moscow barracks in a couple of weeks. Just in time.

Gresko glanced at the general-staff chief, Travkin. He suspected that Travkin was one of the originators of the anti-KGB contingency plans from which Kotsarev and Yushenko were working, but he did not want to know for certain. Undoubtedly the coup would be very difficult without at least the passive cooperation of the chief of staff.

"Here they come," said Dushkin.

Gresko and Kotsarev left the dry grass of the plain and walked back to the dugout where the rest of the observation group waited. Most of the men were operational officers sent by their commanders to study the maneuvers of a crack helicopter-assault regiment. The remainder were people from the ministry of defense and Lev Novikov, first secretary for Leningrad, Boyarkin's watchdog.

He didn't send Morosov, Gresko thought. Or come himself. No, Boyarkin's too clever for that. But he's planning something. He didn't go to Morosov's *dacha* the other night to pay a social call. How much time do we have?

"I hope the fire preparation's well registered," said Novikov as they went down the dugout steps. "I'd hate to get blown up on an exercise."

"Don't worry," Kotsarev said shortly. The minister of defense pushed through the group of officers at the thick glass viewing ports and settled down to watch. Gresko followed him with Dushkin.

At first there was only a sprinkle of dots just above the dusty horizon. A dozen of them, then more. They were heading directly for the dugout and it was difficult to estimate their speed.

"There is an ECM vehicle now operating at five thousand meters," said the air-liaison officer. "The support aircraft will start their runs in thirty seconds."

Slightly above the original dots there appeared a dozen more. They became larger very quickly. They scooted off to Gresko's right and disappeared.

"Run beginning now," said the air officer.

Modern combat aircraft are quiet as they approach; most of their engine sound trails behind them. Shielded by the walls of the dugout, the first the observers knew of the approach of the Sukhoi-17 attack aircraft was a faint keening, which rapidly grew into thunder as the planes shot over the landing zone at two hundred meters. Torrents of cannon shells from the Sukhoi's cannon ripped furrows in the ground; rockets screamed from the hardpoints under the swept wings and bloomed into knots of flame and smoke where they struck. The noise was horrendous; or rather it was not noise but great blocks of moving air that battered the entire body.

As quickly as they had come the Sukhois were gone, leaving a long receding boom behind them. Another sound: staccato flap of rotors. The Mil-24 assault helicopters were dropping onto the landing zone, nose machine guns sparkling. They touched down, driving great clouds of yellow dust into the air. Out of the dust, moments later, came running men: the crack first-battalion troops of the Sixteenth Airborne Assault Regiment. After no more than thirty seconds, the helicopters climbed out of the billows of dust, returning to base to collect the second battalion for the support wave. As the clouds settled the men began to form into combat teams, established over-watch fire and begin to move towards the simulated enemy positions. Firing broke out, accompanied by the thump of small mortars. It was a live-ammunition exercise. There would be a dozen or so casualties by its end, none, perhaps, fatal.

"I want to go up and watch the assault wave," Kotsarev said to Dushkin. "Have you transport?"

"Sir, there's a Mil-3 command helicopter near the access road. You can use that. I'm afraid I have to stay here, if you don't object."

"I don't," said Kotsarev. "I'd like to take Chairman Gresko with me." He smiled. "He needs to know where the appropriations are going."

Dushkin detailed a lieutenant to take them to the command helicopter. As the machine clattered into the sky, Kotsarev shouted into Gresko's ear, above the racket of the engine, "It's started. Yushenko says we've made contact with the others."

Gresko glanced nervously forward to where the pilot sat. The man wore a helmet and earphones; he couldn't possibly hear them. "Good. What do they say?"

"They won't interfere. A liaison team will be inserted."

"What about our man?"

"Returning on the eleventh. The control system and cover are being established. Our man will be apparently trying to recruit theirs. They'll be able to be seen together, for a while, without arousing too much suspicion."

On the horizon, the assault helicopters were coming back. The pilot took the Mil-3 up another fifteen hundred meters. Below, the soldiers were fanning out over the steppe towards the enemy positions.

"Can we be sure the Americans won't betray us?" Gresko asked. "The temptation will be very great."

"We're going on alert at the beginning of the project. As as exercise. As long as they know we're ready to counter any adventurism, they won't do anything but go on alert themselves. They've got too much to gain by cooperating. So have we," he added as an afterthought.

"It's dangerous. If anything goes wrong here, they might try to cut their losses."

"Not with most of our ICBM submarines on position. That's been ordered. I proposed it to the Council of Defense when the *Kiev* task force reached Gibraltar. The active submarines sailed this morning. Boyarkin thought it was a good idea."

"We'd better let the Americans know why."

"We will."

The Mil-24s were disgorging more troops onto the dusty plain. The leading edge of the first wave had reached the enemy positions.

"It's to go ahead, then," shouted Gresko. His eardrums ached.

"Yes," answered Kotsarev. "We have to, now. Boyarkin went to see Morosov last night. Yushenko thinks he's starting to move against us."

The assault troops had overrun the simulated enemy. Gresko thought of the long black shapes, the missile submarines, sliding out into the Artic Ocean, and what the Americans would think of that. He shivered.

If only they give us time, he thought. If only we have time.

Round Lake
August 4

*T*HORNE WAS DRINKING COFFEE at the kitchen table when the driveway beeper went off. He silenced the alarm and carried his cup onto the veranda. It had stopped raining half an hour ago and the trees dripped gently. The air smelled of wet grass and tree bark. The clouds were breaking up; occasional patches of yellow sunlight fled across the lawn.

An anonymous buff Oldsmobile rolled down the drive and drew up to the porch. Northrop got out.

"Morning," said Thorne.

"Morning," said Northrop, closing the car door gently behind him. He looked drawn.

"Where's Major Andreyev?" asked Thorne.

"New York," said Northrop shortly. "We've got a problem. Has this place been swept?"

"No."

Northrop went to the car's trunk and got a leather case out of it. "I want to go over the house, then, okay?"

"Okay."

Thorne went back to the kitchen table and sipped his coffee while he finished reading the Washington *Post*'s front page. The headlines said:

SOVIET MISSILE SUBS AT SEA:
RUSSIAN TASK FORCE ENTERS MEDITERRANEAN

Thorne massaged his temples. The international situation had become even worse since the meeting in Northrop's office on August second. Harper had brought a grim set of RUBICON predictions, which he had pointedly referred to as he outlined the operation. Thorne would stay in contact with GRU plotters in Moscow, pass information back to Washington and do nothing else. Thorne asked whether Joscelyn were involved. Yes, Harper said, she was to maintain communications between Washington and Thorne. She would not leave the embassy and would be carefully instructed as to how much Thorne should know, since he unavoidably risked arrest and interrogation by the KGB. Thorne's salary would be on a high level of the "consultant" grid; there would be a bonus for field work and the usual benefits package. It was all rather like being signed on to work for an insurance company, except for the RUBICON printouts.

All right, Thorne had said. When do we start?

We want to bring the Russian to Round Lake for the briefing, Northrop had told him. We'd rather not use any of the safe houses.

Something's gone wrong, he thought, swirling the last of the coffee. They can't move him here.

Northrop came back from his sweep, snapping down the catches on the leather case. He put it on the table next to the newspaper.

"What's that all about?" asked Thorne, pointing to the headlines.

"We think it's a message from the anti-Boyarkin faction that we shouldn't interfere, only watch. Boyarkin and the KGB don't know that, of course. We hope. They'll think it's to intimidate us over the mideast. Never mind that, we've got more immediate problems. Your link man made it to New York but GRU Washington doesn't dare handle him. The station chief, Karelin, met Harper once too often. The KGB station head wants to know where Karelin was. He thinks Karelin's been running operations without KGB knowledge. Karelin's refused to talk without superior GRU authorization, so there'll be a jurisdictional tug-of-war over that for a few days. In the meantime, the KGB's looking for a loose GRU operative – in other words, Andreyev. We're getting him out of the country, you'll meet him overseas."

"Where?"

"We're going to kill two birds with one stone. Mossad needs to know something about this project, to keep their temperatures down. And we need somewhere the KGB has trouble operating. You're both going to Israel. But the Israelis aren't to know about Andreyev. They don't need to, yet."

Tel Aviv
August 7

STEIN COLLECTED THORNE at Lod Airport. They went through the cool of the terminal into the day's heat. Thorne badly wanted a drink.

"My van's over there," said Stein, and pointed. It was a VW microbus that had seen better days. They got in and Stein started the engine, which wheezed consumptively and then settled down to an uneven clatter.

"Needs new bearings," confided the Israeli. "I haven't had time to get them replaced. Cost more than the bus is worth, anyway." He paused. "How does it feel to be a CIA spook again?"

"I'm not a spook," said Thorne. "I'm a civilian retained for consulting services. My name isn't even on the payroll."

"The names of the spookiest ones never are," Stein pointed out.

They drove without speaking while Tel Aviv drew nearer. It was a disorganized collection of architecture, assembled without obvious planning. A few tower blocks jutted into the Mediterranean sky above a conglomeration of grayish concrete apartment houses and office buildings.

"Not pretty, is it?" Stein observed. "They keep intending to do something about it but we always have a war or runaway inflation before they can get around to starting. But it's not bad in the winter."

"I remember," said Thorne. He had been in Tel Aviv twice before, both times working with Stein to repair some of the damage the Yom Kippur War had inflicted on Mossad-CIA cooperation. That was after Vietnam and Cambodia.

I've been around, Thorne told himself. That, if nothing else.

"What's next?" he asked.

"Meeting," said Stein, maneuvering the VW around a reekingly asthmatic bus. The mid-afternoon traffic was heavy with exhaust fumes and unidentifiable Oriental scents. From the perspective of the United States, Thorne found it difficult not to think of Israel as a transplanted European country, despite the months he had spent there. It wasn't one, though; it was a curious blend of European institutions overlying a much older culture.

"Who are we meeting?" he asked, when Stein didn't continue.

"My boss. Haim Choresh, Mossad head. You met him in 1975. Remember?"

"Yes."

"The other's the minister of defense."

Thorne was startled. "Isn't that rather exalted?"

"He's worried. We're all worried. You know about Syria's new toys, of course?"

"Northrop told me."

Stein braked and geared down suddenly, cursing. An ancient Renault shot past the microbus and pulled in abruptly. Thorne went tense. Stein reached inside his jacket, steering with his left hand. The Renault scurried on up the street.

"Not that time," said Stein.

"Your countrymen don't drive any better than they used to."

"No. Did you see my front bumper? Somebody backed into me and then claimed I'd rear-ended him. Fortunately there was a witness. Anyway, you're coming with some rather exalted credentials yourself. From the DCI, with the implication of others above *him*, no less. We're hoping you've got some help for us."

"Isser."

"I know," said Stein tiredly. He turned the microbus into a side street. "You're going to tell us not to panic, the situation's under control."

Thorne, guiltily, said nothing.

Stein turned off the engine and watched the rearview mirror. Thorne waited.

The staccato beep of a horn on the main street behind: an irritated driver. Other horns responded.

Stein grunted. "All right. We're clear."

He got out of the vehicle, Thorne following. They went into a shop displaying cheap jewelery, metalwork and leather goods, through it, and started up a flight of stairs. Behind, Thorne heard the VW's engine start. Traces being removed.

"There's an apartment upstairs," Stein said. He was puffing as they reached the top. "We rent it from the proprietor for the quiet relaxation of distinguished guests."

"I never heard myself described quite that way before."

"We'd prefer it if you didn't go out," Stein told him.

It was really, by American standards, a bachelorette, with everything except the bathroom tucked into it. The cooking area was screened from the couch – which must conceal a bed, since there wasn't one elsewhere in the room – by a folding wooden divider. A wooden table with two chairs, a standing lamp, a sling-back chair and a coffee table completed the furnishings. Gauze curtains covered the window, admitting light but not the curious gaze.

"Sorry about the air conditioning," said Stein. "There isn't any. It's clean, though."

"In more ways than one, I hope."

"Absolutely." Stein collapsed into the chair. "Forgive me for taking the best seat, but my physical condition isn't what it used to be."

"How's the heart problem?"

"Still a problem." Stein closed his eyes for a moment. "You know," he said, and then opened them, "I almost wish, from time to time, that the damned thing would quit before I have to see what's probably going to happen. I was born here. I fought the Arabs in '48, '56, '67 and '73. I don't know if I want to do it again."

"Isser."

"Anyway, that's what I sometimes think. There's beer in

the fridge. Budweiser. I remembered you like it. Let's have one before they get here, which will be in about ten minutes."

The minister and Haim Choresh arrived as Stein was draining his glass. Stein and Thorne stood up.

"Hello, Dr. Thorne," said the Mossad chief. "We met a long time ago. It's pleasant to see you again. May I introduce you to our minister of defense, Mordecai Seri."

"Minister," said Thorne. They shook hands. Then they all sat down.

Without warning, Thorne experienced a sudden and intense attack of *deja vu*. Momentarily he was certain he had been in this meeting before, in some hotel room or other, Washington, Tel Aviv long before, Saigon, Phnom Penh, Jersualem. He had lost count of how many.

A jet boomed overhead, towards the west. Thorne thought of Los Angeles and a great spire of flame above it.

"Dr. Thorne," Seri was saying, "I gather you have information for us."

Thorne pulled himself together. He was very tired. "I've been instructed as follows. The United States is engaged in an intelligence operation that will remove the threat you face – we all face. There are elements in the Soviet government that do not agree with Boyarkin's policies. These elements are being encouraged to remove him. Those who follow will force Libya and Syria to dispose of their nuclear weapons. We would ask that you not initiate any hostilities, or appear to do so, before the operation is completed."

"I assume 'completed' means 'completed successfully,' " said Choresh. "What happens if that is not the case?"

"In that case we may all have the same problem. General war."

"Full-scale thermonuclear?" asked Seri.

"Almost all our predictions suggest it."

"Almost?"

"There's a ten-percent chance we can avoid it."

There was a long silence. Then the minister said, "I wish you could have stopped Pakistan."

"So do I," said Thorne, remembering Los Angeles and his children. "I do indeed."

"I would like more detail," said Seri. "How are your people intending to execute this . . . interesting maneuver?"

"The GRU wants to retain its autonomy," said Thorne bluntly. "Boyarkin's trying to remove it. The Russian military doesn't want a war they don't start themselves. The politicians are afraid of the purges Boyarkin's started. All we're doing is assuring the anti-Boyarkin faction that we won't strike while they remove him, when there will inevitably be some dislocation of control. The GRU is to inform us of their movements, as insurance against misunderstanding. They've taken out some other insurance as well. Their submarines are out. So are ours."

"So I've read," said the defense minister. "What happens after this coup succeeds? Who orders the Libyans to give up their weapons? And the Syrians?"

"I don't know," said Thorne. "I'm not taken into that much confidence. But if we had an agreement with the Russians that they should be removed, I'm sure they would be."

"Is that a certainty, or your guess?"

"Guess."

The minister considered. "From whom this come?"

"Their highest levels of authority, excepting Boyarkin."

"How long?"

"We think two or three weeks."

"So we are to do nothing for two or three weeks? The Syrians moved another tank division and supporting arms up the Golan this morning. They've done this before. But this time we think they're going to attack. And that they believe we won't dare strike back very hard, because the Americans won't let us risk nuclear war and perhaps their oil supplies."

"Are you expecting a Syrian first strike?" asked Thorne.

"No. Not yet. Our own weapons are well dispersed now; we started that several days ago. This has been communicated to Damascus. Even if they destroyed our cities, we could still destroy theirs. It's a bit like your country and the Russians, isn't it, Dr. Thorne?" Seri's voice was acid.

"Yes," said Thorne. "Just give us time."

"All right," said the minister. "We'll *try* not to do anything rash until you let us know about the development of your project – unless the Syrians or Libyans precipitate something. I'll take your request to the cabinet. You'll have your answer tomorrow evening. In the meantime, Isser, would you like to take Dr. Thorne up to the Golan? It might be useful for him to know, for his superiors' benefit, what the situation is like up there, instead of studying computer printouts in nice quiet rooms in Langley."

Seri stamped out.

Choresh remained momentarily. "I'll arrange transport," he said. "Be at the military compound at Lod at 5:00 A.M." He glanced over his shoulder. "Dr. Thorne, you didn't say quite what he wanted to hear. I'm sorry. For your protection we'll keep a watch on this building until you leave. So sleep well."

"Thanks," said Thorne. He was infuriated. He was supposed to meet Andreyev at ten that evening. With the Israeli surveillance there wasn't a chance of managing that. He hadn't expected security to be so tight, not for a messenger.

This time Northrop had miscalculated. Andreyev would be tying himself in knots by midnight.

At exactly the time Seri left the apartment, Andreyev was debarking from an Alitalia flight at Lod Airport. He had been instructed to go to the Tamar Hotel and wait until Thorne contacted him. He would stay in the hotel until the ninth, fly back to Helsinki, and make his way to Moscow via the Finnish route.

He got a taxi to the hotel. It was fearsomely expensive, but the Americans had supplied him with plenty of money and, somehow, an American Express card. The slip of green plastic awed him; he knew of the western credit system, but the fact that such a complex arrangement could actually work was staggering. The computer power needed to manage such a system was incomprehensible. There was nothing like it in Russia, not for the use of private citizens.

The hotel room was small but bright and clean. Andreyev unpacked and, daringly, went to the dining room to eat, expecting to be asked at any moment for identification. His passport showed him to be one Helmuth Asch, a naturalized American who had emigrated from West Germany at age twenty-one and who was holidaying in Europe and Israel. Andreyev thought the indentity rather perverse – a German visiting the homeland of the survivors of the Holocaust – but no one had taken so much as a second glance at him.

He had relaxed by the time the waiter brought coffee and took a concealed delight in paying with the American Express card. Then he went to his room to wait.

The day lengthened. Andreyev ate again at nine. By 9:45 he was back in his room. Ten o'clock arrived. Thorne did not come.

Eleven. Still nothing. And no fallback.

I can only wait until he comes, Andreyev thought. And if he doesn't, I leave on the ninth.

But what has gone wrong?

Not for the first time, he wondered if he were being betrayed.

Syrian General Staff Headquarters
Damascus
August 7

GENERAL RIAD HALLAK, chief of the Syrian general staff and commander-in-chief of the army, drew the red curtains away from the enormous wall map that faced his desk. The map was a large-scale one, of western Syria, the Golan and the eastern border of Israel. Colored flags and rectangles of card were sprinkled across it, very thickly along the demilitarized zone separating the Israeli-held Golan from Syrian territory.

Surveying the map, Hallak felt a deep satisfaction. For six months he had irregularly built up and then reduced his country's forces along the disputed border, carried out large-scale exercises, ordered more and then cancelled the orders and tried generally to keep the Israelis uncertain of his intentions. This effect had been magnified by some judicious disinformation applied by Syrian intelligence with the assistance of the KGB resident in Damascus. Hallak was well pleased with the aid the Syrian military had received from Moscow; he had not been sure the Libyans would indeed supply the missiles and warheads as agreed. No one could be certain of Qadhafi, but some careful Russian pressure on Tripoli had got Hallak what he wanted. The Israelis knew the weapons were in Syria, of course; if they had not, Hallak would have made sure they found out. The bombs were not actually to be used. They were intended as a deterrent to the sort of savage Israeli counterattack that had brought the Jews to within twenty miles of Damascus in October 1973. Hallak calculated that with the Golan back in Syrian hands, the Americans wouldn't let their proteges in Jerusalem risk a nuclear exchange in an attempt to recover the territory. And Israeli reaction to the Syrian reconquest would be limited by the knowledge of nuclear weapons in Damascus.

Hallak was confident that neither Syria nor Israel would be threatened enough to use atomic weapons. The reconquest of the Golan was a limited operation, after all; Hallak had no intention of trying to drive the Israelis into the sea, no matter what Radio Damascus howled. Once the operation was complete the Americans would try to find a diplomatic solution to the conflict, as they always did when their own direct interests weren't threatened. And Syria's success would raise her prestige – and Hallak's – immeasurably in the Arab world, at Egypt's expense.

The only thing that worried Hallak somewhat was Qadhafi's unpredictable behavior. He was, necessarily, trusting the Russians to keep the Libyan leader under control.

Hallak leaned on the edge of his desk. The worn copy of Rommel's biography was at his right hand. He patted it gently. He had learned a great deal from the German: deception, surprise, carefully selected objectives, reserves engaged at exactly the right moment. Leadership from the front, at the cutting edge. With good reason, he considered himself the best soldier that Syria had produced for a century.

He had even turned to advantage his countrymen's weakness for building up a state of public war fever before going to war. In 1973 Radio Damascus had indulged in weeks of anti-Zionist vituperation before attacking; this time, as far as anyone but himself and the cabinet knew, the same pattern would be followed.

Except that it wouldn't.

His intercom buzzed.

"Yes?"

"General, your staff is here," said his ADC.

"Ask them to come in."

The commanders of the air force, air defense and the navy filed into Hallek's office. His own second-in-command, Lieutenant-General Abdallah El Koussir, followed them. Koussir was an irritant to Hallak. The man was militarily competent but not at the level to which he had been promoted through his family's influence in the Ba'athist regime. Hallak also had doubts about the man's nerve in a crisis. However, Koussir wasn't likely to face one in the present situation.

The chief of staff put the thought out of his mind and said, "You will be happy to hear what I am going to tell you. This time we are not on an exercise. At 9:00 A.M. tomorrow we are returning to the Golan, and we will remain."

Tel Aviv — The Golan
August 8

THE TINY OH-6 HELICOPTER was waiting for them when they got out of Stein's van in the Lod military compound. The machine was little more than a metal-and-plastic teardrop, sprouting a tail boom and a toylike rotor above the cabin. Thorne hadn't ridden in one since leaving Cambodia, hurriedly, in 1976.

"Old-home week," he said as he clambered into the cabin. His eyes felt gritty from lack of sleep.

Stein looked even more tired and gray than Thorne felt. The Israeli collapsed onto the seat beside Thorne's and took several deep breaths. The pilot started the engine and the rotor blades began to whack-whack overhead.

"You're sure you're all right?" asked Thorne, concerned.

Stein nodded and said something. The words were lost in the engine's whine.

"What?"

"I'll do. We had some bad news last night."

Thorne raised his eyebrows.

"Radio Damascus," shouted Stein. "They've started shouting for a holy war, a new Jihad." The OH-6 was lifting off in the soft dawn light. Tel Aviv's suburbs and Lod began to fall away below. "And the Libyans have chimed in with support. Also the Syrian Seventh Tank Division has been put into the line on the other side of the DMZ. More artillery's been moved up."

"They're going to attack."

"Yes. But not within ninety-six hours. They normally take at least that long to work themselves up."

"What are you going to do?"

"I don't know. The general staff didn't tell me." He smiled briefly. "But I wouldn't be surprised if we did a spoiling attack. To chop them up before they can get started. Another surprise for the world, eh?"

Thorne nodded. "What about their nuclear weapons?"

"We don't think the Syrians will strike us unless we're completely overruning them. We've got more warheads than they do, after all. We'll only neutralize their ground and air forces."

"You've got it scripted, then."

"Scripted?" Stein's brows furrowed. "Oh. Yes. You could say that."

"What happens if they don't follow the script?"

Stein looked out the OH-6's window. The helicopter was climbing away from the coastal plain towards the ragged, sun-scoured ramparts of the inner land. The sun was rising, at their altitude a flattened ellipse of fire. Below, the new light had only begun to touch the scarps of the ancient hills. "I worry about that," he confessed. "Their chief of staff's a new breed. Riad Hallak. We don't know much about him, except that he's a great admirer of Rommel."

Thorne's vocal cords hurt from talking over the helicopter's engine noise. "They'll probably follow your script," he said, and began to watch the tormented landscape roll away beneath. Stein slumped into his seat and closed his eyes. The two men remained so all the way to the Israeli base at Kafr Naffakh, not ten miles from the Syrian tank lines at the far side of the demil-itarized zone, on the Damascus Road.

Stein was asleep when the OH-6 landed at the Kafr Naffakh base. As the rotor blades slapped to a stop, Thorne nudged the Israeli, then peered through the plastic bubble for his first look at the installation.

The town itself was a dusty heap of ruined sugar cubes arranged in no obvious order, with a scattering of broken minarets beyond the wire fence of the headquarters compound where the helicopter had landed. As the dust settled, two officers came hurrying from a white building Thorne took to be the HQ block, since there was an Israeli flag outside it.

Stein rubbed his eyes and sat up. He looked disoriented and ill.

"Are you all right?"

"As soon as I get some tea. There's our reception committee."

The two officers led them to the HQ block. Thorne couldn't follow the conversation between them and Stein, since they spoke Hebrew. One of the officers left them at the door of an austere office. The other said, "I'm Colonel Eliad, military administration zone intelligence. Dr. Thorne, I'm pleased to meet you. Major Rath, my ADC, is getting you some breakfast. You can eat here, then he'll take you up to the lines. What exactly did you want to see?"

"I'll let Colonel Stein judge that," said Thorne. "It's really just to get the feel of the situation. I gather the Syrians are building up again."

"For the past two weeks. They've done it before. This time it looks more serious, though." Eliad glanced at Stein.

"He knows," Stein said.

The colonel relaxed slightly. "We *are* expecting an attack. We're being reinforced to deal with it. They outnumber us, as usual, but it didn't matter last time, not in the long run. However, we're taking anti-nuclear precautions."

"Greater dispersal?" asked Thorne.

Eliad frowned. "Yes. That makes things difficult, though – as your own military found out, not from experience, fortunately. If one has enough troops and fighting vehicles concentrated to be decisive in an attack, they're a pretty target for a nuclear burst."

"It's a tricky balance," acknowledged Thorne.

"Anything from general staff on our next moves?" asked Stein. "We didn't get anything on the helicopter radio."

"No changes since last night. Jerusalem thinks that the Syrian movements this time are extensive enough to make an attack likely. But Radio Damascus has only been cursing us since yesterday. So it won't be just yet."

"Are you going to take preemptive action?" Thorne asked, and immediately wished he hadn't.

"I wish I could tell you, Dr. Thorne," said Eliad. "But you'll understand why I can't."

"Of course. I'm sorry."

"It doesn't matter. It pays to be curious in our business. Ah. Here's your breakfast. Major Rath will take you to the forward positions on the Kuneitra Road when you've done."

Half an hour later they were in a jeep bouncing along the Naffakh-Kuneitra Road. Stein and Thorne sat in the backseat, Rath and the driver in front. A heavy 50-caliber machine gun sprouted on a flexible mount in the center of the vehicle. Thorne had to rest his feet on an ammunition container. It was eight o'clock, and already hot as a griddle. The road wound among rough basalt hillocks and conical hills, the remnants of ancient volcanoes. Occasional crumbling walls of small lava boulders outlined barren, untilled fields, long since gone back to sun-baked desolation. The Golan was an inhospitable place, especially in August. Occasionally there were artillery emplace-ments and packets of tanks and troop carriers along the road, all well dug in and camouflaged. The tanks were unfamiliar to Thorne, who was more used to the high profiles of American M-60s or the frying-pan turrets of Soviet armored vehicles.

"Merkavas?" he asked Rath.

"Yes. We've got two brigades equipped with them up here. The reserve brigades are M-60s."

"I haven't seen them before. They look businesslike."

"Yes. They were built for our particular needs."

A Merkava was rumbling slowly along the road just ahead of them, probably heading for a firing ramp. Thorne studied the big vehicle as they passed. The tank was low and wide, carrying a small turret, which was shaped of wedges to deflect hostile shot. Sheets of light armor hung over its tracks and road wheels. The long gun, wrapped in a thermal sleeve, was secured to the front deck by a heavy clamp.

I wouldn't like to be a Syrian tank captain caught in that thing's sights, Thorne reflected. "Laser range finder?" he asked Rath. They were past the Merkava.

The major nodded. "Plus a ballistic computer. That's a

Mark I you were looking at. The IIs have a more powerful engine. We've only a handful of those so far."

"The Mark I looks tough enough."

Rath smiled and returned to watching the road ahead.

At 8:45 the driver stopped the jeep twenty meters short of a bend in the road. Rath got out. "We can have a look at the far side of the DMZ from above," he said, gesturing to a hill that rose on their right. "I don't want to go farther along the road; it's in full view of their batteries. Sometimes they send a shell across."

Thorne clambered stiffly out of the jeep. Stein followed him, with some difficulty. "Do you want to go back?" Thorne asked as they started up through the ragged jumble of stone below the hill's crest.

"I'm all right."

A communications and observation bunker lay just below the crest. Rath spoke briefly in Hebrew to a soldier hunched over a radio and then led Stein and Thorne up into the observation dugout at the summit. An officer was using a pair of binoculars to scan the opposite horizon. Thorne looked past him, across the DMZ, into Syrian territory. There wasn't much to see. Rock, hills, occasional exhausted shrubs and thorn trees, struggling against the sun and dehydration. The Syrian positions were well-camouflaged.

A soldier hurried into the dugout and gave the officer a slip of paper. The officer read it and frowned. He spoke to the soldier and then to Rath. Rath listened, strain lines appearing at the corners of his mouth. Two more soldiers entered the dugout and got up on the fire step, unslinging their rifles.

Rath turned to Thorne. "Radar's plotted incoming targets. They're still on the Syrian side of the border but there are a lot of them. More than we've seen on exercise lately. We'd better get back to Naffakh."

"Are your aircraft up?" Stein asked as they hurried down the communications trench to the bunker.

"Mahanayim and Ramat David bases are scrambling right now."

They went through the bunker. There was palpable

tension in the air. On the slope outside, near the jeep, Rath said hopefully, "It may be another bluff. They've been doing it for weeks."

"But never so big?" asked Thorne.

"No."

They got into the jeep and the driver started back down the road away from the front. Rath unclipped a microphone from the radio under the dash and tried to raise Naffakh HQ. After some difficulty he succeeded. He obviously didn't like what he heard. Thorne glanced at Stein. The Israeli was leaning forward in the pitching jeep, listening intently. Rath signed off and gave a curt order to the driver. The jeep accelerated abruptly.

"Their planes aren't turning back," Stein told Thorne. "It looks as though they mean it this time."

Thorne looked westward. Something glinted beyond Naffakh, high up and traveling fast. The glint disappeared.

Stein had noticed it, too. "Ours," he said.

The jeep careered along for another five minutes. The driver couldn't go very fast because the road was full of rocks and chuckholes, but Thorne's teeth rattled in his head anyway. They were in a narrow defile, with ragged outcrops of stone rising on both sides.

Rath spun around in his seat. Simultaneously, Thorne heard another sound over the grind of the jeep's engine: a low howl with a rasping edge. He turned to look behind.

Four dark shapes hung just above the ridge where the OP and the bunker lay. Gouts of black smoke and dull orange flame were blossoming into the sky behind the dark shapes. The shapes grew larger with appalling speed, black circles hyphenated on both sides by the slashes of the wings, studded underneath with bombs and rockets. The wing roots of the left-most aircraft began to twinkle.

The jeep bounced twice, violently, and ran off the road behind a great boulder.

"Out, out," yelled Rath. The four men threw themselves from the jeep and scrambled behind the rock. Thorne cracked his left cheekbone and elbow on the stone and his arm went numb.

The howl expanded into a roar as the four aircraft shot overhead. Cannon shells exploded in the defile; the jeep's windshield starred and disintegrated. Sukhoi-22 ground-attack planes, Thorne thought abstractedly. I wonder if they got the bunker.

Apparently they weren't sure. They appeared above the far end of the defile, climbing and turning. The roar of their afterburners beat at Thorne's eardrums.

Rath shook his arm, pointing. There were six more dots, high, this time in the west. Two of them separated from the others and began to descend. The Sukhoi-22s were halfway through their turn, heading back towards the ridge. The pair of Israeli aircraft slipped behind them, closing. Pale streaks of smoke pulled away from the Israelis, drawing thin lines towards the Syrian jets. Two of the Syrians were suddenly linked to the Israelis by the skeins of the rocket trails. Puffs of smoke. Bits of the lead Sukhoi began to fall off, then the tail fin spun away like a leaf. The aircraft turned over and plunged out of Thorne's sight beyond the lip of the defile. Another Sukhoi staggered, nose rising, and exploded. The two survivors hurtled off into the east, hotly pursued by the Israelis.

Thorne realized that he had been holding his breath. He let it out slowly. With the scream of the fighters gone, he could hear another sound, sullen and continuous, too familiar. An artillery barrage.

"They foxed us. Shit," said Rath. "Let's get going. They'll be missing me at Naffakh. What a time to go sight-seeing."

"Sorry," Thorne said. "I didn't plan it this way."

"I'm sure you didn't." The Israeli smiled ruefully. "Neither did we. Come on." His face went white. "Colonel Stein?"

Thorne turned. Stein lay facedown, hands clasped over the back of his neck, face turned to the wall of rock beside them. Thorne tugged gently at his shoulder. The hands fell away. Thorne rolled him over. Stein's eyes were open, filmed with dust.

"Oh, Christ," said Thorne. He felt for a pulse at the neck. There was none.

"He wasn't hit," said Rath.

"No. Heart, I think." Thorne knelt over Stein and began cardiopulmonary resuscitation, trying to trigger the heart and lungs back into life.

After ten minutes he knew it was no good. They put Stein – Thorne did not yet think of it as Stein's body – across the jeep's rear seat. Thorne sat on the ammunition box all the way to Naffakh, to keep his friend from rolling onto the floor.

Naffakh was in a state of controlled chaos. One Syrian air strike had reached as far as the ruined town but the attack had missed the HQ area. Three columns of black smoke marked the impact points of a pair of Syrian aircraft and one Israeli interceptor. There weren't many troops or tanks in evidence; the Israelis preferred not to move large formations near the front by day until they had command of the air.

Rath helped Thorne get Stein out of the jeep and they took the body to the base hospital block, where a temporary morgue had been established. Then Rath said, "You have to get back. I'll take care of Colonel Stein's . . . Colonel Stein."

"I know," said Thorne. The Israelis never left their dead or wounded behind, if they had to retreat.

"I'll get your pilot. He'll stay low."

"Good," said Thorne. "I'd just as soon not be taken for a Syrian."

Rath laughed bleakly and hurried off. Thorne went to the OH-6 and got into the front seat. A minute later the pilot joined him and started the engine. He motioned to a headset. Thorne put it on. "I'm sorry," the pilot told him. Thorne nodded.

The OH-6 clattered above the town, toward Tel Aviv. As they passed over the Jordan River and the Golan escarpment Thorne could see plumes of dust along the roads below. Reinforcements. Safe enough, under the fighter umbrella from the bases at Haifa and Herzliya. Several times Thorne saw the glint of aircraft wings well above the helicopter, traveling both west and east. He wondered what was happening on the ridge at the DMZ, around the bunker and the observation post.

"What're things like on the DMZ?" Thorne asked the pilot.

"I don't know very much." The OH-6 dropped into a valley and clattered over a village. "I heard the Syrians were sending tanks and armored infantry across. There was an artillery barrage and air strikes on our front positions." The pilot had a thick accent; Thorne had some difficulty understanding him.

"Anything else?"

"No."

Thorne gestured at the radio. "Can you raise your headquarters?"

"I could. But we've been ordered to stay off the air except for essential traffic. Is this essential?"

"No," said Thorne, and sank back into the seat. Andreyev. Jesus, he had to get to Andreyev.

Andreyev woke to the sound of heavy traffic outside. He went to the window, pulled the drapes aside and looked out. Four stories below, a dozen military trucks were rolling quickly along the Chovevei Zion, heading north. The trucks were shrouded with canvas but through the open tailgates Andreyev could see that they were packed with soldiers.

He looked at his watch. Eleven in the morning. He remembered lying awake, fully clothed, until 3:00 A.M., waiting for Thorne to come. He must have drifted off to sleep shortly after that.

There was a television next to the door. Andreyev fiddled with the unfamiliar controls and was rewarded by a picture of a grim-faced man sitting behind a desk reading something. Andreyev didn't understand the language. He thought it was Hebrew. He left the television on and went to the bathroom to shave.

He was drying his face when the voice shifted from Hebrew to English.

"All non-residents of Israel should pay careful attention to the following. This morning, at 9:00 A.M., Syrian forces attacked our lines in the Golan Heights. There has been extensive fighting in the air and on the ground but no attacks on Israeli territory west of the Jordan River have yet occurred.

"However, all non-residents are urged to leave as soon as possible. To assist you, the following schedule is being arranged. If you are to leave today, please go immediately to your departure area. If you do not have a ticket valid for today, you will not be permitted to enter those areas. Police and army units will enforce this. Non-residents who are scheduled to depart tomorrow should do so. For those whose departure dates follow tomorrow, special arrangements are being made. Please tune to this channel every hour on the hour for details. Do not telephone your carrier or use the telephone system except for emergencies. If you do not need to go out, please do not do so, as it is necessary to keep the streets clear for military traffic."

The man began to repeat the announcement in French. Andreyev turned him off.

Now what?

Where was Thorne?

At least I can leave here tomorrow, Andreyev thought. But if there's delay, and I don't make the contact in Helsinki. . . .

He shrugged off the thought and went downstairs for breakfast. Only half the waiters were present and the hotel guests were in a highly agitated state. Several families were eating hurriedly, their luggage by their chairs, waiting for the airport bus. Andreyev thought of Brigitte. He wondered what would happen to her if there were a big war.

Probably what happened to so many of our children when the Germans came, he thought. Burned, blown up, starved, shot. The Americans have been lucky, they don't know what it's like.

He watched the next table. A young woman was struggling with a small boy who wouldn't eat his breakfast. The father snapped at the child. The child, sullenly, began to eat. Andreyev thought of the napalmed children's bodies he had seen in Afghanistan. They had looked like small, cracked black dolls without any hair.

He pushed his plate away and finally got a waiter. Paying with the American Express card no longer gave him pleasure.

The mother and father and the grumbling small boy left for the hotel steps, dragging their luggage.

Andreyev went back to his room. Another truck convoy was rumbling north below his window. He lay down on the bed and stared at the ceiling. The combination of strain and boredom was beginning to tell; he was sleepy again. At length he drifted into an uneasy doze.

A tapping on the door awoke him. He left the bed noiselessly, went and stood against the wall next to the door.

"Yes?"

"I was told Mr. Thurstan would be here this morning."

Andreyev opened the door. "He's gone to the dining room for a little breakfast. Would you like to wait?"

"I can stay for twenty minutes."

Andreyev closed the door behind the American. Thorne was carrying a suitcase and looked exhausted. A large red scrape disfigured his left cheekbone. He was about two inches taller than Andreyev, and thinner. The two men studied each other for a moment. Then Thorne put out his hand. Andreyev shook it.

"I'm sorry I'm late," said Thorne. "The Israelis had me under protective surveillance, and then I had to go up to the Golan. I don't have much time, we'd better get organized."

Andreyev cupped a hand to his ear and looked around the room.

"The previous resident worked for us," said Thorne. "It's clean."

"All right."

They sat on the bed and began to work out the contact rules for Moscow: fallbacks, indicators to be chalked on lamp posts, a telephone number. It took nearly two hours. At the end of it Andreyev said, "Make sure you always have kopecks for a phone call," and grinned.

Thorne grinned back. He and the Russian had taken to each other, perhaps because of their shared professionalism and dangerous future. "I'll be sure." He got up. "I have to go. See you soon."

"Yes. Soon."

Andreyev burned their notes in an ashtray and flushed the remains down the toilet. When he left the bathroom, Thorne was gone.

Washington
August 8

*T*HE TELEPHONE RANG for the fifth time.

Harper dragged himself out of the lower reaches of sleep.
The disembodied luminous numerals of the bedside alarm
showed 4:10 A.M.. He turned the reading light on and grappled
for the telephone, trying to shake off sleep. "Harper."

"Director? Could you please come to the Situation Room
immediately?"

Harper was instantly awake. The Situation Room, in the
sub-basement of the White House, was used as a crisis-
management center.

"What's going on?"

"The Syrians attacked in the Golan two hours ago."

"Christ," said the DCI and rang off.

His wife, Celestine, turned over and opened her eyes. She
was used to telephone calls at odd hours but had never learned to
like them. "What's the matter?"

"Syrians and Israelis at it again. I have to go to the White
House."

Her eyes cleared abruptly. "Is it bad?"

"Don't know yet. Could be. They've opened up the
Situation Room." Harper was searching over the side of the
bed for his slippers.

"I'll make you some breakfast."

"Don't. I'll manage. Thanks anyway."

She closed her eyes. "Why can't they start their wars
during working hours?"

"They did. It's eleven o'clock in the morning over there."

He put on his robe and went to shave. Somewhere in the

trees beyond the bathroom window a robin chirped sleepily. We'd better go ahead with RUBICON ONE, Harper thought. I hope Thorne's on his way home. The Russian too. Damn. That's the last place we should have sent Andreyev.

He drank coffee and ate half a grapefruit in the summer kitchen at the back of the house. More birds were awake and twittering by the time he opened the garage door. The glow of Washington's lights concealed whatever glimmer of dawn there was in the east. The air was humid, promising a sultry day.

I hope we've got enough time, he thought as he pointed the Oldsmobile towards the central city. Dear God, I hope there's enough time.

The Situation Room was a communications and control center underneath the White House, two levels down. An enormous map of the world was spread across one wall. Blue spots of light indicated American military dispositions. Red ones marked Eastern-block forces. White were NATO and other allies. There was a lot of red. The data projected on the map and the displays under it were processed through the enormous computers out at Langley, after being transmitted from Cheyenne Mountain, SAC HQ at Omaha, and other intelligence installations around the country and overseas. There was probably no other single place on the planet where one could tap such vast quantities of information.

President Law didn't look as though the knowledge consoled him. He was sitting at a long curved table, on which were ranks of telephones and computer terminals, when Harper arrived. A couple of dozen other men, in both military and civilian dress, were sprinkled around the room. Several hadn't shaved. There was a muted hum of telephone conversations.

"Mr. President?" said Harper.

Law turned in his chair to look at the DCI. He was clearly very angry. "Sit down, Cam."

Harper did so. He had been dreading this moment ever since getting out of bed.

"Why in hell didn't your people get wind of this?"

"We did, sir. It was in yesterday's estimates."

"The estimates didn't predict it today. They said it would be several weeks before it happened, if it happened."

"I know, Mr. President. I'll find out what went wrong."

Law's jaw muscles knotted and then relaxed. "You might be consoled by the fact that the Israelis were caught with one foot off the ground, too. We've been monitoring battlefield traffic. The Syrians are doing quite well. Who's behind this attack, do you think?"

"Riad Hallak. Their chief of staff. He came on the scene about six years ago, up from the junior-officer ranks. He's thirty-eight. From what we know of him, he's very clever."

McKay, the secretary of defense, walked hurriedly into the Situation Room. He was carrying a computer printout. "Sitrep from the computer room, Mr. President," he said, laying the printout at Law's elbow. Law read it. "Clever is the word for him," he said. "This says the Syrian armor has penetrated a kilometer past the DMZ and is only fifteen kilometers from Naffakh. Tell me about Naffakh."

"It's the Central Golan Area command center," said McKay. "On the main road to the bridges over the Jordan. It's a key part of the Israeli defenses."

"What kind of resistance are the Israelis putting up?"

"Stiff, Mr. President. They're using a lot of air strikes to hold the Syrians until their armor can group for a counterattack. But their regrouping's slow, as though they don't really want to do it. Also their air attacks are being badly cut up by Syrian missiles. SAM-8s. And the Syrians also have a lot of interceptors in the air."

"Cam?"

"Masses of armor are good targets for tactical nuclear weapons," said Harper. "I would think they want to get air superiority over the battlefield before they concentrate. That way they'd have a good chance of protecting their counterattack from a nuclear strike."

McKay departed after a nod from Law. "What about the possibility of that?" he asked Harper. "Anything? On either side?"

"No. Although," said Harper with a trace of bitterness, "given the Israeli and our miscalculation, I hesitate to make any firm predictions."

"Especially about the Libyans?"

"Especially. But I don't think Qadhafi would dare strike unless the Israelis were in real trouble. And that's not the case yet. Egypt wouldn't give them air clearance and the Israelis know enough to guard the seacoast."

Law nodded, as though preoccupied. Harper waited.

"Cam," said the president at last, while the map displays flickered through their transformations, "your project. What about that?"

"It's where I said it was yesterday. Our man is in Israel. I hope he's on his way back now."

An aide came and spoke softly to the president. Law nodded and said to Harper, "Come with me."

There was a small conference room adjoining the Situation Room. Law closed the door behind them and said, "I'm going to be up to my ears in diplomats and the state and defense department people very shortly, so I don't know what my schedule will be." Law put his right foot on a chair and began to massage his calf muscles. "All this sitting down's hard on my legs. RUBICON ONE. We had better take the next step. How do you feel about it?"

"I think it'd be wise," said the DCI. "Even if it doesn't work out perfectly, we're no worse off than if we hadn't tried it."

"I should repeat that I am not considering even the possibility of a first strike."

"Yes, Mr. President. I hate the idea, too. But none of the successful scenarios have that as a necessary condition. And the unsuccessful ones . . . well, they predict war in any case, even if we didn't try at all."

"I have to go back," said Law. "Get your man to Moscow as soon as you can. I'll square it with the committees. Under the circumstances, they'll be happy to go along. As you said, it's wise."

The Golan
8:00 A.M., August 10

HALLAK WAS BEGINNING to feel tired. Ever since the attack began, he had been shuttling up and down the front, shifting the thrusts of his tank and mechanized-infantry teams whenever Israeli resistance stiffened, always seeking the weak point, widening it into a breach, pouring battalion after battalion around the enemy flanks whenever opportunity offered. The advance had kept up its pace until casualties and resupply difficulties lowered the strength of the antiaircraft units, whereupon the Israeli air strikes had begun to take a considerable toll of the Syrian spearheads.

Nevertheless, he was more than satisfied. The situation map in his battle headquarters at Qatana showed tremendous success: the Golan had been overrun to a line from Mount Hermon south through Masada, Mughur, El Birah, Sada, down to Kafr el Ma, which formed the southern hinge of the attack. The Israelis still retained Naffakh despite the ferocious attacks of the Seventh Armored Division, but Hallak was confident that the soon-to-be-committed Syrian reserves would sweep the Israelis back to the western rim of the Golan. And there, where the ancient Damascus Road crosses the Jordan, he would trap them. For the Benit Yacov Bridge, the main reinforcement route for the enemy forces in the Golan, had been wrecked on the first day of the attack by a special air unit, which had sacrificed itself to do so. That was the key to eventual Syrian victory, for only now had the Israelis been able to concentrate enough tanks for the counterattack that Hallak desperately hoped they would deliver.

He had intentionally stretched a salient out towards the ruined bridge. By night, he had reinforced it with antitank and antiaircraft weapons so thickly and so well concealed that, despite its apparent weakness on the situation map, the salient was a bristling fortress. And when the Israeli tank and infantry battalions and air support had broken their teeth on it, the Syrian reserves, advancing under an umbrella of SAM-9 and SAM-8 antiaircraft missiles, would drive the remnants of the Zionist forces back on the Jordan escarpment and destroy them.

Then there could be talk of a ceasefire.

His senior ADC entered the map room. "*Fariq* Hallak," he said. "The salient commander says the Israelis are starting to move. Your helicopter is ready."

Relief swept through Hallak. He had worried that the Israelis would refuse to concentrate enough armor for a counterattack, out of fear of a Syrian nuclear strike. Apparently they had decided to risk it. It was precisely what he wanted. If the Israelis had decided on a withdrawal, his commitment to the salient would be useless. Like Rommel, he had staked much on the aggressiveness of his enemies.

The Gazelle's rotors were already turning as Hallak strapped himself in. In a billow of yellow dust the helicopter lifted away from the landing pad and turned west. The pilot kept the machine at no more than two hundred meters from the ground; even this far east there was a risk of Israeli interceptors.

As the Gazelle dipped and rose over the folds of the hills, Hallak studied the terrain. At first there were no signs of fighting; then, as they approached Kuneitra, the occasional burned-out vehicle or black splash of a crashed aircraft appeared. The wreckage became more and more frequent as the Gazelle flew on. Near Sindiyana there was a terrible sight: a column of Israeli Centurion tanks caught in a defile by Syrian aircraft. Some were still burning, but there were no bodies.

Somewhat farther on, a Syrian mechanized unit had met the same fate at the guns of an Israeli attack squadron. This time there were corpses draped in the hatches of the armored personnel carriers and lying contorted among the boulders along the track. The dead men all looked black, from fire or from the sun. The smell crept even into the helicopter's cockpit.

Hallak frowned, but not because of the stench. Syrian

infantry carriers should have been moving along this route to form the salient's reserve. They were nowhere to be seen. It was as well he had decided to visit Colonel Dirouzi's headquarters.

The tip of the salient lay around Amudiye, poised only three kilometers from the Benit Yacov Bridge Road. The road, although the bridge had been destroyed, was not one the Israelis could afford to lose, and Hallak had judged that they would fight savagely to keep control of it. He had been proven correct. As the Gazelle settled onto a level patch of ground near the salient command bunker, he could see dust plumes off in the distance, towards the road. The Israelis were on the move.

Colonel Yusuf Dirouzi appeared in the bunker entrance as the helicopter's engine whined into stillness. Hallak had put Dirouzi in command of the salient even as it was being formed. The colonel was one of the few senior officers who approached Hallak's own quality and was an expert at positional warfare, which was exactly what Hallak needed in the salient commander. Hallak himself would pick the time and place of the Syrian counteroffensive, which would start when the expected Israeli attack into the salient failed.

Dirouzi saluted. Hallak returned the salute and said, "I hope I find you in good health."

Dirouzi smiled, displaying a row of crooked, whitish teeth below his mustache. "My health is of no consequence in light of what we are to do today, *Fariq*," he said. "Or especially in relation to your own, which I hope is excellent."

"Yes, excellent," said Hallak. The formalities dealt with, he asked, "Where are the infantry-support units? They should have been on the El Kushniye Road. I saw none."

Dirouzi's smile disappeared. "I was told not an hour ago they were already moving."

"They aren't," said Hallak, cursing inwardly. "Show me where they ought to be."

Dirouzi snapped an order and a staff officer brought a map. "They should be there," he said, pointing, "if they moved when they were supposed to. They're on radio silence, and they won't respond to our transmissions because of Israeli deception measures." He marked off the distance on the map. "I had better go look. It's only half a dozen kilometers, and the road's secure." He looked at his watch. "There's enough time. Radar intercepts don't show an immediate air attack, which is how the Jews will start. And everything here is arranged. The unit commanders know what to do."

Hallak pulled at an earlobe. "I don't like you being away from here, even for an hour. Wait. We'll go over there in the Gazelle; it won't take thirty minutes. When we find the column we can set down and prod them."

"Yes, *Fariq*," said Dirouzi. He turned to the officer who had brought the map and handed it back. "Major Saleh is in charge until I get back."

They climbed into the Gazelle. As the helicopter lifted, Hallak saw a half-dozen flashes and smoke plumes in and around the salient's outer perimeter. Israeli artillery trying to register on its targets. Very difficult in the rock-and-crevice landscape.

Two dozen kilometers away, a Syrian mobile-radar-unit operator was cursing the Soviet equipment that, without warning and after working perfectly for two weeks, had decided to desert the cause. Worse, the backup module didn't work, either. This was serious, as the radar was responsible for early air-raid warning on the arc from Mughur to Suleiquiye. He reported the failed unit to his commander, who began radioing urgently for a replacement – twenty minutes after the radar went off the air.

The Syrian radar failure was noted by an Israeli monitoring aircraft, which in turn notified Mahanayim air control. The information was passed to a flight of four Kfir C2 strike aircraft, which promptly streaked for the gap in the Syrian cover. Syrian radar and ECM installations were priority targets; destroying them while they were unable to defend themselves was an ideal situation.

The Gazelle carrying Hallak and Dirouzi was fifty meters up, halfway between the salient HQ bunker and El Birah, when the Kfirs, which were flying only slightly higher, shot over the horizon. The helicopter lay almost directly in front of the lead Israeli, whose pilot promptly identified it as hostile and snapped a burst of 30-mm cannon shells at it.

It was all he had time for, but it was enough. Twelve shells struck the Gazelle, eight of them in the engine and fuel tank, which immediately caught fire. The nineth and tenth killed the pilot. The final two sheared the rotor couplings and knocked the Gazelle upside down.

Hallak's very last thought, just before the Gazelle struck the road below, was of his second-in-command back in Damascus: *Allah forgive me, I shouldn't have brought Dirouzi. That idiot Koussir won't know what to do. I've failed.*

The Kremlin
10:00 A.M. to 11:00 A.M., August 11

MOST COMMITTEE ROOMS, in Russia as anywhere else, resemble each other. This one was no exception: high-backed chairs, a long table covered with green baize – a characteristic of Soviet committee rooms, for some reason – and, to further identify the room's nation of origin, a portrait of Lenin on the wall opposite the tall windows that overlooked the courtyard of the Kremlin Arsenal. A pair of red flags with the hammer and sickle in gold thread flanked the chair at the head of the table.

The room was used for the monthly meetings of the Soviet Council of Defense, an exclusive body that coordinated the desires of the Politburo with the activities of the ministry of defense and the general staff. The meeting in session on the morning of August eleventh, however, was not a regular one. Occupying the chairs around the table were Boyarkin, chairman of the Council; Morosov, Gresko, Fyodor Klyushin (the new head of the MVD, replacing Blinov, who had been given the Central Committee's first secretaryship), Blinov himself, and the second and third secretaries of the Central Committee. All of them, except Boyarkin, appeared tense and tired. Boyarkin, perversely, looked excited and full of anticipation. His eyes glittered as he looked around the table.

He cleared his throat and said, "Very early this morning I received a communication from President Nahawi of Syria. Because of the deteriorating military situation in the Golan since General Riad Hallak's death, he is requesting a large airlift of weapons and ammunition to replace those destroyed by the Zionist counterattack that began yesterday morning. Minister

Kotsarev, would you recapitulate what has happened in the last twenty-four hours in the Golan?"

Kotsarev flipped open a red-jacketed report and began to read. "At 8:52 A.M. Damascus time yesterday, the Israelis counterattacked the Syrian salient at Amudiye. For reasons not clear until 6:00 P.M., the reserves that were supposed to support the salient's defenders did not arrive. By 3:00 P.M. the Israelis, aided by a breakdown of Syrian command and control in the salient and elsewhere, had penetrated well into the Syrian defenses. The situation deteriorated steadily until 5:00 P.M., when the neck of the salient was pinched out and the Israeli mechanized forces began to penetrate into the Syrian rear areas. At 6:00 P.M. our military mission in Damascus was informed that General Hallak and the salient commander had been killed in an air crash and that Lieutenant-General El Koussir was taking control of the battle. In the opinion of the military mission Koussir was not competent to deal with the situation, but President Nahawi confirmed his command. By nightfall the Israelis were as far as Juwayza, and the Syrian attack on Naffakh was broken off. As of eight o'clock this morning the Israelis were on a line, Masada-Kuneitra-El Bassah, and were showing all signs of renewing the attack. They finally succeeded in repairing the Benit Yacov Bridge during the night, and large reinforcements are being routed from their northern command area. There are also reports that the Americans are mounting a clandestine resupply mission and that several planeloads of war material landed at Mahanayim during the night. This is unconfirmed and it is thought that the resupply will have to remain small because of American difficulty in securing overflight rights from Spain for a full-scale military airlift. There are indications that Syrian air power is beginning to collapse, and the confused withdrawal of their ground forces has damaged morale."

Kotsarev closed the folder and looked up. "It's not surprising about their morale. They went from what looked like certain victory to probable defeat in a space of sixteen hours."

"It's a defeat we can't permit," said Boyarkin. He smiled

without humor. "President Nahawi agrees with me. As well as the resupply he has requested a number of technicians and pilots to stiffen their air defenses. In addition, he has asked that we provide help in the form of ground troops and armored fighting vehicles if the Israelis decide to pursue their counteroffensive into Syrian territory. He does not seem to feel that his forces can resist a Zionist drive on Damascus, particularly since Mubarak of Egypt has declared his country neutral in the conflict. The Israeli rear is secure, and they can turn their full weight on Damascus."

Boyarkin paused. Then he said. "I strongly recommend to this council that we begin to resupply immediately, and that we prepare to lift several mechanized battalions to Syria, if that is necessary – which I hope it will be. A strong Soviet military presence in that country would be very helpful to our closer relations with Damascus."

Despite himself, Gresko could not help admiring Boyarkin's deviousness. Once Russian troops were in the country, and with the Syrian military in a state of shock, the control of President Nahawi's government would be within reach. "But suppose Damascus uses its nuclear weapons?" he asked. "Syria could make a full-scale Israeli invasion exceedingly dangerous."

Boyarkin shrugged unconcernedly. "Then we still win. If the Israelis did not counter-strike with their own bombs, the invasion would end. If they did, and if each country wrecked the other, we'd be seen as the nation that tried to help the Syrians defend themselves, up to and including nuclear exchanges. After all, Damascus is only trying to regain her rightful property. Our hand would be much stronger with the Arabs. And we would help rebuild Syria into a true socialist state."

"And the possibility of a general war?" asked Kotsarev. He had gone red.

"The Americans will not attack us because the Syrians, with or without our assistance, are defending themselves. Nor will they if the two countries devastate each other. What would it gain them? They will protest, no more. And they haven't been comfortable with their Israeli bedfellows for several years, not since Begin started the Zionist hard-line tactics, before he died." Boyarkin surveyed the men around the table. "I make this proposal officially and call a vote."

Kotsarev and Gresko alone failed to raise their hands. "The motion is carried," said Boyarkin. "Minister Kotsarev, will you please see to it?"

"The logistics are difficult," said Kotsarev. "We need to –"

"Stop," said Boyarkin. Kotsarev stopped. There was a very long silence.

"Do you mean to tell me," asked Boyarkin at last, "that with all the planning we have done for this sort of thing for more than twenty years, your ministry cannot carry out its responsibilities?"

"No," said Kotsarev desperately. "But –"

"Can you do it or not?"

After a pause. "Yes."

Damn Kotsarev, Gresko thought. He should have made it look easy. We could have delayed the movements for any number of reasons. Not now.

"Within the time available?"

"Yes. We can do it."

"Excellent. Then do it."

"GOOD," SAID KOTSAREV, although he did not think it was good at all. He looked around the table at the senior members of the ministry of defense: the five commanders of the combat branches, the chief of the political directorate (GLAVPUR) and Marshal Pavel Travkin, chief of the Soviet general staff. Marshal Travkin was the only one present, besides Kotsarev, who knew of the intentions of the GRU. He had, in fact, been involved with Yushenko in the original anti-KGB study.

"Good," Kotsarev said again. "The resupply will begin from the Kiev supply depots at 8:00 A.M. tomorrow. Ammunition first, then antitank and antiaircraft missiles, followed by armored vehicles and medical supplies, with the designated advisors." He turned to the army operational commander. "You're quite certain the advisors will be notified and ready in time for that wave?"

"Yes, minister."

"Marshal Travkin. The six mechanized airmobile battalions will be at four hours' movement readiness until further notice?"

"Yes, minister. Also, we have diverted forty of the Antonov-22 strategic transports to Kiev, for shuttle operations to Syria via Belgrade. They will be available for tank resupply by tomorrow evening. We can lift eighty T-64 tanks to Homs and Es Suweidiya within thirty-six hours of the order to do so, with their crews and some support equipment. Air cover over the landings can be provided by Mig-23 interceptors flown into Latakia two hours in advance of the transports' arrival."

Eighty tanks, thought Kotsarev. A full mechanized regiment with some support. And soon after that, some more for a reserve. With six airborne infantry battalions the Soviet

Union would then have a powerful force in Syria. And with another four days of lift after the initial two-day one, it should be possible to have the combat arms of a mechanized division in the country – if the Americans allowed it.

"See to the details," he said. He turned to the GLAVPUR chief. "There is nothing here that you're concerned about?"

"No. It's all in order."

"Good." Kotsarev stood up, dismissing the meeting.

As the men left the room, Marshal Travkin glanced at him questioningly. Kotsarev gave a fraction of a nod.

The GLAVPUR officer didn't see this, which was just as well.

Twenty minutes later Travkin and Kotsarev were waiting in Kotsarev's office. It had been debugged that evening but Kotsarev was still uncomfortable. Sometimes he felt that the walls themselves were microphones and cameras, recording his every twitch.

A tap at the door. "Come in, "said Kotsarev.

General Yushenko and Colonel Stanislav Vakula entered. They saluted and Kotsarev waved both the newcomers to chairs. "He's here?" asked the minister.

"Yes," said Yushenko. "Downstairs."

"He got back just in time," said Colonel Vakula. "The Americans took him over from GRU Washington and sent him out of the country with his CIA contact. To Israel, of all places."

"Holy Mother Russia," said Travkin. "What were they thinking of?"

"It doesn't matter now," said Kotsarev. "Has the initial meeting been set up?"

"Yes."

"What about Karelin? Is he all right?"

"He should be. The KGB's still making a jurisdictional fuss about uncleared GRU operations in the U.S. but Karelin has a low-level source in the state department. We'll open that one up to them and they'll be happy for a while. Major Andreyev and the American will be able to meet with relative freedom – we're making it look as though we're trying to recruit him. The

Second Directorate will want control of the operation once they find that out, but we can block that indefinitely. Or long enough."

"Fine," said Kotsarev. "Now. Business. The timing of the operation depends somewhat on events in Israel and Syria. The situation isn't yet critical enough for us to get away with suggesting the cover exercise, Suvorov. And we still need time to complete tactical planning. The earliest we can possibly be ready is the nineteenth, since our key military unit won't be back in Moscow until the sixteenth. The twentieth or twenty-first would be ideal, if the international situation permits a test exercise of Suvorov."

"And if it doesn't?" asked Travkin.

"We'll have to move anyway. We've gone much too far to stop now. Sooner or later the KGB would unearth something. It's bad enough that we have to get their agreement to executing Suvorov. Although that may turn to our advantage – they won't be alarmed at the first troop movements, and that will give us a little more time."

"So the period of critical danger for us is between now and August nineteenth," said Travkin.

"Yes. We might try with what we have before then, but we couldn't be sure of success."

The four men momentarily considered the penalties of failure. Then Yushenko said, "Colonel Vakula. You may tell Major Andreyev to inform the American that we will be able to act as early as the nineteenth of August. If absolutely necessary we may move before then but will notify them. Until then, would they please act in a rational manner despite the mideast situation."

Except for the cot and the chemical toilet, it might have been the same room in which Andreyev had met the anonymous general weeks before. As the last time, he was waiting, alone.

There had been no difficulty getting back over the border from Finland. His movement orders, provided by the men slipping him across, had taken him direct from Selznevo to Kubinka Airbase, only that morning. An army car brought him to the general headquarters building and he was put into the room and given food. Now he lay on the cot, staring at the ceiling, wondering what was about to happen to him. According to his watch it was 11:15 in the evening, but he couldn't remember whether he had reset it for all the time zones he had traversed.

There was a carafe of water on the desk next to the remains of his meal. Sighing, he got his razor and soap out of his kit and used some of the water to shave. The blade was dull and the water cold but he felt better after rinsing his face over the chemical toilet. He dried off with the scratchy toilet paper and sat down to nibble morosely at the heel of a loaf of bread.

Without warning, the door clicked and swung open. The man outlined against the corridor was the colonel who had come to the tactical training school. "Màjor Andreyev," he said. "Do you remember me?"

"Colonel Lukashin."

"Not now. Here I am Colonel Vakula. I hope you're well rested. We have many things to do."

Moscow
August 12

THEY HAD BEEN PROVIDED with an office – a small one – on the top floor of the embassy, and with two bedrooms that were normally used by senior officials from Washington. The bedrooms adjoined, but had no connecting door.

Joscelyn and Thorne were waiting in the office. The window behind the desk overlooked the rear of the embassy, towards Bolshaya Street and the northern curve of the Moscow River where it passed under Kutuzovsky Prospekt. It was six in the evening, Moscow time.

"Finn isn't happy, is he?" asked Joscelyn. She was sitting in the chair behind the desk. She had kicked off her shoes and was balancing her heels on the rim of the wastebasket.

"No," said Thorne. His transformation into a CIA agent was still unsettling him, even though he had known it was inevitable. The briefings at Round Lake had been theory; this was real. Beyond the embassy compound there were several tens of thousands of KGB employees who would acquire immediate promotion if they found out his real business.

"You can hardly blame Finn," he said. "If I were CIA station chief I wouldn't like having us dumped into my station either."

"That's true." She looked at the desk clock. "You have to go in ten minutes."

"Yes," said Thorne. He stood up. Joscelyn looked at him. "I hope this works," she said. He had been very subdued since arriving in Moscow. His cover was that of an internal security officer replacing one who had been taken ill, or seemed to the Russians to be ill. Her own place in the embassy scheme of things – again as far as Soviet passport control was concerned –

was that of an additional supervisor for the embassy coding and communications center.

"It'll work," said Thorne. He came around the desk and kissed her. "Don't worry."

When he had gone, she slipped her shoes back on and put her feet under the desk. I wish Stein hadn't died, she thought. That's upset him. That, and his children being in Los Angeles. I wish we had never got into this. I wish I had never broken into that horrible scenario in the 220. They trapped both of us, David and me.

And they're going to tell us to betray the GRU—what Harper called the Fourth Option, back there in Langley, before David came into the office. The KGB will kill Nikolai Andreyev, who is David's friend, and I know it's going to happen and I can't say anything. Because if Dzerzhinsky Square picks up David, he has to know as little as possible. Damn them all, Russians, Israelis, Syrians, Libyans, yes, and Americans, too.

There was a hot, wet streak along the side of her nose. She wiped it off and put herself back to work.

As he expected, Thorne acquired two KGB watchers the instant he walked through the embassy gates. They would have been briefed about his work in Moscow; as a security expert he would bear watching. It would be assumed at Dzerzhinsky Square that he would be happy to recruit the entire Politburo if he were given the opportunity.

He went along the street to the Barrikadnaya subway station, dropped a five-kopek piece into the turnstile, and started down the escalator. They were still there, about fifteen yards back. Big, lumpy men in wrinkled Russian suits. His own western clothes drew curious glances from the drab Soviet citizens on the moving steps.

He reached the platform and glanced around at the station decor. It was opulent by western standards. Mosaics on the walls, chandeliers. Not one splash of graffiti.

No paint-spray bombs available here, he thought. Even if

there were, nobody'd dare take one to the Moscow Metro. Ten years in the Gulag for that.

The train arrived. He wriggled into it in a crush of Muscovites on their way from somewhere to somewhere else. There was an aroma of bodies and twice-breathed vodka fumes. Thorne stood face to face with a middle-aged woman carrying a string bag with some onions in it. She inspected his suit minutely, and then turned her head away.

The enemy is everywhere, he thought. I might steal her onions.

The KGB had moved into the car a yard behind him. The train pulled away south, towards Kievskaya Station. Thorne slowly elbowed his way towards the front door of the car. One of the KGB men edged after him; the other stayed at the center doors.

The train slowed for Kievskaya. Thorne was by now at the doors, with his followers two feet behind. The station slid into view: murals, ceramics, more chandeliers under a curving roof. The second KGB man was standing on tiptoes, watching Thorne over the heads of the other passengers.

The doors hissed open. Thorne got out. The KGB man behind him followed suit. The other waited in case Thorne got back into the train before the first one could follow.

Thorne started for the front of the train. He judged that the second follower would leave the car as soon as Thorne was well away from it. The rear door of the next car was now six feet away. Both of the KGB men should be out on the platform by now.

A young woman carrying a child was just behind Thorne's right elbow. The doors were three feet away.

He had waited long enough. He tripped over his own feet, stumbling half right and sideways and knocking the woman backwards. She in turn staggered into the KGB man. Instinctively, the Russian reached out to support them.

The doors began to close. Thorne slid between them with half an inch to spare. They met solidly behind him and the train began to move.

Thorne didn't look out the window.

The Zalatoi was a kind of self-service restaurant called a *stoloviye*, and was sandwiched between two more fashionable cafés on Gorkovo Street. Thorne entered, walked up to the long counter and waited. After a suitable socialist pause a short, pasty-faced woman waddled up to the other side of the counter and looked questioningly at him. Her eyes flicked over his western clothes.

"*Kotleta*," he said. "*Pazahlsta.*"

"Mm," she said. She put a meat patty on a cracked plate. "Potatoes?"

"Please."

She added the vegetables. "I suppose you want a drink as well," she said. "You Poles always do."

He was taken aback. "Pole?"

"Aren't you a Pole?"

"No."

"A Czech, I knew it. You foreigners. Always trying to sound like us. How much do you want?"

"How much what?"

"Open your ears. Vodka."

He thought quickly. "A hundred grams."

She poured the spirit into a foggy glass. "I bet you don't get vodka like this in Czechoslovakia."

"No," he said. "We don't."

"You should be more like us. One ruble fifty."

He paid and took his food and drink to one of the long tables at the back wall. The knife and fork were spotted with rust and felt greasy. He picked at the grayish meat despondently. Five minutes until Andreyev was to appear, unless they had to use the fallback. He drank some of the vodka.

The tables of the Zalatoi were beginning to fill. Heavyset working men and clerks with thick, unfashionable eyeglasses were shouting for service at the deserted food counter. Shop girls, sprinkled through the line, giggled. Finally the pasty-faced woman appeared.

"Cow," said one of the laborers. "What've you been doing? Making the vodka out of the potatoes? Or drinking it?"

"She looks like she's been drinking it," said his companion. "Look at her eyes. She can't tell when she's got customers."

"Where did you come from?" she asked, slinging a *kotleta* onto a plate. "Magnitogorsk? No, that's not it. Magnitogorsk workers smell better."

Thorne sighed. Russians, if they didn't know each other personally, were the rudest people on earth.

"How did that get in here?" asked a light, feminine voice. Thorne looked up. Half a dozen people in the line were looking at him. The eaters at the tables looked up briefly, then returned to their mastication.

"Don't ask me," said the woman behind the counter. "He just wandered in. Czech. Tourist."

"Another trade delegate," said the thin man at the head of the line. "Trying to tell us how to do it better. Do we need that?"

Thorne was well aware that Russians disliked foreigners, except in particular circumstances. This was obviously not one of the particular circumstances. Thorne looked at the thin man and drank another two grams of vodka.

The thin man picked up his plate and glass and sat at the table in front of Thorne. "What makes you Czechs think we can't do it just as well as you can? What?"

This was getting out of control. "But," said Thorne, "what was the name of the last Czech to design a Soviet spaceship?"

The Russian searched his memory. "There wasn't one."

"Exactly," said Thorne. "You've done it all first. We merely support you."

One of the laborers joined them. "What's he saying?"

"He said they helped us."

"Oh, they did, did they?" He bit off a chunk of meat patty and said around it, "We don't need help from anybody. Fucking Czechs. Fucking Poles. Always trying to slide over to the Americans. My grandfather told me. Czechs helped the White Russians in the Revolution." He spat on the floor.

"I wasn't there," said Thorne. "Please remember, we are comrades now against the capitalist west. We should drink to that. Three on a bottle. Let's all drink to the Soviet cause." He put a ten-ruble note on the table.

The two men looked at him with a different interest. The laborer got up with the money and went to the counter. He returned with a two-hundred-gram bottle of vodka and no obvious change. They poured, drank, then refilled the glasses.

"You're not bad, for a Czech," said the laborer. He began to eat again.

Christ, Thorne realized, it's three minutes past the contact time. I've got to get out of here.

The room was crowded now and full of the buzz of conversation and cutlery rattle. "I'm sorry," said Thorne. "I have to be on my way."

The thin man grabbed his wrist. "Wait. Just a minute. Pyotr," he called over his shoulder, "here's somebody you ought to meet. You've been to Czechoslovakia."

Thorne's bowels contracted. He didn't speak a word of Czech. Why hadn't he said he was East German?

A lanky man from two tables away got up, weaved his way to Thorne's table and sat down. "What?" He was more than a little drunk.

"Here's a Czech. You went to Prague in 1968, didn't you? To stop the counterrevolution?"

Pyotr gazed blearily at Thorne. "I was there. Where were you?"

"Not in Prague. I never got mixed up in that."

"I learned some Czech," said Pyotr. "To talk to the girls. Like this." He emitted a stream of slurred ks and ss.

"Sorry," said Thorne. "Your accent's not exactly what I'm used to."

Pyotr sat up straight. "Are you saying I don't know Czech? Say something in Czech."

Thorne said two sentences in Khmer. Everyone relaxed.

"What did that mean?" asked the thin man.

"I love you and will you be mine forever?"

They all laughed, except Pyotr. "That wasn't Czech," he

said. "I don't know what it was but it wasn't Czech. You're not Czech."

The faces around the table were frozen. Thorne picked up the vodka bottle and poured a bit all around. "All right," he said. "I'm Polish."

"No, you're not," said the laborer. "You're a fucking foreigner. Somebody call the militia."

"Go ahead," said Thorne. He was thinking: if I can just get loose from this bunch I can still make the fallback. But I've got to move fast.

"I will," said the laborer. He started to get up.

"Sit," said a voice above him.

The man twisted in his seat, looking up. Andreyev was standing behind the man's chair. He wore a baggy blue suit.

"Piss off," said the man. "We've got a bad one here."

"You're drunk," said Andreyev. "Sit still." He pulled a chair from an adjoining table and sat down.

"Who the fuck are you?" asked the thin man. He was belligerent with alcohol.

Andreyev took a card from his pocket and showed it to him. The man read it. "Oh," he said.

"Find another table, asshole," said Andreyev. He looked at the others. "You, too."

They left hurriedly, without looking back. Andreyev looked around. There was no one in earshot if they kept their voices down. "I was late but I decided to check here anyway. Were you followed?"

"Yes. I lost them."

"Good. They'll find us together sooner or later, but there's cover for that. Here's what you have to tell your people. . . . Why are you looking at me like that?"

"Just glad to see you. I thought I was screwed."

"Not this time," said Andreyev. "Now. The information. There are preparations still to be made. We can move as early as the nineteenth, but the margin for success would be small. It will be later than that, if possible. We will inform you of the exact date and time just before the action."

"All right. I'll move it along. How long can we pretend you're recruiting me?"

"Long enough. If they do blow us, we can only hope that they don't . . . get the information out of us until it's too late."

"I'll try not to land us in the shit," said Thorne. "That's all?"

"For now."

On the way back to the embassy, Thorne niggled away at a question that kept edging into his mind. The Russians weren't giving anything like the hard information Harper would presumably want. But Thorne had been told not to press them. He thought it was rather odd.

The Golan
8:00 A.M. to 9:08 A.M., August 13

At EIGHT O'CLOCK in the morning of August thirteenth, in the Syrian headquarters at Qatana Lieutenant-General Abdallah El Koussir lost his nerve. An Israeli motorized infantry brigade using extensive artillery and air support had broken through the Syrian blocking position at Khan Ureinibah and was established astride the Kuneitra-Damascus Road. Syrian forces were trying to move up from the southern end of the front, but were making little progress in the face of Israeli air interdiction. The Soviet resupply transports were pouring into Damascus airport, but Syrian command and control systems had broken down so badly that very little of the fresh equipment had yet reached the front.

Nearly all of Koussir's first-line tank crews had been committed to action; there were still sixty or seventy T-64s in the reserve-tank parks but there were hardly any thoroughly trained men to fight in them. And the Syrian air force had lost a third of its strength. There was nothing between the Israelis and Damascus but a pair of hastily assembled infantry groups, not much more than a battalion each, armed with a hodgepodge of weapons, and very few of those.

Had Koussir known of the Israeli decision taken at 7:30 that same morning, which was to halt the advance at the hamlet of Ras en Nuriye, he might not have taken the action he did. In fact, if the Israeli stop-order had reached all the units for which it was intended, he might well have regained his self-control. Neither of those possibilities was fulfilled.

Captain David Goren peered into the eyepiece of the Merkava's turret periscope. There was no doubt about it: the

Syrian infantry position ahead of them had been vacated. He opened the turret hatch and cautiously looked out. The remaining four Merkavas of Goren's tank company were dispersed hull-down in firing positions to the sides of the road. An armored troop carrier was scuttling off into a ravine to the left.

We've still got infantry support, he thought. No reason not to go on.

"Where are we?" asked his gunner.

"Half a kilometer from Halas. It looks wide open. Anything on the radio?"

"No. What are we going to do now?"

"The radio's still screwed?"

"Afraid so."

A round from a Syrian tank had struck an oblique blow on the Merkava's turret an hour ago. It had put the radio out of action. Communications were nearly impossible anyway, because of the Syrian jamming.

"Let's keep going till we run into something. Then we can report it somehow or other." Goren waved the other tanks forward. The four fighting vehicles clattered out of their defilade positions and started up the road. Within twenty minutes they were beyond the abandoned village of Halas. The infantry-support vehicles were on their heels. They stopped a kilometer northeast of the village and dug in. It was half a kilometer too far.

At 8:15 Koussir received a garbled report of Israeli main battle tanks and armored troop carriers past Halas, moving on Damascus. His nerve was already slipping, and this report sent him over the edge. He immediately telephoned President Nahawi, who was in the GHQ bunker well outside Damascus. The president's voice in the earpiece was dry and nervous.

"General Koussir? Yes?"

Koussir gave him the gist of the report. There was a long silence when he finished. Koussir, used to direction from above, grew more and more nervous. He tried to imagine what Hallak would have done. Finally, in a desperate stab in the dark, he said,

"President, I request complete freedom of action. I can stop the Israelis at Halas, but only by the most extreme methods."

Another long silence, muffled, as though Nahawi had put his hand over the mouthpiece of the telephone. Then:

"Do so. We will begin diplomatic action. Also I will contact our Libyan allies for assistance. Take any measures you see fit."

"Yes, president," said Koussir, into an empty telephone line. The president had hung up.

Sixteen minutes later a pair of Mig-27 ground-attack aircraft lifted from Tadmor Airbase into a burning yellow sky. Beneath each plane's belly rode a slender missile, dun-painted, the hue of stone and sand, of the snake in the desert.

The Migs' takeoff was detected within three minutes by an Israeli surveillance RF-4 Phantom orbiting at twelve thousand meters over Dalwah. Syrian air activity had been desultory over the front since dawn, but the Mahanayim fighter controller vectored a flight of four F-16 interceptors after the Migs as a security measure.

At 8:52 four Mig-23 fighters took off from the Homs airbase north of Damascus, and a similar force from Dumeir followed six minutes later. Both sorties were detected by the Israeli surveillance aircraft, and two flights of F-15 Eagles were brought forward from Ramat David and Haifa. At this point the Mig-27s with their dun-colored weapons were eighty kilometers from Halas and David Goren's four tanks. The Mig-23s were above the attack aircraft, flying top cover.

"I have them," said the pilot of the lead F-16. "Very low, a hundred meters, eleven o'clock. All copy?"

"Copy," came from the other three interceptors.

"They're loaded. Three, four, you watch for their top cover." The pilot turned a knob on his transmitter. "Jephthah leader to Tanit. Where's our mosquito repellent?"

"Over you now. Coming down."

The Eagles would be dropping towards the Mig-23 covering aircraft. The 27s were keeping low, hoping to escape detection. Already a forlorn hope.

The pilot rolled the F-16 into a steep dive, his wingman following, towards the flitting Mig-27s below. The Migs began to jink haphazardly; they had been warned of or had detected the closing Israelis. The Syrian jets were traveling as fast as they could at low altitude, swing-wings swept full back, the orange glow from their tail pipes betraying the use of afterburners.

They'll use all their fuel before they get home if they keep on reheat, reflected the pilot as the F-16 closed towards missile range. Worry began to nibble at the back of his mind. The Migs were taking hardly any evasive action at all. By rights they should have jettisoned their bomb loads and swung to meet the Israeli attack. Bait? He glanced up through the clear bubble of his canopy. Nothing. The cockpit alarms that would warn of a missile lock-on were silent. Somewhere up above, the Eagles were dealing with the Mig-23 escorts.

It was suddenly at the front of his mind, as though he were back in the briefing room. "Cruise missiles," the intelligence officer had said, "at least those of an early generation, must be launched inside a very small approach window. An aircraft attacked while carrying such a missile cannot take extreme evasive action at the time of launch as this will place the missile-guidance system outside its target-acquisition envelope. The Pakistani missiles the Syrians and Libyans are said to have acquired are of such an early generation."

That's them, thought the pilot. "Jephthah two. These are the big ones. I think they're nuclear. Put the Sidewinders right up their backsides. Take the right-hand one."

"Copy," said his wingman.

The pilot pressed the firing studs for the AIM-9L Side-winder missiles at the F-16's wingtips. The rockets leaped ahead trailing blooms of flame, homing on the Mig's exhaust, riding the heat signature towards the engine.

The trails of the two missiles had reached halfway to the Mig's afterburner glow when a brilliant plume of flame spurted from beneath the Syrian aircraft. A pale shape was momentarily visible beyond the Mig's nose, accelerating rapidly; then it disappeared as the Sidewinders blew the aircraft to pieces. The pilot wrenched his F-16 around the cloud of debris and flame and searched frantically ahead. There it was, going like the devil. Damn, the Syrian had launched it. "Jephthah two," he called. "Did yours launch one?"

The other voice was faintly shaky. "He tried. But it hit the ground. I flew over it."

"We have to catch that thing. Go."

The throttle was full forward but he pushed at it anyway. "Tanit from Jephthah one," he transmitted. "A cruise missile is headed your way. I suspect nuclear. Altitude one hundred meters, holding. I check it at Mach point eight. Chasing but you should vector an intercept."

"Copy, Jephthah one," said Tanit control.

The cruise missile was eight kilometers from Halas.

David Goren was standing in the net-camouflaged turret of the Merkava, watching the dogfight to the east through a pair of binoculars. It was a fair-sized one, although not as big as some he had seen earlier in the fighting. Already there had been three black plumes and one yellow explosion up there in the bright, hazy blue, although it was impossible to tell the identities of the burning and exploding aircraft.

He swept the binoculars down from the sky to their proper business, scanning the terrain ahead. There hadn't been a sign of Syrian troops.

There was a dot, an aircraft, just above the ridge to the east, flying very low. Another dot, above and behind it. The upper dot was twinkling. Cannon fire. The two aircraft were approaching very quickly.

"Air attack," he shouted into the hatch, and began to slide back into the safety of the turret, still watching the sky.

The nuclear warhead detonated less than half a kilometer away. Except for a momentary impression of a very bright light, like an enormous flashbulb, David Goren never knew anything about what killed him.

Cairo
1:00 P.M., August 13

THE EMERGENCY SESSION of the Egyptian National Assembly had been a stormy one, lasting well into the normal midday break period. At eleven o'clock, when the members were informed of the nuclear explosion in the Golan, there had been a stunned silence followed by a renewed cacophony. Normally docile in the presence of President Hosni Mubarak, the assembly began to call for sanctions against Israel for its violent counterattack into Syrian territory, although it was not yet clear whether the bomb had been Israeli or Syrian.

Anwar, Anwar, your hopes are falling in ruins about my head, thought Mubarak as, surrounded by bodyguards, he made his way down the steps of the assembly building to the limousine that would take him back to his office. He was not looking forward to the afternoon. Everyone, Russia, America, the Arab states, would be angry and frightened. Badly frightened. The nightmare was beginning to come true. Egypt had walked the edge of a knife ever since Sadat and Begin met at Camp David that summer so long ago: on one side of the knife, the Israelis with their gleaming, deadly war machine; on the other, the rejectionist Arab states led by Syria and by Libya under that madman. . . .

"Mr. President?"

Mubarak stopped. Nessim Saïd, his chief of intelligence, was slipping through the ring of bodyguards. "Colonel Saïd. Have you more information?"

"Yes, Mr. President."

Mubarak considered. "Meet me in my office at two."

"Sir, it's urgent. If I could ride with you –"

"All right. Come."

They got into the backseat of the armored Lincoln. Motorcycles fanned out in front and behind as the car moved away into the sweltering heat of the Egyptian capital. The sky was a hot blue shading to yellow at the horizon.

"Do you know yet who used the bomb?" asked Mubarak.

"It was Syria's," Saïd told him. "We're almost certain. The Israelis weren't in enough trouble to need to use it. The Syrians were."

"How much damage did it do?"

"We don't know yet. Israeli radio traffic appears to be near normal volume. This would suggest that not much harm was done." Saïd looked pale and nervous and was sweating perceptibly even in the air-conditioned Lincoln. He half undid his tunic.

"We are in a very dangerous situation," said Mubarak.

"Yes," agreed Saïd. Mubarak waited for him to go on, but he didn't. Saïd was looking intently through the windshield at the street ahead.

"You said there was something important," prompted Mubarak.

As he spoke, an army truck hurtled out of a side street, swerved, swept three of the six motorcycle escorts off their machines and slammed to a halt in front of the Lincoln. Soldiers tumbled out of the rear of the truck, raising weapons. The Lincoln's driver put the car into a skid, trying to turn the heavy vehicle more quickly by breaking the rear wheels loose. The two men in the rear seat lurched sideways with the turn. Saïd was dragging a pistol out of his tunic.

"They're at it again," said Mubarak. "This time –"

Colonel Saïd shot him three times through the heart.

The Eastern Mediterranean
3:00 P.M., August 13

THERE WAS NOTHING SUBTLE about the Libyan attack on Haifa and Tel Aviv. Like the Syrian attempt of six hours earlier, it was composed of Mig-27 attack aircraft and Mig-23 escorts, but many more of each: in all, nearly two-thirds of Libya's front-line fighter and attack strength, spread out in a great gaggle of delta shapes roaring in from the sea.

The ubiquitous Israeli surveillance aircraft detected them first, as they left the Libyan base at El Adem. Within a few minutes their mission profile became obvious: high out at sea, then a high-speed dive to low level for the attack itself. The Israelis could not hope to shoot down every one of them. The Libyans had presented them with a variation of the shell game, with nuclear warheads for peas and several dozen Migs for shells.

In fact only two of the Migs carried the ex-Pakistani cruise missiles, but the Israelis had no way of knowing this. They scrambled every available interceptor and vectored them seawards, then drew off some of their air strength facing the Syrians. They also armed six F-15 Eagles with AGM-88s, air-to-ground missiles. Each missile was tipped with a ten-kiloton nuclear warhead. The Eagles were put on five minutes' standby.

The great air battle was joined two-hundred kilometers from the Israeli coast, as the Libyan jets slid into their attack curves.

Captain Mahmoud Hajj glued his eyes to his instruments, particularly the alarm light that would supposedly warn of any Israeli radar-homing missiles locked onto his Mig-27. In four minutes he would be in the cruise-missile launch window and would no longer be able to take evasive action if attacked. Not that that would do much good anyway, against the Israeli Sidewinders and Shafrirs. The weight of the missile under the Mig's belly made her clumsy and slow to respond to the controls.

He could not jettison the missile to turn and fight, either. He was ordered to launch it properly or die with it, and nothing else.

A bright flash somewhere ahead and above. Smoke and flame. There were plumes of burning aircraft all over the sky. He prayed inside his oxygen mask and kept flying. Two minutes, with the help of God, to launch.

Four kilometers to the southeast, the pilot of a lone Israeli Kfir interceptor slipped past a wildly gyrating Mig-23 and fired a Shafrir air-to-air missile at a target he identified as a Mig-27. The missile struck the Mig between the leading edge of its tail plane and the trailing edge of its swept wing. Several kilograms of the Mig's airframe were driven into the whirling turbine blades of its engines, which promptly tore themselves to pieces. The cruise missile under the Mig wrenched away from its support pylon and began to tumble lazily towards the sea. Its rather primitive fail-safe devices worked and the warhead did not explode.

As Captain Hajj reached the ten-second mark of his countdown, the lock-on alarm on his instrument panel began to flash. With a tremendous effort he prevented himself from triggering the cruise-missile firing circuits. The clock crept on, slow as the desert.

Four.

Three. The Israeli must be firing now.

Two.

One.

Zero. He triggered the firing circuit.

Nothing happened for the longest time. Hajj waited.

The panel clock's second hand snapped onwards one-sixtieth of a minute.

The Mig jumped as the missile dropped away from its grapples. It came into view ahead of the Mig's nose, accelerating rapidly, trailing flame.

Hajj rammed his throttle forward, rolled the Mig and dove.

He was three-quarters of a second too late. A Falcon radar-homing missile blew the Mig in two.

By the time the cruise missile settled into its course, the Libyan strike force had been badly savaged. Its commanders had assumed – with some justification – that the Israelis would be so preoccupied with the Syrian nuclear threat that they would respond slowly to the attack from the sea. But the Israelis had taken a calculated risk in pulling their interceptors back from the Syrian front, and the risk appeared to have paid off. Numbers of Libyan fighters were already breaking away from combat, near the end of their fuel, and turning for El Adem.

No one noticed the tiny radar or heat signature of the cruise missile as it flew a hundred meters above the waves towards Tel Aviv. The ten-kiloton warhead was now fully armed. It would not totally flatten the city, but it would wreck its industries, kill half its population, drive the rest into the fallout-stricken countryside and burn what could be burned of the rubble.

Captain Ayi Kaplan swung his F-15 onto a course for the Herzliya Airbase. His had been one of the first of the interceptors to attack the Libyan strike force, and his fuel was running low. As well, his aircraft was nearly disarmed. He had fired all his missiles and the weapons-status display showed only a dozen rounds left for the cannon. It was definitely time to go home. He put the Eagle into a shallow climb and throttled back. No other aircraft were visible through the cockpit canopy, but the radar display reflected in his windscreen showed a dozen strong blips at varying distances. Other Israeli aircraft, returning to base.

The Hughes radar in the Eagle's nose cone also showed a very small target sixty kilometers ahead and well below.

Kaplan's eyebrows drew together. It was a very soft blip, even to the Hughes equipment.

A light aircraft? This far out?

Preoccupied by his climb and the fuel situation, Kaplan had failed for a few seconds to note the speed of the small target. When he did, it was with surprise. The vehicle was traveling much too fast for a light plane.

Kaplan swore. His briefing had been hurried, because of the need to attack the Libyans well out to sea, but he and the other pilots had been warned of the weapons the enemy might be carrying. And here was one of them not sixty kilometers away.

He went to afterburner and switched to the general frequency. "All intercept aircraft from Thunderbolt one. I have a target answering cruise-missile description sector 15, heading 092, speed 900. Intercepting."

A short silence. Two blips on the headup display abruptly changed course. "Nesher six to Thunderbolt one. We have it. What is your range-to-target?"

"Sixty kilometers."

"You get first slice. We're at eighty. What weapons have you left?"

"Twelve rounds of cannon." The Eagle's acceleration was pressing Kaplan back in his seat. "Have you any hostiles?"

"No."

Two other voices broke in, one the Herzliya controller on the general frequency, calling for aircraft within intercept range to vector on the position Kaplan had reported. The other was lost in a blur of static or jamming and went off the air.

At this low level the F-15, especially on afterburner, ate fuel at an appalling rate. As Kaplan closed on the target and its trace became harder and harder in the display he began to worry about his chances of reaching the seacoast after the interception.

No time for that, he told himself. Knock it down first, then worry about home.

Three minutes passed and he still couldn't get a visual contact. The missile had to be very small. He armed the cannon and selected the missile's blip as the target for the Eagle's combat computer.

There. It was a dove-gray with a pale orange flame at its tail, stubby wings and triform fins. His Eagle was overhauling it at about three-hundred-twenty kilometers per hour. Kaplan touched the controls delicately until the fighter was in the proper attack profile. The cannon hammered.

Four of the twelve shells hit the missile. The first two sheared off its tail and engine and the third penetrated the fuel cell. The fourth did two things. It separated the warhead from the missile's airframe and triggered its detonation mechanism.

Without a ripple, the expanding fireball swallowed the F-15, Kaplan, the rags of the cruise missile and an errant flock of seagulls that had strayed too far from home.

Washington
2:40 P.M., August 13

'HERE'S THE TRANSCRIPT, Mr. President," said the aide and put a sheet of paper at Law's elbow. Law, Harper, Secretary of State Edward Presniak, Defense Secretary McKay, Chairman of the Joint Chiefs of Staff General Torrance and several other senior government officials were sitting at the conference table in the room adjoining the White House Situation Room. There was an odor of pipe and tobacco smoke and nervous sweat, despite the air conditioning.

Law skimmed the transcript and set it down. "This," he said, "is a transcript of a Radio Cairo broadcast picked up at 7:10 P.M. their time. It confirms the earlier report that President Mubarak is dead and indicates that . . . well, I'll read it. It says, 'The Rejectionist Front under General Shazli, with the approval of the National Assembly, has removed the pro-Zionist traitor Mubarak from office and assumed control of the People's Republic of Egypt. All military personnel are to report to their mobilization points without delay. The unforgiveable nuclear attack by Israel on her neighbors and those Arab nations supporting them is a criminal breach of international relations and must be treated as such by all people who prefer peace to war. The execution of the traitor Mubarak is only the first step in the weeding out of all those who would see Egypt a satellite of the Zionist-American neocolonialists.'"

Law put the sheet aside. "It goes on like that for several more paragraphs, then ends with another demand for all military personnel to report. What's going on over there? Cam?"

Harper said, "NSA intercepts indicate that the Egyptian army is mobilizing, at least partially. Satellite data shows considerable vehicle movement in the Sinai. However, Cairo isn't prepared for any large-scale attacks on Israel; we estimate that they are trying to draw pressure off the Syrians."

"Will the Israelis attack them to slow the mobilization?" asked Presniak.

Law put up a hand. "I think we'd better recapitulate before we go any further." He looked down at a handwritten sheet. "One. It is apparent that the Syrian nuclear strike this morning did do some damage, but not much, to the Israeli forces in the Golan. Two. There was no immediate damage at all from the Libyan attack, which included at least one nuclear weapon. The fallout damage depends upon the winds for the next day or so. We don't think it will be great, since the bomb went off over water. The Syrian explosion will be more dangerous in fallout, but unfortunately for Damascus the winds are blowing the debris away from Israel. Three. I have contacted the Israeli prime minister. He indicates that the military situation is obscure, especially since Mubarak's death. However, he says Jerusalem has no immediate intention of using nuclear weapons unless forced to do so." Law looked around the table. "More than that I wasn't able to get out of him. He said he was very busy."

This didn't raise the ghost of a smile from anyone.

"Four," Law went on. "We have issued a strong protest against the Libyan and Syrian actions and have stated that we are considering drastic means to prevent a recurrence. Five. Soviet radio traffic surrounding their airlift has increased again, and a very large lift of strategic transports left Belgrade a few hours ago for Syria. We have not been able to determine whether they are carrying troops or only equipment and ammunition, as they have been for the past two days. We *do* know that the Soviets have had several airmobile battalions at readiness for at least thirty-six hours. We have accordingly informed the Russian ambassador here that we take a dim view of their clients' use of nuclear weapons, and a much dimmer view of outside military interference in the conflict. Moscow has not so far responded.

"Six. Our Sixth Fleet is moving towards the eastern end of the Mediterranean. That task force the Soviets sent through Gibraltar a while back is shadowing it." Law paused. "That could be an extremely volatile situation." There were nods around the table.

"Last. In case there are Russian troops in those transports, I am ordering the Eighty-second Airborne component of the Quick Reaction Force to be at six hours readiness to move. For the moment we will remain at Defense Condition Four: normal peacetime activity, except for the QRF. Have I missed anything?"

Heads shook all around.

"Mr. President," said Presniak, "we haven't decided the exact conditions for inserting the QRF into Israel."

"I don't want any exact conditions yet," said Law. "Beyond the principle that Russian troops advancing into Israel proper would not be acceptable. The situation's too fluid at the moment.

"But –"

The aide came back into the room and put a note beside Harper. They waited while Harper scanned it. He put it down and said, "The Russian strategic transports landed at Damascus and Es Suweidiya an hour ago. There were Russian aircraft covering the landing. We got satellite pictures with the last light. The planes were unloading troops and light airborne vehicles. Radio intercepts confirm this. And there's another transport wave on the way from Kiev via Belgrade."

"Jesus Christ," someone muttered.

"They're crazy," said General Torrance. "They have to be aware we won't put up with that."

Law looked at Harper, who shrugged infinitesimally and said, "I would remind us all that the current Soviet leadership may not be in control much longer. This may not be the time to overreact."

McKay said irritably, "Has it occurred to my colleague at the CIA that this entire RUBICON ONE project may be handing the Russians time to shift the Middle East balance of power decisively? So decisively that there won't be any point in our reacting at all? That perhaps we're playing into a deception set up by the KGB and the general staff together?"

"It's occurred to us," said Harper evenly. "But we don't think that's what they're doing. In any case, the Russians aren't beating on Jerusalem's gates just yet."

"Nevertheless," said Law, "we'd better give them a signal. I propose we move to DefCon Three."

They agreed on it quickly.

At 10:15 P.M., Washington time, the order went out to all United States forces around the globe: assume Defense Condition Three, all troops on standby, all leaves cancelled.

There were still two defense conditions short of war: DefCon Two, troops ready for combat, and DefCon One, troops deployed for combat. DefCon Two had only been reached once, during the Cuban missile crisis.

DefCon One had never been reached at all.

Moscow
August 14

A T 7:30 A.M., four minutes after leaving the one-bedroom apartment he shared with his wife and six-year-old son, Colonel Stanislav Vakula was walking along Prosternaya Street. He was on his way to the Preobrazhenskaya Metro station, heading for work. It was hot, the sky dull with the threat of rain, and damp. The gray overcast made the street's gray stone and concrete buildings look even grayer. Vakula's neck inside his uniform collar felt sticky.

"Colonel Vakula?"

Vakula's stride faltered momentarily. The man, dressed in a shabby blue suit, had overtaken him on the side away from the curb. Instinctively, the colonel looked back. There was no black car sliding quietly up to the curb behind him.

He looked at the man: broad features, snub nose, cheerful-looking, military haircut. "Yes. What do you want?"

"I'm Colonel Grinev. KGB Second Directorate." He waved an identification card at Vakula. "I wonder if I might walk along with you to the station."

And what if I said no, thought Vakula. "Whatever you like. Is this official?"

Grinev dropped into step beside him. He was four inches shorter than the GRU officer. "Well, in a way. My business with you is being developed through normal channels but my superiors decided I might as well have a word with you in the meantime."

Vakula's nerves were tingling. "Always glad to cooperate with the KGB," he said easily. "If I can, subject to my own orders, of course."

"Of course." Grinev's voice dropped. "It's about this

GRU operative working out of GHQ. Major Nikolai Andreyev."

With a tremendous effort, Vakula kept his voice steady. "What about him?"

"He's after a rather big fish, isn't he? To my superiors' irritation. And it was so quick, too. The American's no sooner off the plane than he's slipping away – very professionally, I might add – from a routine surveillance and popping into a worker's café to meet your young major. I hope Andreyev's control knows what he's doing."

Balls, thought Vakula. We'd hoped they wouldn't catch the two of them together until the second meeting at least. Somebody in the café must have told the militia afterward. At least they don't seem to know I'm controlling him. "The ground was prepared overseas," said Vakula. "I can't say anything more than that."

Grinev sighed theatrically. "I do wish we could start working together again, like we used to. Then we wouldn't be tripping over each other, right?"

"Right," said Vakula. "What's your concern at the moment?"

They were a hundred meters from the Metro station. A few large drops of rain spattered on the pavement. Another splashed on the bridge of Grinev's nose. He brushed it away, blinking. "As I said, an American embassy security man's a big fish. Too big, in fact. We're wondering if he isn't working on your Major Andreyev, rather than the other way round. Remember, we've got resources military intelligence doesn't. We might be able to find out things you couldn't."

Vakula stopped. "What you're saying is the KGB wants to deal with the American."

"That's what's going through channels. I must say your people have become uncooperative over the past few years. Anyone would think you'd got something to hide." He laughed. "But we thought we'd have a chat with you personally, anyway. We have to cooperate at some level, don't we, if we're going to get anywhere? Even if the cooperation is unofficial. And remember, a friend of the KGB always has a friend."

They want me to pass information to them, thought Vakula, if they can't officially get their hands on Thorne.

"I'll consider it," he said neutrally. They were at the Metro. There was quite a spattering of rain now. The street smelled of water and dust and warm asphalt.

"You do that," said Grinev. The blue eyes were now cold. "Because if it turns out that this catch of yours is really a CIA provocation, you're going to need a friend."

He walked away. Vakula, sweat trickling uncomfortably in his armpits, thought, they're serious about this. We'd better play them along. It's only until the nineteenth or the twentieth. Only until then.

At three that afternoon, Kotsarev wrote Travkin an interdepartmental memo:

TOP SECRET – EYES ONLY
FROM: F.Y. KOTSAREV
TO: P.A. TRAVKIN
RE: PRACTICE EXERCISE SUVOROV

The practice exercise has been approved by the requisite authorities and you are directed to carry it out on the night of August 19/20, in cooperation with the KGB and MVD. As internal security is one of the items to be tested by the exercise, no one below the rank of unit commander is to be informed in advance. All appropriate preparations must be complete by the morning of the nineteenth.
Kotsarev

As he signed it Kotsarev breathed a sigh of relief. The American alert had made Morosov and a preoccupied Boyarkin if not keen on Suvorov, at least acquiescent. The exercise had slipped neatly into the pattern of the Soviet alert. In fact, the Sixteenth Airborne Regiment would move thirty minutes before the scheduled start of the security exercise so that the troops could secure the vital points before the KGB and the

MVD could react. There were several other army units involved in the official exercise, but they could be left to themselves while the Sixteenth carried out the real business of Suvorov.

Now if Yushenko could only stall the KGB's attempt to take over the American. The GRU chief could give the brothers false information about Thorne's recruitment for a while, but direct KGB control of Thorne would be disaster.

It's only until the nineteenth, he thought, echoing Vakula. Only until then.

"I have to be quick," said Andreyev. He was standing beside Thorne in front of an enormous painting on the second floor of the Tret'yakov Gallery. The painting was by Ilya Repin and was called *The Execution of the Streltsi*. There was no one else in the big room, whose walls were jammed haphazardly with pictures all the way to the ceiling.

Thorne nodded. "I was followed, as I expected. But they didn't try very hard to hang onto me. Do you know anything about that?"

"Yes. The KGB knows about us. But the cover's holding. My own tail's downstairs; he'll be up in a minute. Two things. One, we're set for the nineteenth. Two, the airlift won't stop because of your alert; we're moving battle tanks now, elements of a mechanized regiment. Not yet decided whether to use them. It depends on what the Israelis do."

"Good," said Thorne. "Next place?"

"Lenin Museum, tomorrow, 12:30 P.M. Fallback 5:00 P.M. at the Historical Museum. If I'm not there, there's nothing to report. Call the number I gave you for the next location."

Thorne grimaced. He didn't want to work all the way through Moscow's supply of museums. "All right," he said.

But Andreyev was gone.

At 11:00 P.M. Moscow time the Israelis, desperately worried by the Egyptian mobilization, the steady movement of Syrian troops from the south end of the front line towards the Damascus-Kuneitra Road and the stream of Russian equipment

and men arriving in Syria, began a night attack intended to
smash the Arab offensive capability by the following evening.
The Israelis were trusting that their command of the air and
known nuclear armament would deter a repetition of the nuclear
attack of the thirteenth, and that the threat of American intervention would keep the Russians out of the fighting as long as
Damascus itself was not threatened.

Their axis of attack, therefore, swung away from the
Syrian capital, into the southeast and the Damascus-Der'ā Road.

The Golan
August 15

MAJOR RATH STUDIED the situation map. He was in the Golan headquarters command bunker, under the ruins of Naffakh. The town, wrecked in the Six Day War, had never been rebuilt and had not been much more than a ruin when the Syrians attacked. The attack had transformed the ruins into heaps of broken stone and brick.

Nevertheless, the HQ was functioning. Reports were beginning to filter in from the units attacking towards Der'a; confused at the moment but beginning to make sense as the information was transferred to the map table. So far it appeared that the Syrian tank-infantry spearheads advancing from the southern end of the line had been caught either at rest during the night or disorganized and off guard.

Rath looked at his watch. Almost dawn. The Syrians would soon be receiving the full weight of the Israeli Air Force; the air attacks would go on at least until noon. Then a number of squadrons were to be drawn off to the Sinai front in case the Egyptians decided to continue their provocative movements. Rath sighed. It was all so pointless. The Arabs were going to lose again, and all for what? Even their nuclear weapons hadn't helped them.

Although there had been an unbelievably tense few hours after the mushroom cloud rose over Halas. For a little while Rath had thought the end had truly come, but then it had not.

It could yet, though, he reminded himself. No one's even mentioned a cease-fire yet.

For no particular reason, Rath thought of Stein and the enigmatic American he had brought up to the line the morning the war began. That morning, and even Stein's death, seemed unutterably far away. Rath wondered momentarily what had happened to the American.

"Ninth Brigade has some prisoners," said Colonel Eliad, coming into the map room from the radio section. "They're part of a mechanized battalion following the Syrian lead elements."

Lieutenant-General Medan, commander of the Golan front and the northern military region, looked up from the map. "Any unit identification?"

"Not yet. Brigade HQ hasn't talked to them yet."

"Make sure they let us know," said Medan unnecessarily.

"Right," said Eliad. Medan had a reputation for requesting the obvious. It was a mark of his meticulousness.

Rath went and sat on a raggedy couch in the corner of the map room. He was exhausted, but the command bunker was not a good place to sleep. It was too noisy: the crackle and snap of transmissions in the radio section next door, messengers and officers in and out, HQ staff talking to each other and, under all, a steady vibration, a faint rumble. Heavy artillery supporting the attack by shelling the Syrian roads behind the front. Interdicting fire, it was called, if you were firing it. You referred to it otherwise when it was falling on you.

An aide hurried in from the radio section and handed Eliad a message. The map room's lighting was not good but Rath thought Eliad paled slightly.

"We have a positive indentification on the Ninth's prisoners," he said.

"Yes?" asked Medan impatiently.

"They're Russian."

The background conversation in the room stopped. Then Medan said, "Oh, fuck."

By 9:00 A.M., though, the situation didn't seem so critical. There didn't appear to be very many Russians, and what there were, were using only light weapons. Obviously they were the airborne troops, or some of them, that the Russians had moved into Es Suweidīya at the beginning of their airlift.

Both Rath and Eliad hoped the Russians were only stiffening for the Syrians. There were a lot of Soviet tanks and troops in Damascus now, but the Israeli general staff's assessment was that they were there to deter an assault on the Syrian capital itself.

By ten o'clock it was clear that the Syrians' northward advance had been severely mauled. No less than 120 tanks and many infantry were pocketed by the Ninth and Tal Brigades around the village of Nawa. With the reduction of the pocket, which should be possible by last light, almost all Syrian offensive strength would be gone, and during the night the Israelis would withdraw to less exposed positions. Two reserve brigades were moving up from Kuneitra in support, to relieve the tired troops of the Ninth and Tal units.

The only flaw in the situation, from Rath's viewpoint, was the stiff resistance the Syrians were putting up. Israeli aircraft losses were higher than expected, partly because of the Russian antiaircraft-missile resupply, and partly because the Syrian fighter pilots seemed to have gotten better.

Or perhaps they were not Syrian but Russian. Reconnaissance flights the previous day had spotted Mig-23s with Soviet markings at Homs Airbase, but none had yet been seen in combat. Two Israeli surveillance aircraft had disappeared in Syrian airspace during the morning, but with so much air traffic and radio jamming it was hard to tell exactly what had happened to them.

Jerusalem was still ruminating on the implications of the Russian prisoners. There were reports of troop movements southwest of Damascus, near the Kuneitra road. A dry wind was blowing across the Golan, towards Der'ä. Fallout was beginning to settle invisibly onto the basalt plain. The previous sunset and the sunrise had been spectacular because of the debris kicked up by the Syrian bomb.

At 12:02 P.M. a column of T-64 tanks, BMD air-portable personnel carriers and BMP infantry-combat vehicles roared down the Damascus road towards Kuneitra. Reconnaissance units fanned out ahead of the column. The Soviet markings on the tank turrets had been painted over, but there had been no time to replace them with Syrian designations. The column contained the major combat elements of the 672nd Independent Mechanized Regiment and two score Syrian tanks from the Damascus reserve. They were driving straight for the Israeli relief forces moving into Kuneitra, preparatory to continuing their movement to the pocket at Nawa. High above the column, Mig-23s from Homs Airbase orbited in the clear blue.

The light Israeli forces protecting the flank of the southward attack made contact with the Russians at 1:46 P.M. They fell back, informing Naffakh HQ. Medan ordered the two reserve brigades to deploy to meet the threat two kilometers from Kuneitra, but sudden and intense radio jamming prevented his orders from getting through. He then dispatched a message by jeep to the command element of the reserve column and hoped.

Meanwhile, the reserve roared on into the heat of the Golan, towards the advancing Russians.

The Soviet commander, Lieutenant-General Ranov, intended no more than a push through the enemy's screening forces to threaten the Israeli rear, thus reducing pressure on the Syrians and the Russian airmobile battalions to the south. If he could get the Israelis to withdraw in disorder, prey to antitank ambushes, so much the better. His orders were to strike the Israeli infantry as hard as possible – because the men's deaths would cause more distress in the small country than would the loss of armored vehicles – but not to destroy the Israeli forces in the Golan. That would be tempting Jerusalem too far.

Lieutenant-General Koussir acted alone, without contacting either President Nahawi or the Soviet military mission in Damascus, or even the staff of the 672nd Regiment. Fatigue and despair had unbalanced him: he had placed much faith in the nuclear strike at the Israelis, and it had failed. He had not dared another. But now the Israelis were destroying the southern forces that should even now be screening Damascus. And the capital was defended by the Russians, with a ragtag of Syrian troops at their heels. It was a shame beyond bearing.

He made one telephone call from Qatana. Half-an-hour

later, one of Syria's few remaining Mig-27s took off from the Palmyra runway into the west.

The Mig probably would have been caught had not the Israeli Air Force been dealing with the air cover of the Russian advance, supporting the attack on the Nawa pocket and simultaneously withdrawing some units for the Sinai front. The Mig was able to launch its missile without interference. The device exploded precisely over the two Israeli armored brigades at Kuneitra as they were deploying to meet the Soviet advance. The delay caused by the radio jamming cost them dearly; they were a well-concentrated target for a nuclear burst.

Rath was in the radio section listening to the badly jammed transmissions of the reserve brigades. They had changed frequencies several times but the jammers kept chasing them around the radio spectrum.

"Try –" he said, and stopped. There was a sudden shrill squeal from the relay loudspeaker, which was set to the Sixth Brigade's command frequency, and then a patter of static. A lot of static.

"What's that?" he asked the operator urgently.

"I don't know."

The bunker roof was weak from the shelling of the first Syrian attack and the ground shock of the nuclear detonation over Halas. When the ground wave of the Kuneitra explosion struck the roof it collapsed, burying Rath, Medan, Eliad and the entire Golan command staff under six tons of stone and dust.

The northern military district headquarters in Israel proper knew within fifteen minutes what had happened, both from pilot reports and from the fact that the Naffakh battle HQ had gone off the air. As well, they were unable to raise the reserve columns, which should have been in the region of Kuneitra.

Then air reconnaissance reported an enemy tank column picking its way along the Damascus-Kuneitra road, directly into the rear of the Ninth and Tal Brigades fighting the Syrians in the pocket at Nawa. Ten minutes after that, it was obvious that the reserve brigades were in no condition to interfere with the advancing tanks. One of the surviving brigade officers – he was clearly in shock, or already suffering from radiation sickness – reported by radio that the Israeli column had been very nearly at ground zero. He had survived, for the moment, only because his tank had broken down well behind the main body.

Northern HQ contacted Jerusalem and reported that the Ninth and Tal Brigades were as good as lost if they could not disengage from the Nawa pocket and withdraw to a defensible line. The enemy forces out of Damascus had to be delayed long enough for the Israelis to pull back. The loss of the reserves meant that if the Ninth and the Tal were destroyed, there would be nothing between the enemy tank column and Israel but a few weak infantry units.

The Israelis had no way of knowing that the Russian commander did not intend a full-scale battle, nor that he was as surprised as they were at the Syrian nuclear attack. Ranov, following his orders, continued to advance into the Israeli rear.

For an hour-and-a-half the Israeli Air Force tried to stop the Russians by ground attack alone. SAMs, antiaircraft fire and Russian-piloted Mig-23s cut the attacks to pieces. The Israeli pilots were desperately tired; their opponents were not. The T64s and personnel carriers, with occasional losses, ground towards Nawa, where the Ninth and Tal Brigades, with considerable difficulty, were trying to disengage from the Syrians.

It was obvious by 11:00 A.M. that they were going to be taken in the rear. If the attackers advanced another four kilometers, the last chance of extracting the two brigades would be lost.

The general staff chose not to lose it. When the Soviet tanks were still eleven kilometers away from the Nawa pocket, at 12:40 P.M., an Israeli nuclear weapon with a 9.2-kilotons yield detonated squarely above the center of the Russian advance.

Four hours later the battered vehicles and troops of the two Israeli brigades were taking up positions outside the nuclear-blast zone southwest of the place where Kuneitra had been. The path into Israel was, for the moment, secure.

Moscow
August 16

ANDREYEV AND THORNE WERE WALKING under the lime trees in the Alexander Gardens, which lie along the western wall of the Kremlin. To their right lay Manege Square with the white-columned Central Exhibition Hall flanking it. The vivid flowerbeds of the gardens were luminous in the noon light. The rain had stopped early that morning and the city smelled of wet pavement. In the gardens hung the odors of flowers and damp grass.

"They're starting to wonder how I meet you so easily," said Andreyev. "They can't understand why you're not under some kind of surveillance from your own people."

Thorne nodded. He still felt that to be a weak point in his cover. It would make it easy for the KGB to believe he was trying to recruit Andreyev, instead of the other way around.

"My control's worried," said Andreyev. He looked morose and tired. Thorne felt a twinge of compassion for the young man. Thorne might be risking expulsion from the country but the Russian was risking his life – not to mention the lives of his relatives, given the recent mood of the Kremlin.

"Why?" asked Thorne.

"He thinks the KGB's trying to take you over from us. He's also worried that a purge of the GRU is being put together. They'd only need something like this."

"Yes," said Thorne. "But it won't be long now."

"The unit leading the action is returning to its barracks today," said Andreyev. "From an exercise. I was supposed to tell you that."

"Good," said Thorne. "I'll pass it along."

"And one other thing."

"What?"

"The Iraqui government is badly frightened by the Israeli bomb. The staff of the Twenty-third Airborne Division's being sent to Baghdad today, in case the Iraquis request military support."

"Christ," said Thorne. "My people won't like that. On top of the Israelis and the Syrians throwing bombs at each other."

"You knew many of our troops were killed in the Israeli attack?"

"Yes. Is Boyarkin going to go berserk because of that?"

"My people don't think so. They think he's glad it happened. It will give him an excuse to send more troops to Syria."

"He's crazy."

"Yes."

"Was there anything else?"

"Not now."

They arranged the next meeting and separated. Thorne walked along the edge of the gardens towards the Metro station. The scent of flowers in the humid air was heavy and thick, sickly and too sweet.

Washington
August 16

"WHAT'S THE FEELING over at the state department?" asked Law. He was leaning on the edge of the great desk in the Oval Office.

"Tense," said the secretary of state. Presniak moved his shoulders uncomfortably to get the ache out of them. "They're tense on the Hill, too. The pro-Israeli lobby's screaming for a statement that we'll intervene if the Russians put one soldier across the 1973 cease-fire lines in the Golan. If we don't do something along those lines it may cost you the next election."

"If we do, there may not be a next election," said Law. "Cam, anything else on the Iraqui situation?"

"No, sir. There have been four flights into Baghdad in the last twenty-four hours but we have no positive ID on Soviet staff officers yet."

Law drummed his fingertips nervously on the desk. "The Saudis won't like Russian troops on their doorstep. Do you think we should tell them about the possibility? They may already know, of course."

"I'm not in favor of it just now," said Harper. "If the Russians know we found out about it that quickly the KGB may start searching for leaks. That could be very bad."

"All right," said Law. "We'll hold off for a few hours then."

"Are we to go to DefCon Two?" asked McKay. "I don't advise it at this time."

"I agree. Everyone's already tense enough. When does the cease-fire proposal start to move?"

Presniak looked at the rank of clocks, showing the world's

major time zones, on the wall of the Oval Office. "Ambassador Tate is presenting it to the Israeli foreign minister in an hour, at five o'clock their time. We have also informed the Soviet ambassador here of the proposal and have requested an immediate reaction."

"Any response?"

"No. Only prevarications. He's been very hard to see the last few days. When I have seen him, he's been edgy. I think he's frightened."

"Who isn't?" asked Law. "Try to keep the lid on the Israelis. Everybody's a bit shocked because of yesterday's exchange. We're going to protest it to both the Israelis and the Syrians but I don't think it will do much good. And when the shock wears off both Damascus and Jerusalem may be tempted to go for broke. And everybody's waiting to see what we and the Russians are going to do. Ed, what's happening in Damascus?"

Presniak said, "A copy of the cease-fire proposal's being delivered to Nahawi at the same time the Israelis receive theirs."

"What's the military situation generally, Nathan?"

"Everybody's digging in," said McKay. "Egypt's slowed down its mobilization and the Libyans are screaming blue murder but so far they've stayed carefully within their own airspace. They've lost a lot of planes. The Jordanians don't want to have anything to do with the war but they've reported a number of cases of radiation sickness to UN Health. Fallout."

"Was that for certain a Russian tank column the Israelis hit?" asked Law.

Harper nodded gloomily. "It's confirmed. But Moscow hasn't uttered a peep about it. There's been a lot of coded radio traffic between there and Damascus, but so far nothing else."

"So far," repeated Law. He straightened up. "Nathan, Cam, come with me. Ed, would you mind the store for me over at state? I'm going back to the Situation Room."

"Mr. President," said Presniak, "if you wish, I'll go to Jerusalem. I – "

Law shook his head. "The Kissinger days are gone. And

we don't have the time he did, short as that was. Also it's too dangerous. I don't want to have to go looking for a new secretary of state if they decide to hit Tel Aviv or Jerusalem."

"Very well, Mr. President." Harper couldn't tell whether the secretary was relieved.

As they rode down to the Situation Room in the elevator, Law said to McKay, "The newscasts don't make the situation look good, do they? There are a lot of very frightened people out there."

"There are also," McKay pointed out, "a lot of very frightened people in here." He paused. "I hesitate to ask this, but is the First Lady staying in Washington?"

"I asked her if she wanted to leave," said Law. "She wouldn't go."

"She really ought to."

"You tell her that." Arlene Law was noted for her decisive nature.

"I'll pass on that, Mr. President, thank you."

The crisis-management team had assembled in the conference room: the joint chiefs of staff and General Torrance, their chairman; the deputy director of state; and Northrop. The vice president was out of Washington, just in case.

"The DCI will give the situation report," said Law formally when everyone had settled down.

Harper did so. When he finished, the faces around the table were uniformly grim.

"What do your computers say?" asked McKay, after a short pause.

"It's not good," said Harper. "We are well and truly into the danger zone. It got worse during the night when we programmed in the way the Kremlin's stonewalling us on joint cease-fire proposals. So we've gone ahead with a proposal, unilaterally. The Kremlin isn't nearly as cooperative now as they were in October '73. And they weren't very cooperative then, until the Israelis surrounded the Egyptian Third Army. It appears that Boyarkin hasn't made up his mind whether the Syrians have lost or not."

"Neither side's in any condition to go on the offensive," said Torrance. "They're still picking themselves up from the nuclear strikes."

"What about our airlift to Israel?" asked McKay. "We have to do something about that soon."

"That's a tough one," said the deputy director of state. "We're getting a clear message from several NATO countries, particularly Spain, that they don't want to be used as a staging base for our airlift and that they don't like to permit resupply overflights by our transports. Logically enough, to them. They don't want their oil cut off, and they don't want to be any farther up the Soviet target list than they are now."

"The Kremlin was counting on that," said McKay.

"Naturally."

"Damn," said Torrance. "I sometimes wish we had the control over our allies the Russians have over theirs."

"So do I," said Law. "Unfortunately, we don't. I think we'd better try every diplomatic means for a cease-fire before we start throwing our weight around among our allies."

"But the Russians aren't talking."

"The Syrians may be willing to. The bombs the Russians helped them get haven't done them a lot of good."

Harper scratched his nose. "The Russians may not have intended the weapons to help Syria. There's good reason to believe they want to put Israel, and thereby us, into an impossible situation. Which will strengthen them enormously in the mideast. Boyarkin may – may, I repeat – be gambling that we won't go to war over a serious Israeli defeat. That if he draws the crisis out long enough, domestic pressure and fear of war will stop us from supporting Jerusalem as far as we might. He wouldn't want to destroy Israel, but he might want to neutralize her. The implications of that for us are very serious. But he may believe we'll try to recover our losses later rather than go to war. We may have to decide whether he's right."

There was a long silence.

"Is he?" asked Torrance. When no one answered, he said, "If it comes to that, Mr. President, we may have to consider a first strike."

Law regarded him stonily.

"Mr. President," said McKay, "it had to be said. We've been skirting it for a day now."

Law switched his gaze to the secretary of defense. "Yes," he said. "It has to be considered. But not now. We have not exhausted all the alternatives. Boyarkin may be removed."

"Jesus Christ, Mr. President," said Torrance. He slapped the table hard. "Are you going to commit this country's survival to the pipedreams of a handful of rebellious Russian politicians? Even if they're not playing us for fools anyway?" Torrance's eyes shot to Harper and then back to the president. "There's no guarantee that their plot will succeed, if there is a plot. We're losing time. I want to go to DefCon Two. Let them know we're willing to push just as hard as they do."

"No," said Law mildly. "I admit the situation is more serious than any we've ever faced. But the Soviets are on no higher an alert than we. I hardly see that as a reason to consider the incineration of the citizens of Moscow or Novosibirsk or anywhere else, for that matter."

One of the telephones burred softly. It wasn't the red phone. The president picked it up. "Law here," he said, and listened. Then he put the receiver down, looking faintly relieved.

"That was Ed Presniak," he said. "The Saudi ambassador just contacted him and said that there were indications of a Russian military move into Iraq. And that they don't like the idea of Russian ground forces in Syria. And could we confirm anything about the Iraqui situation. Ed said yes, we could confirm it, and could we help. To cut a long story short, the Saudis have asked us to consider endorsing – that was how their ambassador put it – their territorial integrity against outside forces if the Russians actually do move troops into Iraq."

"Well, I'll be damned," said McKay. "There's our oil. And Europe's. And the airlift."

"Possibly," said Law. "The situation's still fluid, remember. But we can certainly leak the Saudi request. General Torrance, can we start moving the Seventh Fleet's Indian Ocean task force towards Saudi Arabia?"

Torrance had brightened considerably. "I'll see to it right away."

"Good," said Law. He turned to Harper. "You'd better get your magicians to pop this into their computers. It might help."

"Yes, sir," Harper said. He studied Law for a moment as the president turned back to the faces around the table.

He loves this, realized Harper. Moving ships and planes and men all over the earth. He knows it's deadly, but he loves it anyway. We all do. We're decent and intelligent men, but we love it anyway. Power.

Four hours later the ships of Seventh Fleet Task Forces Seventy-seven and Seventy-nine, consisting of two aircraft carriers, twenty-three other combat vessels and troop transports carrying four reinforced battalions of marines, swung their bows northwest towards the Arabian Sea. Out on the horizon, shadowing them, lay the hazy forms of Russian frigates and missile cruisers. For now, they held their distance, like hawks circling in the upper air.

Moscow — Washington — The Golan
August 17

DURING THE EARLY AFTERNOON of August seventeenth, Soviet Foreign Minister Distanov transmitted to the Russian Embassy in Washington the text of a cease-fire proposition. Unlike the American plan, in which both sides withdrew to their prewar lines, the Soviet proposal was brutal. It demanded that the Israeli forces in the Golan lay down their weapons where they stood, whereupon they would be interned by Soviet forces in Syria and repatriated to Israel within three weeks. The note acknowledged that the conditions were harsh, but that this was justified by the unprovoked Israeli nuclear attack on Soviet troops who were doing nothing more than helping allies retain their sovereign territory. The world must be made to see that Jerusalem's piratical aggressiveness towards its neighbors would no longer be tolerated.

The proposal went on to state that if the invaders did not comply with the conditions, or one agreed on with other concerned governments (this was the escape hatch) by August twentieth, noon Moscow time, then any necessary measures would be taken by the Syrians and their allies, whoever they might be, to remove the aggressors from Syrian soil.

The proposal was also delivered to the Israeli foreign minister via the Swedish ambassador in Tel Aviv. There was no immediate response.

An addendum to the note, which went only to Washington, protested the maneuvers of the Seventh Fleet, referring to them as "extremely provocative."

President Law, when he received the ceasefire proposal and the addendum, requested via the hotline an immediate conversation with General Secretary Boyarkin. He was informed that the general secretary was not available owing to the extreme pressure of mideastern events. He would contact the American president as soon as possible.

"He wants to play poker, does he?" said Law when this information was relayed to him. Within two hours the United States had gone to DefCon Two, and twenty-six minutes after that the Soviet war machine adopted the same posture. Within the hour, satellites reported extensive tank movements in Eastern Europe and electronic intelligence detected a sixty-four percent increase in Soviet military radio traffic. Most Russian naval units had by now put to sea.

At a late-morning press conference Law outlined the situation, called publicly on the Soviet Union for talks to deal with the crisis and announced that an airlift of ammunition, aircraft and tank spares and medical supplies was to begin "as soon as the necessary arrangements are made."

On the west coast and elsewhere there were demonstrations against nuclear war. A steady and increasing trickle of the wiser or more timid began to leave the larger cities. Stores began to run short of canned goods and gun shops enjoyed a growing boom in sales.

Anguished outcries began to arrive from the various European governments that might be asked for overflight rights for the airlift. They were not mollified by the tenuous understanding between the Saudis and the United States. The secretary of state had to inform the Israeli ambassador that without some commitment by Jerusalem to withdraw from the territory it had overrun, the airlift might be indefinitely delayed. Some signs of resolving the conflict had to be evident before the United States could reasonably press for overflight permissions.

Jerusalem digested this, emitted a sharp complaint about the US attempt to force a resolution without concessions from the Syrians and then kept its own counsel. On the Golan front, where Syrian troops, stiffened by Russian support and re-supply, had launched a series of attacks to further wear down their opponents, the Israelis looked to their defenses.

In numerous capitals of the world, the conviction grew that the superpowers had finally let things slide out of control.

At six that evening, Moscow time, Thorne strolled through the main entrance of Gorky Park and turned in the direction of the amusement area. Above the trees in front of him the slowly rotating upper half of the Ferris wheel came into view.

There were few strollers in the park. The KGB purges begun in July had made many Russians prefer to stay home. Also there was the critical international situation. Unpleasant rumors, fueled by the angry anti-Israel and anti-American diatribes of *Pravda*, were making the rounds. There had been, for a few days, many uniformed men in the streets: reservists called to their units. Then, suddenly, there were fewer soldiers than normal; all leaves were cancelled. The mood of the Soviet capital, in short, wasn't good.

Thorne reached the open area near the Ferris wheel and watched as it slowed to a stop. The cabins discharged a clutch of children and a sprinkling of adults.

"You can see all over Moscow from the top of the wheel," Andreyev said from behind him. Thorne nodded and walked away from the wheel towards a tree-shaded gravel walk. There was a bench a few yards inside the dim green tunnel. Thorne sat down on it. Perhaps two minutes later Andreyev joined him.

"My people are worried," Thorne said. "You know our alert's increased."

"Yes," said Andreyev. "So's ours."

They fell silent as a man and a woman accompanied by two small girls hurried along the path in front of them. The children were chattering about the Ferris wheel. When they were out of earshot, Thorne said, "They want to know exactly what you're planning to do, and when. They haven't decided yet on the level of our help to the Israelis. But we have our factions, too. One of them wants a much stronger response than we're giving at the moment."

"The nineteenth is still the earliest date," said Andreyev.

He sounded surly. "They won't give you an exact time yet. A diplomatic settlement still is possible."

"Would your people move anyway?"

"I don't know."

"Did they tell you about Boyarkin's cease-fire proposal?"

"Only that there has been one."

Thorne outlined it. When he finished, Andreyev said, "I was instructed to tell you this. You must not interfere, the cease-fire problem will be dealt with at the appropriate time. Only be patient, and don't give in to Boyarkin's pressure. If the general secretary succeeds in isolating Israel, his policy will be seen to be correct, and he will be unassailable. However, he cannot afford to fail, because if he does he will lose most of his support, as Khrushchev did. Your policy must not err too much in forcing him in either direction."

"The cease-fire proposal is only buying time for him, then," said Thorne. "Enough time for the United States to lose its nerve."

"I think that's correct."

"I'll inform Washington," said Thorne, "of your concern. When will you be able to give us an exact time for the start of the action?"

"I haven't been told that."

"We will have to have some warning. Tell your control."

Andreyev stood up. His face was drawn. "I'll tell him." He paused. "Do you think we'll be able to get out of this one?"

"I don't know," said Thorne.

"Call me," said Andreyev, and was gone.

"There's no doubt about it," said Yushenko. "Morosov's trying to arrange things so he can force my dismissal or resignation. His try at taking over the American is a first step."

Kotsarev studied Yushenko's office ceiling. "He's really after me. No offense intended. If he can show that you've made a shambles of an important operation, and it was approved by me, I'll be out as well. That's what Boyarkin wants. Then Gresko will be isolated."

"He would pick on this operation," grumbled Yushenko. "It could have been any other. But no, it had to be this one. If he only knew."

"Be thankful he doesn't," said Kotsarev sharply. He had been exceedingly irritable for the past three days, because of the tension. His wife hardly dared speak to him. That morning she had decided to go to the Black Sea villa for a week. Kotsarev had agreed, preferring her to be out of Moscow during the coup. His son and daughter, fortunately, were on holiday in the south as well.

He preferred not to think about what would happen to them all if Suvorov failed. Even if there were no war.

"He's got his eye on some others as well, I think," said Yushenko. "Travkin, for one. And GLAVPUR would like to have one of their own in charge of the Strategic Rocket Service." He paused. "Could we consider moving before the nineteenth?"

"No. You said yourself we need the Suvorov cover. Suvorov was agreed for that date. I don't wish to risk suspicion by moving it up."

"Well," said Yushenko, "the Syrians won't be dropping any more bombs. What was that madman thinking of? Koussir, I mean."

"Nahawi's relieved him, anyway. He may not survive the war, no matter who wins."

"That's right," said Yushenko. "Now if the Americans can only keep the Israelis under control . . . and don't push too hard themselves."

"Exactly," Kotsarev said. "In the meantime, we wait."

Minutes of the Emergency Session, Council of Defense Moscow 10:00 hours, August 18

PRESENT:

Vitaly A. Boyarkin, General Secretary, CPSU
Viktor V. Gresko, Chairman, Council of Ministers
Fyodor Y. Kotsarev, Minister of Defense
Aleksandr T. Morosov, Chairman, KGB
Boris N. Distanov, Foreign Minister
Leonid F. Shurygin, Secretary for Defense Affairs
Pavel N. Travkin, Chief of the General Staff
Sergei S. Zabotin, Chief of the Military-Industrial Commission

Secretary Boyarkin opened the meeting with a report on the political situation vis-à-vis Israel, Syria and the United States. Minister Kotsarev presented a report on military preparedness with regard to the alert. There was no discussion.

Secretary Boyarkin stated that the Israeli government had summarily rejected his cease-fire proposal but had shown some interest in the American one, provided certain guarantees were provided by Syria.

Chairman Gresko asked what these guarantees were. Minister Distanov stated that they were not specified in the note.

Marshal Travkin asked what the response to the American proposal was to be, given the Israeli interest in it.

Secretary Boyarkin explained that it was only necessary to say to the United States that the matter of the cease-fire should be explored further. In the meantime, the attritional attacks launched against the Israelis on the seventeenth would continue to wear down the Zionist forces until Jerusalem was ready to sue for peace on any terms. Also, that the United States would not begin a general war simply to protect Israel from such a defeat, as long as the country itself was not invaded. To deter Israel from using atomic weapons again, Secretary Boyarkin stated that ten nuclear devices with their delivery vehicles should be airlifted from the Rostov logistics center early on August twentieth, and that Israel should be informed of their presence once they were deployed.

Several members spoke at once. Then Chairman Gresko asked what would be done if the Israelis, rather than suing for peace, launched an attack with their nuclear armament.

Secretary Boyarkin responded that the Americans would prevent the Israelis from doing so, since this would risk general war. But if they did carry out such an attack, the Americans would back down from a full-scale confrontation, since it was pointless for them to destroy their own country merely to save Israel. And that Russian troops had the right to defend themselves by any means available should such an attack occur.

Minister Kotsarev asked whether the secretary had read any of the last two months' strategic analyses regarding American determination to prevent the Soviet Union's extension of control farther into the Middle East.

Secretary Boyarkin responded that he had, and that the analyses were inaccurate and timid.

Minister Kotsarev asked how the secretary had reached that conclusion. The minister made a reference to the reading of tea leaves.

Secretary Boyarkin stated that military officers who feared confrontation with the enemy should consider resignation before it was forced upon them. The secretary made reference to the commissar system of Stalin, under which recalcitrant officers were summarily disposed of.

Chairman Gresko stated that he hoped those days had been left behind.

Secretary Boyarkin said that the point of the meeting had been lost, and that he wished the Council to decide on the dispatch of nuclear weapons to Syria, where they would be retained under Soviet control, not to be used without endorsement by a quorum of the Politburo.

A vote was called. In favor of the motion: Boyarkin, Morosov, Distanov, Shurygin, Travkin, Zabotin. Opposed: Gresko, Kotsarev.

The motion was declared carried. Adjournment was at 11:15 A.M., August eighteenth.

Gorky Park
6:40 P.M., August 18

THEY WERE SITTING at a white-painted iron table. On the table were two half-filled glasses and a bottle of Mukuzani red wine. The table belonged to an outdoor cafe next to one of the model-boat ponds in the park. Thorne watched a small blond boy place a wooden sailboat in the water and point its bow to the pond's opposite rim. There was no wind, and the boat's sails hung limply. The boy's father knelt beside him and they both blew on the sails. The boat, reluctantly, moved a meter-and-a-half and stopped. The father reeled it in. The child's face was desolate.

"There'll be a wind soon," said Andreyev. "When it's cooler."

"Good," said Thorne. "No one likes being becalmed."

The boy's father was holding up a wetted finger, testing for a breeze. There was none. It was still quite hot. The boy sat down on the grass next to his father and began adjusting the boat's rigging.

"What do your people say?" asked Andreyev.

"That they won't give in to Boyarkin's cease-fire proposal. And that the Israelis will be controlled." Thorne thought momentarily about the afternoon's communication from Washington. He hoped that Harper was still his control, rather than Northrop. He did not trust the deputy director for operations. The messages he received from home, via Joscelyn, who was still at the embassy, did not indicate who had originated them. "Also that our own hawks are still unpopular with the president."

The boy put the sailboat back into the water. It still did not move.

"Hawks," said Andreyev. "That's a good way of putting
. The rest means nothing very much."

Thorne refilled their glasses from the bottle. "What have
ou for us?"

Andreyev frowned. "You won't like it." He covered his
nouth with his hand, as though he were coughing. "The
ecretary has ordered that nuclear weapons be moved to Syria.
On the twentieth, the day after tomorrow."

Thorne stared at the boy, who was pulling the sailboat
ack to shore by a string attached to its mast, and then at
Andreyev. "Dear God," he said. "Why?"

"I think, from what I've been told, that he doesn't think
ou'll go to war."

"We can't not go to war."

"Do you want me to tell my control that?"

"No," said Thorne. "I said it. It's not policy."

"It won't matter anyway," said Andreyev. "He'll be gone
by then."

"This is madness," Thorne said. "Both sides."

"Yes."

A breath of cooler air moved past Thorne's cheek, a faint
breeze.

"It'll go now," said Thorne, meaning the sailboat. The
child and his father were still fiddling with the sails. "They want
to know exactly when your move is beginning, so no misunderstandings will occur."

"Tomorrow you'll be told. Two hours ahead of the start
time. That has to be enough."

"All right."

Andreyev looked up the path that led to the scatter of white
tables. "The brothers are here."

Two KGB men were walking along the path to the outdoor café.

"We don't have a lot of time left," said Andreyev. "It's as
well it's tomorrow."

Thorne nodded. The sails of the toy boat had finally
caught the breeze, and the blond child was trotting around the
pond to meet it at the other side.

Moscow
August 19

"I WONDER," SHE SAID, "how much more tense it can get before somebody's nerve breaks."

Thorne was looking out their office window at the late afternoon skyline of Moscow. "I don't know," he said.

"Being in the middle of a major target doesn't help one's attention span, does it?"

Thorne turned from the office window and sat on the edge of the desk. Joscelyn put her hand on his arm. "I'm sorry," she said. "It's more dangerous for you."

He covered her hand with his. "At least I have things to do," he said. "You have to sit and worry."

"My social life isn't what it was, that's true."

Thorne nodded. They had kept contacts with regular embassy staff to a minimum. They were resented as intruders, particularly by the CIA station chief, who was infuriated by the priority they had on his communications equipment. He also disliked Thorne's contact with an unidentified Russian agent, fearing that Thorne's activities might endanger his own, which were not very secure to begin with. The KGB crackdown since Leschenko's death had dried up or otherwise disposed of a number of his sources.

"If they manage to succeed...." Thorne's voice trailed off.

She bit her lower lip and said "What time is it? I left my watch in my room."

"Five minutes past five."

Communications from Washington normally arrived at 5:15 each afternoon. "Damn," said Thorne. "I hope they give me something solid to tell Nikolai. Our promises have been so vague."

"What could they expect? The Russians, I mean. A signed protocol?"

"This has happened so God-damned fast," Thorne said. 'Two weeks ago the world was in its normal state of chaos. Now we're staring World War Three in the eye. Not the limited kind, either. The go-for-broke. Why do we *do* these things to ourselves?"

"I don't know," she said. "It doesn't make any sense."

"It's like 1914," said Thorne. He was biting at a thumbnail. 'The wrong combination of circumstances. . . . You can't risk the chance that the other side will move first. Once we both take that to its logical conclusion – "

A faint chime came from inside the desk. "It's early," said Joscelyn. She unlocked the desk, pulled up the mini-terminal and tapped briefly on its keyboard. Several dozen code groups appeared on the screen. She frowned. "It's very short." She keyed in the decode sequence. The screen went blank and then displayed its message:

MARK ONE AUTHORIZES OPTION FOUR.
CONFIRM.

She closed her eyes for a moment. Then she opened them and typed.

UNDERSTOOD

The screen responded.

PREPARE BACKGROUND AND REPORT INITIALIZATION TIME AS SOON AS KNOWN, EXECUTE/ABORT INSTRUCTIONS WILL BE GIVEN AT THAT POINT, THIS CHANNEL LOCKED OPEN TO MARK ONE.
CONFIRM.

Joscelyn rubbed her cheekbones with her fingertips and typed.

UNDERSTOOD.

The screen cleared itself to a dull amber.

"What the hell's that all about?" asked Thorne. He had come around to stand behind her. "Joscelyn."

She had put her hands over her face. "Damn, damn, *damn*," she said, her voice muffled.

"What's going on, Joscelyn?"

She took her hands away from her face as he went around to the front of the desk. "I can't tell you," she said dully.

"For Chist's sake, Joscelyn," he said for the third time, feeling stupid at the repetition. "I have to be out there in two hours. *I have to know what's going on.*"

She was silent. Thorne went cold as understanding swept over him. He couldn't understand how he had overlooked it. "It isn't a communications link, is it?" he said. "It's RUBICON ONE. They decided to use it. You've known all along."

She nodded, not looking at him.

"Why didn't Harper tell me?"

"They didn't want you to know enough to blow the operation if you were picked up. I had to know in case we lost communications with the coup."

"They took a risk. I might have guessed earlier than this."

"They thought you wouldn't, I guess."

"Option Four," said Thorne. "That's the Heydrich option, isn't it?"

"I don't understand."

"Heydrich," said Thorne. "Head of the Nazi SD. In 1938 he planted false information on Stalin that the Soviet Army was going to overthrow him. Stalin exterminated the officer corps. When the Germans invaded all the experienced Russian commanders were dead." He smiled at her without humor. "It was brilliant. So we've decided to try a rerun. They're not after Boyarkin at all. They want the Russian officer corps."

"But they *do* want Boyarkin." Her voice was strained. "They want us to inform the KGB of the plot, but not soon enough to save Boyarkin. They want both him and the officers out of the way. They think the KGB will survive, and then purge the officers, if Morosov knows at the right time."

"But they'll settle for either Boyarkin or the officers if they can't have both. That's why Harper didn't push the GRU for their exact plans. He didn't care. He just wanted to know when they were going to start. To the minute."

She nodded, face cradled in her hands, staring at the desk top. The amber terminal screen reflected delicately on the surfaces of her fingernails.

"Damn you," he said. "You and Harper and Northrop. You've been playing me like a fish on a line. Ever since July. That wasn't an accidental meeting at Langley, was it? And you were following orders when you came to the lake. You set it up so I'd get involved with you again. So if you were sent to Moscow I'd agree to be the other part of the link."

"Please, David. It wasn't like that. I –"

He was at the door now. "I don't suppose it occurred to you that if they go through with it the KGB will kill Nikolai. And a lot of other people. All right. I'll bring back the start time and see what they want us to do. But I don't God damned well promise I'll do it."

The door slammed behind him.

Joscelyn stared at the terminal screen for some time after he left, trying to feel innocent and wronged. She could not.

"This is exceedingly interesting," said Morosov. He leaned back in his chair and surveyed his great desk with its colored telephones. From this desk, in minutes, he could reach any of the sources of political power in Moscow, or any regional headquarters of the KGB in the Soviet Union, or any of the overseas stations tucked away in the corners of Russian embassies. The thought usually made him feel secure and comfortable, but today there was a niggling worry at the back of his mind.

He sat forward and tapped the two dossiers. Lieutenant-General Pryakhin, chief of the Second Directorate, looked at him expectantly. Morosov's stomach growled; it was nearing suppertime.

"Thorne," said Morosov. The top dossier concerned the American; the KGB had hastily accumulated it from various American sources since the man arrived in Moscow. "He was a CIA employee. Computers and political-military modeling.

Ex-field agent. What did he have to do with security of the embassy sort? Did he learn it after he left the CIA?"

"We haven't yet been able to find that out for certain," Pryakhin said. "But it doesn't look as though he did. If his position at the embassy is computer security, though, he may have trained in it at Langley five years ago."

"Like the woman." Morosov pushed Thorne's dossier aside and opened Joscelyn's. "They worked in the same place. Now she arrives here and so does he shortly afterwards. But she's never been seen outside the embassy. Not even for sight-seeing. You would think that she and Thorne, being old acquaintances, would have done some of that together."

"They were more than old acquaintances," Pryakhin reminded him.

"Yes. That makes it even more peculiar. Unless they aren't speaking to each other any more because of that. Or something along those lines."

"It's possible, but unlikely. Even the Americans would be more sensible than to make a posting like that."

"And he's been seeing a lot of this GRU field man–"

"Andreyev," supplied Pryakhin.

"Who's his control?"

"Someone's running Andreyev out of the GSHQ out on the Ring. It might be Vakula. He was aware of the operation."

"The control is highly placed, then."

"Yes."

"There's no sign the GRU was working on Thorne before he left the United States?"

"They've given us information about the approaches made to him back there. But it hasn't been independently corroborated."

"The whole thing is too pat," said Morosov. "There's very rotten fish here somewhere." He tapped a sheet of paper lying beside Thorne's dossier. "And your contact in GRU says that Andreyev's control is worried that Andreyev has been turned by Thorne. Unlikely, but possible. . . ." He thought for a moment and said, "This may be precisely what we're looking for to hang Yushenko and his . . . never mind who." Moroso smiled toothily. "Success in this wouldn't do your career any harm, either, general." The smile faded. "What's the mood in the streets?"

"They are upset. The secretary's, ah, cleansing operations have disturbed some of the more timid. But what they are worried about now is the Americans."

"Good," said Morosov. "At the moment it's better to keep their attention focused on an outside threat; it binds them closer to the new regime." He picked up a pen and tapped his front teeth with it. "Although we have to be careful with them. The masses so easily fail to recognize their true needs. Speaking of which, are you ready for Suvorov tonight?"

"Completely, chairman." Pryakhin wondered why Morosov had digressed.

Morosov regarded him intently. "If Thorne and Andreyev are indeed playing games, and we can find that out before Suvorov begins, then tonight would be an ideal time to arrest Yushenko. Our actions would be considered part of the security exercise until the last moment."

"Ah," said Pryakhin. "Very ingenious, chairman." Actually he was thinking that Morosov was an idiot. Arresting Yushenko at general staff HQ would be politically unwise; better to do it far more quietly. However, if ordered, it would be done. Most of the senior KGB were not impressed with Chairman Morosov's competence. That, of course, was why Boyarkin had given him the post. Morosov as head of the KGB was no rival.

"I'm glad you think so," said Morosov. "For the moment, don't touch Andreyev. If it turns out that they have really recruited Thorne, we'll simply take him over and let the GRU go whistle. If the reverse is true, we'll deal with the whole mob as soon as Yushenko's detained. I want you to collect Thorne as soon as he's outside again, which might be this evening, right?"

Pryakhin nodded.

"Take him before he reaches Andreyev. We haven't much time. Bring him to the Lubianka and call me immediately. I'll want to talk to him myself."

"Yes, chairman."

"Go do it."

The lieutenant-general was halfway to the door when Morosov said, "One other thing. The woman, Petrie. Bring her in, too. Get her out of the embassy somehow. If something's going on, she may be involved. And Thorne will tell us faster if he knows we have her."

"The embassy will object when they find out."

"Let them. At the moment the Americans have more on their plate than these two. And we can always make up a reason for collecting them, if we have to." He grinned ferociously. "It may not be necessary."

I have to stop feeling so sick about this, Thorne told himself as he left the Park Kultury Metro station and hurried under the traffic causeway towards the Krymsky Bridge. The evening sun lit the facades of Moscow to a pinkish glow, luminous against the cloud-darkened southern sky. There would be rain by nightfall. Off to Thorne's right the wedding-cake spire of the Moscow University tower thrust into the slate-colored masses of the oncoming thunderstorm.

Damn, I should have remembered my raincoat, he thought. And then: I should have talked to her before I left. But this. How could she have done it? I thought I knew her better than that.

Maybe she was trying to tell you when you slammed out of the office.

But you were in your room for two hours before you left and she didn't come.

Well, why would she, after that?

Shit, Thorne swore at himself. Leave it. You've got work to do. Meet Nikolai, get the time, get back, tell Washington, maybe I can persuade them to drop the Heydrich option at least and. . . .

He was nearing the approaches to the bridge. Traffic was light, as usual in Moscow. A nondescript gray car passed him slowly, very near the curb, and stopped ten feet farther on. A man in civilian clothes got out and walked towards Thorne. Thorne felt his sphincter loosen and altered his direction slightly to pass the man. The man cut him off, stopped and said.

"May I see your papers, please?" Thorne took his embassy documentation out of his jacket.

"Who are you?" he said in Russian.

"State security. May I see them, please?"

Thorne suppressed a useless urge to run and handed them over. The security man flipped through the pages and nodded. "You're Dr. David Thorne? American?"

"That's what it says," said Thorne. "May I have them back? I want to get home before it rains."

The policeman nodded and put the documents in his own pocket. The driver had stepped out of the car and was leaning, but not idly, against the near front fender. "Would you please get in," the first man said, gesturing at the open rear door. "Your papers are not in order and they must be seen to immediately."

"My papers are in order," said Thorne, not moving. The driver straightened up.

The first man, without warning, hit Thorne hard in the solar plexus. Thorne doubled over, gasping. He felt himself thrust into the car onto the gray plastic seat, hard against its occupant, who dragged him all the way in. The door slammed and the vehicle accelerated quickly.

When he could sit up, the first security man was watching him closely. Something hard was jammed into Thorne's ribs. He did not need to look down to know that it was the barrel of a gun.

Several hundred feet behind the car, Andreyev, who had followed Thorne from the Metro station, had already turned on his heel and was walking unhurriedly away.

Joscelyn was back in the office, doing nothing, when the telephone rang. She snatched it up. A voice she did not recognize said, "This is your friend's friend. He hasn't arrived. I can't wait much longer. Please be at the Pushkin Monument in thirty minutes. Carry a scarf in your right hand."

"What –" said Joscelyn, into an empty line.

She took the precaution of telling the CIA duty officer where she was going, although not why, and that she expected to be back within two hours. If she wasn't, he should inform the station chief, who should inform the director of central intelligence using any priority he had to. The duty officer raised his eyebrows but agreed.

Five minutes later she was on her way. She hadn't a scarf, but had managed to borrow a yellow handkerchief. As she passed through the embassy gates she looked unobtrusively around her; the usual KGB loiterers were present, but as she crossed Tchaikovsky Street to the bus stop no one appeared to be following her. She waited, disciplining herself not to pace up and down, while a bus approached. The air was thick with humidity; off to the southeast a line of thunderheads was approaching.

The bus took her north to Vostanniye Square and its hulking Stalinesque apartment complex, where she got off; still there were no obvious followers. She walked along Barrikadnaya Street to the Metro station and waited impatiently for the escalator to deliver her to the platform. By the clock suspended from the tiled roof she had no more than fifteen minutes to reach Pushkin Square.

At least I don't have to brush off any tails, she thought. Even if I knew how to do it properly I don't have time. David. Oh, David, if only they haven't caught you. This was madness from the beginning. Perhaps Andreyev will know where you are, maybe I can find a way to get you out. Diplomatic immunity. But what I'm about to do is betray Andreyev to the KGB.

The train roared in. She squeezed into the car ahead of a pair of young men in ill-cut Russian jeans. They looked at her appreciatively. She went and stood at the other end of the car.

The ride to Pushkin Square Station was both too long and too short. At the station, the escalator to ground level was closed down for repairs. Joscelyn hurried up the stairs. At the top she was out of breath. She had five minutes.

If they do have David I'll have to carry his end of the operation as well as my own, she thought. If I can, if I will. Was David right? He likes Andreyev; Andreyev is a decent man. Would David go ahead with it, what did he call it, the Heydrich option? What would that make us?

She crossed Strastnoi Boulevard; the statue of Pushkin stood somberly in its park in the leveling light. She took the yellow handkerchief out of her purse, patted her damp forehead with it and walked slowly towards the statue.

She reached the base of the statue and turned. The two youths from the train were twenty meters behind her. Fear rose in her.

Two more men rounded the statue's base. These were middle-aged, thick looking. They took her by the upper arms and dragged her towards a car that drew up at the curb. She struggled uselessly. At the car one of them pulled the yellow handkerchief out of her hand and threw it away. The square of bright cloth floated to the pavement, hesitated, then fluttered away in the strengthening southeast wind like a startled bird.

Andreyev reached the GHQ building at a few minutes before nine. In normal times the offices and corridors were quiet at this hour, but since the beginning of the mideast crisis it seemed that they were busier by night than by day. There were officers everywhere, all wearing tense expressions.

He reached Vakula's office and knocked.

"Come in."

Andreyev closed the door behind him and said, "The KGB has Thorne."

Vakula sat up straight. "You know this for certain?"

"I saw them pick him up at the Krymsky Bridge."

Vakula picked up the telephone. "Get me General Yushenko," he said into it. "Yes, I know he's in the Crisis Center. Get him anyway." He waited. "General Yushenko. I apologize for disturbing you. We have lost a very important communications link. Yes, that one. Yes, general, right away." He put the receiver down and stood up hurriedly. "Come with me."

Moments later they were in Yushenko's office. The GRU chief was already there. "Marshal Travkin and the minister are coming," he said. "What happened?"

Vakula told him. Andreyev, uncomfortable and nervous, stood beside the door.

"Shit," said Yushenko as Travkin and Kotsarev entered. "It wasn't –"

"What's going on?" asked Kotsarev.

Vakula repeated what he had told Yushenko.

"This is a balls-up," said Kotsarev. "When did it happen?"

"Major Andreyev?" said Vakula.

"Thirty-five minutes ago."

"They won't have it out of him yet," said Yushenko. "Not if they're unsure what they're after."

"Suvorov is supposed to be signaled at eleven o'clock," said Kotsarev to Travkin. "We were going to start at ten-thirty. Can we move that up an hour?"

Travkin's eyebrows drew together. "That's a lot of lead time. The half-hour advance was intended to catch the MVD and KGB in transit, without enough time for Dzerzhinsky Square to change the orders. Morosov's people will be calling to know what's going on. We can't stall them for ninety minutes."

"You'll have to tell them they have an incorrect copy of the Suvorov timetable," said Kotsarev. "Confuse them just long enough to get troops to Dzerzhinsky Square. We have to get the American out alive. He's our only link at the right level."

"What *about* the Americans?" asked Travkin. "We're risking a lot if they don't know what's happening. It will look extremely suspicious."

"We have to risk it," said Kotsarev. He was very tired. The strain of the alert and the mobilization coupled with the Suvorov exercise was draining him. Travkin's face was pinched and worn; only Yushenko looked relaxed and unconcerned. "We've dealt fairly with them until now and they'll have to take us on faith," Kotsarev went on. "As soon as we recover the American we'll re-establish contact. Marshal Travkin, call Colonel Dushkin immediately and give him the revised Suvorov orders. I will call Chairman Gresko and tell him to come here immediately. Major Andreyev."

Andreyev straightened to attention. "Yes, sir."

"Join Dushkin's troops when they reach Dzerzhinsky

Square. Find Dushkin. Tell him the American has to be brought out alive. Make sure he is."

"Yes, sir."

Kotsarev turned to Yushenko. "You're sure Deputy Minister Zhigalin's at home right now?"

"Positive, minister."

"Good. The deputy minister will get a surprise in a few hours, with any luck. We may need a new KGB chairman before midnight."

COLONEL DUSHKIN WAS WAITING by his telephone. He had received one earlier call, at 9:15, during which an anonymous staff voice had told him to be ready to start Suvorov on a moment's notice. Dushkin was confident. He had, as ordered, not informed his subordinates of the exercise, but had taken a number of unofficial precautions to ensure that his part ran smoothly. The alert helped, anyway; all ranks except senior commanders were confined to the regiment's base on the northwest edge of Moscow, and all leaves had been cancelled.

The telephone rang. Dushkin grabbed it up and said, "Dushkin here."

The voice at the other end was familiar from the Kirov exercises. Dushkin felt a momentary surprise that the chief of the general staff was handling Suvorov, but he listened carefully.

"Colonel Dushkin. I have urgent news for you. Suvorov has been put forward. We have received information that elements of the KGB are planning to arrest the Politburo and assume direct control of the government and the army. General Secretary Boyarkin has ordered the army to suppress this. I want you to immediately arrest your regimental political officers and hold them incommunicado; we don't know whether they're involved or not. Then send two companies of your First Battalion to secure KGB headquarters in Dzerzhinsky Square. You go with them. That's the most important objective. The Third Battalion is to occupy the First Directorate building on the Ring. The Second Battalion will surround the Ninth Directorate barracks in Beskudnikovo District and disarm the troops there. Two companies of the Third Battalion are to secure the radio and television stations; the third company will deal with the telephone exchange. Take no orders except from myself or Minister Kotsarev. You have the command frequency. Very important: there is one officer, Major Nikolai Andreyev of the GRU, who is to join you at Dzerzhinsky Square. He will be at the Metro station entrance, bearing a signed note from me. He is to remove one particular prisoner from the Lubianka. You will assist him as required. Do you have all that?"

Dushkin was scribbling furiously. "Yes, marshal."

"You must be on the move before 10:00 P.M. Call me as soon as you are ready to go."

"Yes, marshal," Dushkin said into a dead telephone. He passed his hand briefly over his eyes and rang for his executive officer.

Travkin put the telephone down. "He's moving."

"Good," said Kotsarev. "So is Minister Gresko." He picked up the telephone and dialed. "Chairman Morosov, please." He listened momentarily, said, "I'll call there," and hung up. "Dear Aleksandr is at Dzerzhinsky Square. Shit. I wanted to collect him at home. The secretary's still at the Kremlin?"

Boyarkin had taken up residence in Stalin's old apartments earlier in the summer, rather than live like the rest of the Politburo in relatively vulnerable comfort.

"Yes," said Yushenko. "He called me in the Crisis Center not an hour ago. The call was put through the Kremlin exchange."

"Fine," said Kotsarev. "Major Andreyev, on your way. General Yushenko, have GRU security arrest all GLAVPUR personnel in the building. Marshal Travkin will start phoning the local division commanders and have them arrest their political cadres. Colonel Vakula, take your unit and pick up Boyarkin. If you can't get him back here for any reason, shoot him."

They had taken his watch away, with his clothes. He thought it was about an hour since his arrest, but it could have been less. He had been sitting strapped to the chair in the pitch dark for some time and it had distorted his sense of time.

He was frightened, very frightened. He had known in the abstract that this could happen, but the knowledge had not prepared him for the reality.

The reality was quite different.

He tugged against the straps, knowing it was pointless, and waited some more.

The door behind him rattled and the overhead light went on. Thorne saw that the room contained a wooden table with three chairs behind it. There was an ashtray on the table. Next to Thorne's chair was another one, also with straps. With a chill of apprehension he saw that there was a rubber groundsheet under the other chair. He looked down. His chair sat on one as well.

Tidy, he thought dazedly. Tidy. But they couldn't be going that far. They couldn't afford the diplomatic row. It's just to frighten me.

Three men he did not recognize walked around his chair and looked at him. One was short, chunky, with prominent jowls and faded blue eyes. His hair was cut very short and he wore a well-tailored suit. The second was tall, with black hair combed straight back and a seamed face. His tunic bore a lieutenant-general's twin stars. The third was utterly nondescript except for a large mole on the right lobe of his chin. His insignia proclaimed him a major. Thorne mentally christened them Jowls, the General and Mole.

"What do you mean by this?" asked the General of Mole. "Get his clothes back immediately."

Mole twitched his shoulders apologetically. "General, they've been taken to the depository for registration. I –"

"Get him a blanket then. And undo the straps."

Mole loosened the buckles and then got a greenish-gray army blanket from a small metal trolley by the door. The trolley was draped in another blanket. Thorne took the rough cloth and covered himself.

"I hope you're not cold," said the General. Jowls was watching Thorne expressionlessly.

"Not now," said Thorne. "I want to place a telephone call to my embassy immediately. All my papers were in order."

Jowls and the General sat down. Thorne sensed Mole standing just behind him and to the right.

"You speak excellent Russian, Dr. Thorne. One might think you were a Leningrader."

"Thank you. Return my clothes and papers and take me to a telephone."

"Your papers were in order, in fact," said the General. "That was not the problem, whatever you were told. The problem is your connection with a GRU major named Nikolai Andreyev. You don't deny you know him?"

"I know him," said Thorne.

"I would like you to tell me the substance of your conversations with him."

"Why don't you ask the GRU?"

"They have indicated that Andreyev was recruiting you, because of your position at the embassy."

"That's right."

"Then there should be no difficulty sharing whatever information you gave him with us. We are, after all, on the same side."

Jowls spoke for the first time. "There is some suspicion that you were recruiting Andreyev, rather than the other way around." His voice was low and rasping.

The General frowned slightly, as though Jowls were intruding, but he did not comment. Thorne had begun to sort out the heirarchy. The General was in charge of the interrogation. He was the "soft" one, who would try to gain Thorne's trust by protecting him against Mole, the thug. Jowls outranked them both, if he dared break in upon the meticulous structure of an interrogation.

"This is an extremely serious matter," said the General. "So serious, in fact, that KGB Chairman Morosov had decided to join our discussion." He gestured at Jowls.

That shook Thorne badly. If Morosov were here, they meant business. The rubber groundsheets suddenly seemed less pointless. "I'm honored," he said with a dry mouth. Morosov inclined his head slightly.

"Were you eliciting information from Major Andreyev?"

"No. I was passing it to him. I –"

"When were you recruited?"

"In Washington. Two years ago." Thank God he was word-perfect at his cover. But it was not deep enough to stand up for more than a few hours. Two, perhaps three. They would trip him up by that time. What time was it? When was the army going to move?

"By whom?"

"I didn't know his name. But I think he was your military intelligence, not KGB."

"How do you know?"

"Because I'm here and not at GRU headquarters."

Morosov laughed with a snort. Mole shifted uncomfortably in Thorne's peripheral vision.

"Quite so," the General said equably. "What led you to cooperate?"

"The CIA kicked me out. I didn't feel I deserved it."

"Why did they do that?"

"Somebody who had friends up top was after my job. They shuffled me off to a junior post in the state department. That's how I got into embassy security."

"That is a lot of pigswill, Dr. Thorne. After you left the CIA – for whatever reason – you went to live in New Hampshire. You have published two books on military history since then. You have not been near the state department."

So much for that cover, Thorne reflected bitterly. But it wasn't intended to stand up to this sort of scrutiny. Somebody at state's working for the KGB. Harper will want to know – unless Harper has thrown me to the KGB as part of RUBICON ONE. Unless Harper wanted me to blow the GRU this way.

Fuck them, Thorne told himself. I might have done what they wanted. Betray Nikolai. But not if this is how they're going to do it. I can hold out until midnight, or one o'clock. Surely the GRU and the army will have moved by then.

Joscelyn? Did she know Harper was going to do this? If he has done it?

Something of his thoughts must have shown in his face. "Well, Dr. Thorne?" asked the General with a trace of amusement.

"Your information's wrong. You'd better check your sources."

Morosov grunted impatiently and said, "We don't have a lot of time, Pryakhin."

General Pryakhin sighed. He nodded at Mole. Thorne heard the door open and close.

"Dr. Thorne, the CIA would never let a man they had kicked out work in embassy security. The risks would be far too great. You have been doing something else. What is it?"

"Perhaps you should ask the GRU. I'm their property, not yours."

"We cannot allow you to go in these circles indefinitely."

There didn't seem to be an answer to that, so Thorne shrugged. His feet were like ice.

Morosov folded his arms over his chest. One sleeve rode up, exposing his watch. Thorne's eyes shot to it and then away. It was ten o'clock.

Pryakhin was smiling at him indulgently. "So it's time-sensitive, whatever it is, eh, Dr. Thorne? Why should you be so interested in the time?"

He can't know that much, Thorne reminded himself. "Wouldn't you be if you were in my position? You've kept me disoriented. Now I know how long I've been here. When I get back to the embassy every minute is going to cost you people. A lot."

The door opened and closed. Two pairs of footsteps approached. Thorne didn't turn around.

One pair stopped behind Thorne. The other continued and halted on his left.

"Sit down, please," said Pryakhin.

"David," said Joscelyn.

It had begun to rain. The streets were deserted. Andreyev waited at the Dzerzhinsky Square Metro station across from the Lubianka. Although the building was no longer the head-quarters of the overseas espionage and intelligence service, the

First Directorate, it was still the seat of the chairman of the KGB, and its cellars were still in use. The more so now, with Boyarkin as secretary.

Andreyev thought of Thorne in there and shivered slightly, perhaps from the chill of the rain. A pair of MVD men walked slowly along the side of the square, by the Lubianka's pale facade – mustard-yellow in daylight – and disappeared behind the statue of Felix Dzerzhinsky.

From the north, almost blown away by the southerly wind, there was a grumble of heavy engines punctuated by squeaks and clatters. Tracked military vehicles. The sound disappeared in the rain's hiss.

They've been able to start, at least, thought Andreyev. We might actually make it work.

The MVD men reappeared from behind the monument, walking unconcernedly. They hadn't heard the vehicles. Andreyev reminded himself that Suvorov itself was legal, although an army unit overruning the Lubianka would destroy that cover quite thoroughly.

The sound came again; it did not fade but grew louder. The MVD men stopped, listening.

Masked headlights up Dzerzhinsky Street, moving towards the square. Andreyev watched several of the lights swing away into a side street. They were surrounding the Lubianka block.

The roar and clatter and squeak was louder now. Two KGB guards had left the Lubianka's entrance and were peering through the rain towards the noise. One of them called something to the MVD men; Andreyev couldn't hear what. The MVD didn't respond.

The lead vehicle rolled into the square and swung around the statue towards Andreyev. It was a BMD air-portable troop carrier. Several others followed it. The squat shapes of a pair of ASU-85 assault guns, their hulls glinting wetly in the diffused glow of the streetlights, rumbled past the BMDs, swiveled on their tracks and stopped with their guns pointing at the Lubianka's facade. Troops began to pour out of the BMDs and to form into squads. In several of the Lubianka's lighted windows, silhouettes of men appeared.

A tall figure dismounted from the lead BMD and strode towards Andreyev. The man wore a military rain cape. Beads of water hung from the peak of his cap.

"Major Andreyev?"

"Yes."

"I am Colonel Dushkin. May I see your identification?"

Andreyev handed him Travkin's note. The colonel tilted it to catch the reddish light from the Metro sign. Drops of rain splattered on the paper; the ink began to run.

"Good," said Dushkin and handed the note back. Andreyev tore it into squares and scattered them on the pavement. "Come with me," Dushkin said.

At the BMD the driver passed the colonel a headset and microphone on a long cord. Dushkin spoke briefly into the command net. Then he nodded to Andreyev. "Stay by me. We'll find your man when the building's secured."

"Can you do the cellars quickly?" asked Andreyev. "He's likely down there."

"Accordingly to plan," said Dushkin briefly. He got up onto the deck of the BMD and waved his arm at the Lubianka. The troops shook out into a skirmish line and began to move forward. There were four KGB troopers at the front door now. The MVD men were standing off to their right.

Another man came out and stood behind the guards: an officer. "What's going on?" he called.

Dushkin blew a whistle. The line of men broke into a trot. The KGB guards unslung their weapons and levelled them. Someone fired a shot and the KGB officer collapsed. The guards began shooting; muzzle flashes lit up the square. Return fire knocked them against the doors. The MVD men fled, only to be shot down within three meters. Dushkin's paratroops reached the doors and began to pour inside. More firing, this time from the interior of the building, then a dull boom. Andreyev could hear the crackle of automatic weapons from the rear of the Lubianka. The paratroopers were closing the ring.

"Look," said Pryakhin. "Miss Petrie, I believe you know something about Dr. Thorne's activities. All we want to know is what he was doing with a Major Andreyev of the GRU. Once we know that, you can both go. By morning, at the latest."

Joscelyn had not uttered a word since sitting down. She did not do so now.

Mole walked around her chair, grabbed her blouse at the collar, and wrenched. The light fabric tore away from from her shoulders. She yelped with pain and Mole struck her across the mouth. Her head jerked under the blow. Pryakhin watched Thorne. "Was she your link to Washington?" he asked.

Thorne's bare feet were resting on the concrete floor. The floor had been vibrating minutely for the past two or three minutes. The others, shod, did not appear to have noticed. "We have nothing to do with each other," he said.

"I am losing patience," said Morosov, to Pryakhin rather than Thorne or Joscelyn. Pryakhin shrugged and nodded to Mole, who went to the cart beside the door and brought it into the middle of the room. He stopped next to Thorne.

"Miss Petrie," said Pryakhin. "You've probably heard all sorts of stories about the things that happen in these cellars. They are all true."

Mole pulled the blanket off Thorne and tightened the straps that held his arms and legs to the chair. Another belt went around his waist. "We normally carry out interrogations over a considerable period, to avoid damage to the subject," Pryakhin went on. "However, we are occasionally pressed for time, and have to disregard physical safety. Or mental. We're fortunate in having the two of you, for reasons I'm sure you can guess. I'm going to make you responsible for Dr. Thorne's health. We know, by the way, that you speak fairly good Russian, so pretended ignorance is no escape. Now if you don't speak fairly quickly, we will reverse positions and apply the technique to you. I don't think you have been trained to withstand that degree of agony. So remember that you will talk to us sooner or later. Do so now and you'll both be able to leave."

Thorne looked at Joscelyn. She looked back distractedly. Her lower lip was bleeding.

"She doesn't know anything about this," he said. "And you're out of your minds if you think I'll talk while she's here."

"Still holding the cover," said Pryakhin. To Mole: "Clip him up."

Mole took the blanket off the cart. On it was a gray metal box with an electrical cord at one end; at the other were a pair of wires to which were attached large alligator clips. The top of the box bore a dial and two toggle switches.

I could get out of this, Thorne told himself. Give them Nikolai and the GRU. Joscelyn might get off scot-free. A labor camp for me, ten, fifteen years. But not dead.

If Nikolai's people haven't come by midnight, I'll give them to Pryakhin. Bit by bit. If I can last till midnight I might make it to one o'clock. Give them a little at a time.

Joscelyn could get us out, too. But I don't want her to. This is what Pryakhin wants us to think. Oh, he's clever. Make each one responsible for the other; try to break down our bonding.

"There are two clips," Pryakhin was saying to Joscelyn. "With males, one is attached to the tip of the penis, the other to the scrotum. An electric current is passed between the clips, through the body tissues. The strength of the current can be varied to produce any effect between a tickle and a convulsion." He paused. "With females, of course, one of the clips is replaced by a probe."

Joscelyn closed her eyes. Mole unraveled the two wires. A knock at the door.

"Who is it?" asked Pryakhin.

A KGB officer stuck his head into the room. "Chairman, your pardon, but there are army troops outside. Paratroops in BMDs. They've dismounted."

"Suvorov," said Morosov. He looked at his watch and frowned. "We haven't started yet."

"No," said the officer. "It's half an hour still."

"What the devil," said Morosov. "They must have begun an hour ago to be here now. I'd better call staff HQ." He looked at Joscelyn. His lips were loose and damp. "Don't go on until I come back." He left the room with the officer.

"Do as he said," Pryakhin told Mole. Mole put the wires and clips back on the cart. "This is temporary," said Pryakhin. "But it will give you time to think."

Silence descended. Pryakhin brushed lint off his tunic. Mole hovered.

A faint rattling seeped through the thick door. Pryakhin straightened. The rattling came again, still muffled but much louder. Assault rifles on full automatic.

Pryakhin ran for the door, Mole after him. A dull boom reverberated through the walls. The two KGB men shot into the corridor. The door slammed behind them and clicked.

"The ground floor's secure," said Dushkin to Andreyev. "Let's go in."

They trotted across the wet pavement, stepped over the bodies at the door and went inside. The walls were bullet-pocked and there was shattered plaster on the floor. Gunsmoke hazed the air. Dushkin and Andreyev drew their pistols. A paratrooper in a camouflage smock was kneeling at a cross-corridor. Brass cartridge cases littered the floor around him.

"Where's Major Zavada?" asked Dushkin.

"Down the hall, colonel. He's starting down into the cellars."

"Good."

They went along the hall. Half a dozen KGB men were sitting against the wall, hands clasped on heads, watched by the paratroops. A body in a KGB uniform sprawled halfway out of an office door. There were several pools of blood on the floor and splatters of red on the walls.

"Major Zavada," called Dushkin. A short, muscular officer turned to look at them. "This is Major Andreyev. He wants someone out of the cellars. Help him."

Zavada nodded. "We're going down now."

"Have you located Morosov? He's supposed to be here."

"No one of that description yet."

"He may be upstairs. Bring him to me if you find him." Dushkin went back along the hall.

"Go," said Zavada. Six paratroopers got up from their crouch, kicked open a door and ran through it. Andreyev heard their boots clattering down steps. He followed Zavada into the stairwell.

At the bottom of the stairs they came under fire. One of the soldiers tossed a concussion grenade into the hallway and yanked the stairwell door closed. A terrific bank and the firing stopped. In an instant three of the paratroops were through the door and spraying the hall with their AKMs. The other three followed them, turning the opposite way. Four more soldiers clattered down the stairs and out into the hall. Zavada and Andreyev followed them, crouching low. More shots, a scream and a shout from a cross-corridor. Another grenade. Andreyev's eardrums popped with the concussion. He stumbled over a body on the floor: a lieutenant-general with long black hair and a seamed face clutching a pistol uselessly in his hand. A meter farther on lay another man, a mole on his chin half-obscured by blood.

The shooting stopped. The air was smoky; Andreyev's eyes smarted from the fumes. He took a deep, reeking breath and shouted, "David!"

Very faintly, he heard Thorne's voice from up the corridor. Andreyev sprinted for the sound.

Thorne was banging on the door at the end of the hall. "I've got you," said Andreyev. "Is there anyone in there with you?"

"Nobody dangerous. The door's locked."

"Get away from it. I'm going to shoot the lock off."

"Go ahead."

Andreyev leveled his pistol and fired. The lock shattered. He kicked the door open. Thorne, naked, was standing against the wall beside it. A young blond woman was next to him.

"Who's that?"

"Dr. Joscelyn Petrie. The other part of the link. The KGB got her out of the embassy and picked her up."

"Tell me later," said Andreyev. "We've got to get you back into contact with your people. I'm to bring you to GHQ; we'll establish a channel from there."

"All right. Joscelyn better come, she knows the communications protocols." Thorne was picking a blanket off the floor. "Can you get me some clothes? And a shirt for Joscelyn?"

"I'll try."

They hurried along the corridor and up the stairs behind a clutch of KGB prisoners being prodded along by Dushkin's paratroops. "Morosov was in the interrogation room," said Thorne. "Have you found him yet?"

"I don't know," said Andreyev in a preoccupied way. "What do you think your people are doing? They're worried about that at GHQ."

"Get me there as fast as you can. Washington won't be happy."

Dushkin was in the main hall when they reached it. He had a cheerful look on his face. "You found him." He saw Joscelyn and frowned. "I didn't know there were two. It doesn't matter. You can verify to Marshal Travkin that we're secure here. The other objectives are also under control. There's still fighting over at the Ninth's barracks, but it's tapering off. I hope the secretary's safe."

"I'm sure he is," said Andreyev, remembering that Dushkin was not aware of Suvorov's real purposes.

Three paratroops, led by a captain, approached down the smoky hallway. A prisoner in civilian clothes, head down, stumbled in front of them. He looked up as they approached.

"That's Morosov," said Thorne.

"Good," said Dushkin. "Where did you find him?"

"An office on the top floor," said the captain.

"Put him in a BMD with a guard and take him to GHQ. Then come back here. Major Zavada."

"Colonel?"

"Take the rest of the prisoners downstairs and lock them up. Make sure they're in empty cells or their own prisoners will kill them. Put out a perimeter guard and get ready for any counterattacks. I'm going to Morosov's office to contact Marshal Travkin. As soon as everything's cleared up, meet me there. Major Andreyev, you may do whatever you're supposed to."

"May I have transport back to GHQ? And clothes for these two?"

"Put a BMD at this officer's disposal, Major Zavada. Have some of the casualties stripped for clothes. Anything else?"

"No, sir," said Andreyev.

"What time is it?" asked Thorne.

"Eleven fifty-five," said Dushkin.

"Christ," said Thorne. "We haven't any time to lose."

"NOTHING YET, MR. PRESIDENT," Harper said. His face was drawn and wretched.

"Judas Priest," said Law. "What the hell is going on over there?" He studied the rippling displays on the curved wall of the crowded Situation Room. The great map of the world was thickly sprinkled with spots of red, green, blue and white lights. A dense cluster of red lay along the West German border: activated Soviet Army units. The blue dots facing them seemed very few.

Chief of Staff Torrance put down a telephone. "The Israelis have been pushed out of Ain Dhakar. They've fallen back to positions half a kilometer farther west."

"All right. When will our transport begin to arrive?"

"They'll be landing at Lod in half-an-hour."

Jerusalem had finally begun to consider the American ceasefire proposal officially, and on the strength of that the state department had finally wrung overflight permission from a reluctant Spanish government. But the airlift was only starting and its results had not reached the Golan front line. The Israelis were slowly being exhausted by Syrian and Soviet pressure. Another Russian airmobile brigade had been flown into Damascus the previous night.

"Mr. President," said Presniak, "I hate to say this, but it looks very much as though the Russians have played us for fools. You've lost contact with your link to the GRU. The DCI has admitted that the GRU plot may be a deception, a delaying tactic. The Russians are into Syria so deeply now that even if we give up on RUBICON ONE the country's as good as occupied. And the way things are going, the Israelis will soon have to accept even the most unfavorable ceasefire, unless we support them with troops as well as with equipment. The Kremlin likely thinks we won't do that. When they turn around in a day or two and say 'Sorry, we fooled you,' we'll be in an impossible situation. Diplomatically, maybe militarily as well."

"Cam?"

Harper said miserably, "Ed may be right. It's clear Joscelyn and David have been picked up. But there's no telling yet. I –"

"Ambassador Simpson is on the line again, Mr. President," said an aide.

Law grabbed up the telephone connecting him to the American embassy in Moscow. "Hello, Alan. Anything yet?"

The voice at the other end of the line was remarkably clear for having been coded, scrambled, bounced off two satellites, relayed and decoded. "Not regarding your two strays, I'm afraid. But one of our attachés came in a few minutes ago. He said there were roadlocks and troops around Dzerzhinsky Square and he heard shooting."

"How much?"

"A lot, he said. And several if not all of the Moscow phone exchanges are out. Not the diplomatic lines, though. I've checked with the Canadians and the British."

"Have you got through to Distanov yet?"

"The phones at the foreign ministry aren't working. Just a moment, Mr. President. The CIA station chief wants to speak to me."

Law heard muffled voices. Then, "We've found your people, Mr. President. The man Thorne just called. Joscelyn Petrie was with him. He said to give you the phrase 'Mark One.' Is he bona fide?"

"Yes," said Law. "Where the hell is he?"

"This is a bit of a surprise. He's at the Soviet general staff headquarters. He wants to set up a voice link from there to here to you."

Law exhaled slowly, saw Harper looking at him with an agonized expression and gave the DCI the thumbs-up sign. "Can your technicians handle it?"

"Yes. Within half an hour."

"Please do it faster if possible. What else did he say?"

Again the background conversation at the Moscow end. "That everything seemed under control for the moment. Nothing else."

"Put me through to him as soon as the link's established." Law hung up.

Most of the people in the room were looking at him. Law stood up and led Harper, Torrance, Presniak and the deputy director of state into the conference room. "It's looking better," Law told them, and outlined what Simpson had told him.

"No word about the success of the coup, though," Presniak said.

"No." Law glanced at the bank of clocks at the end of the room. "It's 12:55 in the morning over there. They may still be tidying up."

"Or they may be collapsing," said Harper. "The KGB isn't without resources. It depends on whether they got Boyarkin and Morosov. Option Four is still open." He ran a tongue over his lips. Option Four still tasted foul.

"There's no sign of their alert winding down," said Torrance.

"Too early for that," said Presniak.

"We'd better not lower ours yet," Law said. "But it looks as though we've all got a chance. At last."

THE TAIL BEACON of the last of the Antonov-22 transports lifted above the faroff runway-perimeter lights and slowly receded into the star-flecked sky. The base commander watched it until it became no more than another star, blinking rhythmically, fainter and fainter, until it winked into oblivion.

The regional GLAVPUR chief came to his side. "That's the last?"

"Yes." The night breeze over the walkway surrounding the airbase control tower carried a slight chill; the base commander shivered. "That's the last of them."

"The first wave got off satisfactorily?"

"Yes. I wonder. . . ."

"What?"

"Why they were sent directly from here. They were supposed to go via Kiev and Belgrade. Originally."

"Originally, yes." The commander sensed the other's shrug. "The routing was changed very high up. Send them by the southeast route, even if we have to violate Iranian airspace a little. The Iraquis won't complain if we overfly them." Pride in the voice, now. "The secretary himself gave me the orders."

"It's odd."

"Our strength is that we follow orders." Curtly. "There was no need for you to demand verification of the instructions. You know I shall have to report that as obstructionism."

"I apologize." Privately the base commander wished he had gotten verification from GHQ Moscow anyway. But the GLAVPUR man was far too powerful. The commander hoped the incident wouldn't interfere with his chances of promotion. The reviews were coming up in September.

"Why don't we go to my office and discuss it?" he asked. "I have some very good French cognac. . . ." He trailed off.

A silence. "That would be pleasant. By the way, I've always thought you a very effective officer. Oh, incidentally – "

"Yes?"

"Have you been in touch with Moscow in the last two or three hours?"

"No, you said there was no need for verification. I assure you, I haven't – "

"I tried to contact GLAVPUR headquarters at ten o'clock, to tell them that the first wave had gone. First I couldn't get through; then when I did they said there was trouble with the exchange, and to call back later."

"I'll have communications check into it. This is no time to lose contact."

Both men went silent. The alert was fraying everyone's nerves. It was clear that the problem with the Americans was very serious, although not much official information had been released. But war was in the air.

"First the cognac, though. We'll drink, then call communications, right?"

The base commander led the way into the control tower. Far away now, to the southeast, the Antonovs of the second wave were reaching for their cruising altitude. The first wave, another five transports, was two hours ahead of the second. In the cargo bays of the great aircraft rode ten SCUD-A short-range guided missiles, their transporters and ten tactical nuclear warheads, all bound for Syria.

Kotsarev had decided not to arrest the regional political chiefs until Moscow was secure. It was a terrible miscalculation.

Washington — Moscow
1:35 A.M. to 5:26 A.M., Moscow time

THE GRAY TELEPHONE RANG. Everyone in the conference room looked at it. Then Law picked up the receiver. McKay, Presniak, Torrance and Harper put extensions to their ears.

"This is Jason Law," said the president. He heard the simultaneous translation begin and cursed inwardly because his caller didn't know English. Or because he himself didn't know Russian; he wasn't sure which.

"Mr. President, this is Acting Secretary of the Communist Party Viktor Gresko. Until recently I was chairman of the Council of Ministers. I still am, for that matter."

"We haven't met," said Law. "But I've been told a good deal about you."

A dry chuckle. "Particularly recently, I suspect. Well. I am happy to tell you that all is under control here. There is still some scattered resistance from the, ah, opposition, but we are dealing with it."

"I'm happy to hear that. Secretary Gresko, we must move immediately to arrange a ceasefire in the Golan. I suppose you realize that it has been only the existence of your . . . project that has prevented us from moving our troops in to assist the Israelis. They are very tired. You must know also that we cannot allow their defeat at the hands of Russian troops. I have been under great pressure to intervene directly."

"I can understand that. We never intended, incidentally, to allow our forces or the Syrians to cross the 1973 cease-fire lines."

Law glanced at McKay, who raised one eyebrow, unconvinced. "That's immaterial at the moment," said Law. "How soon will you begin your withdrawal?"

"There is some face to be saved on both sides," said Gresko. "I have been thinking along the following lines. An immediate cease-fire, after which both sides return to their original positions. This will require some withdrawal by the Israelis but they could style it as a planned move following their successful punitive expedition against Syria. We on our part will say that after helping our allies repel and defeat Israeli aggression, we are removing our forces as a gesture of peace, with the unstated proviso that they can be expected to return if Israel tries to. . . . You will perceive my drift. We rely on you to keep Jerusalem under control."

"As we do on you for good sense in Damascus," said Law. "I think this will do to start with. But nobody is going to like it."

"It is better than the alternative."

"Almost anything is," said Law. "When can we begin the cease-fire negotiations?"

A sigh. "I would like to say immediately. However, there is a great deal of reorganization to do here, and some of it will not wait. I must consolidate my position with my colleagues in the Politburo. They are on their way here now."

"When, then?"

"I will speak with you again within four hours. You may need to contact me during that time, so I have taken the liberty of asking your Dr. Thorne to handle such communications. As a gesture of good faith. You knew he was here?"

"Yes. That will be satisfactory. You will understand if we maintain our alert until you're, ah, settled."

"I was hoping we might both relax the bowstrings a little."

Law glanced at Torrance, who shook his head emphatically.

"We would not feel comfortable with that just now."

Again the sigh. "I understand. We will maintain our own readiness, then."

"Should I inquire about your predecessor?"

"Comrade Boyarkin? He is here, safe. Also Morosov, the KGB chairman. Erstwhile chairman, rather. They will be dealt with appropriately."

Law felt a faint chill. Remember, he told himself, that these

re the heirs of Stalin. "I would be grateful if you would let me
peak to David Thorne."

"Of course. He is a very brave man. Dr. Petrie I find
qually courageous. I will speak with you before 5:30, our time.
Good-bye, Mr. President."

"Goodbye."

A click, and silence for some time. Then, "David Thorne
here, Mr. President."

"Dr. Thorne," said Law. "You have my gratitude. I can't
ay anything more without sounding pompous. When you
come home there'll be a warm welcome for you."

"Thank you Mr. President." Law thought the voice was
ired and tense, which was hardly surprising. Harper was
ooking at him expectantly. Law nodded.

"David," said Harper. "It's Cam. We were worried about
you. What happened?"

"KGB collected me," said Thorne briefly. Law thought
he voice had taken on an angry edge. "Nikolai got me and
oscelyn out of the Lubianka just before things turned ugly."

"How did they get her?"

"They lured her out. She thought it was Nikolai."

"She had strict orders – "

"She also knew what you needed to know. And why. She
chanced it." The voice was definitely angry now.

"All right. You're staying put?"

"Yes."

"It makes sense," said Harper. "You've been in it since
near the beginning. You might as well see the end of it. Thank
you, David."

"You're very welcome."

The tone bordered on sarcasm. Harper glanced at Law.
"Dr. Thorne," said Law, "we had better all go back to work.
I'll probably be talking to you later."

"Yes, sir. Good-bye."

"Good-bye."

They broke the connection. After a moment Law said,
"He knows. And he doesn't like it."

Harper nodded. "Yes. But he's hardly likely to tell them.

We got most of what we had to have, anyway, even if the scenario didn't run its full course."

"To tell the truth, Cam," said Law, "I'm just as glad it didn't. It was a little gritty."

Harper nodded. He wasn't sure if he were disappointed or not.

There was a samovar on the chest next to the round conference table. Beside the samovar stood two bottles of vodka in buckets of ice, and glasses. Thorne studied the bottles, realized that vodka would knock him off his feet, and poured a glass of tea from the samovar. "You too?" he asked Joscelyn.

She looked up from the red plush couch on the other side of the room, beyond the table. The plastic of the telephones on the table reflected dully the dim overhead lights. The dimness exaggerated the shadows under her eyes.

"Please."

"There's sugar but no milk."

"I don't mind."

The room seemed very empty now that Gresko and the others were gone. Thorne handed her the glass and sat down at one of the conference table's chairs.

"It looks as though we got out of it after all," he said, breaking the silence.

She nodded.

"Joscelyn, I'm sorry about what I said. No, how I said it. But I trusted you. So did Nikolai."

She looked down at her glass. "You didn't hear my side of it."

"Okay. Tell me."

She took a deep breath, not looking at him. "In July, after we had supper in Washington, just after you came down from New Hampshire. . . ." She stopped, looked around the room and cupped a hand at her ear.

"I don't think they'd bug their own conference room," he said. "Anyway, it doesn't matter now."

She shrugged and went on. "I went back and broke into RUBICON ONE. I wanted to find out what they were trying to get you to do. I knew they were using me to shove you into something. They had it all planned. There was a trapdoor in the program. They caught me. After that it was cooperate or face the consequences. But I didn't know about Option Four. Not until just before they sent me over here. Then it was too late. And it didn't seem real – not until the KGB picked me up."

"It would have been real enough to Nikolai."

"I know. I kept hoping that they'd decide not to do it. Or that something would go wrong."

"It did."

"Yes. It did."

"At Round Lake. You knew about the project then."

She opened her eyes. "Not everything. I put what I did know out of my mind. And I wanted to see you; I would have come to the lake even if Northrop hadn't told me to."

He was very angry. "Those bastards. Harper. Northrop. Even the president. He knew."

"It wouldn't surprise me."

"I'm finished this time. No more."

"I think I am, too."

A long silence. Then she asked, "Are we finished, too, along with the rest of it?"

He swirled the tea in his glass. "I'm still too angry to know. Give me some time."

"All right." She leaned her head against the red plush and closed her eyes again. "God, I want to sleep."

"Go ahead."

"I'm too keyed up. I – "

The door opened and Andreyev came in. He went straight to the bottles, poured vodka and drank. His uniform was still plaster-dusted from the Lubianka fighting.

"What's going on?" Thorne asked.

Andreyev poured another ounce of vodka and turned around. "The KGB at the Ninth's barracks is putting up more resistance than we expected. They got some ATGMs and knocked out some of our armor. We're putting them down but it's taking time. Marshal Travkin's ordered in a brigade of guards. A couple of hours yet, I think."

"That's why Gresko was looking so worried."

"I think so," said Andreyev. "Dr. Petrie, I haven't had time to greet you properly. I am happy to meet a colleague of David's."

She smiled tiredly at him. "I'm afraid my Russian isn't as good as David's. But I'm pleased to meet you, too."

"What's next?" asked Thorne.

"Now we wait until the Politburo session is over. They're all here now."

"There is no argument, then?" Gresko asked mildly. He looked around the table at the other members of the Politburo. Morosov and Boyarkin were conspicuous by their absence. The atmosphere in the room, while tense, had none of the oppression those two had carried with them.

"There is no argument, Comrade Gresko," said Distanov, the foreign minister. "The previous secretary and KGB chairman have forfeited their positions by their rashness. They have brought this country to within a whisker of destruction."

"Thank you, Minister Distanov," said Gresko dryly. "May we then proceed with the vote?"

It seems unlikely that they will refuse, thought Gresko, with Kotsarev, and by implication the Red Army, glowering at them from down the table.

"Is there any dissent," asked Kotsarev, "to Chairman Gresko's assumption of the general secretaryship, on an acting basis?"

There was not. "Carried," said Kotsarev. "Is there any objection to Deputy Chairman Zhigalin's assumption of the KGB chairmanship?"

Again none. "Carried," said Kotsarev.

"There will have to be further reorganization," said Gresko smoothly. He suppressed an inner exultation: he now held the secretaryship, the chairmanship of the Council of Ministers and, by default, Boyarkin's other post, chairman of the Presidium of the Supreme Soviet. The three key positions of the Soviet government. "The command structures of the KGB and the MVD must be overhauled," he went on. "Chairman Zhigalin and Minister Kotsarev will see to that in the next few days." As he spoke, he considered which of his allies he would give the Council of Ministers to. There were several members of the non-voting or candidate block of the Politburo who were possibilities. He did not like to divest himself of any of his power, but retaining too much might turn a majority against him – perhaps even Kotsarev. Kotsarev might do well with the Council of Ministers, if it came to that.

"I have been in contact with President Law," he continued, "and informed him of our change in policy. He was much relieved." That raised a couple of half-smiles around the table. The smiles might disappear if those present knew how long Gresko and Kotsarev had been in contact with the Americans. It might leak out eventually, but by then it would no longer matter. "We will both be winding down our alerts soon, with a cease-fire as part of the procedure. Minister Distanov, we must begin to prepare a proposal for that. The rest of you might prefer to remain here until the streets are fully secure."

It was not precisely an order, but Gresko did not think that any of them would leave.

"Do you wish to begin now?" asked Distanov.

"Directly," said Gresko. "Minister Kotsarev, is there a room we can use? Other than the Communications Center?"

"Left down the hall, second door on the right. May I suggest to those not involved that the officers' mess on the eighth floor will be happy to offer hospitality until morning."

All but Distanov, Zhigalin, Gresko and Kotsarev departed. After a silence, Kotsarev asked, "And Boyarkin?"

Distanov stood up hurriedly. "I will be waiting for you, Secretary Gresko. Down the hall."

When he was gone, Kotsarev said, "He's willing to eat the crumbs, but he doesn't want to cut the loaf."

"What do you think?" asked Gresko. Zhigalin looked from one to the other, waiting.

Kotsarev shook his head. "There is only one thing to do and we all know it."

"Chairman Zhigalin?"

Zhigalin started as though the use of his new title surprised him. "I concur. They are both still extremely dangerous."

Kotsarev got heavily to his feet. "I will take the security detachment down myself."

Boyarkin and Morosov had been put in adjoining rooms in the sub-basement of the building. Two Army guards stood at each door. The GLAVPUR staff were imprisoned on the floor above; it had not been considered wise to put Boyarkin and Morosov near them.

Kotsarev, with the six-man security detachment behind him, stopped at the northeast door. "Bring them both out," he said to the guards. "You and you. Join this group."

The guards opened the first door. Boyarkin stood in the opening. His eyes were flat and black. He studied Kotsarev and said, "Well, minister. I should have guessed."

"Morosov," called Kotsarev. "It's time to go."

The ex-KGB chairman was rumpled and dusty. He had removed his tie, which now dangled from the pocket of his jacket. The green wool was streaked with dirt.

"The courtyard," said Kotsarev to one of the guards. "Morosov, Boyarkin, follow him."

"You are going to execute us," said Morosov. There was a slight hesitation in his voice.

"Go on."

They went along the corridor and up the stairs to the steel door leading to the courtyard between the rear wings of the building. The yard was planted with grass and small trees. There were wooden benches; the staff clerks often sat on them to eat their lunches. The light from the building's upper stories touched the trees but did not illuminate them.

The rear of the courtyard was a masonry wall with a steel door in it. A floodlight high up on the southwest wing glared down onto the door.

"Over there," said Kotsarev.

Boyarkin and Morosov went and stood in front of the door. They blinked in the hard light. Kotsarev snapped his fingers. There was a rattle as the security guards cocked their assault rifles.

"Comrade," said Morosov hurriedly, "remember that I can still be useful. I. . . ." He stopped.

"You know what has to happen," said Kotsarev. "Don't disgrace yourself now."

Morosov opened his mouth and then closed it. Kotsarev looked at Boyarkin. Boyarkin's eyes were fixed on his, filled with murder.

"Fire," said Kotsarev.

Morosov put his hands out, uselessly, as though to stop the bullets. The gunfire pinned both men to the steel door and then let them drop. The courtyard echoed.

Kotsarev walked over to the two bundles on the ground, drawing his pistol, but he didn't need it.

Thorne's eyelids were paralytic with exhaustion. He had drunk enough tea to feel ill; or perhaps the nausea was from fatique and tension. Joscelyn had succumbed and was sleeping on the couch. Her hair was tangled and damp; the building retained the day's heat and the air conditioning was marginal. Andreyev had disappeared again.

Thorne looked at his watch. It was 4:20 in the morning and Washington still had not called.

He rubbed his forehead and thought, how did I come to be sitting in a room in the general headquarters of the Soviet staff? Good God.

He tried to pursue the thought but it eluded him. He considered going out into the corridor but when he had put his head out thirty minutes ago there had been a guard outside the door. The guard had eyed him nervously.

The door opened and a chubby staff officer came in. The man stopped and smiled faintly at Thorne. "Good morning, Dr. Thorne. I'm General Yushenko."

"Good morning, general."

Yushenko went to the sideboard and poured himself a glass of vodka. Thorne wondered again at the phenomenal Russian capacity for alcohol. Yushenko walked over to the table, pushed a telephone out of the way and sat on the table's edge. "Dr Thorne, I have an apology to offer. You might transmit it to Cameron Harper; he will probably find it amusing, and perhaps informative."

Thorne looked at him. "What are you apologizing for?"

"Major Andreyev would likely make the apology if he knew of the circumstances. I would prefer that he didn't. Briefly, I'm sorry that we had to arrange your stay in the Lubianka. You were there longer than we expected. We thought the KGB would pull you in after your meeting with Major Andreyev. As a result of their haste we had to move the coup forward an hour. That didn't matter, as it turned out."

Thorne didn't feel particularly surprised. Harper was exonerated for that, at least. "Why?"

"I'm sure you can guess. We did not really want your people, for all their assurances, to know exactly when we would move. Balancing the risks, we decided it was better to break communications temporarily, until we succeeded. Naturally we preferred not to hold you ourselves, in case you had taken security precautions we weren't aware of." The smile disappeared. "You might also inform your director of intelligence that we are not historical illiterates. Heydrich's destruction of our officer corps in 1938 is carefully studied here as a classic of espionage."

There was no point in arguing. Thorne made a noncommittal gesture.

"I admit Harper concealed it well," said Yushenko. "And it was a sufficient variation of the technique that we didn't suspect it until two days ago. It was one of the deciding factors in lending you to the KGB. In fact, we still don't have any hard evidence that this was what you were doing." He smiled minutely. "I don't think it would be diplomatic of us to try to extract confirmation from you."

"I'd prefer you didn't," said Thorne.

Yushenko got off the table. "Tell Cameron Harper what I said. Also that we won't respond in kind . . . this time. But that he should not try it again."

"All right," said Thorne.

"Good night," said Yushenko, and left the room. Thorne closed his eyes. It was 4:30 in the morning. At 4:33 Thorne was asleep.

Voices in the room awakened him. He dragged himself upright in his chair. Joscelyn was stirring on the couch. Gresko, Kotsarev and a man Thorne hadn't seen before were standing at the far end of the table. Gresko saw Thorne wake up. The secretary's hair was untidy and there were dark half-moons under his eyes.

"Dr. Thorne," said Gresko. "My apologies for waking you. I am about to call your president. You are welcome to stay. I think at this point we need to be more open than we have been, all of us."

"Yes, Mr. Secretary," Thorne said.

"This is Foreign Minister Distanov," said Gresko. "We have worked out a cease-fire proposal. I hope that it will be acceptable to everyone."

Distanov and Thorne nodded at each other. The three Russians sat down.

One of the telephones, a green one, rang. Joscelyn came awake, blinking. Gresko picked up the phone and Kotsarev and Distanov put extensions to their ears. Gresko waved at Thorne and Joscelyn and pointed to two black extensions. Rapid clicks and beeps in Thorne's ear. Then, "This is President Law." The voice was very clear.

"Secretary Gresko," said Gresko. The simultaneous translator, somewhere in the communications net, started up. Thorne realized that he was being used as a check on the accuracy of the translation.

"Have you drafted a proposal?" asked Law.

"We have. And you?"

"Likewise. We have also told the Israeli prime minister that Soviet foreign policy is undergoing a rapid change, and that a cease-fire proposal is under draft."

"His reaction?"

"Somewhat reluctant, I'm afraid to say. He is unwilling to trust either of us completely. But his forces are very tired.

Jerusalem will likely accept anything reasonable. But we must be very careful that they do not feel pushed to the wall. They have been looking nuclear war in the face for some time and they may overreact if there is any sign of escalation, or a really unfavorable peace."

"That was also our analysis," said Gresko. "Our information is less coherent than yours because of the recent . . . upheaval here. But we came to much the same conclusions. May I present our draft?"

"Please do."

"Withdrawal of both sides to the 1973 lines within twenty-four hours. A seventy-two-hour cease-fire to be established immediately. Cessation of US and Soviet airlifts of military supplies and equipment within four hours from now. A moratorium on such shipments for a minimum of fourteen days. Withdrawal of our troops from Syria within two weeks, and the establishment of UN ceasefire supervision, conditional on the following."

"Yes?" said Law.

"Withdrawal of all nuclear weapons possessed by Libya, Syria and Israel, or the disposal of same. The area be declared a nuclear-free zone."

There was a short silence. Then Law said, "I sympathize with your desire for that, but the Israelis will never agree to it. Not while Libya still possesses the devices. Nor, likely, even if they don't. The weapons are too easy to acquire."

"We will make the Libyans give up their bombs."

"Can you be sure of that?"

"They will," said Gresko. "They cannot survive without our technical support."

"There would still be the problem of the Israelis. I cannot see how they could be made to agree."

"They are your allies," said Gresko. "If we can remove the Libyan and Syrian threats, you should be able to do the same with Israel."

"We operate on rather different principles," said Law snappishly. "In respect of sovereign governments."

"I could argue that," said Gresko equally shortly, "but I won't. Describe to me your draft proposal."

Law did. It was much the same as the Russians', except for the weapons-disposal clause. On that Gresko seemed fixed. The two men bargained for twenty minutes. Thorne listened with growing despair. Now that the immediate crisis seemed over, the two nations were reverting to their normal intransigent behavior.

The sticking point, of course, was the Israeli reaction. Thorne could not imagine Jerusalem giving away what some day might be her last bargaining counter.

Towards 5:25 Gresko softened a little. It might be enough to prevent acquisition of nuclear weapons from powers outside the Middle East. Countries such as Israel could retain domestically produced bombs but undertake not to produce any more. Inspection teams could monitor this. The problem of Iraq someday producing her own devices was a difficult one but that could be dealt with later. The result would be that Israel would remain the only nuclear power in the region, but in return she would have to submit to inspections of her nuclear-weapons industry.

Law thought Jerusalem might consider it.

"Very well, Mr. President," said Gresko tiredly. "See what they think of it. At this point we might reduce our alerts, don't you think?"

"Gladly," said Law. "It's 5:35, your time. We will go to DefCon Three from DefCon Two at 6:00 A.M. your time. Will you reciprocate?"

Gresko glanced at Kotsarev, who nodded.

"Yes," said the general secretary. "We will do that."

"I'll call you with the Israeli response in two hours," said Law.

Ten kilometers from Damascus airport, the last of the Antonov transports of the second wave was slipping into its final approach. The sun was just above the horizon; the aircraft's metal surfaces glinted red-orange in the early light. On the airport taxiways the other four Antonovs were rolling slowly towards the waiting trucks and their Russian guards. The SCUD missiles and the warheads of the first shipment were already moving along the highways north and east to their launch sites.

The Israeli attack came in at 3000 meters, out of the southwest. From the time the dozen Kfirs of the raid crossed the front lines at Kuneitra, they had been supported by four Phantom ECM aircraft carrying new jamming equipment supplied by the American airlift. The jammers were tailored to the radar suppression of the Soviet SAM batteries and the ZSU antiaircraft guns clustered thickly around Damascus airport. They worked very well indeed. The defense's target-acquisition displays disappeared in a fog of green spikes and unintelligible radar returns.

The Kfirs, well spread out, rolled into forty-five-degree dives. The airport guns switched from radar to manual control and began to hose dense streams of cannon shells at the attackers.

Two of the Kfirs, caught by intersecting lines of fire, staggered out of their dives, turning westward. The first exploded in a gout of flame before completing the turn; the other flew directly into another burst of shells. Shorn of its tail, it turned on its back and plummeted into one of the suburbs near the airport.

The remaining ten aircraft were able to press their attacks home. Pulling out of their dives, they released their ordnance onto the taxiing aircraft and the runways.

The bombs were a mixture of fragmentation and concrete-digging weapons. Six of the nine Antonov transports on the ground, together with several other aircraft, were cut to pieces by the first explosions. The tenth Antonov, which was just settling onto the main north-south runway, was struck by a fragmentation bomb, which entered its fuselage just behind the raised canopy and exploded two meters to the rear of the cockpit, killing the crew instantly. A second bomb, this time one of the concrete-diggers, penetrated the upper right portion of the transport's cargo bay. The weapon's delay fuse detonated it as it was passing within a meter of the crate containing the ten-kiloton nuclear warhead for the SCUD missile farther back in the bay.

The digger bomb's shock wave first tripped the warhead's fail-safes, and then, against all odds, detonated one of the lenses of the spherical explosive charge, which was the actual trigger of the device. This segment, in its turn, set off the others. The result was, technically, a "fizzle yield," since the compression of the uranium core by the explosive was not uniform. As a result, the warhead yielded barely half its rated power.

It was quite enough to obliterate the airport and a good share of the eastern half of Damascus. The weapon's core gasified instantly, producing an intense burst of gamma radiation. The resulting magnetic pulse induced electrical surges that traveled along power lines, antennas, pipes and even railroad tracks outside the zone of initial destruction, and that burned out most electrical and communications equipment in the Damascus power and communications networks. The thermal pulse that followed, as the fireball took shape, charred or ignited combustible materials, including human flesh, within a radius of one and a half kilometers. The ensuing blast wave flattened hundreds of buildings, crushing or burying their occupants and in the rubble, fires, fed by overturned braziers and spilled cooking oil, began to burn. Where the airport had been, the fireball roared upward, condensing water from the atmosphere into a mushroom cloud, dragging with it tons of debris, which were converted into radioactive ash and spewed into the middle atmosphere, where the wind began to drive it southeast.

DefCon One
6:00 A.M.

Someone had brought in trays of cucumbers, cold sausage, warm bread and butter. The samovar, recharged, hissed on the sideboard. Kotsarev had disappeared to start the process of winding down the alert. Andreyev, back from wherever he had been, sat in one of the chairs at the conference table, looking blankly into space. Gresko, Yushenko and Distanov were talking quietly by the sideboard. The general secretary had a glass of vodka in one hand and was nibbling at a slice of cucumber. He shrugged at something Distanov said and turned to look at Thorne and Joscelyn. "Dr. Thorne, Dr. Petrie, come here, eat, drink. Soon we will all be able to go home to bed. Major Andreyev, you as well."

They gathered at the sideboard. Thorne was famished. He cut off a thick slice of bread, slathered it with butter and bit off a chunk. Gresko poured shot glasses of vodka and handed them around. "Toast," he said. "To world peace and understanding."

They all drank. Thorne felt the spirit's warmth spread through his arms and legs. Joscelyn cut rounds of sausage and handed them around. The sausage smelled of herbs and garlic. Thorne ate a piece and started on another slice of bread.

"There will be decoration or promotion in this for everyone, major," Gresko said to Andreyev. He switched his gaze to Thorne. "I hope your government is also generous. It was –"

A telephone rang. It was the only red one on the table. Gresko frowned, left the sideboard and picked up the receiver. He listened for a moment and then put the instrument down. His mouth was a tight line. The others looked at him expectantly.

"That was Minister Kotsarev," he said. "We must all leave

immediately for Vnukovo Airbase. You Americans will come, too. Perhaps you will be able to convince your president that we will not retreat indefinitely from our position. I had thought there had already been enough treachery but apparently your government does not agree."

"But what's happened?" asked Joscelyn.

"The Israelis have bombed Damascus with a nuclear weapon."

"They've *what*?" asked Law. The conference room was dead silent.

"Twenty minutes ago," said Harper. "We monitored it by satellite. The dazzle in the sensors was characteristic of an initial nuclear flash. When the dazzle stopped there was the signature of a small ground burst."

Law put his head in his hands. "How small?"

"Not yet certain, but it was under ten kilotons. Photo intelligence shows at least half of the city's gone. A lot of the rest is burning. No estimate of casualties so far. Ground zero was at the airport. There were at least ten Russian heavy transports there."

"Christ almighty. Why would they do that now? Why a nuclear attack to stop the airlift when the Russians can just divert to Homs or Palmyra?"

The intercom buzzed. Law pressed a switch. "Mr. President," said a voice from the speaker. "Your call to Prime Minister Reisman is through."

Law snatched up the telephone. "Mr. Prime Minister. Do you know what has happened at Damascus?"

Reisman's voice was hesitant, like that of a man in shock. "It was reported to me ten minutes ago. Mr. President – "

"Why in hell did you do it?" burst out Law. "My call was originally about a cease-fire proposal. The Kremlin's in new hands, they want to stop this. But now – "

"Mr. President," said Reisman. A flash of anger drove away the hesitancy. "Before you interrupt again, listen to me. We did not do it."

"You what?" said Law.

"We didn't do it. The detonation coincided with an air raid we were making on Damascus Airport. But our planes were carrying only conventional weapons." He paused and said bitterly, "None of the twelve aircraft of the raid have re-established communication. We assume they were all destroyed in the fireball. We also assume that the weapon that did explode was Syrian. Or Soviet. Not that anyone will believe us when we say that."

"Oh, God," said Law. "They sent them."

"What?"

"The previous Soviet government. Damn. This is what I was calling you about originally. The coup in Moscow has definitely succeeded. I've been talking to Gresko; he wants an immediate cease-fire and a wind-down of our alerts. We're starting to resolve the crisis. Or we were. The Boyarkin government was planning to ship nuclear weapons to Syria. It now looks as though Gresko's people either didn't know the bombs had already been sent, or were letting them go anyway."

"What were the Russian cease-fire proposals?"

Law told him. After a long pause Reisman said, "We cannot agree to the dismantling our nuclear capability. Especially not with Russian warheads in Syria."

"The Kremlin may agree to a return to the prewar situation," said Law. "There is the option of retaining your weapons, but submitting to inspection procedures. There is room for negotiations. Please, Mr. Prime Minister, consider it. We are very near the point of no return, since Damascus."

"That is all very well," said Reisman. "But you have not looked at the situation from our perspective. Damascus has been leveled by an atomic bomb. It looks as though Israel has initiated nuclear warfare against urban targets. Our general staff is expecting a nuclear counterstrike at any time on our own cities. One of our options is to devastate any part of Syria in which any nuclear weapons, Soviet or Syrian, might be based. We are running out of time. Today the wind is blowing east, so the fallout on our country will be minimal. Who knows which way it may be blowing tomorrow? Need I say more?"

"Prime Minister," said Law, and there was a desperation in his voice that chilled Harper's blood, "I beg you to wait. I will call Secretary Gresko this instant and ask him to verify that there were Russian nuclear devices in Syria, and that it may have been one of those that exploded. If he accepts that possibility, will you hold your attack?"

Reisman said, "I will accept anything reasonable that frees me from either indulging in or submitting to genocide. I will wait by the telephone. Please hurry."

Law stabbed buttons. "Get me Secretary Gresko," he said into the mouthpiece, and then, cradling it on his shoulder, he said, "Well, Cam, what do your computers say we should do now?" Without waiting for an answer, he went on to Torrance, "Do you think the Israelis did it?"

"No," said Torrance. "But everyone is going to think they did. Especially the Russians, if Gresko really doesn't know the weapons reached Damascus."

"Could it have been a Russian bomb, Cam?"

"There is a possibility," said Harper, "that Gresko and company know that the warheads went to Syria after all. They were supposed to be shipped about now. That could put them in Damascus at the right time to be caught by the Israeli raid. If Gresko simply let the weapons go through, for some purpose of his own, they could plead an oversight if we found out. . . ."

Law was gesturing impatiently. "Keep trying," he said into the telephone. "Try for Dr. Thorne or Dr. Petrie."

There was an instant tension.

"All right," said Law. He put the receiver down and studied it. "Gresko isn't available," he said. "An aide said he was in conference. There is no one else available. Gresko will call us back."

The door to the Situation Room opened. "Excuse me, Mr. President. General Torrance, ELINT reports that the Russians are going on maximum alert."

A silence. Then Law said, "Well, that answers the question of where they are. They've left for their airborne command post. General Torrance, go to DefCon One. Alert Andrews

Airbase that we'll be needing the NEACP aircraft in twenty minutes. Secretary McKay will get everyone on the Blue List there."

Law, Torrance and McKay all reached for telephones. Law reached Reisman on the first ring.

"Well, Mr. President?"

"I have to tell you that I can't contact Gresko. The Soviet alert level has increased. We think that Gresko and the Soviet military staff are going to their airborne command post. We are also raising our alert and will be in the air shortly."

"I see," said Reisman. "It's finally come to this."

"Not necessarily," Law said. "I am going to try Secretary Gresko again, as soon as we're in the air. If there is no immediate sign of Soviet or Syrian retaliation against you, I beg you to exercise restraint."

"Be sensible, Mr. President. By the time we detect such signs, it will be too late. You are in the same position, on a larger scale."

"Yes," said Law. "I know. Give me one hour."

An interminable silence. Then, "Very well, Mr. President. One hour. I cannot guarantee that we will not act after that. Good-bye."

"Good-bye," said Law, and hung up.

"Mr. President," said Torrance. "Are we to be at launch-on-warning or launch-on-impact?"

"What's your opinion?"

"Their alert is several minutes ahead of ours."

"Launch-on-warning. If one of their ICBMs so much as sticks its head out of its hole, we'll have to hit them."

The floor of the Ilyushin-76 strategic-command aircraft remained at a steep angle. Thorne tightened his lap belt and watched as puffs of cumulus receded even farther below. The plane was at ten-thousand meters at least, and still climbing. Among the scattered white patches of cloud the Russian landscape was slowly blurring into a bluish-green haze. Thorne could make out no landmarks.

He turned to look at Joscelyn. She smiled back with an

obvious effort. Across the cabin Andreyev was strapped into another seat. They were the only ones in the compartment, which was at the Ilyushin's stern, and contained, besides a double row of seats, a set of bunk beds, a small galley and a rack of communications equipment. On the other side of the compartment door lay the command and control section of the aircraft, which Gresko and Kotsarev, with several other officers and civilians, had entered as the Ilyushin took off. Thorne had glimpsed what lay on the other side of the door: rank on rank of computer consoles, radar screens, blinking lights and steady lights, rows of enigmatic green cabinets with louvers in them. In this aircraft was now established the control of Russia and all her military strength.

And out there somewhere also flew the Russian equivalent of Looking Glass, the United States' airborne Strategic Air Command headquarters, controlling the huge intercontinental missiles with their multiple warheads, silent pale obelisks in their silos; the Backfire bombers circling with their tankers in the cold blue above the Arctic Circle; the ballistic-missile submarines cruising at thirty knots, two hundred meters below the waves off Seattle and Boston; the tactical nuclear missiles under the trees in East Germany and Hungary and Poland, waiting beyond the Hof Gap and the plains south of Hamburg. Eighteen-thousand megatons. Eight-hundred-and-fifty-thousand Hiroshimas.

The Ilyushin leveled off. The door opened and Gresko entered the compartment, followed by Kotsarev. They were very angry and frightened.

"Well, Dr. Thorne," said Gresko. "Your country is at its maximum alert. First you let the Israelis bomb Damascus, then you go on an alert such as we have never seen. To ask us what we're going to do about it. What do you think of that, eh?"

"Don't blame me," said Thorne, too tired to care. "I didn't bomb Damascus."

Gresko scowled at him and went to the communications console. Kotsarev studied Thorne coldly, then turned away to stand behind the secretary.

Andreyev was looking pointedly out his window. Always

the ancient Russian paranoia, Thorne reflected. The eternal viper at the bottom of the Christmas stocking.

"Is the patch through to Washington?" Gresko was saying. "Good. Then complete the call. I will wait for five minutes."

The National Emergency Airborne Command Post, the NEACP – inevitably transmuted to "Kneecap" – was a Boeing 747 jumbo jet modified to carry tons of electronic gear and the personnel of the Blue List, those members of the government deemed essential to the fighting of a nuclear war. At the time Gresko's call was patched through Washington, the Boeing was flying a random course at ten-thousand meters over Virigina, tending westward.

Law took the call in the Central Communications Center on the aircraft's main level. With him were Presniak, Harper. Defense Secretary McKay, Torrance, Torrance's three joint chiefs of staff, Chairman Wands of the National Security Agency and General Howatt, commander of SAC. The call was routed through a speaker phone. The ten men listened intently as the device hummed, clicked and then delivered itself of Gresko's voice. The words were faint. Law turned up the volume as the translator took over.

"Mr. President?"

"Yes, Mr. Secretary. I'm here."

"Good. I expect you have determined where I am."

"Yes."

"You are no doubt in a similar place. I note that your alert is now at Defense Condition One. Which means, if I remember correctly, that you are deploying for combat."

"That's right," said Law. "Your alert left us no choice. I must also tell you that we are at launch-on-warning."

"I thought that you were going to restrain the Israelis Instead you have permitted them to bomb Damascus. You must realize that whatever our wish to avoid a wider war, we cannot overlook an attack such as this." Even over the small speaker and obscured by the simultaneous translation, the fury in

Gresko's voice was unmistakable. "How are we to arrange a settlement now? I –"

"Mr. Secretary," Law broke in. "I have spoken to Prime Minister Reisman about Damascus. He has stated categorically that his forces did not explode a nuclear device over that city. Could it possibly have been a Syrian weapon? Or perhaps one of yours? There were Antonov-22s on the runways when the bomb detonated."

Law waited in the ensuing silence. Then he said, "Mr. Secretary? Are you still there?"

"I cannot accept your explanation," said Gresko. "The remaining Syrian warheads are under our control and are not in Damascus. We have sent no nuclear weapons to Syria. This is an Israeli prevarication, a lie. And you know it."

"I know no such thing," snarled Law. "Do you seriously believe the Israelis would destroy Damascus and then refuse to admit it? If they meant such an attack as a deterrent, they would have to say that they had done it."

"There are no Soviet nuclear weapons on Syrian territory."

Law breathed deeply for a moment. "We are on the edge of a holocaust. Before you assume that Jerusalem is at fault here, you might at least verify what you have just said. Are you sure Boyarkin did not order the shipment of the weapons before you dealt with him?"

A silence. Then Gresko said, "We will check."

The speaker clicked as the connection was broken. Law looked at the clock on the bulkhead. He had to contact Reisman within twenty-four minutes.

He swept his gaze around the table. Harper as looking down at a thin sheaf of computer printout, his chin cupped in his left hand.

"What does RUBICON say about this?" asked Law.

Harper looked up. "We once ran a scenario like this, Mr. President, with an accidental nuclear occurrence during a crisis. It was not specific to the Arab-Israeli situation, but –" he tapped the printout, "this is the scenario output. It advises an immediate first strike by the unaffected power, because his opponent will assume the detonation, if it is on his own territory, to signal the start of an attack. He will react accordingly."

"So we should go to war because a computer advises us to," said Law sadly. "Who would ever have thought it would come to this?"

"I don't believe –" said Torrance.

"Be quiet," said Law, "and let me think."

He knew they assumed him to be considering a first strike. But he had already thought beyond that precipice to what would come after: the great white flashes of light, hundreds and thousands of them, over the missile silos, the airbases, the seaports; over Washington, Moscow, San Francisco, Kiev, Leningrad; the thermal pulses, the radiation, the blast waves interlocking from Los Angeles to Boston, from Riga to Vladivostok. In one-and-a-half-million square kilometers of the United States – a sixth of the country – the initial thermal pulse would burn all exposed living things to death. The blast waves that followed would entomb the survivors under the debris of whatever structure had protected them from incineration, and then the debris would begin to burn. In the regions of concentrated attack there would be no escape: to flee one detonation would be to be irradiated, blown apart or simply vaporized by another. There would be no doctors, no hospitals, no emergency services: all would have been consumed in the first minutes after the missiles fell. And after that, not a tree, not a blade of grass, not a man nor a woman or a child remaining, only the seared rubble under the gently falling rain of radioactive ash.

In an account of the Hiroshima attack Law had come across an image that for some reason had become fixed in his mind. An expectant mother lay dead in an ash-drenched street. Beside her knelt her four-year-old daughter, trying to make her mother drink from a broken cup. Around them survivors stumbled like sleepwalkers through the rubble, no one noticing the weeping child.

And it will be worse than that here, Law thought. So much worse that neither I nor anyone else in this room can begin to imagine how it will be.

"General Torrance," he asked. "Where exactly are *John F. Kennedy* and *Kitty Hawk*?"

"A hundred miles east of Haifa."

"I have to call Reisman in twenty minutes. I want a strike force from those two carriers in the air by that time. Arrange it so that there is such a force available at all times, airborne, within five minutes' flying time of all northern Israeli airbases. The strike force must be able to stop aircraft from taking off from those bases, or intercept other planes flying from southern ones. They will also prevent Syrian-based jets from entering Israeli airspace."

"Mr. President," said Lussing, the chief of the air staff, "that will mean we are violating Israeli airspace."

"Do it anyway," said Law. "I have decided that we will not permit Israel to launch a nuclear attack on Syria – even if we have to shoot down Israeli aircraft ourselves."

A stunned silence. "Mr. President," said Presniak, "this is an attack on one of our own allies. It's a diplomatic catastrophe."

"There's another catastrophe waiting in the wings," said Law. "And it's not a diplomatic one. Do it."

Torrance stood up. "I cannot obey that order, Mr. President."

"You what?"

"I cannot obey. Please reconsider. This is not a rational decision."

Law wondered momentarily whether Torrance would try to declare him unfit for command. There was no precedent for it, and it was illegal, but he might try. "It is my decision," he said. "I hereby relieve you of your post as joint chiefs of staff chairman. You may leave this meeting."

"What do the rest of you think?" asked Torrance.

"General Torrance. You may leave."

No one said anything. Torrance turned heavily and went to the door. He looked at Law for a long moment, shrugged and left. The door closed noiselessly behind him. The only sound in the compartment was the distant whine of the engines and the rush of air sliding past the Boeing's skin.

"Well?" Law asked the chief of the air staff.

Lussing said, "I'll see to it immediately," and followed Torrance out the door.

"Cam," said Law. "Go with him. Make sure he does. In the meantime, is there anyone else who wants to resign?"

Silence.

"Good. In ten minutes I am going to tell Reisman what we've done. We need time, gentlemen. This is the only way I can think of to gain it. Time to talk to the Russians, time to save ourselves from this . . . juggernaut. At whatever cost . . . diplomatically or otherwise."

"It will take us years to repair the damage if we attack Israel," said Presniak. "None of our allies will ever trust us again."

"Do you prefer the likely alternative?"

"Mr. President," said McKay, "with a first strike we might at least –"

"No," said Law. "I want to find out what Secretary Gresko has to say about those bombs."

Seven minutes later he ended his conversation with the Russian leader. Gresko was more hostile than ever. They had not finished checking but there had been no weapons shipment through Kiev and Belgrade. Law was frightened by the implications of Gresko's words: clearly the Soviet leader did not believe the Israeli denial of responsibility, and was half convinced that the time needed to check their claim was only to let the United States complete its military preparations. The sole gleam of hope was that Gresko was willing to accept that risk. Even the mission of the American strike force had not seemed to impress him, although he had agreed to try to keep Russian and Syrian aircraft on their side of the border.

"Get me Reisman," Law said to the speaker phone.

Out in the eastern Mediterranean the catapults of the *John F. Kennedy* and the *Kitty Hawk* were slamming the Tomcats and the F-18s of the strike force into the sky, up towards the indigo of the stratosphere, and the coasts of Israel.

"Prime Minister," said Law. "Have you come to a decision yet?"

"I was awaiting your information," said Reisman.

"The Russians do not know whether it was one of their weapons or not. They are trying to find out."

"They have not admitted it was not ours?"

"No. But there is still time."

"Yes. Time for them to decide to strike. I think they are going to present you with a *fait accompli*, Mr. President, and that is the reason for these delays. Good-bye."

"Wait," said Law. "What are you going to do?"

"That is a decision we will take by ourselves," said Reisman. "We have listened to others for too long."

"Prime Minister," said Law. Reluctance was clear in his voice. "I have to tell you that we won't permit you to execute a nuclear attack on Syria. I request you in the strongest terms to bring all your aircraft back to base and keep them there. To provide you with defense against Syrian attack, we are sending Tomcats and F-18s from the Sixth Fleet. We have told the Russians that we are doing this. Your radar will have detected our aircraft by now."

"Jason Law," said Reisman. "You cannot be serious. I cannot believe you have just said what you have."

"I mean it," said Law. "Get your planes onto the ground. We have ordered our pilots to shoot down any aircraft attempting to cross your border with Syria, in either direction. The Russians have promised to keep their planes back." And I hope they can, Law thought. God knows what their communications are like after losing Damascus. "Secretary Gresko will be contacting me very soon. If he admits responsibility, we will withdraw our forces. If not, we'll maintain our interdiction until some other resolution is achieved. No matter how long it takes."

"If you violate our airspace we will shoot your planes down," said Reisman. "Always this interference in our affairs.

You and the Russians did not let us finish the Syrians and Egyptians in 1973, nor in 1967, nor in 1956. If you had, this would not be happening. You arm both us and the Arabs to the teeth, you force us to wreck our economies to buy your weapons, and you are full of self-righteousness when we use the machines you were so eager to sell. You and the Russians, you are both mad. We will listen to you no longer."

"Prime Minister," said Law. But Reisman had hung up.

"Will they try?" asked Presniak.

"We can't possibly seal the border completely," said Lussing. "We don't have enough planes, especially if the Israelis fight."

"I know," said Law. "I can only hope they will decide not to. And that if they decide to strike at Syria, we will be able to stop them."

The Boeing jolted slightly in an air pocket. Law felt a sudden rush of doubt that made him want to shout at the others. Help me, in the name of God, I'm not sure what I should be doing, give me an answer that will guide us away from this abyss. . . .

What was Gresko doing? Was he, at this very instant, losing the courage to wait, lifting the red telephone or whatever the Russians used, calling out the order that would open the silo doors, turn the bombers out of their circles in the cold Arctic stratosphere, draw the submarines up from the deep water towards their launch depth?

He thought again of the child in Hiroshima, the pathetic broken cup in her hand.

Over the airbases of northern Israel, Kfirs, Phantoms, F-15s and F-16s marked with the Star of David clawed for height, climbing for the American strike force curving in from the sea. In the approaching Tomcats the weapons officers armed the long-range Phoenix missiles and began to track the rising Israelis.

"There is no doubt?" asked Gresko. His face looked dead and gray.

"None at all," said Kotsarev. "Boyarkin must have ordered the shipment personally, before we acted."

They were standing at the main communications console just behind the cockpit of the Ilyushin. Kotsarev had a momentary vision of Boyarkin, his chest blown away, blood on his mouth, laughing with monstrous delight. "No doubt at all," he repeated. "Ten Antonovs were dispatched from Rostov, not from Kiev, in two waves. There are now at least five SCUD-As with nuclear warheads in Syria. The other five we can assume were destroyed in the explosion at Damascus."

"And the Damascus bomb was ours."

"I think it very likely," said Kotsarev.

"The Americans will think we knew all the time," said Gresko. "We have forced them into threatening an attack on their own allies. They will think we planned it."

"Secretary," said Kotsarev. "We cannot be sure that Law was telling the truth about threatening Jerusalem. The planes from their Sixth Fleet may actually be on their way to Syrian targets. If we admit we put the bombs there they will have justification for that. But we cannot accept an American strike on Syria." He paused, looked at Gresko and said:

"We have to strike. We cannot wait any longer."

"There is one possibility yet," said Gresko. "If the Americans and the Israelis fight. . . ." He turned to the communications officer. "The Tupolevs shadowing the Sixth Fleet. They are monitoring the American strike force, aren't they?"

"Yes, secretary."

"Contact the aircraft nearest the probable combat area. Tell the pilot to report immediately whatever he detects."

Nine-thousand miles away, the chief of the air staff said, "They're not backing down. They're trying to call our bluff."

"It's not a bluff," said Law. "God damn Reisman. Why won't he call his planes home?"

The American and Israeli jets engaged just inside Israeli airspace. Vapour trails drew a pale mesh against the high blue. Captain Robert Winter, flying one of *Kitty Hawk's* Tomcats, turned easily inside a Kfir and fired one of his Sidewinders. The missile blew one wing off the gyrating interceptor, which turned on its back and began to flutter earthward, burning.

Winter considered what he would do after he fired his other three Sidewinders. The mission profile specified that the long-range Phoenixes were to be kept for aircraft approaching the Israeli-Syrian border, and Winter didn't like using the Tomcat's cannon for dogfighting while the plane was still loaded with the heavy Phoenixes.

He also didn't like shooting at Israelis.

It might have been this reluctance that slowed his reactions when the under-attack alarm went off. The air was so thick with missiles and jets that the Tomcat's electronics had taken a long time to identify Winter's Tomcat as the target of the Israeli Shafrir, and he was left with only a tiny margin of error. It was not enough. The Shafrir struck the Tomcat in the starboard fuel tank, just outboard of the swing-wing pivot, and the fighter blew up.

"They are shooting each other down," said the communications officer. "The Tupolev's radar shows at least two aircraft destroyed. They can't tell whether Israeli or American."

"Tell me he must be certain. Can he see anything?"

The officer spoke briefly and listened. "He says he sees smoke, two explosion bursts – another flash, something blew up. . . ."

"That's enough," said Gresko. "Come with me," he told Kotsarev.

"I think it's going to happen," Joscelyn said listlessly. She was leaning against Thorne's shoulder, her hand in his. "They don't seem to be able to control it. Maybe they don't want to. I wish we were home. What will happen to us if there's a war?"

"I don't know," said Thorne. "I think this plane has the range to escape. But I don't know where they'd go."

"Not having a country any more," she said. "It's sad. It didn't have to happen."